LOLA
ON
FIRE

Also by Rio Youers

Halcyon

The Forgotten Girl

LOLA ON FIRE

A NOVEL

RIO YOUERS

wm

WILLIAM MORROW

An Imprint of HarperCollins*Publishers*

This is a work of fiction. Names, characters, places, and incidents are products of the author's imagination or are used fictitiously and are not to be construed as real. Any resemblance to actual events, locales, organizations, or persons, living or dead, is entirely coincidental.

HarperCollins books may be purchased for educational, business, or sales promotional use. For information, please email the Special Markets Department at SPsales@harpercollins.com.

FIRST EDITION

Library of Congress Cataloging-in-Publication Data

Names: Youers, Rio, author.
Title: Lola on fire : a novel / Rio Youers.
Description: First Edition. | New York, NY : William Morrow, [2021]
Identifiers: LCCN 2020017798 (print) | LCCN 2020017799 (ebook) | ISBN 9780063001008 (hardcover) | ISBN 9780063001015 (trade paperback) | ISBN 9780063001022 (ebook)
Subjects: GSAFD: Suspense fiction. | Mystery fiction.
Classification: LCC PR9199.4.Y667 L65 2021 (print) | LCC PR9199.4.Y667 (ebook) | DDC 813/.6—dc23
LC record available at https://lccn.loc.gov/2020017798
LC ebook record available at https://lccn.loc.gov/2020017799

ISBN 978-0-06-300100-8

21 22 23 24 25 LSC 10 9 8 7 6 5 4 3 2 1

THIS NOVEL IS DEDICATED TO

Lily Maye Youers and Charlie Samuel Youers

All you have to do is dream . . .

LOLA ON FIRE

PROLOGUE

THE UNSTOPPABLE LOLA BEAR

(1993)

The car boomed toward Lola, its headlights cut so that she wouldn't see it in the darkness. The driver didn't factor in the engine noise, though. Or maybe he did but gambled on her not hearing it above the gunfire. He for damn sure didn't factor in the streetlight reflecting off the windshield, clear as sun-flash off a sniper's lens.

No time to think. An overworked expression, and one that riled Lola. It applied to reflex, not survival. To *not think*, Lola knew, was to lie down and die.

She calculated: Four seconds until the car was on top of her. It might not kill her outright but would do enough damage to render her ineffective.

Four seconds. She had time.

Tony Broome was taking cover ninety feet away, tucked behind the front wheel of a stationary Buick, which was smart, but every time he inhaled, the top of his head lifted above the hood. Not by much, only an inch or so, but an inch was enough. Lola liked Tony. They'd worked numerous jobs together. He was good people.

It would take a second to steady her hand, aim, pull the trigger. 0.08 seconds for the bullet to meet its target. Then two seconds to move.

Lola leveled her pistol, pumped off a shot. The peak of Tony's skull disappeared in a splash of blood. With that threat erased, Lola turned back to the car. Its engine snarled like a wild thing caged. She would clear more distance by rolling, but it would take longer to reset. So she pirouetted, staying on her feet, her gun hand still poised.

The car missed her by a gasp, the distance between her and

it tight enough to trap a sheet of paper. She lifted details—some crucial—as it whistled past: a 1992 Mercury Sable in reef-blue metallic. A cracked windshield. A dented fender. Paul Mostly rode shotgun (his surname the fuel for many inane gags: Paul *mostly* doesn't know shit from Shinola; Paul *mostly* has his thumb jammed up his ass). He had a custom bullpup M14 across his thighs. Some jerkoff she didn't know was behind the wheel. He had a cornerstone jaw sprinkled with beard and wore a patch over his left eye. Jimmy wouldn't usually hire someone with an eye patch. It exposed how desperate he was.

A good sign.

Lola aimed and fired twice at the back of the driver's headrest. The second shot was for insurance, in case the first was deflected on its passage through the rear windshield. The Sable ran out of blacktop with the driver too dead to react. It mounted the sidewalk and struck a steel security fence with a concertina boom. The passenger-side door dropped off its hinges a moment later and Paul reeled out, spitting teeth from his blood-filled mouth. He flailed with the bullpup. Spent rounds glittered like broken glass.

Paul *mostly* misses with every shot.

Lola sighted down the barrel of her Baby Eagle: 9mm, Israeli-made, and decidedly lethal for something so daintily named.

Paul *mostly* dies from a gunshot wound to the throat.

The quickest way onto Jimmy's property was to vault onto the Sable and over the fence. It was also a guaranteed way to get herself perforated. The crash—not to mention the gunfire—had announced her arrival like a railroad flare. Too many sights focused on that point. Lola could use it as a diversion, though. She knew Jimmy's property. There were other ways in.

She skirted the eastern wall where shadow kept her hidden.

There'd be men posted here. Two, maybe three. Lola would hear them first—their quick, unsteady breathing in the darkness, in sync with the jitter of their hearts. She paused, listening, then moved on. Tony (another Tony) Marconi stood sentry midway down, trying to look everywhere at once, not trusting his peripheral vision, his hearing, his instinct. Tony M. was a twenty-eight-year-old brute with a skull as tough as quartz. He had black belts in judo and tae kwon do. Lola could drop him with a bullet, but a bullet would betray her location.

She had to strike silently.

Timing her movement, Lola hit him like rain, first across the right wrist, disarming him, then with a punch to the throat that disabled his vocal cords. She brought him down with a low kick that exploded his kneecap. A fourth strike, delivered with bewildering force and precision, snapped his neck like wet bark.

...

Lola took a breath and felt the blood rushing through her body. She waited a minute for it to slow. There were shouts from beyond the wall—Jimmy's men on alert, panicked crows with semiautomatics clutched in their trembling claws—and the throaty, wheezy snarl of Doberman pinschers. There were seven of them, named after the seven samurai from the movie of the same name, still on their leashes, judging from their frequent yelps and yowls.

She imagined Jimmy with his hands nervously flexing, stealing glances out the window, a bluish vein ticking in the hollow of one temple.

You can do this.

Lola gritted her teeth. She had no patience for positive reinforcement—a cousin to weakness.

It's already done.

She crept through the shadows toward the rear of the house. Benjamin Chen, her Xing Yi Quan instructor, floated to mind. Shifu Chen was beautiful and ocean-like and always welcome. Lola once asked him—appealing to his passion for metaphor—how to stay dry when caught in a storm. Shifu Chen had responded with a question, and a metaphor, of his own:

"How do you fly a kite?"

Lola had waited with everything open, eager for education, for betterment. Shifu Chen looked at her for a second, then made a kite out of his left hand. "You ride the wind," he'd said, making his hand sway and swirl. "You gauge its strength, make adjustments. In a sense, you become the wind."

"Right."

"So, to keep from getting wet . . ."

Lola finished for him, "You become the storm."

Another thug she didn't know guarded the south gate. He didn't wear an eye patch but may as well have; Lola came up on his blind side and drove the heel of her palm into his face. It was a direct, efficient strike, ninety-eight percent of her internal power funneled into the end of the move. The thug's face bones caved. Eggshell splintered his brain. He collapsed and foamed at the mouth and his long limbs jangled.

Lola slipped through the gate. The house glimmered beyond the elms, a contemporary multimillion-dollar structure purchased with blood and wile. Every window was illuminated. Muscle barricaded the doors. She heard a sound to her right and found cover in the shadows. It was Mickey Grieco, searching the grounds with the help of Katsushiro—one of the Dobermans. The dog caught her scent and pulled Mickey close. Lola took off her jacket, placed it on the ground, and moved. Katsushiro found her jacket and showed all his teeth, and when Mickey picked it up with a puzzled expression, Lola struck from behind. Mickey died quickly but Katsushiro took longer. She strangled him with his own leash.

Lola pulled her jacket back on and moved toward the house.

She had sent a message through Carver City's grimy underbelly, using call girls and bootblacks and crooked cops, but also painting it across the exterior walls of the Steel Tiger, where every mobster and degenerate was certain to see it.

**I'M COMING FOR JIMMY AND YOU KNOW WHY
GET IN MY WAY AND I'LL KILL YOU TOO**

...

She left a trail of bodies—human and canine—on her way to the house, most of them on the lawn, Heihachi in the pool, which had turned from aqua to cherry-red. She maintained stealth for as long as she was able but had to switch to the Baby Eagle. That was okay. Let Jimmy hear the gunshots. Let him hear the panic, the screams.

Lola entered the house through the three-car garage and took a bullet to the shoulder.

It was Marco Cabrini—the first soldier she'd worked with, a know-it-all motherfucker born into the life—and he'd positioned himself at the far corner of the foyer, in the perfect amount of shadow. Lola saw the zeros of his eyes but too late. Marco fired four times and the third shot found her. She slammed back against the door with a white-hot coal burning into her left shoulder and a new weakness in her legs. Her return fire was lucky in that she only half aimed. She caught Marco in the shin and he dropped shrieking. Lola reloaded and popped one into his skull.

She holstered her pistol and examined her shoulder for an exit wound. It was there, a raw pocket of exposed tissue beneath a hole in her jacket. Lola nodded grimly, recalling an axiom of her grandfather's: *Entry wound bad. Exit wound good.* She smeared blood and sweat from her brow, readied her gun, and pushed deeper into the house.

Then Jimmy came at her with a flamethrower.

...

Jimmy Latzo had always been a crazy son of a bitch. Lola used to think it was all for show—to color his reputation—but the more she got to know him, the more she realized that he was hard-wired that way. Or perhaps it was a short circuit, some synapse in his brain that struggled to connect to a considered response. Either way, Jimmy was a loose cannon. He once took a chainsaw to a man who'd cheated him out of $3,600 in a poker game. It wasn't the money—$3,600 was a piss in the ocean for Jimmy. It was the fact that he'd been *cheated*, that somebody thought he'd be stupid enough not to notice. On another occasion—shortly after Lola started working for him—he roped a snitch to the back of his Cadillac and drove him through the city streets, like some outlaw from the Wild West being drawn by a horse.

Jimmy had butchered, bribed, and hair-triggered his way up through the ranks of Carver City's criminal empire. He had crooked cops and politicians dangling from strings and would make them dance to whatever tune he was playing. He always got what he wanted.

With one exception . . .

Lola smelled the diesel first, so out of place in Jimmy's pristine house. A warning light flashed in her mind and she made the connection at the same moment she heard the click of the ignition charge. Jimmy had bought the flamethrower eighteen months ago—a reconditioned M2, World War II era. He sometimes wore it to business meetings and when addressing subordinates. "Burn, bitch," he squealed now, and a thirty-foot jet of flame squirted across the living room. It set fire to the silk drapes and the sectional sofa. It lapped across the walls and ceiling in red and orange tongues. Lola hit the deck and rolled. The hole in her shoulder limited her speed and movement. She felt her skin prickle in the heat.

Pain bolted through her. She watched fire purl across the ceiling. *Crazy bastard*, she thought. But that was Jimmy. He wouldn't blink an eye at burning his house to the ground if it meant she would burn, too.

"Fucking *bitch*!"

Lola dived and rolled again as Jimmy lashed another rope of fire across the room. She positioned herself behind a pony wall with antique vases displayed on it, each of which exploded in the heat. Flames curled around and over the wall. Her clothes caught in several places and she doused them with her gun hand. Jimmy triggered another ignition cartridge. She heard him cackle before a third cord of flame scorched the air.

Her lungs contracted. She felt a tight collar of panic, as alien to her as an exoplanet. *How do you fly a kite?* she thought, the heat pushing down on her like a predator pinning its prey. She ran multiple scenarios through her brain, along with probable outcomes. *Six seconds.* Lola latched onto this with all the fury in her soul. *Six seconds of burn time in that old M2. That's all.* Blisters bubbled across the backs of both hands and she felt her jacket melting into her skin. She covered her mouth and nose against the burning fumes and calculated. Jimmy had fired three bursts, totaling four seconds.

Two seconds remaining. Then he'd be spent.

Flames snapped at the walls and rippled across the ceiling. The living room was a furnace. Above all else, Lola knew she had to break cover and move. Her body could ignite at any moment.

She sprang from behind the pony wall, pushed through a window of flame. Fire crawled up her back and caught the tips of her hair. In that lunatic moment she heard two sounds clearly: the strings of Jimmy's grand piano snapping with odd melody, and Jimmy's whooping, victorious laughter. He squeezed another thread of fire toward her, thinking she had nowhere to go, but she hit the double doors leading into the dining room.

The heat blast pushed her to the back of the room. It pushed her free.

...

Lola yanked off her smoldering jacket. She slapped at her hair and legs. Her pants had burned away in places, revealing patches of reddened skin. There was small comfort in knowing that it could've been worse.

It was a long way from over.

"Bitch!"

The double doors Lola had crashed through burned like phoenix wings, keeping Jimmy at a safe distance. For now. There was another entrance into the dining room—an arched opening that led to the front hallway. Lola pushed herself to her feet and staggered through it just as Jimmy reached the hallway from the living room side. She raised her gun and fired awkwardly, managing two shots before Jimmy let loose with the flamethrower again. Lola retreated into the foyer. She tumbled over Marco Cabrini's corpse, half pulling him on top of her as the air crackled.

"It's all over, Lola," Jimmy cried. She saw him at the far end of the hallway, bordered by flame. He shimmered, appearing taller, *smokier*, closer to the devil he was. "No vengeance for you. Dumb fucking skeeze."

She'd get off a shot, but her right arm was underneath Marco, and even if she could aim with her left—if she didn't have a goddamn tunnel running through her shoulder—how accurate would her shot be? Jimmy flickered and swayed. He didn't look real.

Six seconds, she thought.

"I mean, I'm Jimmy fucking Latzo. I don't lose. You fucking *know* that. And guess what, baby doll . . . you tried to bring me down—fucking *end* me—and I brought *you* down. The unstoppable Lola Bear. I'm going to go from legendary to godlike."

And if he killed her, he probably would. It didn't matter that his army was torn apart and his house in ashes; killing Lola Bear would add considerably to his résumé.

Six seconds.

He started down the hallway with fire boiling around him, looking for all the world like some madman spat from hell. Lola watched him advance, her mind whirring. She needed time to clamber from beneath Marco Cabrini, steady her aiming hand, and put a bullet through Jimmy's heart. Her having that time depended solely on whether those fuel tanks were spent.

Jimmy stopped at the threshold between the hallway and

foyer, twenty feet from where Lola lay. She saw his face clearly, his pig-mouth drawn downward, his eyes alight. He winked and aimed the flamethrower at her.

The house burned behind him. Windows shattered and chunks of the ceiling fell. Smoke mushroomed.

"You could've had everything," he said.

...

Jimmy ignited another cartridge and a bright pilot flame sizzled at the tip of the flamethrower's muzzle. Lola got ready. She pushed with her strong shoulder, easing herself from beneath Marco's corpse. With equal effort, she raised the Baby Eagle. The sights wavered. Jimmy still shimmered.

He roared maniacally and hit the firing trigger, but instead of a long strip of burning fuel, there was only an anticlimactic dribble of fire. His expression collapsed. "Motherfucker," he gasped. He shook the flamethrower's wand and jiggled it up and down, like rattling a spray paint can to eke out the last few squirts.

Nothing.

Lola looked at Jimmy down the sights of her gun. She got to her feet and stumbled closer. She didn't want to miss.

"You're out, Jimmy."

"Out," he repeated numbly.

"Out of fuel. And shit out of luck."

Lola pulled the trigger.

...

She shot him where it wouldn't kill him—not right away—but where it would cause excruciating pain: in the gut. She imagined the bullet ripping through the soft mass of his stomach, spilling acids and bacteria, then barreling on to his colon, perhaps his spleen, before lodging in his kidney.

Jimmy screamed brilliantly, falling to his knees, then onto his back, where he rocked this way and that on the flamethrower's tanks. Lola stood over him, the gun targeting his face now.

"You couldn't let me have that one thing," she said. "You had to take it away."

"You don't know it was me." Blood bubbled from Jimmy's mouth. The tendons in his throat were as tight and thick as bass strings. "You don't know shit, honey."

"But I do."

The fire had spread down the hallway, jumping between the walls and ceiling, snapping across the floor. Something in the living room came down with a spectacular crash. Sparks flashed like lightning in roiling clouds of smoke. Lola blinked and spluttered. She'd have to do this soon.

"Love letters," she said, reaching into her pocket with her left hand. Pain corkscrewed from the hole in her shoulder, all the way to the tips of her fingers. "Beneath his tough exterior, Vince was a hopeless romantic. He used to write these little notes and leave them in places I'd least expect: under the sun visor in my car, so it would drop into my lap while I was driving, or inside a box of ammunition. Sweet nothings, you know: *Crazy about you, girl . . . Love you madly.* That kind of thing."

"Gah, I'm gonna fucking puke."

"His favorite hiding place, though"—Lola coughed and tilted away from the gathering smoke—"was inside my left shoe, beneath the insole. Always the left, because it was closer to my heart."

"*Gah.*"

"When I picked up Vince's . . . personal belongings from"—
she coughed again—"the coroner, I noticed the insole of his left
shoe was sticking up just a bit. So I lifted it, and sure enough, I
found a little note beneath."

Lola took her hand from her pocket, a folded piece of paper
clasped between her trembling fingers. "Not a love letter, though.
Not this time." She unfolded the paper and showed Jimmy what
was written there. A single word in smeared, brownish uppercase:

JIMMY

Another crash from the living room, the sound of breaking
glass, the tuneless thud of the grand piano collapsing. More
smoke dirtied the air above Lola. In a modest house with nar-
rower spaces, she probably would have died from smoke inhala-
tion by now.

"And yeah, Jimmy, it's written in blood. Vincent's blood. I had
it checked." Lola crouched, in part to breathe the fractionally
cleaner air, mostly to jam the pistol's muzzle beneath the ridge
of Jimmy's jaw. "He must've found time to write this after you
cut his ears off, but before you plugged a bullet in the back of his
skull."

Jimmy gagged and gurgled and spat blood. His eyes were spinning records, playing some shocked, disbelieving tune.

"You couldn't stand that I chose him over you," Lola said.

"Fuck you."

The fire had reached the foyer, climbing the high walls, black-
ening the windows. Something popped and sizzled. The door to
the downstairs bathroom burned off its hinges and fell with an
oven-hot clap.

"You couldn't stand losing. But here's a news flash for you,

Jimmy." Lola straightened, retreating a step in the heat. She kept the sights locked on Jimmy. "You were never in the running."

"Bitch, kill me if you're going to."

"I don't have to kill you, Jimmy. You were brought down by a woman—*one* woman. Even if you survive that bullet in your stomach, your reputation is in pieces. You won't recover from this."

"*Gah*." Jimmy kicked his legs in agony. His right hand was clapped to his gut, knuckle-deep in blood. His left hand was splayed, trembling, on fire. He didn't appear to notice.

"But I didn't suffer these burns, and kill all your men"—Lola looped her finger around the trigger—"just to let you live."

Smoke ballooned, obscuring Lola's vision. She waited for it to clear, although her eyes were red-raw and watering.

"You lose, Jimmy."

She fired twice and saw both bullets hit. Jimmy's body hopped like he'd taken a couple of quick zaps from a defibrillator. He tensed for a moment, as if all the feeling in his body were rushing toward one point, then slumped.

Lola tossed the last note Vince Petrescu ever wrote onto Jimmy's chest, where it curled and browned. She staggered backward, then butted through the front doors and out into the night. The first gulp of clean air pushed a wave of dizziness through her. She folded to her knees and vomited.

Sirens blared, extremely close.

Lola hurried from the scene, burned and limping. Blood trickled down her arm and dripped from her sleeve.

Become the storm, she thought, looking at the sky.

PART I
ONE-INCH
PUNCH

CHAPTER ONE

The "gun" was a Zoraki M2906, a replica, a prop for movies and training. It had the heft and feel of a real pistol, all working parts, except it fired blanks, not live rounds. The orange cap lodged into its muzzle, distinguishing it from handguns of a more lethal variety, had been removed a long time ago.

Brody Ellis sat behind the wheel of his shitbox Pontiac, parked in the shadows. His gaze switched between the stale yellow glow of the convenience store and the replica handgun lying on the passenger seat. The clock in the dash—part of the stereo, which had a CD and cassette player; that's how old and shitty his shitbox was—displayed 4:28. Brody had read somewhere, or maybe one of his loser buddies had told him, that four-thirty to five A.M. was the best time to rob a convenience store. The cash register would be fatter, for one thing. More important, the cashier, not to mention any cops in the vicinity, would be nearing the ends of their shifts, and were likely to be tired, not as responsive. Brody wasn't sure if this was reliable information. Maybe some cops started their shifts at four A.M., and some no doubt became more focused as the hours wore on. But it sounded plausible, and Brody needed every advantage he could get. He'd never robbed a convenience store before.

And you don't have to now, he thought. *You can still back down from this shit.*

Yeah, he could, but what then? Tyrese was hounding him for half the rent. Same as every damn month, only this month Brody was out of cash. His overdraft was maxed and his credit rating was for shit. There was nowhere to go for the money, and Tyrese was not a man of limitless patience.

"I'm just a big ol' teddy bear," he'd said when he showed Brody around the place, but yesterday that big ol' teddy bear had pinned Brody to the wall. "Get your half to me, or you and your damn sister will be out on your asses. I'm not fucking around." The muscles packed into Tyrese's arms had thrummed with dangerous energy.

Brody had pondered how different life would be if he were on his own. Jesus Christ, it was 2019, and at twenty-four years old, he could be the goddamn poster boy for free-spirited millennials. He could live out of his car, if needed, or crash on a friend's sofa. Just for a couple of weeks, until he found a job and pulled enough scratch together to get another place. But he wasn't on his own. Molly complicated things. She needed comfort and care, much of which came by way of her medication. How many more nights would he lie awake with her, holding her while she cried with the miserable pain of it all, the muscles in her delicate legs trembling and jerking?

...

4:34. The convenience store's light spilled across Independence Avenue like it had been tipped from a barrel. Buddy's, it was called. 24-HR VALUE WITH A SMILE! The owner's name wasn't Buddy. It was Elias Abrahamian, a middle-aged Armenian with a gold tooth and a neck tattoo. Drove a Beamer. Never smiled. Elias would be at home sleeping next to his young wife while reliable, bespectacled employee ANT—HERE TO HELP worked the register. Ant—130 pounds of piss in skinny jeans—would be fading, playing *Candy Crush Saga* on his phone to stay awake. Nobody had been in or out of the store for twenty-three minutes.

...

4:41. Brody picked up the replica, leveled his arm, aimed at the windshield. His hand trembled. He cupped his right wrist with his left palm, which helped but only a little.

"Empty the fucking register, motherfucker! Right fucking now!"

Should he scream, like a hair-trigger sociopath, or make his demand in an even but menacing tone, as if blowing Ant out of his Vans were all in a day's work?

"You know what to do, kid. Don't give me a reason."

He preferred the latter option. Keep it cool, controlled, and quick. But he'd never sell cool if he couldn't keep his goddamn hand from shaking.

Brody tried again.

"Let's fucking do this—"

Again.

"Gonna ask you once—"

Brody had done his homework. He'd reconnoitered Buddy's and several other stores this side of the Freewood Valley delta. They all had pros and cons, but Buddy's came out on top. No bulletproof glass. Only one employee running the night shift (Ant on Mondays, Tuesdays, and Thursdays). Clear routes in and out. Busy enough to put some stacks in the register, but quiet enough—particularly between three and five A.M.—for the store to be empty for longish periods.

"One wrong move and I'll—"

Three miles from the nearest police department, which didn't account for patrols, but Brody was hoping for some luck. Christ knows, he was due. Only two surveillance cameras, one above the checkout counter, the other at the back of the store. It was possible that Ant had an alarm button or .45 beneath the counter, but Brody depended on him being too shit-scared to use them.

"Don't be a hero, kid—"

...

Brody had bought the replica from a wheelchair-bound meth-head who was done with rolling the dice.

"Every time I stick someone up," he said, "you can see 'em weighing up their chances. As if having no legs makes a bullet slower."

"But there are no bullets," Brody said. "Right?"

"Shit, *they* don't know that. I mean, the Zoraki is a grade-A replica. They use that shit in movies."

"But it's harmless? I don't want to . . . you know, *hurt* anybody."

"Harmless to everybody except you. Cop sees you waving that around, you're going to catch a bullet."

"Don't I know it. So what's your asking price?"

"That model sells for about one-fifty on eBay."

"One-*fifty*? Fuck that. I was thinking, like . . . twenty bucks."

"Get the fuck out of here with twenty bucks. Jesus."

"Hey, man, I can probably get the job done with my hand in a paper bag."

"Good luck with that. See how confident you feel with your hand in a goddamn paper bag. That's what I'm selling here, man. *Confidence.*"

"Shit, I'll give you fifty."

"I'm looking at a yard, man. At least."

"A yard? You want to buy a yard?"

"No, a *yard*. You know, a hundred bucks."

"Right. Yeah. I can give you sixty, man. That's all the money in my world."

"Sixty and that Panthers lid."

"Deal."

...

4:48. Brody put his gloves on.

Go time.

...

He popped the car door and kept to the shadows until there were no shadows, only that lemony splash of light from the store. Approaching the automatic doors, he hooked a ski mask from his jacket pocket and rolled it over his face. The replica gun was in his other pocket, snug beside his wallet. Before reaching for it, a voice at the back of his mind once again insisted that he didn't have to do this, that he could back out and find another way. It wasn't the memory of Tyrese pinning him to the wall that kept him going, but of Molly trembling in his arms, trying hard—trying *so* damn hard—to be brave.

"Do it," he whispered to himself. "In and out. Thirty seconds."

A quick glance to his left and right before entering, to make sure no cars were pulling into the lot. Brody snatched the replica from his pocket and the weight of it in his hand—here, in the store lights, in the *open*—sent his heart cannonballing into his throat. He fumbled the gun, nearly dropped it, reeled into Buddy's with his lips peeled back behind the ski mask, his right hand jitter-bugging, the tip of the barrel swaying like a metronome. The colors—all the boxes and packets and labels—were too bright and the fluorescent lights had sunlamp intensity. Brody wondered, had the gun been real, if he might have pulled the trigger in the sheer rush of it all.

Ant saw him and shrank, his thin arms crossed over his face.

"Jesus Christ, man. No, please—"

"You know what to do. Make it quick."

"Aw, Jesus. Aw, fuck."

"*Now.*"

It didn't matter that Brody's hand trembled, because Ant couldn't see it. Ant cowered behind his crossed arms, knees knocking. He'd started to make a squeaky-door sound—*reeee, reeeeeee*—and his shoulders jerked with every shrill breath. Brody was the apotheosis of cool in comparison.

"The money, dickwad." Brody rapped the butt of the replica on the counter. "I'll put a bullet in your knee, I swear to God."

Ant yelped and curled into a loose ball. He made no move for the cash register. Brody clenched his jaw and looked behind him, checking that no one had slunk into the store. He scoped the lot, too. No headlights. No early birds heading to Buddy's for a pack of smokes and a shitty cup of coffee. It was just a matter of time, though.

"*Reeee, reeeeeeee—*"

Abort mission, the voice at the back of Brody's mind snapped. *This isn't working. Get the hell out.*

But he didn't want to abort mission. He'd come this far, and he wasn't sure he could muster the moxie to do it all again.

So what are you going to do? Give Ant a cuddle? Ask nicely?

Ant's keycard hung from a lanyard around his neck, twirling

slowly as he trembled. Brody had watched the store's cashiers use their keycards on previous occasions, touching the QR code to the scanner to open the register. It was that simple.

"*Reeeeeeeee—*"

Brody vaulted the counter in a wild, liquid move. Heart revving, he snatched at the plastic card around Ant's neck. Ant squealed and flailed with one arm.

"*No, please . . . nooooooo—*"

Ant's right elbow glanced off Brody's jaw. It didn't hurt but Brody staggered backward. He reached for the keycard again, grabbed it in one fist, and yanked. The lanyard didn't break.

"Mother*fuck*—"

Brody gave it another firm tug but the card remained around Ant's neck, and now Ant—probably unaware of what he was doing—grabbed a fistful of Brody's ski mask, trying to push him away, but succeeding only in shoving the mask up and revealing half of Brody's face to the surveillance camera. Brody growled, one eye rolling toward the front doors. How long before they opened and someone entered the store? How long before Ant realized that his assailant was a bumbling amateur who had no intention of using the gun?

Brody looked from the doors to the camera above the counter. There was a small black-and-white TV beside it, and Brody—the left half of his face uncovered—was the star of the show.

"*Reeee, reeeeee—*"

This (attempted) robbery had been somewhat planned, but what happened next was raw impulse. Brody raised the replica and brought the butt down on Ant's skull. It wasn't a shocking, forceful blow, but the skin cracked and blood flowed. Ant let go of Brody's mask and flopped backward. His eyes rolled in a giddy way that made Brody feel sick inside.

"Stupid asshole." Brody pulled his ski mask down. "You *made* me do that."

He looped the lanyard from around Ant's neck, leaped to the cash register, scanned the card. The drawer opened, revealing coins and banknotes—mostly tens, nothing larger than a twenty. None of the stacks were deep. Brody guesstimated a take of about two hundred bucks.

You're shitting me? he thought deliriously. *All of this for two hundred dollars.*

He grabbed the money, stuffing it into a paper bag he'd pulled from beneath the counter. It took seconds. Ant groaned and squirmed on the floor behind him. Brody was about to haul ass when he noticed the cash tray shift loosely. A tiny bell in his mind chimed, cutting through the chaos. He lifted the tray and tossed it, scattering coins. Beneath were more coins in neat rolls, and receipts and vouchers—also a bundle of bills with Benjamin Franklin's kindly face on the front. He was neighbored by more presidents in fatter stacks. Brody stared at the money for several out-of-body seconds, wondering if there was usually this much in the register, or if Elias had neglected to drop the day's take at the bank. Although it could have been two days' take—shit, a whole *week's*. There had to be two thousand dollars in there. Maybe three.

Brody removed the cash with an odd mix of euphoria and guilt. He considered, *very* briefly, leaving some behind, but took it all, even the four rolls of quarters—another forty bucks there.

"I'm sorry, brother," he said to Ant. "I hope your head's okay. I just . . . just . . ."

"Fuck you, man. My boss is going to kill me."

"Yeah." The bag in Brody's hand was quite full. "Dude's going to be pissed."

"Reeeeee—"

Brody twisted the top of the paper bag to close it, rolled over the counter, and headed for the doors. He moved quickly, sneakers skimming over the floor, his pulse echoing through his quavering limbs. Above the euphoria and guilt was the knowledge that he would never be able to undo what he had just done. Maybe later he would analyze how that made him feel—try to find some peace in it.

The doors opened. He stepped outside.

The girl came out of nowhere.

...

Brody collided with her. She staggered backward and he instinctively reached to steady her. "Sorry, I . . . I . . ." They danced awkwardly for a second or two, then she looked up—noticed the ski mask, the gun in his hand. Her eyes widened and she jumped back, and in that moment Brody registered how striking she was. Not pretty, but unusual, with penciled eyebrows, wagon-red lipstick, a scar beneath her left eye. She wore an Oakley beanie, purple hair looping from beneath it, framing her jaw and slender neck.

"Jesus!"

"Sorry," Brody muttered again. He bolted past her and ran without looking back, into the shadows where his car was parked.

...

He drove a mile with his head pounding, vision swimming, and finally pulled over on a side street lined with dark, dozing houses and mature trees. He killed the engine and inched the window open, listening for sirens. The city of Freewood Valley was silent, but for the sporadic hiss of traffic on Kimber Bridge.

Brody waited there until the sweat coating his body had dried, then he wiped his eyes—he'd been crying a little—and drove the nineteen miles to Rebel Point, the town he called home.

...

There was a twenty-four-hour CVS on Century Road. Brody swung into the lot and parked out of the spotlight. He fished the paper bag loaded with cash from the passenger-side footwell, dug his hand inside, and took out a sheaf of mixed bills—enough to cover Molly's prescriptions. He reached for his wallet with his other hand, but it wasn't in the pocket he thought it was in. Brody frowned. He remembered it being there, snug beside the replica. Hell, he'd *felt* it as he strode toward Buddy's.

"What the—"

Brody's heart dipped. A cold, unpleasant feeling leaked to the balls of his feet. He checked his other pocket. Maybe he'd switched it at some point—a little detail he'd forgotten in all the excitement.

No wallet.

"Shit." Brody tossed the bills into the passenger seat and rooted in both pockets again, going as deep as the stitching would allow. He found a candy wrapper and a bottle cap and an old receipt for breakfast at Applebee's. He bounded from the car, rifled his jeans. There was a firm rectangle lodged into his back pocket. A second's relief washed through him, but no, that was his phone.

"Jesus Christ, *no*."

Brody checked the car next: beside and beneath the seats, the center console, the glove compartment. He even checked the backseat. There was no sign of his wallet, which meant he'd dropped it, probably while pulling the replica from his pocket, but maybe while tussling with Ant. It was somewhere on the scene, and he couldn't exactly go back to look for it. His only hope was that it hadn't been found, but he thought it more likely the cops had it in their possession and were comparing the face on the driver's license with the clumsy, half-masked assailant on the store's surveillance video.

...

He bought Molly's pain management, antidepressant, and anti-spasticity medications, pulling the crumpled bills from the front pocket of his jeans and handing them over with trembling hands. The pharmacist asked if he was okay. Brody vaguely replied that he'd just come off a night shift and was dog-tired.

Two long miles to Palm Street, to the shotgun house he shared with his sister and teddy bear Tyrese. He expected to see police parked outside, two cruisers blocking the tight driveway, lights beating. The street was quiet, though, accented by a colorful wisp of morning light in the east.

Brody sat for a while, then gathered his things and went inside.

CHAPTER TWO

The house was laid out like a trailer, and not much bigger. The living room backed onto the kitchen, then a tiny bathroom, then two bedrooms fronted by a narrow hallway. Brody and Molly shared a room. A curtain divided the space, affording each of them a degree of privacy, although it was, altogether, too confined a house for secrecy.

Brody snuck in just after six A.M., faced with the challenge of hiding the bag of cash somewhere Molly or Tyrese would never find it. He didn't want their questions or accusations. Dealing with the police would be enough. His lame strategy, when they came, was to deny everything, let his public defender fight the battle. It was likely a losing battle, but denial was all Brody had. He'd already dumped the ski mask—threw it into a storm drain at the edge of town. Now he had to hide the cash.

He tipped the armchair and used the replica's barrel to punch a hole through the gauzy fabric beneath, then stuffed the cash and replica inside. It wasn't perfect, but it would do for now. He then walked as silently as possible into the bedroom he shared with Molly and placed her meds on the shelf above her headrest. He watched her sleep for a minute. She had two melted ice packs and a damp towel wrapped around her left leg.

Brody wanted to sleep, too—God, he was *exhausted*—but knew he couldn't. His mind was too active. He went back into the kitchen instead, made himself coffee, peered through the living room blinds as the day warmed, checking for cops. Tyrese woke at seven-fifteen, poured himself a monstrous bowl of Cheerios, dropped his considerable ass into the armchair in which Brody had stashed the cash and replica pistol.

"I want to see some money today," he grumbled.

"I'm on it."

"Better goddamn be." And a moment later Tyrese narrowed his eyes and asked, "What are you looking at?"

Brody lowered the blinds and stepped away from the window.

Molly hobbled in after Tyrese had left for work. At twenty-one, she was three years younger than Brody. Sometimes she seemed like a kid to him still, with a glimmer in her eye and a hopefulness in her demeanor. Other times she looked older, wearier. This was one of those times, and not only because she'd just woken up. She stood in the kitchen, propped on her crutches, looking at the stacks of dirty dishes, a bundle of laundry on a folding chair, the overflowing garbage, a calendar that hadn't been flipped since June.

"This shithole," she said.

"I'll clean today."

She nodded, went back to their bedroom, and returned a few minutes later with her medications. She set the boxes down hard on the kitchen table and for some time Brody couldn't look at her.

...

Molly had been born with the umbilical cord knotted around her throat and was deprived of oxygen for two and half minutes. MRI scans indicated mild brain damage. At age two, she was diagnosed with spastic cerebral palsy. Brody had an early memory of visiting his little sister in the hospital, her legs wrapped in casts from the knees down, still drowsy after what would be the first of her five surgeries. As Brody sat at Molly's bedside and cupped her small hand in his own, he knew that she would one day be strong enough to walk on her own, but that if she ever needed someone to lean on, he would be there.

She fell often. She picked herself up. The walker she used until she was six years old became a hated thing. She graduated to forearm crutches, which she still used. Molly was capable of walking unassisted, but not very far, and falling, she said, became tiresome. The left side of her body lacked response, but her ambition had no boundary. She could skateboard, drive a car, ride a horse. "Disabled?" she'd say. "It's just a matter of perspective, right?"

She was Brody's world. His whole damn world.

"You want to explain this to me?"

Molly took a seat at the kitchen table, opposite Brody, who regarded her with raccoon-black eyes and a not-now expression. His gaze jumped to the three boxes of medication—Motrin, Lexapro, Lioresal—on the table in front of her.

"I picked up your meds," he replied dryly. "Three cheers for Brody."

"You know what I mean."

"The money?"

"Yeah, the money." She sat back in her seat, arms crossed. A vein in her forehead pulsed. "Tell me you didn't steal it."

"I didn't steal it." He looked at her briefly. "I won it in a card game."

"Bullshit."

"What can I say? I got lucky."

Her speech was slurred, the left side of her mouth pulled downward. Her words were often incomplete—the result of muscle weakness, not lack of intelligence, as many people thought.

Brody understood her perfectly, always had. As he often said, he was fluent in Mollyese.

"You need money to win money." She had no problem conveying attitude. Skepticism, for instance, or outright disbelief. "Even scratch cards cost a dollar."

"Threw my car keys into the pot." Brody had thought this lie out. "That old shitbox is worth a hundred bucks. Probably."

The kitchen window was broken, wouldn't latch, so they heard more neighborhood sounds than they wanted to. TVs and cell phones, conversations, fights, sometimes gunshots. Now they heard a car turn onto Palm Street and drive toward their house, slowing as it approached. Brody tightened inside, his hands clenched beneath the table. He imagined a Rebel Point cruiser easing to a stop outside, doors opening, two broad-shouldered cops stepping out and heading toward his front porch. He held his breath, but the car passed by and was soon out of earshot.

They would come, though. Surely.

"You're not in trouble, are you?" Molly asked. "Jesus, Brody, I couldn't stand to lose you, too."

...

He reached across the table and took her hand, and would wonder later if this was more for his comfort than hers.

"Everything's going to be fine, Moll."

She pressed her lips together, her fingers tightening beneath his palm. Brody thought she would pull away from him but she didn't. Her eyes dropped to the medications. She'd already taken the Motrin and Lioresal, and that was good.

"I came into some money." He cleared his throat, looked reflexively toward the armchair, then the window. "Enough to get

Tyrese off our backs. Enough to make ends meet until I get another job."

Now she pulled her hand away.

"It'll be an entry-level job. Shitty hours. Minimum wage." Brody spread his hands, looked at her earnestly. *Whatever it takes, sis.* His jaw trembled. "But I'll keep my head down, stick at it. We'll get out of here—get our own place."

"It's hard to believe you."

Their mom had bailed on them in 2007. Brody—a deer-eyed twelve-year-old—had kissed her good night, as usual, and when he woke up in the morning she was gone. His starkest childhood memory was of trying to pacify Molly while she bawled, banging her crutches against the wall, blaming herself. Their father had shouldered the extra load, and he never complained, never faltered. Brody believed him superhuman.

Seven months ago, Ethan Ellis leaped from the roof of the Folgt Building—fourteen stories, 160 feet—and hit the road below like a moth hitting the headlight of a speeding Mack truck. His suicide was too much to come to terms with, not least because it made no sense. "If the world made sense," the police officer who'd delivered the death notification said to Brody and Molly, "I'd be out of a job."

Brody had been working at Wolfe Aluminum in nearby Racer, a non-unionized catch basin that had him pulling twelve-hour shifts for chump change. He buckled, understandably, after his old man's death, and found solace at Rocky T's—a dive bar on Carbon Street. His boss at Wolfe held his job for all of a week, then cut him loose. Brody bounced then from washing dishes at the Watermark to serving coffee and donuts to delivering Domino's. His last job was working the drive-through at Chili Kicks,

but he got fired after launching a Hot Tamale Burger at a customer who'd flipped him the bird.

He was a young man—he'd turned twenty-four in August—
who struggled to balance his grief with the responsibility of
looking after his younger sister. Evidently, he'd made some bad
decisions. Robbing a convenience store—dropping his goddamn
wallet at the scene—was just another.

A mud dauber buzzed at the kitchen window, trapped between
the torn screen and the glass. The sky beyond was metallic blue
scuffed with cloud. Brody looked at it wistfully, then wiped his
eyes.

"Not just out of *here*," Molly said. She gestured at the cramped,
dirty kitchen and everything else. "I want out of this town. Somewhere brighter. Cauley, maybe. They have the river."

"Buster's Ice Cream."

"Parade Park."

"Dad used to take us there." They said it at the same time, then
found their smiles, which, despite Molly's palsy, were identical.

"Can we?" she asked.

"Sure." *If the cops don't bust my ass.* "We set our legs. Balance."

"One-inch punch this."

Molly had suffered a succession of bullies, from the moment
she took her first awkward steps, spoken her first awkward words.
The worst was Trevor Hyne, with his barbed-wire attitude and
broad neck. It was hard to call a kid heartless, given they're
always shaped by their nearest and dearest, but if ever a child
was born with a hole in his chest, with nothing to influence,
to warm or nurture, then that child was Trevor Hyne. It wasn't
just that he mimicked Molly's way of walking, ridiculed her way
of talking. He would elbow her, pull her hair, kick the crutches

out from under her. Brody stood up to him several times, but Trevor—heavier and so much stronger—mowed him down like dead grass. "I want to learn karate," Brody had said to his dad. He was ten years old at the time. Too young to get into fights, but old enough to look after his little sister. "I need to get tough." But his dad insisted that fighting was never a solution. His mom apparently disagreed, and directed him quietly toward a YouTube video that offered step-by-step instructions on how to master Bruce Lee's one-inch punch. Brody watched the video over and over, learning how and where to position his body, how to twist his hips and flick his wrist upward a millisecond before impact. He practiced on a pillow duct-taped to a post in their backyard, gradually generating more and more power at extremely close quarters. "Strike just once with this punch," the grandly mustachioed instructor said, "and *if* you get it right . . . your opponent will think twice before confronting you again." Brody never got to use the punch on Trevor, though, because Trevor was crushed to death by a fifth-wheel trailer when Hurricane Ernesto cut across Salamander County (hard to argue with the gods on *that* call). Brody never forgot the instruction video, though, and the phrase—"one-inch punch"—had become his and Molly's euphemism for rallying against the odds, for making something out of nothing.

...

Midday rolled around and still no sign of the cops. Brody started to believe he'd dropped his wallet a safe distance from the store, and experienced the first sliver of hope, although he couldn't keep from peeking between the blinds every time he heard a car on Palm Street.

Molly had a part-time job at Arrow Dairy, punching sales data into a Mac. It earned enough for her to contribute to the bills, pay for her cell phone, and make occasional—but always practical—clothing purchases. She left for work shortly before one P.M. With the house to himself, Brody grabbed the bag of cash from inside the armchair, made some space on the kitchen table, and spread the notes out. He counted $2,360. There'd be no wolves at the door for a couple of months, at least. Molly would get her prescriptions, perhaps a few physical therapy sessions, which she hadn't had since Dad had died. Tyrese would get his rent. If Brody found a job quickly, he might even have enough for the deposit on a place in Cauley.

He counted the take again. Still $2,360.

Brody pushed $400 in tens and twenties into the front pocket of his jeans. He put the rest in the paper bag and found a new hiding place, beneath a loose floorboard at the back of his closet. He stashed the replica there, as well. Brody had no plans to use it again, but couldn't bring himself to toss it in the trash. It had cost sixty bucks, after all.

With that sliver of hope broadening, Brody sat on the front porch with one of Tyrese's beers and watched Palm Street breathe. Tiredness caught up with him, though. He dozed while the sun inched westward and the shadows grew—woke up to the sound of the bottle slipping from his hand and hitting the porch boards.

It was after four and still no cops.

...

"I ain't even asking, man." Tyrese counted the money, his deep eyes throwing quick, mistrustful glances at Brody. "Shit."

"It's all there, T. I even threw in a little extra for your troubles—

oh, and because I helped myself to one of your beers." Brody jammed his hands into his back pockets and exhaled. "Think you might get off my ass now?"

"Well, you know, I been thinking, man." Tyrese peeled off the last twenty, considered for a moment, then started counting again. "This is the third month in a row you been late. Shit, man, you only paid on time once since you been here."

"Yeah, well . . . I had some bad luck."

"I hear you, brother, I do. But your bad luck is becoming *my* bad luck, and that shit don't seem fair to me."

"Right, but"—Brody pointed at the notes in Tyrese's hand—"things have really turned around for me. It'll be better from here on out."

"Heard that song before."

"I know, T, but—"

"All things considered," Tyrese interrupted, "I think it's time you find yourself another place to live."

Brody nodded slowly, feeling something cold swim through his gut. He told himself this was no big deal. He and Molly were going to ditch this shithole, anyway. It was just a question of when. He had a little money now, and that was good, but he'd never secure an apartment in Cauley, or anywhere, without first getting a job. He'd need to prove earnings, to build his credit rating. It would take time.

"You'll, um . . ." Brody puffed out his cheeks and looked up at Tyrese. "You'll wait until I've got a new place first, right? I mean, you're not going to throw me out on the street . . ."

"You got until October tenth."

"Shit, T, that's two fucking weeks."

"And that's what happens when you're two weeks late with your rent." Tyrese finished counting the notes for the second time. He nodded and tucked the bills into his pocket. "I warned your dumb ass time and again. You only got yourself to blame."

"I'll give you another month's rent today," Brody countered. "Like, right fucking now. That'll give me until November."

"Not happening." Tyrese shuffled into the kitchen, pulled a jumbo bag of Cheetos from the cupboard, and poured them into his mouth. Bright orange crumbs popped from between his lips when he spoke. "I'm tired of your shit, Brody. It's over."

"Jesus, Tyrese—"

"I'm sorry as hell to be doing this, with your sister and all. Maybe that's why I gave you so many chances." More crumbs exploded from his mouth and peppered his sweatshirt. "I just can't afford to carry your ass no more. Shit, man, I work at Starbucks."

...

Brody helped himself to another of Tyrese's beers. He'd paid for it, after all—given the son of a bitch an extra ten bucks, for all the good it did. He drank it in a gloomy corner of the living room, mind pinwheeling, his anxiety amped.

Two weeks, he thought. His fingers tapped a mad rhythm on the bottle neck. *Out on our asses, if I'm not already behind bars.*

Brody knew only a tiny portion—five percent, maybe—of his anxiety could be attributed to Tyrese. The rest was down to the missing wallet. Sure, the police hadn't come knocking, but that didn't mean they wouldn't. They were probably trying to make him sweat. He'd be easier to break that way.

Another, more terrifying possibility occurred to Brody, and one he couldn't shake: Buddy's owner, Elias Abrahamian, hadn't called the cops because he'd decided to take matters into his own hands. He knew where Brody lived, of course, and tonight, or tomorrow night, or a week from now, he and his friends from the Armenian mob would pay him a visit. They'd kick down his door, put a bullet in Molly, then knock the shit out of Brody and cram him into the trunk of Elias's BMW. Brody would wake up in a damp cement room, peering through bruised eyes. *Steal from me, you fuckin' piece-of-shit, skinny-ass bitch?* Elias would say, selecting one from a multitude of torture implements arranged on a wooden bench. *Let me show you what I do to motherfucks who steal from me.*

Brody tossed the beer without finishing it, then dashed to his room and checked the jacket he'd been wearing yet again. He checked his jeans, too, front pockets and back. No wallet. He ran out to his car and went through it, using the flashlight on his cell phone to peer into all the small corners.

Nothing.

He drove to Freewood Valley and parked down the street from Buddy's, exactly where he'd parked some fourteen hours before. Knowing it was desperate, and pointless, he kicked at the trash and dead leaves at the edges of the sidewalk, and in the shallow gutter running beside the road. He ventured all the way down to Buddy's lot, and might have gone farther, but stopped when he saw the black-and-white cruiser angled in one of the parking spaces. A coincidence? Maybe. But Brody thought it more likely that the FVPD had finally gotten around to investigating the robbery, and were in the process of viewing security footage of Brody hitting Ant the salesclerk with the grip of his pistol, then lifting two-thousand-plus dollars from the cash register.

...

Molly said, "You didn't clean," which was a kinder way of saying what she *really* wanted to: *Jesus, Brody, can't you do anything?* She sat on the sofa and started to cry. Brody went to her. He held her, but his arms felt thin and feeble.

"It'll be okay." His words were feeble, too.

"October tenth. That's fifteen days away."

"I know. I'll think of something."

He couldn't see beyond the more immediate problem, though: jail time or the Armenian mob. If, by some miracle, he came out of this unscathed, then he could think about a long-term living solution.

"What are we going to do?"

Running was an option, he supposed—shacking up at a Motel 15, a long way from town, until this whole crazy shitstorm blew over.

"Brody?"

"I need time to think." He kissed Molly's wet cheek and touched his forehead briefly to hers. When he stood up to go into the bedroom, his phone started ringing.

...

Unknown number. Brody stared at his phone's screen for a long time. He imagined Elias Abrahamian at the other end, snarling, his gold tooth winking. *I'm coming for you, bitch*, he'd say as soon as Brody answered. *Like a jackal*.

He let it go to voice mail, then checked his messages. There were none. His phone rang again ninety seconds later. The same number. This time Brody answered.

"Hi, Brody."

"Who is this?"

It wasn't Elias Abrahamian, that was for sure. The voice was female, high-spirited. He imagined it belonging to a punk-haired

Manga character or sk8er girl, somebody tattooed and pierced and unafraid.

"Your new best friend," she said, and giggled.

"I know who you are." Because he did. He drew a quick and accurate line from the robbery to this moment, and saw a girl with purple hair looping from beneath an Oakley beanie, wagon-red lipstick, a scar beneath her left eye. He'd collided with her on his way out of the store.

Brody smiled, despite everything. He sensed a beat of excitement across the line—of *daring*.

"So," the girl said, and giggled again. "Do you want your wallet back?"

CHAPTER THREE

Nothing ever changed at Rocky T's. It was the same colorless décor, the same dour faces lining the bar, the same heartland rock on the jukebox. Even the bartender, Macy, was the same. She'd served every drink Brody had downed there, no matter the time of day, and never with a smile. Brody wondered if she kept a sleeping bag behind the bar that she rolled into when Rocky T's closed its doors at three A.M., and rolled out of again to begin work a few hours later.

He ordered a Bud Light and took a seat at one of the booths. TVs ran sports highlights and Bob Seger sang about—what else?—that old-time rock and roll. Brody looked around without making eye contact with anyone. There was no sign of the girl with the purple hair.

Brody was early, though. Twenty minutes early. His relief that the cops didn't have his wallet was enveloped only by his need to get out of the house. He couldn't stand to look one minute more into Molly's sad eyes.

...

"Waitin' for yer date to show?" Macy asked when he ordered his second beer ten minutes later. Her bleak eyes found his for a moment, then dropped like weights. She had a fat lip on its way to healing—somebody had clearly popped her in the kisser. "You finally hit up Craigslist, find yerself a cum dumpster?"

"Jesus, Macy, you found your calling in customer service.

No doubt about it." Brody threw a five on the bar. "Keep the change."

He returned to his booth, sank half of his beer in a single draw. Tom Petty belted from the juke—"Don't Do Me Like That."

The girl with the purple hair arrived in a dropkick of color.

...

Not a beanie but a yellow headband that lifted her hair into a vibrant sheaf. Her earrings and jacket were the blue of a new pool table. Shockingly red lipstick. The scar beneath her eye caught the light like broken glass. She slid in across from Brody and everybody turned to see.

"Heya."

Brody nodded and made a tight sound in his throat. He had hoped to appear strong. Badass. He had failed already.

"You look," she said, "*so* different without your ski mask."

"Jesus Christ." A glance toward the bar. All eyes on their booth. Even Macy was looking, her fat lip curled. "You want to lower your goddamn voice?"

"Whoops. Sorry." Her eyes shimmered. She whispered, "*You look so different when you're not robbing a convenience store.*"

"Jesus Christ."

Brody didn't have a game plan, but he thought he might play ignorant, deny all knowledge of the robbery, grab his wallet—give Miss Purple Hair a $20 reward—and go home. He saw now that this wasn't going to work. The girl was sharp, and all sharp things had to be handled with care.

He said, "You have something of mine."

The girl nodded, reached into her jacket pocket, and took out a Chase Bank Mastercard. She pushed it across the table. It was *his* Mastercard, of course, with its 23.9 percent APR and $7,500 limit (maxed).

"Where's the rest?" Brody asked.

"I have it. Not with me. But it's safe. I brought this"—she tapped the card with one bright pink fingernail—"so you'd know I'm not lying."

Brody sat back in his seat and looked at her through narrowed eyes. His chest tightened with impatience. He knew what she wanted: a take of the money. And how could he blame her? In her situation, he'd do the same thing.

"How much?"

"What?" She attempted an innocent expression, but there was too much mischief to cover. Her red lips twitched.

"Your cut," Brody said. "To keep quiet. That's what this is all about, right?"

She barked a short, hollow laugh. "Shit, Bro, do I look like I need money? These boots . . ." She lifted her right leg and clomped her boot on the table. It had a block heel, glimmering studs and buckles. "Valentino Garavani. Fifteen hundred dollars. This jacket. Seventeen hundred dollars. A birthday present. And you know what? I was pissed when I opened it because I wanted the one with the silver buttons."

Brody angled his head, his eyes still narrowed. He wondered what a girl who wore $1,500 boots was doing, alone, at Buddy's Convenience Store at 4:55 in the morning. The question touched his lips, but instead he asked:

"So what *do* you want?"

"You can start by buying me a drink." There was a dog-eared drinks menu on the table. She grabbed it, danced her finger over the cocktails. "Eeny, meeny, miny, moe." Her finger came down. "Sex on the Beach. Lucky me."

"That's an eight-dollar fucking cocktail," Brody gasped. "How about a shot of Tiger Breath? Tastes like shit, but it's only a buck fifty."

"Tempting, Brody. Very." She dropped a wink that pulled at something inside him. "Sex on the Beach. Make it snappy."

Brody rolled his eyes, went to the bar, ordered the drink.

"Shit, boy," Macy remarked. Still no smile, but her broken lip lifted. "She's got you wrapped around her finger."

"You don't know the half of it."

Macy mixed. Brody waited, looking at his sneaker tops, not at the old drunk next to him who'd started to sing along to Mellencamp, getting the lyrics wrong—

". . . *hold onto six piece, long as you can, Chinese come around real soon mixing women and men . . .*"

—and then Macy pushed the cocktail toward him, tall and orangey-red and served in a murky glass. Brody thanked her with a nod, reeled away from the bar, handed the drink to the girl with the purple hair as he took his seat in the booth. She closed her lips around the straw, cheeks dented as she sucked. "Dee-fucking-lish." She giggled, sucked again, and Brody, male, red-blooded, flushed from the groin out. He cleared his throat and mopped a film of sweat from his nose.

"I know a little about you, Brody," the girl said a moment later, swirling her drink with the straw. "I looked you up on Facebook. Everybody's favorite glory hole."

"Cute."

"Twenty-four years old. Star sign, Virgo. Dropped out of high school at seventeen—"

"To help my old man pay the bills."

"You like Foo Fighters, Arcade Fire, and *Stranger Things*. Is *The Matrix* really your favorite movie?"

"It's a classic."

"Seventy-nine friends. (By the way, some of them aren't *really* friends.) Relationship status: *nada*. Worked at Wolfe Aluminum—past tense. Your sister, Molly, has cerebral palsy."

"And yet I know nothing about you." Brody swigged from his beer, warm now, and flat. "I don't even know your name."

"Blair."

"As in, Witch Project?"

"Oh shit. That's an *old* one, Bro." That short, hollow laugh again. "I expected better from you."

"I guess I left my A-game at home." Brody sneered. That was the second time she'd shortened his name, or perhaps she was calling him *bro*, as in *brother*. Either way, it felt too familiar, too goddamn chummy, and he didn't like it. "So what *do* you want, Blair?"

"I'm getting to that." She sucked on her straw again, managing to smile at the same time. Her eyes had a cunning he couldn't help but find alluring. "You know all about loss, don't you, Brody? That deep, soul-sucking hurt. I'm guessing you still feel it."

Brody cleared his throat again.

Blair said, "Your father died seven months ago. Suicide. I read about it online. He jumped off the Folgt Building."

"What does any of this have to do with my goddamn wallet?" Brody leaned across the table. He gripped the edges with hands that had started to tremble.

"Your mom's not around, huh? Did she run away with her boss? Her brother-in-law?" Blair leaned across the table, too, her eyes digging into his. The glow around her dimmed. "Is she dead?"

"Dead to me." There were sparks in Brody's voice. He let go of the table and flexed his hands. "You know what, keep the wallet. I don't need this shit."

"I'm not going to keep it, Brody. What the fuck do I want with an empty wallet?" Blair sat back, sucked playfully on her straw, all candy and rainbows again. "I'll just hand it over to the police, tell them where and when I found it. Armed robbery is a felony, Brody. I think you know that. But did you know that here, in South Carolina, it carries a mandatory minimum sentence of ten years in prison?"

Brody covered his tired eyes.

"Up to thirty years. Thirty fucking years, man, with no shot at parole for the first seven." Blair whistled through her teeth. "Who's going to look after your sister while you're stamping license plates at the state pen?"

"The cops'll want to know why you didn't hand the wallet over at the time," Brody ventured. It was a desperate, straw-grasping plea, but it was all he had. "Withholding evidence—obstruction of justice—is an offense, too, Blair. Is that a chance you're willing to take?"

"I'll tell them I feared for my life," Blair said, and grinned. "You'd seen my face and . . . yeah, you had this *crazy* look in your eyes, and . . . well, I was just so *scared* you'd find a way to track me down." Her grin disappeared. She turned her lips down and her eyes swelled—huge brown O's brimming with guilelessness. "In the end, and despite the danger, I decided it was the right thing to do."

Brody groaned. He felt drained.

"You know, I think they'll be so jazzed with the evidence, and so busy dealing with you, that they won't bother with me." She grinned again. "Or maybe not. But hey, is that a chance *you're* willing to take?"

The jukebox switched tracks. The pinball machine flashed.

Someone at the bar cracked a joke and there was a clamor of laughter. Macy didn't smile. Brody took all this in with his tired eyes.

"I've got you where I want you," Blair said.

"Okay." Brody opened his arms, expanding the target. "So what's this about?"

Blair leaned across the table again. Everything about her was reckless, dangerous, exhilarating. She touched his hand—stroked it, suggestively, and Brody's heart clanged like a rock against an empty barrel.

She said, "I want you to steal something for me."

...

"I'm not a thief."

"There's surveillance video at Buddy's Convenience Store that says differently."

"That was a one-off. I was desperate."

"You're *still* desperate."

Brody had no answer to that. He tried to hold her gaze—to show some damn backbone—but she outshone him, as intense as a light in an interrogation room. He stared at the dregs of his warm beer instead, his fingers drumming idly on the tabletop. When he looked up again, Blair had slumped back in her seat. Her head was down.

"I know about loss, too." Her voice was almost too soft to hear. She had switched from manic to forlorn in a matter of seconds. "I can't remember the last time I had a good night's sleep. And all this . . ." She gestured at her purple hair and savagely colored lips. "It's a mask, Bro, hiding that deep, soul-sucking hurt I was talking about. Sometimes it feels like an anchor strapped to my ankle. I can float. I can ride the waves. But I'm always stuck in the same place."

"You've known me twenty minutes," Brody said. The iciness in his voice was a barefaced attempt to jump on her when she was down—to take back an iota of control. "You can call me Brody."

"Well, ex*cuse* me, BRO-*deeeeeee*." She rolled her eyes, then lowered them again. "My mom died nineteen months ago. February twenty-sixth, 2018. One year—to the day—before your dad died, in fact. So I guess, despite the sugary frosting and Valentino Garavani boots, we've got something in common."

Brody's jaw throbbed. His throat was so dry that he drank the dregs of his beer anyway, and shuddered all the way to his pelvis.

"She had bone cancer," Blair continued. "It took her out quickly. From diagnosis to dead in four months. She was forty-six years old."

"I'm sorry. That's . . ." Anything Brody said would be redundant, so he closed his mouth.

"There are a few things you need to know." Blair looked up again. Some of the flare had returned to her expression. "First, my mom was my best friend. We did everything together, and her death stopped me in my tracks. I attempted suicide three times, and came close once—had to have my stomach pumped at a hospital in Munich. The second thing you need to know is that my asshole father was cheating on her—even during her illness—with a woman named Meredith. Now, you've never met Meredith, but you *know* her. Just picture every hoity-toity, money-grubbing bitch you've ever seen in any movie or soap opera, like, ever."

Brody gestured to indicate he had such a picture in his head.

"That's Meredith," Blair snapped. "She's a fucking vile human being. An upper-level *biznatch*. And get this . . . she's my step-mom now."

"Well, shit, I'm sorry about your luck." Brody rubbed his eyes. "With that, and not getting the exact seventeen-hundred-dollar jacket you wanted, my heart just fucking bleeds for you."

"Asshole."

"You want to cut to the chase?"

"Oh, I'm sorry, do you have somewhere else to be?" Blair raised her voice. "JAIL, maybe?"

Brody stiffened in his seat, then looked the length of the bar to see if Blair had drawn any extra attention. She had; several whiskery faces had swiveled their way. "Punch her in the eye," one of those faces growled—Brody wasn't sure which one. "Mind your goddamn business," he barked back emptily. "I'll punch *you* in the eye."

"The third thing you need to know," Blair continued, unruffled by the attention, "is that my mom promised me her diamonds. It wasn't in her will or anything. It was something we talked about—an understanding between the two of us." She gestured at her ears and throat. "A pendant. Matching earrings. From Harry Winston. Not their top-of-the-line set, but probably worth fifty thousand dollars."

"Jesus," Brody said.

"They were a graduation gift from Nancy Reagan."

"Holy shit. Really?"

"My mom was from good stock, Brody." Blair finished her drink, looking away from him, and for just a second he saw the hurt in her eyes. "The idea was that I'd wear them on my wedding day, so that some small part of Mom would be with me." Blair blinked, scuffed the back of one hand across her cheek.

"And then my daughter, or daughter-in-law, would wear them on *her* wedding day, and so on . . ."

Brody nodded. His old man didn't have any money, and didn't leave them much beyond a closet full of faded clothes, a vinyl collection from the 1980s, and a five-year-old Chevy Malibu with monthly payments they couldn't meet. Brody sold what he could and took the rest to Goodwill. He kept one thing, though: a leather biker jacket that his dad had bought as a teenager, fully intending to one day buy the motorcycle to go with it—a Harley, of course—and ride from New York City to Los Angeles. Sadly, this life goal was never accomplished, but that didn't mean it couldn't be reinvented. Sorting through his old man's things, Brody found the jacket, hung it in his own closet, and had fostered ever since the fantasy that he might one day zip himself into it, and make the cross-country journey for them both.

He understood, as well as anybody, that people can survive in the things they leave behind.

"I took off after Mom died," Blair said. "I couldn't handle that shit. I went to Europe, India, Thailand. I was gone for eleven months, and when I returned to America, Dad and Meredith were married. And do you know what Daddy's gift to Meredith was?"

"Mommy's diamonds," Brody said.

"Ding-ding-ding. We have a winner."

"I've got to admit." Brody looked at her with some sympathy. "That's an asshole move."

"You're damn right it's an asshole move."

"And, what . . . you want me to break into your parents' house, steal the diamonds for you?"

"Ding-ding-ding." Blair beamed. Her smile was off slightly—

a few crooked teeth—but brilliant, nonetheless. "Shit, Brody, maybe you *did* bring your A-game."

"Maybe. And it's telling me to stay the hell away from this."

"Why?"

"Listen, I dig your bouncy rebel vibe, I really do, and I even feel a shred of sympathy for you." Brody held his thumb and forefinger half an inch apart. "But don't you think, when the diamonds go missing, that you're going to be prime suspect *numero uno*?"

"No, because I'm going to be with my dad when you steal them." Blair was still beaming. "The perfect alibi."

"But you won't be able to wear the diamonds. Or flaunt them. Or whatever the fuck else you do with diamonds. So what's the point?"

"The point, Brody, is that they'll be in the possession of their rightful owner. It's a matter of principle." Blair pushed her empty glass to one side, propped her elbows on the table, and leaned closer. "And no, I won't be able to wear them, but I've rented a safe-deposit box at a bank in Freewood Valley. That's where they'll stay, at least for the foreseeable future. And then, when God finally answers my prayers and strikes Meredith dead, I'll wear them to her fucking funeral."

Brody fetched an exhausted sigh. In lieu of sleep, he bought another beer. He bought Blair a drink, too, the same eight-dollar cocktail. Macy served him without comment. The old drunk mumbled along to Springsteen.

"Thanks." Blair nodded at the drink.

"Sure."

A strange silence seeped between them as they tended to their drinks—strange in that it was comfortable. Despite Blair's brash, brattish exterior, Brody had warmed to her. Just a little.

"This is not an impulsive thing, Brody. You should know I've been thinking about this for a long time." She licked her lips and shrugged. Her eyes, Brody noticed, were subtly different colors: brown and a lighter brown. "I thought about hiring someone. An ex-con, you know? But shit, I don't know anybody like that. I'm just a spoiled girl from the Valley. And then, when I bumped into you and your wallet dropped at my feet . . . well, I guess I saw that as a sign."

"Right." Brody glugged his beer, wiped his mouth, nodded. "I can see that, I guess. But, Blair, I'm *not* a thief. I know what I did, and I know what I'm capable of. And trust me, you need a professional, someone with lockpicks and wire cutters and . . . Jesus, whatever else thieves use. I'm just a jerkoff with a fake gun. I *will* fuck this up."

"Next Thursday. October third. One of my dad's business interests is throwing him a big, swanky party at the country club." Blair raised her penciled eyebrows. "I'll be there with my dad and Meredith. Our house will be empty."

"And I'm guessing that empty house will be rigged with a high-end alarm system and light sensors. Maybe a guard dog."

"No dog," Blair said. "Light sensors in front only. And yeah, there's an alarm system, which *will* be activated if you go through any doors or break any glass. Sunrise Security will be on the scene within five minutes." Her cheeks pulsed as she sucked on her straw. "But I've planned this out, Brody. Every detail. You're going to ghost in, then ghost out again. Invisible. You won't even need your ski mask."

"Good," Brody said. "Because I've already dumped it."

"My bedroom window will be unlatched," Blair said. "It's on the south side of the property. Second window from the right.

You can access it by climbing onto the pool house. It's an easy climb. I've done it myself, like, a *thousand* times."

"Sneaking in from all-night parties?"

"You know it." She grinned and touched his hand again. "Bad girl, right?"

"I guess." He lowered his eyes.

"Okay, so once you're in my room—and oh, excuse the mess, by the way, it's just, *ugh*, like, you know . . ." She threw her hands up, exasperated, as if troublesome pixies snuck into her room while she wasn't there and threw her shit all over. "Anyway, go straight through and on to the landing. My dad and Meredith's room is to the right, the double doors at the top of the stairs. Oh, and I'm *sure* I don't need to remind you to wear gloves, so you don't leave any paw prints on the door handles."

"I may not be a thief," Brody said, "but I'm not an idiot, either."

"You dropped your wallet at the scene of a crime, so . . ."

Brody rolled his eyes and gestured for her to continue.

"Their room is *hyoooooge*. Two walk-in closets, his-and-her bathrooms, a bed the size of Alaska. I'm not kidding, Bro, they'd need GPS to find each other and fuck."

"Wow, so . . . elegant. So refined."

"Always." Blair smiled and lifted her chin. Her sheaf of purple hair swished. "Okay, the important part: Meredith keeps her jewelry in her dresser. It's the one against the far wall, between the two picture windows. It has three mirrors and a stool in front with a gold cushion. There are hair-spray cans and makeup boxes and a few other things on top. I suggest throwing all that crap on the floor, emptying the drawers—"

"You want it to look like a robbery," Brody said. "Like the thief was after anything of value, not just your mom's diamonds."

"Exactly." Blair snapped her fingers. "I knew you were the right man for the job."

Brody slurped his beer and shrugged.

"The diamonds are in the top middle drawer on the right-hand side." Blair said, just above a whisper. "That drawer will be locked, but you can jimmy it easily with a flathead screwdriver. Now, I've served this on a platter for you, Brody—given you a blueprint for success. But you're going to have to bring your own screwdriver."

An imperceptible nod, but he hadn't agreed to anything. Not yet.

"The diamonds are in a black case with the Harry Winston logo on it. That's an uppercase *H* above an uppercase *W*. Leave the case, but grab the pendant and earrings. It'll look like you weren't after that case, specifically. You feel me?"

"I feel you."

"I'm stating the obvious here, but don't just take the diamonds. That *would* look suspicious—like, you know, I'd hired someone to steal them."

"Or blackmailed someone."

Blair's face, already cartoon-bright, lit from within. She smiled and everything shone. "Damn, I *like* you, Brody. You're so cute. Maybe, after all this, we can get together and paint the town a wicked shade of red."

Don't count on it, Brody wanted to say, but the words wouldn't come. Blair was heedless and loud and utterly refreshing. He thought going on a date with her would be like swimming with a stingray or BASE jumping from El Capitan, but it might be just the kick in the ass his dismal life needed. So he shrugged and lifted one eyebrow.

"Maybe," he said.

"Take whatever else you want," Blair continued. She took a long pull on her straw and a third of the drink disappeared. "Meredith has a lot of jewelry. *Too* much, that goddamn pig. Do whatever you want with it. Pawn it, give it to your sister, I don't give a fuck. All I care about are my mom's diamonds."

Brody tried to resist, but couldn't keep from indulging in a brief fantasy: hitting up several pawnshops across the state, racking up the stacks, then checking in to a safe, clean hotel (not the Motel 15, with its invariable assemblage of crackheads and whores) and staying there until he'd turned things around. If everything worked out, he and Molly could be in their new apartment—in Cauley, of course, maybe overlooking the river—by Christmas.

Brody pursed his lips. He knew it was foolhardy to give this fantasy even brief life. But if—just *if*—Blair's plan went as smoothly as she said it would . . . well, things could really work out.

"Bring me the diamonds," Blair said now, rattling her pink fingernails against her glass, "and you'll get your wallet back. If you *don't* bring me the diamonds—shit, if you can't do this for me, Brody, then I'm going to the police. And don't think for one second that I won't do it, because I will."

Of this, Brody had no doubt. He finished his beer and said, "I guess you really do have me where you want me."

Blair made a pistol out of her right hand. She aimed at Brody, pulled the trigger.

"This is crazy shit," Brody said. He ran his hands through his hair. His scalp was slick with sweat. "My dad always told me that two wrongs don't make a right."

"But maybe two wrongs *can* keep your ass out of jail." Blair drained her glass of everything but the ice cubes. "I've made this very simple for you. Do exactly what I say, and it can't fail."

"I guess you've never heard of Murphy's Law."

"'Whatever can go wrong, will go wrong.' Yeah, I've heard of it. And it's pessimistic bullshit."

"You're talking to a guy who dropped his wallet the *one fucking time* he robbed a convenience store, whose mom ran out on him when he was twelve years old, whose dad decided to swan-dive off a fourteen-story office building. Trust me, Blair, I'm very used to things going wrong." He took a deep breath and looked at her squarely. "Jesus Christ, I should change my last name to Murphy."

"Yeah. So sad. Did I mention the ten-year minimum sentence?"

"Would you cut me some slack?"

"I'm cutting you a *deal*, Brody. That's how things get done." Blair counted off the pros on her fingers. "You get your freedom, my dad gets a sizable insurance payout, and I get my mom's diamonds. Everybody comes out on top."

"Yeah, right."

"So what do you say?"

Brody slumped in his seat. So many thoughts ricocheted around his mind. He pressed the heel of his hand against his forehead and sighed.

"This is a no-brainer, Brody, but I can see you're tired—probably not thinking straight—so here's what I'm going to do." She tipped a wink and flashed her smile again. "I'm going to let you sleep on it. *That's* the kind of girl I am. But I *will* call you tomorrow morning, bright and breezy. And if you don't pick up the phone, or if you *do* but don't tell me what I want to hear . . ."

She made a siren sound—"*Weeooooow-weeooooow*"—and used her forearm to mimic a cell door slamming. "*Bam!* Don't drop the soap, brother."

"There must be another way," Brody muttered. "I'll wash your car for a year . . . I'll clean your goddamn room—"

"I've told you what I want." Blair got to her feet, standing all of five-five in her designer boots, but appearing so much taller. She leaned over and dropped a moist kiss on his cheek, very close to his lips. "I wasn't kidding when I said you were cute."

Brody squeaked something in reply, then she was gone, bounding exuberantly from the bar, leaving nothing behind but the print of her lipstick on his face.

...

He'd made his mind up before the door had even closed behind her, and became certain of his decision on the long walk home—to the point where he nearly pulled up her number on his phone and called her back. He didn't, though, because he was tired, and she was something else, and he wanted a clear head the next time he spoke to her.

Molly had fallen asleep in the armchair, her crutches resting against the cluttered coffee table, within reach. Brody sat on the arm beside her, brushing strands of light brown hair—the same color as his—from her brow. He recalled that memory from so long ago, its power refusing to fade over time: of standing resolutely beside her hospital bed, his hand joined to hers, promising to be there if she ever needed someone to lean on.

Brody lost himself to sleep soon after and dreamed brightly.

...

His phone rang a little before nine A.M. He was already awake, propped against his pillows, waiting.

"Did you dream about me?"

"I don't dream."

"Everybody dreams, Brody."

He smiled—yes, this was true—and listened to her breathing over the line, the near-silence of anticipation.

"So?"

He imagined her in her messy room, cross-legged on the bed, colorless without makeup but vibrant within, maybe dressed in Winnie-the-Pooh pajamas and chewing her lower lip.

"So," he said.

"You going to do this?"

"Yeah."

"The right decision."

"We'll see."

He heard Tyrese singing in the shower, the neighbors quarreling, Molly's crutches thonking across the kitchen linoleum. These were delightfully normal, unexciting sounds, and Brody thought in that moment that he could listen to them forever.

Blair said, breaking the ordinariness, "I live at 1186 Windsor Grove. That's in Freewood Valley. The Laurels. You know it?"

"I know it."

"Okay." Blair took a deep breath. "I'm going to run through the plan one more time. Are you listening?"

"I'm listening."

"Good."

CHAPTER FOUR

Brody had been to the Laurels only once in his life. His father had driven him and Molly through it shortly after their mom took to her heels. "A possible future," he'd said, rolling their old car past multimillion-dollar homes set back from the roads (private roads, not a crack or pothole to be found), pointing out the multiple-car garages and lustrous lawns, the security gates at the ends of long driveways, the fountains and sculptures. "You can live in a place like this if you work hard, if you go to college and give it everything you've got." From the get-go, he took his single-parent responsibilities seriously. Indeed, the only big fight he and Brody had—it nearly came to blows—was when Brody dropped out of high school to get a job, help out with the bills. "You can kiss your house in the Laurels goodbye," his dad had stated resignedly, and there were tears in his eyes.

Brody didn't think he'd ever return to the Laurels, but his life's script had been flipped again.

He was back, not to buy a house, but to steal from one.

...

He parked half a mile from Blair's house and walked across Poplar Common—just a regular dude out for an evening stroll. The car being so far away didn't bother him; if this went the way Blair insisted it would, he wouldn't need to make a quick getaway.

Windsor Grove bordered the common on its northwest side. Blair told him that the simplest way onto her property—to avoid being seen or triggering the light sensors—was to cut through the dense woodland that ran between the common and her back-yard (although "yard" was an extremely modest term for an area of real estate that could host the next Panthers game). "Those woods are thick," Blair had warned him. "I suggest you navigate them early evening, while there's still some light in the sky, then hang loose until it gets dark. We'll be out of the house at seven, and home by nine-thirty. That gives you plenty of time."

Brody crept into the woods a full hour before sunset. He twisted through an acre of crowded trees and blackened brush, and soon arrived at the perimeter of Blair's backyard. An eight-foot chain-link fence stood in front of him, but didn't present a problem. Chain-link fences were designed to be climbed, with their numerous little rungs and handholds, and the house was so distantly removed from its neighbors that no one would see him do so.

Hopefully.

He remained between the trees and scanned the back of the property. The light was dropping fast, but he saw the soft, green-ish shimmer of the swimming pool and pool house beyond. Just like Blair said, its position offered easy access to her room—the second window from the right. He nodded. Her intel had, so far at least, been accurate.

Yeah, that's great, a voice in his mind spoke up—the same voice that had advised him to back down at Buddy's Conve-nience Store. *But you're not even on the property yet.* Anything *can go wrong.*

"Thanks for the vote of confidence," Brody whispered.

She's a loose cannon. You can't trust her.

"I have no choice."

He checked his phone, shielding the light with his hand just in case someone caught a flicker of it from the house. 6:29. He retreated a few feet, found a dark space between the trees, and waited.

He scaled the fence at 8:10.

...

His heart hammered as he crossed the sloping lawn toward the pool house, moving on loose legs, the breaths punched quickly from his lungs. *I can't believe you're doing this again*, the voice in his mind persisted. *Are you fucking crazy?* He provided an answer by imagining—for the thousandth time—his and Molly's cool new apartment in Cauley, their beds separated by a wall, not a flimsy curtain, Molly wearing nice clothes, eating healthy foods. A rainbow of possibilities arced through his mind as he wobbled across the grass, around the pool, and pressed himself tight to the pool house wall. He wasn't doing the right thing here, he knew that. But there was sometimes a difference between what was right and what was necessary.

The voice in his mind fell silent.

Brody took a moment to work the jitters out of his legs and steady his breathing. His ungainly bustle across the lawn had triggered no lights or alarms, summoned no dogs. So far, so good. He plucked his gloves from his jacket pocket and pulled them on, then peered around the side of the pool house. A single spotlight shone on the water, coaxing a kaleidoscope of inviting reflections. More lights burned inside the large house, probably to offer the illusion that someone was home. Brody was caught, briefly, by the grandness of it. Old stone and rich timber, its faux-rustic structure offset by an extravagance of glass. He peered through this glass and saw Oriental rugs hanging on the walls and modern sculpture and a vast aquarium bristling with exotic fish. Blair's old man may as well have decorated the joint with hundred-dollar bills.

Brody watched for movement and listened for any sound—a TV playing, a creaking floorboard, a running faucet—that would indicate somebody was home.

Nothing. The exotic fish were the only sign of life.

"Okay." He took another deep, draining breath. Silvery spots flashed across his field of vision. "Let's do this."

He ducked around the other side of the pool house and used two solid pipes to clamber onto a heater the size of a refrigerator. From here he pulled himself onto the roof, then crawled carefully toward Blair's bedroom window. This provided the biggest challenge yet; the roof was slick and pitched at an angle. He came close to slipping twice. It would be just his luck—Murphy's Law in full effect—to slide off the goddamn roof and impale himself on the flathead screwdriver he'd tucked into his jacket pocket. He imagined Blair's bitchy stepmom stepping out for her midnight skinny-dip, and discovering him moaning, near death, bleeding into the pool.

He grasped the window ledge with both hands. When he was sure he had his feet beneath him and that he wasn't going to slip, he transitioned his grip to the bottom of the frame. Blair had told him she'd leave the window unlatched. He closed his eyes and lifted.

A part of him wanted the window to be locked in place. That way he could abandon this nonsense. *Hey, I tried,* he'd say to Blair. *You forgot to leave the window unlatched. This shit is on you, honey. Now give me my goddamn wallet back.* Another part expected an alarm to sound—for a helicopter to appear suddenly and hover overhead, its searchlight covering him.

Neither of these things happened. Blair's bedroom window slid up smoothly. Her lacy curtains billowed against his face.

"Shit," Brody said.

He went inside.

...

Another reliable piece of intel: Blair's room really was a mess. It may once have been the over-pink refuge of a spoiled Valley teenager, but had deteriorated since into mayhem—*fashionable* mayhem, as if an F3 tornado had spiraled through a branch of Nordstrom. There was a suggestion of the rebel inside: posters of Jim Morrison and Che Guevara, an Ayn Rand quote stenciled on her closet door: THE QUESTION ISN'T WHO IS GOING TO LET ME; IT'S WHO IS GOING TO STOP ME.

Brody picked his way across the room, wondering why she hadn't cleaned up at least some of this shit, given she was expecting a "guest." But then, maybe such uncharacteristic behavior would arouse suspicion. If this was the case—as opposed to pure laziness—then Blair really had thought of everything.

"I'm beginning to trust you more and more," he said under his breath, opening her bedroom door and skulking onto the landing.

This trust would last another ninety-eight seconds.

...

A light at the far end of the landing illuminated the double doors to the master bedroom. There was a potted yucca to either side and to the right a framed Warhol-style painting, not of Marilyn Monroe, but of a middle-aged woman with the same teased hair and sultry expression. This, Brody assumed, was Blair's step-mom, and in that moment he believed everything Blair had said about her to be true.

He paused on the landing for a second or two, listening to the house, for any whisper of life. He heard a dim, motorized buzzing. The refrigerator, perhaps, or the aquarium. Other than that . . . a perfect stillness. Brody scurried toward the master bedroom. The right door was ajar. He pushed it, tiptoed into darkness, stroked the wall for a light switch.

Click.

Brody's jaw fell two inches and he turned a full circle, awed. The house he shared with Molly and Tyrese would fit twice in here, with enough room left over for dancing. The bed was indeed Alaska, with its mountain range of greige pillows and glacier-white comforter. There were three chandeliers, several animal-skin rugs, a balcony with a hot tub and a Glassy Mountain view.

"Jesus Christ."

This was all so far removed from Brody's world that it took him a moment to notice the blood splashed across the hardwood floor. He almost stepped in it, in fact, drawing his foot back with a surprised gasp.

"What the—"

All thoughts of Blair's diamonds vacated his mind. His jaw still swaying, Brody followed the blood across the room—its pattern beguilingly signpost-like—and everything inside him turned cold when he rounded the side of the bed and saw the corpse.

...

It was the woman in the Warhol-style painting, easily recogniz-able with her teased blond hair and Botox lips. She was slumped in the corner, one arm tucked behind her head, her body twisted at an unnatural angle. Her bathrobe had rucked up to her thighs, which were smeared with blood. There was more blood on the walls and a circular puddle on the hardwood floor. It ran down her arms and drenched her body. She'd been stabbed multiple times. The knife—a *big* knife—was still lodged in her chest.

Brody's legs crumpled. He fell to his knees with a deep moan and stared at the dead woman until an increment of awareness returned. "Oh Jesus. Oh fuck." It took several weak attempts to get back to his feet but he managed, using the bed for support. "Jesus . . . this isn't . . . oh shit."

What was happening here?

A memory surfaced, clear and bright. He saw Blair sitting across from him at Rocky T's—punky, rebellious Blair, with her burning lipstick and dangerous eyes. *And then*, she said, talking about her precious diamonds, *when God finally answers my prayers and strikes Meredith dead, I'll wear them to her fucking funeral.*

"Blair," Brody said in a small, cracked voice.

The voice at the back of his mind was firmer. *Time to haul ass, Brody.* It jerked him to his senses, as potent as ammonia. *I told you she was a loose cannon. Now get the fuck out of here—this isn't your shit to deal with.*

"Blair," he said again. He shook his head. Could she really . . . ?

GET OUT!

Out. Yes. Right now. To hell with Blair and the diamonds. To hell with his wallet. He floundered backward. His sneaker slipped in Meredith's blood. "Gah . . . Christ." He wiped it thoroughly on one of the rugs. He'd seen *CSI*; leaving a footprint—even a partial footprint, the barest edge of one sneaker—could unfold badly for him.

Brody loped across the large room, through the double doors, and onto the landing. The staircase curved before him, leading to a lavish entranceway—to a door out of this place. He lunged down five steps before remembering something else that Blair had told him: that the alarm system would be triggered if he went through any doors or broke any glass. It didn't matter that he'd left no prints behind; this would still unfold badly if Sunrise Security caught him trying to climb over the front gate.

He had to go out the same way he came in.

Brody bounded up the stairs and back onto the landing. He took a single step toward Blair's room, then froze when he heard that buzzing sound again. He'd thought before that it had come from downstairs—the refrigerator, perhaps, or the aquarium—but no, it was closer than that, and smaller.

It sounded like a cell phone vibrating on a flat surface, or like the motorized zoom on a digital . . .

"Camera," Brody groaned.

It was positioned in the right-hand corner, focused on the staircase and doors to the master bedroom. Brody hadn't noticed it before because of the angle of the wall.

"What the fuck?" Here was something else—along with the corpse in the bedroom—that Blair had failed to mention.

That sly bitch, he thought, and on the back of this a single word that jumped on his brain like a fat kid on a trampoline. *FRAMED . . . FRAMED . . . FRAMED . . .*

The camera buzzed again. A small but serious red light blinked on one side. Its blank eye stared at Brody, full of accusation.

He had no strength in his legs but ran anyway.

. . .

Blair's window was still open and he all but dived through it. He hit the pool house roof on his shoulder, rolled twice, and fell to the stamped concrete below. With his only stroke of good fortune that evening, he landed like a cat, feetfirst.

Around the pool, across the broad lawn, thunder in his mind and booming through his limbs. He didn't stop running until he hit the chain-link fence. It catapulted him backward and he landed on his ass with a grunt. Slowly, crying now, he regained his feet and jumped at the fence, made it over in a mad, trembling scramble.

"What the fuck?" He'd whimpered this—and variations thereof—since he noticed the surveillance camera. "What the *fuuuuck*? What the actual fuck?"

Thin branches whipped and snagged at him as he crashed through the woodland, swinging his arms like machetes. He collided with trees, stumbled over roots, fell numerous times. Blood leaked from a shallow cut on his neck and his left glove was torn, hanging from his wrist by a strip of fabric. He got lost twice and had the presence of mind to use the Google Maps app on his phone. Eventually he wavered from the tree line and onto Poplar Common, bedraggled and breathless.

Ornate lights swept across the common, illuminating paved walkways dotted with people. Brody stuck to the shadows, brushing burs and leaves from his clothes as he moved. He climbed the wall and dropped onto Cardinal Street, then briskly walked the two blocks to where he'd parked his car.

His heart pounded. Tears dripped from his eyes.

What the fuck?

He got behind the wheel, worked the key into the ignition, but didn't crank it. He was in no condition to drive. Not yet. A short, tight scream ripped from his chest. He knotted his hands into fists and cried until his head was empty.

It was 9:27, according to the clock in the dashboard. For the next ten minutes, Brody tried to think through the situation. Should he go to the police? Would they believe him, a street kid from Rebel Point, who'd robbed a convenience store less than a week ago? Or would they believe Blair, whose mom had known Nancy Reagan, and who was clearly from good stock?

Would *not* going to the police make him look more guilty?

There were answers, he was sure of it. But they defied him, at least for now. His mind whirred hopelessly. It was like a computer that kept shutting down every time he issued a command.

"Help me," he cried.

9:33. His cell phone rang. He snatched it out of his pocket and saw Blair's number on the screen. A searing rage flared inside him. He clenched the device so tightly the casing cracked.

You bitch. You goddamn—

Brody pushed the green answer button and lifted the phone to his ear.

"Blair," he growled. He wanted to scream but his throat seized.

Nothing for a moment. He heard her breathing—imagined her sitting somewhere, her stupid fucking boots propped on the arm of a chair or on a table, a dirty smile tilting one side of her mouth. And then she spoke. Her voice was like battery acid.

"Heya, Bro," she said.

CHAPTER FIVE

Brody drove home with his mind slowly returning, like daybreak in a forest, gradually uncovering the dewy understory and the shapes of leaves, but predominantly illuminating the trees—so many tall and twisted trees—that he would have to navigate. They'd always been there, of course, but now they were deeper, denser, more uncertain.

And now there were wolves. Hungry . . . predatory. They had his scent. They were coming.

He ran a red light on Musgrove Road—pure absentmindedness—and his heart skipped at least five beats, but there were no cops in sight. All the Rebel Point cruisers would be nosing around Tank Hill, *his* neighborhood, where he was headed. But they weren't looking for him.

I've got some good news, some bad news, and some real *bad news.*

Tyrese's car was parked in their driveway, but positioned so that Brody couldn't pull in behind it. There was space for two if they went bumper-to-bumper. Tyrese was already reclaiming his turf, and that was fine. Brody didn't need until October tenth. He and Molly would be out before Jimmy Kimmel had finished his opening monologue.

Brody parked on the road and went inside. His front door key still worked, so there was that.

"Sup?" Tyrese asked without looking at him. He was watching *Thursday Night Football*, one hand wrapped around the remote control, the other dipped inside a bucket of KFC.

Brody ignored him. He shuffled through to the bedroom he shared with Molly. She was on her side of the curtain. He heard the unsteady clomp of her crutches across the floor, then the creak of the bedsprings. He stood for a moment, mopping tears from his eyes with his sweatshirt.

"Brody? That you?"

He took a jittery breath, fanned at his damp eyelashes with one hand. "Yeah, it's . . . it's me."

She heard it in his voice, of course, in those few brief, broken words. His anguish. His pain. The bedsprings creaked again. The curtain skated open and Molly was there. Without another word, she pulled him into her arms. Brody was straighter than her, his muscles were more firmly developed, but in that instant—as in so many other ways—she was the stronger of the two. She closed herself around him, her arms crossed behind his back, and held him like she'd never let go.

He cried onto her shoulder.

"Brody," she said. "What's wrong?"

Beat feet, Bro. Out of town. Out of state. Nowhere is too far.

"Moll," he managed between sobs. "I'm in so much trouble. And I think you might be, too."

...

The call had lasted almost seven minutes, according to the readout on his phone. In that brief time, Brody went from being utterly directionless to having his immediate future determined.

"Heya, Bro."

She said it just once but he heard it dozens of times. It dripped onto his brain—*drip-drip-drip*—and trickled into all the important grooves and crevices. The air inside his car turned acrid. He struggled to breathe.

"What did you do?" he managed at last.

"What I needed to," Blair replied. Her voice was remarkably controlled for someone who'd just knifed her stepmom to death. "Meredith was a gold-digging bitch, and my dad was blind to it."

"Jesus Christ, I know what you *did*." Brody's vision tripled. He blinked rapidly but it didn't help. "I mean, what did you do to *me*?"

"It's nothing personal, Brody. You dropped your wallet at my feet. I saw an opportunity and took it."

"You *took* it? You just fucking—"

"You're a high school dropout with no future. They used to send guys like you to Vietnam. To fucking *die*." She shrugged. Brody couldn't see this, of course, but he sensed it. She shrugged those wealthy, trouble-free shoulders. "You've taken the fall for the greater good. You're a sacrificial lamb."

"A sacrificial . . ." Brody gasped and spluttered. He had to thump his chest to get talking again. "You won't get away with this. I'll fight you every step of the way. I'll fucking *bury* you."

"Your public defender against the best lawyers in South Carolina. Good luck with that."

"You dumb bitch," Brody snarled. "I've got your calls logged on my phone. Your number. Times and dates. That proves—"

"It doesn't prove shit, Brody. I've been using a burner, which I'll destroy after this call." Blair spoke with such unnerving confidence that Brody didn't doubt her for a second. "I've spent so much time planning this, putting the pieces into place . . . do you honestly think I'd be stupid enough to call you on my cell phone?"

No, he didn't. He recalled her sharpness when they'd met at Rocky T's, and thinking that he'd have to handle her carefully. But he hadn't, and he'd been cut. Deeply.

There was something else, though . . .

"We were *seen* together," he said, unable to keep the desperation from his voice. "At Rocky T's. Jesus, you turned heads. *Everyone* saw you."

"Half-drunk assholes."

"The bartender wasn't drunk."

"Okay, but what did she see? You talking to some punk chick with purple hair." Blair made a sound, almost a giggle, mostly an exasperated sigh, as if she couldn't believe Brody's gullibility. "I don't *usually* look like that, you silly boy. I was incognito."

"I'll find something," Brody vowed, and then it came to him. He snapped his fingers. "Shit, yeah. Time of death. It won't match the timestamp on the surveillance footage."

"It'll be close enough," Blair responded coolly.

"I'll also take a lie detector test," Brody said. "I'll *insist*."

"Go for it. I've heard polygraph testing is only sixty-five percent accurate. At best."

"I'll make sure you take one, too."

Now she did giggle. A maddening sound. "Oh, Brody, I admire your spirit, but you've got nothing on me. If you squawk, it'll be your word against mine. And who's going to believe you? You're just a dirtbag from Rebel Point."

Brody closed his eyes. It felt like he was sliding down a steep embankment, grabbing at roots and rocks that appeared solid, only to have them come away in his hands.

"My bases are covered," Blair said. "But we're getting *way* ahead of ourselves. Listen a sec."

"I don't want to listen to you."

"I've got some good news, some bad news, and some *real* bad news."

Brody wanted to cut the call, but two of those words—"good" and "news"—sank their shiny hooks into him, dragged him along.

"The good news," Blair revealed, "is that the police are not looking for you. Well, not you *specifically*. My dad didn't submit the surveillance footage as evidence. He removed the tape before the police arrived."

"Why?" Brody asked. This didn't sound at all believable, but he stiffened attentively, like a starving fox that has caught the scent of food.

"That leads me to the bad news," Blair said, and sighed. "My dad has never been a huge admirer of our nation's judicial system. I mean, sure, you can get the death penalty in South Carolina for murder, and our lawyers would push for that to happen. But you could live a long time before they stuck that needle into your arm. Shit, my dad would probably die before you, and what kind of justice is that?"

Brody gritted his teeth. He knew where this was going.

"He's coming for you himself, Brody." Her voice conveyed an uncharacteristic gravitas, as if she'd gone from strewing flowers to pounding nails. "He wants to take matters into his own very capable hands."

"Capable," Brody repeated. Not really a word, more a vague grunt.

"And so we come to the *real* bad news."

"Don't tell me," Brody said. "Your old man is a former Navy SEAL badass. He cracked skulls in the Middle East—put the bullet in Bin Laden."

"Hmm, he's a badass, but he's no hero." A pause. Brody imagined her somewhere quiet, out of the way, while police and forensic units worked inside her house, snapping photographs, dusting for prints. "You never asked what my surname was—and to be fair, I'd have lied if you had. But I can tell you now: it's Latzo. My father is Jimmy Latzo. Have you heard of him?"

"No." Brody pressed a hand to his forehead. "I don't know. Maybe. I'm not exactly thinking straight right now."

"He's . . . a man of influence."

"A mobster, you mean."

"He doesn't like that word." Blair made a *tut-tut* sound, as if Brody were four instead of twenty-four. "Google him. There's a whole bunch of stuff online. Not all of it is true, of course. That whole thing about him tying some guy to the back of his Cadillac and driving him through town—heck, I don't believe *that*."

"Jesus," Brody said. His vision tripled again. He cranked the window and took a chestful of night air.

"Feel kind of sick, huh?"

"Oh Christ. What have you done to me?"

"Aw, come *on*. I never asked you to rob that convenience store. You brought at least some of this on yourself." She tutted again. "*Bad* Brody."

"You're evil," he whispered. "You're the devil."

"I have my moments," she said. "But anyhoo, back to the matter at hand: Believe all of what you read about my father, or none of it. I don't care. But take it from someone who shares a house with him . . . he is one mean son of a buck. And he's looking for you."

Brody's vision had cleared, but it dipped and swayed. He tried to focus on a single point: the black and yellow Waffle House sign on Carnation Boulevard. It bent like a tree in a storm, leaving pretty streaks against the sky.

Blair continued, "He knows what you look like, but he doesn't know *who* you are—"

"Yet."

"Right. But he's already got people working on it. His top guys. It'll likely take them a couple of days to track you down.

No longer than a week. You should use this time to get the hell out of Dodge."

"Why are you telling me this?"

"I don't know. Maybe I'm not the devil you think I am."

He blinked hard. The Waffle House sign bent the other way.

"Or maybe," she said, "some part of me really *did* want to paint the town red with you. Either way, consider this a courtesy call. I don't know, Bro, it kinda feels like the least I can do."

"You're going to hell," he said, and cracked a mad smile.

"And talking of courtesies . . . this may seem trivial now, but I took the liberty of destroying your wallet. Soaked it in gasoline and set that sucker on fire. No chance it can be used as evidence, so you don't have to worry about that little convenience store thing anymore."

"Oh," Brody said. Should he be grateful for this? Maybe, but it felt a little like Blair had handed him a Kleenex to wipe his boogery nose, moments before blowing his brains out with a shotgun.

"Run," she said now, the pounding-nails tone back in her voice. "I'm serious, Brody, if my dad finds you, he's going to hurt you in a hundred different ways. And then he'll hurt you again."

"My sister," Brody said weakly. More tears crept from his eyes.

"If you're lucky, he'll kill you first."

"I hate you."

Silence between them. Ten seconds. No longer. The Waffle House sign bent all the way to the Waffle House parking lot, then snapped back, straight as a flagpole. The flash it left behind was breathtaking.

"Beat feet, Bro. Out of town. Out of *state*." Her voice was still remarkably controlled. "Nowhere is too far."

"Yeah."

"I have to go. The police need to question me."

"Yeah," he said again, but she'd already gone. He lowered the phone, looked at the screen. Call duration: 6:46. His eyes flicked to the cracked, faded dashboard and the cassette/CD player and the fat odometer, and he wondered how far this old shitbox could take him.

...

Molly tried to hold on but he broke away from her, not wanting to—*needing* to. He dropped to one knee, grabbed an old gym bag from beneath the bed, and placed it in Molly's arms.

"Pack anything you absolutely can't do without," he said. His voice was a little firmer now. "Leave the rest."

"Brody, what—"

"We have to go. Tonight."

She stared at him. Her mouth formed a trembling, down-turned line that had very little to do with her palsy. "What are we running from?"

Not what—who. He had Googled "Jimmy Latzo" shortly after his call with Blair, when a fraction of his mind had returned and his hands had stopped shaking enough for him to punch the letters into his phone. He didn't go deep, though. He *couldn't.* Partly because time wasn't on his side. Mostly because the first thing he read put him off digging any deeper.

Blair had told him that not everything he read would be true, but the source—*The Mighty Penn Online*—appeared credible. There was a photo of Latzo, circa 2010. He was dressed like Gotti, had the same pompadour hairstyle, but terrible facial scarring. They looked like burn scars, Brody thought. The accompanying article reported that Latzo was being questioned by authorities in connection with the brutal murder of Art Binkle, a music industry executive from New York City. Binkle's label, Purple Mule Records, had allegedly declined to sign Latzo's nephew (not named), despite a generous monetary "contribution" from Uncle Jimmy. Soon thereafter, Binkle wrote an email to his close friends and business partners, saying that he feared for his life. He was found decapitated in his studio a week later, his severed head mounted on a turntable and spinning at 45 rpm.

"I'll tell you everything soon. I promise." Brody kissed Molly on the cheek. "Please, sis. Pack as quickly as you can. We need to get out of here."

"Are we coming back?"

"No."

"Never?"

"Never."

"But . . ." Tears shone in her eyes. "I have work tomorrow."

"Not anymore."

He left her standing with the gym bag in her arms, and walked through to the living room. The football game was on commercial break. Tyrese was using that time to rifle through the bones in his bucket, looking for any pieces of deep-fried bird he might have missed. He didn't know he had company until Brody said:

"We're out of here."

"Whu?" He had a bone in his mouth, too.

"It's what you wanted, right?" Brody's hands were still shaking. He rammed them into his back pockets. "Well, you got it. We're taillights."

Tyrese spat the bone from his mouth. "When?" He licked his lips and his fingers.

"Tonight."

"Whoa, damn. Really?"

"Really. We're just throwing some shit together, then we're out of your hair for good."

Tyrese considered this, then shrugged and shook his bucket. Bones rattled. He dug a greasy hand in and came up with half a thigh. "Where you going?"

"What's it to you?"

"Shit, man. Just asking."

Brody took his hands from his pockets, folded his arms, shuffled his feet. "Sorry, T, it's just . . ." He lowered his gaze. "We're going to Maine. I have an aunt there who—"

"You told me you don't have no family."

"Right. And we don't. She was a friend of my dad's. A close friend. We just called her aunt, you know? Aunt . . ." His mind blanked. A name. A female name. *Any* female name. ". . . Cherry. Aunt Cherry."

"Cherry, huh?"

"Cheryl, actually." Brody wiped his eyes. They were still damp. "Anyway, she said we can crash with her for a while, and she knows a guy who can set me up with work. Basement conversions, I think."

Tyrese nodded, sucking meat through his teeth, wiping his fingers down the front of his sweatshirt. "Right on."

"So, yeah . . . our bus leaves at midnight."

"You ain't driving?"

"Shit, my car wouldn't make it to Rock Hill, let alone Maine." Brody pushed out a laugh. His chest hurt. "I sold the car. Got two hundred bucks for it. The buyer's picking it up outside Rebel Point Central."

The commercial break ended. Joe Buck's voice welcomed viewers back to the game. Tyrese turned up the volume. "Okay, brother. Sure." He flapped a hand in Brody's direction. "Take her easy, man."

Fuck you, Brody thought. He returned to the bedroom. Molly packed silently and wouldn't look at him. He dragged a second gym bag from beneath his own bed and started throwing stuff in. Underwear, a pair of jeans, a few tees and sweatshirts. His dad's leather jacket wouldn't fit in the bag, but he refused to leave it behind and so put it on. It was too large for him; his dad had been bigger, even as a younger man.

Brody pulled the curtain for privacy, lifted the loose floorboard at the back of his closet. The last things he packed were the replica handgun and the fat bag of cash that had gotten him into this mess.

"You ready, Moll?"

"Nearly," she said coldly.

They were on the road fifteen minutes later.

...

They drove southwest, away from Blair and her mobster daddy (and in the opposite direction from Maine and their fictitious Aunt Cherry). Molly didn't ask any questions, and for that Brody was grateful. She took her medication and eventually drifted off to sleep. By midnight they had passed over the Tugaloo River into Georgia, the first of many state lines Brody hoped to cross within the next few days.

He fueled up west of Gainesville, wondering wryly which would last longer, the car or the tank of gas. They rumbled through the suburbs of Atlanta an hour or so later. The engine groaned and clattered but the car kept running. Brody angled the rearview so he didn't have to look at the shocked, unhappy man staring back at him. He focused on the road ahead, locked to the speed limit. He wanted to make the Alabama state line before stopping for the night.

Molly slept, occasionally half waking to stretch and knead the stiffness out of her legs.

...

Stardust Motel. Mallory, Alabama. Sixty rooms off a litter-strewn parking lot, this populated by aging pickup trucks and cars with expired inspection stickers. The rooms were off-white boxes with insincere splashes of color: fire-orange blankets on the beds; a russet carpet; paintings of birds. It was no different from the Motel 15 chain dotted across South Carolina, or the thousands of other motels across the Lower 48. The disadvantages with places like this—quite aside from the lack of comfort—were the vomit and/or piss in the stairwells, the junkies that oftentimes loitered in their doorways, the stained towels and sheets. The (only) advantages were the price and the fact that all they required was cash up front. No ID. No credit card.

"What are we doing here, Brody?"

"I messed up, sis." Brody ran his thumb over a cigarette burn on the nightstand. "I don't know if there's a way out of this, but if there is, I'll find it."

Brody's phone had switched over to central time. Two-ten A.M. They ate corned beef subs and Twinkies that Brody had bought at the gas station. He slept afterward, but woke early from a shocking nightmare. No chance of getting back to sleep, so he showered, then sat at the window and watched daylight spill across the parking lot and Interstate 20 beyond.

They were 220 miles from Rebel Point but he didn't feel safe.

...

The TV was small, Clinton-era, bolted to the wall. Brody flicked through the news channels, but there was no mention of Jimmy Latzo's murdered wife. The stations were out of Alabama and Georgia, though. Perhaps they weren't interested in out-of-state news. Or perhaps—and Brody prayed this was the case—Latzo's infamy wasn't as far-reaching as Blair had led him to believe.

He checked South Carolina's WIS and Live 5 websites on his phone, scrolled through several pages, but found nothing. Now Brody wondered if Latzo had used his influence to keep his wife's murder out of the press—at least until the guilty party had been tracked down. Bad for business, maybe.

Molly woke up at 7:37 with a numbness in her left hip and her leg shrieking in pain. Brody gave her two Motrin and helped her with some basic range-of-motion exercises. She swore at Brody throughout—told him she couldn't do this, she was going home.

"We don't have a home," Brody said.

Once the pain had faded and most of the feeling had returned, Brody helped Molly into the shower. He held one hand behind the curtain while she washed herself with the other. After she'd toweled off, Brody gestured at her cell phone, placed on the nightstand between the two beds.

"You can't tell your friends," he said, "where we are, or where we've been. No texts. No photographs. Okay?"

Molly nodded.

"If they ask—if *anybody* asks—tell them you've gone to live

with your Aunt Cherry in Maine. Your brother got a job opportunity. Too good to pass up."

Tears filled her eyes. She dropped onto the bed and wept silently. Brody gave her a minute. When he tried to hug her, she
pushed him away.

"I don't understand," she said irritably, "why we can't go to the
police. They can help us. *Protect* us."

"Not an option."

"Why? Is that who you're running from?"

"No. Not exactly." Bitterness swished through his stomach, as
brown as the nicotine stains on the ceiling. "I'm going to tell you
everything, Moll. But first we need distance, then I have to figure
out what we're up against."

She gave him a look, as if the room she had in her heart for
him were diminishing. "I miss Dad." She wiped her eyes on the
bedsheet. "He'd know what to do."

*Yeah, good old Dad. But let's not forget that he started this shitball
rolling when he killed himself.* Brody pushed his hands through
his hair, clenched them behind his head.

"Let's go," he said. "I want to be at least two states west of here
before the sun goes down."

...

They were midway across Mississippi when Jimmy's men caught
up to them.

CHAPTER SIX

The car gave up on the outskirts of Bayonet. It spluttered and lurched, gradually losing speed, until it surrendered with a disagreeable cough on the shoulder of Route 82.

"What now?" Molly asked.

Brody struck the wheel. His only plan had been to put at least a thousand miles between them and Jimmy Latzo. He'd been considering Oklahoma. A small town in the Panhandle, perhaps, where they could catch their breaths and contemplate their next move. Maybe they'd assume aliases and stay awhile. Brody could find work under the table—hang at the corner of a Home Depot until some contractor picked him up for eight bucks an hour.

But could they do that here, in Bayonet? THE SHINING LIGHT OF MISSISSIPPI, according to the sign at the edge of town, but also famous for the Byrnes Theater Massacre. It seemed an ominous place to hang their hats. Moreover, they were only five hundred miles from Rebel Point.

Not far enough.

"Talk to me, Brody."

"I'm thinking."

Two choices: ride the Greyhound, or repair the car. The former was appealing; they could sit back, talk things through, maybe sleep awhile. Brody was reluctant to give up the car, though. It was chewed by rust and breathing its last, but they might have to live in it, at some point.

He flipped a coin in his mind. It came down tails.

"Brody?"

"We get a tow to the nearest garage." He fished his phone from the console in the dash. "See how much it'll cost to get this shit-box back on the road."

...

The tow set him back $110—a sixty-dollar hookup fee, then another fifty bucks to pull his car three miles to Kane Bros. Auto. Brody was certain he'd been stiffed, but the tow-truck driver had an air of misery about him, so he elected not to contest.

The brothers Kane weren't much cheerier. Silas and Mort, whippet-thin twins with black greasy hands extending from the sleeves of their coveralls, their Adam's apples as stark as elbows.

"Prob'ly the fuel pump," Mort said.

"Yup," Silas agreed soberly. "The fuel pump."

They had arrived at this diagnosis without popping the hood. They simply circled the car, rubbing their whiskery throats, frowning.

"How much?" Brody asked.

"Shoot," Mort said. He leaned his narrow frame across the hood, looked at the VIN stenciled at the bottom of the dash. "She's a '99. Old."

"Old," Silas echoed.

"We can check Timmy's Salvage—might get lucky and pull a halfway decent replacement from a junker. That'll save you heartily. Otherwise, we'll have to call our supplier, see if we can get something reconditioned."

"Cheaper than new," Silas said. "A mite, at any rate."

"A mite. Yup. And besides, new won't matter much." Mort's Adam's apple yo-yoed as he spoke. "That'd be sorta like giving a new hip to a man with terminal cancer. If you follow me."

"I follow you. But how much?" Brody spread his hands. "Can you ballpark it?"

"Nope. Too many variables." Mort touched the wheel arch with the tip of his steel toe cap and rust sifted down. "Leave a number and we'll call you tomorrow."

"I'm paying cash," Brody said.

"All to the good, but that don't make us work no faster." Mort stepped around the hood and clapped an oil-dark hand on Brody's shoulder. "We'll get you moving as soon as. In the meanwhile"— he pointed south—"if you're looking for a place to rest your head, Katie's Motel has beds. Go five blocks on Main, then hang a right on Biloxi. She's across from the flea market."

Molly had absented herself from this conversation, and Brody wished he could have done the same. She stood to one side, shielding her eyes from the late afternoon sunlight. With business concluded, at least for now, the brothers turned their attention her way. They nodded curiously, scratched their bristly faces, and didn't quite whisper.

"Crutches, huh?"

"Yup. Crutches."

...

Katie's was of marginally higher quality than the Stardust Motel. There were no used condoms under the bed, no rat turds in the back corner of the closet. It was also more expensive: $69 a night. Katie—in her late fifties, but with the cut biceps of a professional arm wrestler—asked for a credit card to cover incidentals.

"What incidentals?" Brody asked. "Minibar? Valet parking?"

"We got cable." She cocked an eyebrow and smirked. "Adult entertainment."

She settled for an extra $20 cash, which put the room a buck shy of $90. Added to Mr. Happy's tow charge, Brody's bag of cash was $200 lighter than when he'd set out that morning. It was worrisome, not least because he still had to pay for repairs on the car, and they were still a long way from the Oklahoma Panhandle.

"How much cash do you have left?" Molly had always been able to tune in to his concerns. "You know . . . your winnings."

"Enough," Brody replied. "Don't sweat it."

He ordered pizza that night and they wolfed it down watching *Happy Days* reruns on TBS. They didn't laugh often, but when they did it was from deep down and wonderful. Several times, Molly started to say something to him, then stopped herself, at least until she'd taken her medication and pulled herself into bed.

"I know what it is." She looked at the ceiling, painted the same drab tan as the walls. "You know . . . the reason you're in trouble."

"You think you do," Brody said. "But believe me—"

"You didn't win at poker. You cheated. I don't know how, but you did. And the people you cheated . . . they're heavy guys. Mobsters, maybe."

Brody stripped to his boxers, climbed into his own bed. The sheets were cold, clean. They felt good.

"You fucked with the wrong people, Brody."

"Maybe. Or maybe I was just in the wrong place at the wrong time."

"The police can help. Think about it." Molly puffed up her pillow and lay down with her back to him. Brody sat against the headboard, knees drawn. He had to tell Molly everything, and soon. It wasn't fair to have dragged her into this without telling her why. But doing so meant confessing to robbing Buddy's Convenience Store, an act he was desperately ashamed of. Molly would be disappointed in him. Heartbroken, even. On top of everything else, he wasn't ready for that.

He flicked the TV off. Motel ambience filled the air: a shower running in a nearby room, a car pulling into the lot and idling, muffled voices from behind thin walls. Soon Molly's light snoring joined the chorus. Her body barely moved beneath the sheets.

Brody closed his eyes. He slept, but only for a moment. He awoke with his knees still drawn, his gaze fixed on the window. The aqua neon of Katie's sign showed through the curtains. He rolled his head, looked at Molly. She hadn't moved.

Five hundred miles from Rebel Point. Not enough distance. But perhaps enough to dig a little deeper into Jimmy Latzo's infamy. If Brody had any hope of getting out of this, he needed to do his homework.

He picked up his phone.

...

While the Gambino family—with John Gotti at the helm—called the shots in New York City, Don Esposito held sway over western Pennsylvania. This was in the mid- to late 1980s. Jimmy Latzo was, at that time, a young soldier with Rudy Tucoletti's crew, who controlled the action in Carver City, a remodeled commuter town south of Pittsburgh. Even then, Latzo was known for his short fuse. He once ran three teenagers through an industrial meat grinder for vandalizing a hardware store on Tucoletti's turf.

Allegedly.

In those early days, Latzo's reputation gave pause to anybody who thought to challenge him. A soldier from Nicky Scarfo's South Philly Mob had suggested that Latzo's methods lacked finesse, and that he brought shame to La Cosa Nostra. Soon afterward, this soldier was found strangled by his own large intestine, his mouth crammed with bull feces.

Jimmy Latzo feared no recriminations. Thirty years old, stylish, ostensibly untouchable. He was one of Tucoletti's big earners.

"This fucking kid didn't like to lose," Michael DeCicco wrote in his controversial memoir *Point Blank: A Keystone State Mob Story*. "And I mean at anything—business, gambling, women. I once saw him shoot some chick in the kneecap after she refused to dance with him. Boom. Down she went. And everybody turned a blind eye because of who Jimmy was, and what he might do. I swear to God, the kid was a fucking powder keg."

The consensus was that Latzo would blow himself up. It was simply a matter of *when*. In 1989, Rudy Tucoletti got himself whacked with the cancer stick and was dead within months. His cousin Frankie—"A fucking gutless pussy bitch," according to Michael DeCicco in the same tell-all—took the reins in Carver City. He didn't last long. Frankie was gunned down on the eleventh hole at Pin High Country Club, by order of Don Esposito's consigliere, Alfonso Monte, who'd heard that Frankie was in bed with the Feds. Jimmy Latzo—reckless, yes, but his ambition couldn't be questioned—was promoted to caporegime and given control of Carver City.

He was thirty-three years old. A 1990 article in the *Carver City Herald* referred to Latzo as "the Prince of Pennsylvania." Other monikers included "Chainsaw Jimmy" and "the Italian Cat," this latter on account of him always getting the cream. Certainly he lived the high life for the next few years. Fast cars, beautiful women, associating with celebrities and politicians. Carver City officials—those with enough clout to matter—ate from the palm of his hand. Not out of hunger, but fear.

Most of the legends regarding Latzo stemmed from the three years he presided over Carver City. They were many and colorful. Among them: setting fire to a restaurant in Greensburg that had refused him entry to a private function; the beheading of an associate who'd ill-advisedly described Latzo as having "little legs, even for a wop"; tying an alleged informant to the back of his Caddy and driving him through Carver City until only "rat scraps" remained (Blair had said she didn't believe this particular story, but Brody wasn't so sure). It was the suggestion of violence, too—the countless threats and intimidation. Several sources claimed Latzo occasionally wore a World War II–era flamethrower to business meetings to ensure proceedings went the way he wanted them to.

Such violence and arrogance garnered a multitude of enemies, some of whom tried to take him down. There were several failed hits, apparently, and a year-long racketeering trial that went quickly south following the apparent suicide of an FBI informant.

But no one is truly untouchable.

Accounts of what happened in 1993 were varied and unreliable. The authorities suspected gang warfare—Latzo had, on numerous occasions, overstepped the mark with the Russian mob and the tongs, and his actions may have caught up to him. Other sources claimed it was dissent in the ranks; with both Little Nicky and John Gotti behind bars, the East Coast families were in disarray. Folks were squealing left and right, trying to cut deals. There was inevitably bloodshed. Another theory—favored among those on the inside—suggested it was the work of one person. An unnamed soldier with an ax to grind.

Whatever the cause, it resulted in Jimmy Latzo's downfall. Most of his crew was wiped out, and his luxury house in Carver City was burned to the ground. Firefighters pulled Latzo from the flames. He suffered second-and third-degree burns to thirty percent of his body. He'd also been shot three times.

There followed a long process of surgeries, reconstructions, and convalescence. Latzo was rarely seen. Brody found one picture of him at a hospital in New York City, hooked up to numerous machines, wrapped almost entirely in bandages. It was haunting. Several cases were brought against him during this time, but all collapsed due to lack of evidence. No one turned on him, probably because he still had protection from Don Esposito, and there were bigger fish—and better deals to be cut—in Jersey and New York City.

Latzo wasn't finished, though. He was back on his feet by the late nineties, a "legitimate businessman" with interests in commercial real estate and property development. Over the next two decades his name was linked to multiple misdeeds, including insurance fraud scams, a counterfeit money operation, illegal gambling, and the murders of several high-profile businesspeople, with Art Binkle (his severed head spinning at 45 rpm) being the most gruesome and well-known case.

Latzo maintained his innocence, and always managed to slip the noose. He claimed he was being victimized because of previous and deeply naïve business dealings, and had worked to counter this with his "openhearted community efforts" and donations to local charities. According to the last article Brody read, Latzo continued to operate out of Carver City, but had homes across the United States.

"A lot of guys got away with shit back then," Michael DeCicco wrote at the end of his chapter on the Carver City mob. "But

Jimmy wasn't one of them. The kid answered for his crimes, and he's got the scars to prove it. Okay, maybe he isn't at the bottom of the Ohio River or pulling laundry shifts in Marion with the Teflon Don, but he still has to look at his burned-up face every day, and I know that fucking kills him."

...

They ate breakfast at a family restaurant called Missy Lean's. It was southern home style—biscuits and gravy, country-fried steak and eggs, everything served with a generous helping of "God Bless America." Molly ate like she hadn't seen food in a week. Brody, quite the opposite. His appetite was history. He nudged his food around the plate and glanced out the window every time a car pulled into the lot.

"You going to eat that?" Molly pointed at his cheese grits.

"Knock yourself out."

Most of the vehicles were Buicks or Chryslers driven by oc-togenarians wearing plaid shirts and baseball caps. Some were pickup trucks with either a rebel flag on the tailgate or a shotgun racked on the back glass. Occasionally a late-model Toyota or a loaded SUV pulled into one of Missy Lean's parking spaces, and that was when Brody clenched inside. He expected all four doors to open and the cast of *The Sopranos* to roll out. His late-night reading had influenced his imagination, hence the loss of appetite.

He hadn't slept much.

Reading about Jimmy Latzo was one thing, but knowing what to do with that information was another. The dude wasn't simply a corrupt businessman, he was a *mobster*, a fully fledged omertà-swearing-hanging-out-with-John-fucking-Gotti wise guy. How could he, Brody, neutralize that? Hide in Oklahoma and hope for the best? Informants went into witness protection to escape the mob. New towns, new identities, new lives. They had a practiced team behind them, and a shitload of money to set them up. All Brody had was a movie-prop handgun and a crapped-out Pontiac.

"Hey, remember that guy who used to visit when we were younger? A friend of Dad's, I think." Brody raised a hand above his head, indicating a greater height. "Tall. Six-three, maybe. Boston accent."

"*Bawston*," Molly said, and smiled. "Yeah. Karl somebody. Janko, maybe? Or Jankowski?"

"Karl Janko." Brody snapped his fingers. "That's him."

"Always wore tight T-shirts." Molly wiped cheese grits from her chin. "He was Mom's friend, not Dad's."

"Oh. Right."

"Why are you asking?"

"Options, I guess. Keeping them open." Brody picked up a piece of toast, considered it, then dropped it back on the plate. "I'm putting together a mental list of people we know."

"In case we need a favor?"

"Right."

"Okay, but there are people we know, and people who, maybe, would help us. Not too many names on that second list."

"Tell me about it."

"And Janko is a bad dude. I remember Dad telling me he'd been to jail a couple of times."

Brody shrugged vaguely, as if he'd forgotten this detail, when in fact it was at the forefront of his mind. A man like Karl Janko might know a place they could lie low for a while. He might even know someone who could hook them up with false papers.

It was a long shot, no doubt, but maybe their best, if not only, shot.

Molly finished her breakfast, then swiped the toast from Brody's plate and finished that, too. Brody looked out the window. A truck pulled in, USA flag rippling from the antenna, country music making its panels quake. Right behind it, a tar-black Yukon with tinted glass. A stone dropped into the pool of Brody's gut and sent unpleasant ripples through his body. He watched the Yukon muscle into a tight space, then the driver and passenger doors opened. The passenger was thirty-something, tan, dressed in an open-throat shirt and mirrored aviators.

Oh fuck.

The driver was older, in his fifties, silver-haired.

Oh fuck. Oh fuck.

"Brody? You okay?"

The rear doors opened. Brody waited for more wise guys to spill out, smoking Padróns, shooters wedged into the waistbands of their slacks. It was two women, though, the same age as the men, dressed more casually. The older woman wore an Ole Miss Rebels sweatshirt. They joined their men and the two couples walked hand in hand toward the restaurant.

"Brody?"

A sweet, relieved sigh escaped him, and he cursed himself for being so damned paranoid.

"I'm fine," he said.

He got the check.

...

Mort Kane called a touch before ten with good news, he said, and not so good.

"We'll get you on the road by midafternoon. Say, three. That's the good news. Unfortunately, we couldn't yank the parts at Timmy's, and our supplier can only get his hands on aftermarket."

"Aftermarket," Silas said in the background.

"You're looking at six hundred bones, parts and labor. If you're still paying cash, we can bring that down a mite."

Brody closed his eyes, imagining his dwindling bag of cash. He'd been thrifty since emptying the register at Buddy's, but there'd been expenses: food, gas, motels, Molly's medication, paying Tyrese. He'd have to count, but he guessed this repair bill would drop him to below a grand. And that was it. All they had left.

"How much would you give me for the car?" he asked Mort. "You know . . . take it off my hands."

Mort laughed. "Shit, son, you dropped a ton and a half of garbage onto our lot. You'd have to pay *us* to make it go away."

"Pay you?"

"Hundred should do it."

Silas: "Hundred."

"But you could fix it up," Brody said. "Sell it for a profit. Easy money."

"Nothing easy, son. We'd spend a grand fixing her up and sell her for five hundred. That's all she's worth, running smooth-like."

"Shit," Brody said, thinking that the six hundred bucks he was faced with spending was too much for a five-hundred-dollar boneshaker, but that the Pontiac Motel might be their go-to domicile in the weeks to come.

"What you wanna do?" Mort asked.

"Fix her up," Brody said.

Checkout was midday, but Molly, leaning heavily on her crutches, persuaded Katie to extend it to three—no additional charge. At 2:40, Brody covertly took six hundred bucks from his haul, pulled on his jacket, and started for the door.

"I'm going to get the car."

"Okay," Molly said.

"I'll be twenty minutes, give or take, then we're getting out of this shithole." He ran his hand along an imaginary highway. "Next stop: Oklahoma."

"I'm not going," Molly said.

"What?"

"You heard me."

"Yeah, but . . ."

Molly sat on her bed, hair strung across her face, one hand scrunching the sheets. Her crutches leaned against the nightstand. She grabbed one of them and threw it on the floor at his feet.

"I'm not leaving this room until you tell me what's going on." Spots of color found her cheeks. "Fuck you, Brody. I've got a right to know."

He picked up Molly's crutch, placed it on the bed next to his bag, neatly packed, ready to go. Molly's stuff was still dotted around the room.

"Yeah," he said. "You do."

"So?"

He ran a hand down his face, shook his head, and sighed. "Okay, listen, sis." He didn't know where to begin. What he *did* know was that he wasn't having this conversation now, in the motel room. "We've got six hours until we hit the Oklahoma state line. That's a long time, and a lot of highway. I'll tell you everything while we're driving. *Everything.* You have my word. But please, let's just get the hell out of here."

"No. Tell me now."

"There's not enough time. We've got to hand the key in at three." It was moments like this that he wanted to appear strong, show her that he had everything under control. Instead, his chin quivered, his shoulders slumped. "Please, Moll. Let's hit the road. I'll tell you everything, I swear."

She brushed the hair from her eyes and looked at him. He hated doing this to her. She was his best friend, his single source of light. He didn't know then that it was about to get much worse.

"I'm finding it harder and harder to believe you."

"I'm doing the best I can."

His phone chimed. Mort Kane. "Your car's ready," he said, and Brody told him that he'd be right there. He looked at Molly, his chin still quivering. She nodded.

"Don't fuck with me, Brody. You'd better tell me every goddamn detail, or I swear to God I'm jumping out on the move."

She'd do it, too, to prove a point, that she didn't take shit from him—not from *anybody*. He imagined her popping the door lock and bailing on Interstate 40. There one second. Gone the next. And he'd see her in the rearview, tumbling across the inside lane, crutches kicking sparks off the blacktop.

...

Repairs were $540 cash, but Brody haggled them down to five even. A minor victory. The car started like a champ, purred for a time, then everything started to rattle and smell, reminding him that it was still the same old shitbox, after all.

He drove to the motel and rolled into the space outside their door. As he stepped out of the car, Katie hollered to him from the main office.

"Good timing, kid. You got a phone call."

Brody frowned. Exactly nobody knew he was here, and his very few acquaintances—should they call—would hit him up on his cell.

"Got the wrong kid," he hollered back.

"Don't think so. She described you pretty good, right down to the shitty car and crippled sister."

This hooked him. Any anger he felt at Katie describing Molly as crippled was dissolved by her use of the word "she." He didn't have a girlfriend. His mom had deserted him. His buddies— such as they were—were all male. He knew women, of course, lots of women, but only one who would call him.

"Blair," he growled down the phone. It seemed he couldn't speak her name without growling.

"Listen to me, Bro—"

"How do you know where I am?"

"That's the reason I'm calling, you dick. I know where you are because *they* know where you are."

"What?"

"It didn't take my dad long to figure out who you are. Your face is *way* clear on the security footage."

"They know where I am?"

"As soon as he had your name, he had your cell number. You ever hear of geolocation, Brody?"

"Geo *what*?"

"Location. It's a way of tracking the exact whereabouts of a web-based computer or cell phone. There are *programs*. I can't believe you didn't dump your phone. How fucking stupid are you?"

Very fucking stupid, Brody thought. He felt the awkward shape of his cell in the ass pocket of his jeans—imagined it sending out signals, bleeping, like a dolphin with a tracking device strapped to its skull.

"What . . . ? How . . . ?" He shook his head. Too many thoughts, so many questions, hijacked his mind. He looked vacantly around Katie's office, her smelly plastic phone pressed to his face. There was an Alberto Vargas calendar on the wall, a dog in the corner, curled up like a dropped scarf, that startled him when it yapped. A half-eaten TV dinner was pushed to one side of Katie's desk, next to a thick novel with a bookmark parked midway through—Faulkner, Brody noted, which surprised him as much as the dog.

He gathered his thoughts.

"Why are you tipping me off?" It didn't add up—something was wrong with this picture. "You framed me. Why not just let me hang?"

"Maybe I like you more than I thought," Blair responded. There was no warmth in her voice. "You probably don't believe me, but I want us both to get away with this."

He *didn't* believe her. Something else was going on.

"How long have I got?" he asked.

"I don't know. Just get out of there. Right now. And if you know anybody who might protect you, now's the time to look them up."

"No shit."

"And dump your fucking phone. My dad will hack it for contacts, which is why I'm calling you on the motel's landline."

Brody slammed down the receiver and reeled from the main office, bumping his hip on the edge of Katie's desk and knocking her TV dinner to the floor.

"You *shithead*," Katie shouted as he ran across the lot. "That's an incidental!"

He made it to their room in a series of bounding, Impala-like strides, shouldering the door open—

"Molly," he gasped. "We've got—"

Brody froze. Everything appeared in stale snapshots. The tan room and crappy, mismatched furniture. His and Molly's bags on the bed—she'd packed up at last—ready to go. The slick mobster grabbing Molly from behind, with one forearm around her throat and the muzzle of a semiautomatic pistol locked to the conch of her ear.

"Man of the hour," he said, and ran his fat, pale tongue across Molly's brow. "Welcome to the party, motherfucker."

CHAPTER SEVEN

et her go," Brody said, both hands raised. "Please, man. She's got nothing to do with this. I'm the one you want."

"Shut your mouth, kid. You're in no position to deal."

There was a second mobster behind the door. Brody didn't see him until the door banged closed and he grabbed Brody by the upper arm. He was wide and sweaty, his puffy face crowned by a mop of black, boyish curls.

"Ain't nothing to this kid, Leo. Look at him—scrawny little bitch." The thug shook Brody by the arm. "I could break him in half, throw him in the trunk."

Molly squirmed against Leo. Shaky, terrified breaths rumbled from her chest.

"Please," Brody said. "I'm begging you, man. Leave her out of this."

Leo responded by tightening his hold on Molly, squeezing so hard that her feet left the ground. Her eyes swam with helplessness, fear, confusion. It was how she'd looked when the cop told them that their father was dead.

"Come on, man," Brody implored. "Just let her—"

"This is how it's going down," the mobster gripping his left arm interjected. His face was close enough for Brody to smell the nicotine and cooked meats on his breath. "You two assholes are coming with us. You, shit-for-brains"—he shook Brody again—"are riding trunk-class. Play nice and we only have to tie you up and gag you. Try anything stupid and we start breaking bones. That'll make the long trip to Pennsylvania even longer."

Pennsylvania, where Blair's daddy was waiting.

"Please, guys, *please*—"

"The cripple can ride in back with me. But one wrong move"—
the mobster jabbed a finger toward Molly—"and into the fucking trunk she goes."

Brody shook his head. There was no reasoning with these thug
assholes, and he wasn't going down without a fight. That might
result in broken limbs, but it was better than being led like a
sheep to Jimmy Latzo—to a long and miserable death.

He had to do something.

His eyes scanned the room. Could he grab Molly, hit the
bathroom, lock the door, and jump out the window? Could he
bounce the TV off Leo's skull, snatch the pistol, shoot them both
in the legs so they couldn't give chase? *The pistol*, he thought, and
his gaze flicked to his gym bag. The replica was inside, tucked
toward the bottom. Having it in his hand would turn this into a
different conversation.

"Let's go," Leo said. "Right fucking now."

"Yeah," Brody said, and yanked his left arm free of the mobster's grip. At the same time, he curled his right hand into a firm
knot and launched it. His knuckles connected with the big guy's
mouth—smashed his lips against his teeth. It wasn't a lights-out
punch by any means, but it knocked him back a step. Brody
lunged for his gym bag, and managed to get it unzipped before a
sweaty hand grabbed him by the back of his neck, squeezed hard,
turned him around. Another hand smothered his face, pushed
him backward. Brody's head thudded against the door and stars
shimmered.

"Son of a *bitch*," the thug bellowed. "I should pop this motherfucker, Leo, I swear to fucking God."

"You can't pop him, Joey."

"I'll break his fucking teeth."

The stars dispersed. Brody saw the big mobster, Joey, directly in front of him, eclipsing the room, but what he *really* saw was a bully, mean and mindless—a grown-up version of Trevor Hyne, who'd relentlessly mimicked Molly's way of talking, who'd pulled her hair and kicked the crutches out from under her. A gallon of anger raced through Brody. He recalled a certain video on YouTube, in which a lavishly mustachioed instructor tutored the technique behind a punch made famous by Bruce Lee. Brody also recalled a pillow duct-taped to a fence post in their backyard, hit so many times it had to be doubled over and taped again.

Blood filled the gaps between Joey's teeth. His eyes were flames. "I'm gonna take your fucking—"

Brody moved so suddenly it surprised even him. He formed a fist with his right hand and thrust forward, covering four inches—not one—with improbable force and speed. Maybe it was muscle memory, or pure luck, but his form was exquisite. The power didn't come from his wrist, or from his right arm, but rather from his entire body, transferred from the ground up, channeled into a fist-sized pocket of explosive energy.

It worked.

Joey—easily a hundred pounds heavier than Brody—spilled backward like he'd taken a sledgehammer to the gut. On another day, he might have dropped to one knee and recovered after several deep breaths, but this was not that day. His feet tangled and he fell with the density of a dropped cylinder block. The back of his skull met the edge of the nightstand with a tremendous crack. His eyes fluttered before he lost consciousness.

Good night, Joey.

Leo's face was a stupid question mark. The pistol slumped in his hand. Brody, meanwhile, didn't miss a beat. He pounced at his gym bag, dug his hand inside, came up with the replica. It felt immediately powerful, dependable, *good*—the opposite of how it had felt when he'd robbed the convenience store.

Brody pointed it at the mobster. His hand was remarkably steady.

"Okay, you son of a bitch," he said. "Let's deal."

...

Could Leo tell, from across the room, that Brody's gun was fake? Was there an obvious giveaway that someone who knew his way around a firearm—a mobster, say—would pick up on immediately? He studied Leo's face, waiting for him to crack a smile or roll his big brown eyes.

He did neither. Nor did he back down.

"Bad fucking move, kid," he said.

"Let her go."

"You don't get to call the shots." Leo curled his lip, adjusting his hold on Molly so that she covered more of his body. "Drop the piece, or I'll put a bullet in this bitch's eye."

Brody took a step closer and leveled his arm to more determinedly aim at Leo. He cracked a smile of his own; Leo couldn't tell that the gun was a fake. That was good. He also believed that Brody had killed Jimmy Latzo's wife, and a man crazy enough to do *that* should be approached with extreme caution.

This was the advantage he had to press.

"You really want to negotiate with *me*?" Brody's eyes and nostrils flared. He gestured at Joey. "Why don't you ask this fat fuck how negotiating with me works out?"

Leo's gaze flicked toward Joey, who was slumped against the nightstand, his neck bent at an awkward angle.

"Now let her go, or I'll shoot you right between the eyes."

Brody showed his teeth, his lips still tilted into a kind of smile. "You know I'll do it."

"Maybe you will," Leo said, lifting Molly a little higher. "Or maybe you hit her instead."

"I doubt it," Brody said. "But that's a chance I'm willing to take."

Molly cried out and shook her head. She looked at Brody, still with the fear and helplessness in her eyes, but there was something else . . . a bewilderment, a distance, as if she were seeing something she thought was red, but had just learned was actually blue. This hurt Brody more than these goons ever could. He wondered if she'd ever look at him the same way again, or if he'd lost some vital piece of her forever.

"You need to think about the situation you're in," Leo said, and maybe he sensed a frailty in Brody; he appeared to expand beyond Molly. The gun at her ear was darker, deadlier. "There are more of us on the way. Another carload. Bad hombres. They'll be here any moment. You can't take us all on, kid."

"I'll worry about that," Brody said, "when they get here. *If* they get here."

"Oh, they'll get here. Jimmy wants you. And Jimmy always gets what he wants."

Brody flinched at the mention of Jimmy's name, betraying just how scared he was.

"And what are you going to get?" he asked Leo. "A bullet in your skull?"

"I don't think so."

If there was a balance, it had shifted in Leo's favor. It wasn't just that he had backup en route, but that he was becoming more confident that Brody wouldn't—or couldn't—pull the trigger.

This standoff had to end.

"Let's talk about *your* situation," Brody said. "You have a gun to my sister's head, but you're not going to pull the trigger. You're not going to shoot me, either. Why? Because Jimmy wants us alive. Those are his orders. And Jimmy always gets what he wants."

Leo snorted and said, "You better goddamn believe it."

"I killed his wife, right? That's what you think. Stabbed her, what . . . fifteen times? Twenty?" Brody couldn't look at Molly when he said this. He kept his gaze riveted to the mobster. "I'm a crazy son of a bitch. Approach with caution, am I right? So tell me, Leo, how confident are you that I won't pull the trigger?"

"I don't know about crazy, but you *are* a stupid son of a bitch." Leo tensed his forearm, drawing Molly yet closer. "You really think I'm scared of you?"

"You should be," Brody said. "Because I'm exactly three seconds away from splashing your brains all over these fucking walls."

"Fuck you, kid. You won't do it."

"You sure about that?"

Leo sneered and dragged the pistol from Molly's ear to her cheekbone, pressing so hard that her eye closed.

"Let her go," Brody said.

"You got some fucking balls."

"One."

"Jimmy only wants *you* alive, you stupid fuck. He don't care about the cripple."

"That's my sister, you asshole." Brody took another step forward. The tip of the replica was threateningly close to Leo. "Two."

It wasn't only that Brody's hand was steady; in the last few seconds, he became aware of a change *inside*, something running through his veins. It paralleled his fear, then overtook it—as cold as steel, and as solid. He was quietly confident that he *could* shoot Leo, if the gun were real, then turn and bang a round into Joey. The abruptness of this realization unnerved him, but didn't stop the imagery from flowing through his mind: pulling the trigger twice, two deafening reports, two Italian corpses.

"You're dead," he said, as if the things he'd seen in his mind had come to pass.

Leo must have sensed this hard shift in Brody, because he lifted the gun from the side of Molly's head and raised both hands. "Bad fucking move, kid," he said for the second time, taking a step backward.

Brody exhaled. Every muscle in his body clicked down a couple of notches. He kept the gun locked on Leo, though.

"Come on, Moll."

He thought Molly might collapse on the bed in tears, and he'd have to pull her from the room. But, always full of surprises, she grabbed her crutch from where it rested against the nightstand, held it like an oar, and drove the tip into Leo's gut.

"Who's a fucking cripple?" she said.

Leo doubled over, his cheeks blown out. Molly switched hand position on the crutch, holding it more like a baseball bat now. She placed her weight on her stronger right side and swiveled. The crutch whistled through the air and the tip clocked the ridge of Leo's jaw. His head rolled sharply to the right. He dropped to his knees.

Molly staggered toward Brody. She fell into his arms.

"Get us out of here," she said.

Brody grabbed their bags from the bed and together they spilled from the room. Before the door closed, he saw Leo getting to his feet and taking one groggy step forward. Blood smeared his mouth and chin.

The car—thank God for fleabag motels—was right outside, seven feet away. Brody opened the passenger door and Molly flopped across the seat. He loaded both bags on top of her, then slammed the door and rolled across the hood to the driver's side. As he jumped behind the wheel, the motel room door opened. Leo staggered out, one hand looped around his pistol.

Brody yanked the keys from his pocket and gunned the ignition. The car started like a champ again. He threw it into reverse, backed out of the space. Leo took a shot at the front tire and missed.

Molly screamed, scrabbling at her seat belt. Brody didn't wait for her to buckle up. He cranked the wheel and whipped the front of the car around. In the rearview, he saw Leo raise the gun to take another shot, then think better of it and rush toward his own car.

"Go, Brody!" Molly yelled.

"I'm *going*!"

He jammed the transmission into drive, plugged his foot to the floor, and lurched out of the lot. An oncoming Jeep Cherokee swerved and missed them by a beat. Brakes hissed. Horns howled. Brody raced east on Biloxi, turned left on Main, and ripped toward the edge of town.

A glance in the rearview showed not one car in pursuit, but two.

There are more of us on the way, Leo spoke up in his mind. *Another carload. Bad hombres.*

"Shit," Brody said.

They'd catch up to him on Main—four lanes of straight blacktop. They'd shoot out his tires or go one in front, one behind, and force him to a halt.

"Shit, *shit*."

The light at the next intersection was red. Brody slowed but didn't stop. He steered between traffic—horns everywhere—and hit the gas on the other side. "Got to get off this road," he said, then made a sliding right onto a side street lined with parked cars. He traded paint with a few of them, then found his lane and floored it.

The mobsters weren't far behind. They appeared in the rearview and gained fast. Molly looked over her shoulder.

"Oh shit, Brody."

"Yeah." He gripped the wheel. "I know."

"If we get out of this, I'm going to kill you myself."

Brody made another sharp turn, then another. Both cars followed, smoke pouring from their tires. The rush of air past Brody's window, the engine clatter, the overworked grumble of the exhaust, were nothing compared to his sister, who looked over her shoulder again and screamed through the rags of her hair.

"Faster, Brody. Go . . . *go!*"

CHAPTER EIGHT

Blair's phone rattled against her right hip. She plucked it from her pocket, glancing at the screen as she slipped from the room to answer.

"Where is he?"

"Tear-assing out of Bayonet," Leo replied. Blair heard his car's engine roaring in the background. "Keeping to the backstreets. A better chance of losing us that way."

"Is he scared?"

"Kid's got some fucking balls."

"Is he *scared*, Leo? Tell me you put the fear of Christ into him."

"Are you kidding me?" A horn blared. Tires shrieked. "I took a shot at his front tire. Missed on purpose. But yeah, he's pissing in his pants right now."

"Okay." Blair closed her eyes and smiled. This whole thing was playing out exactly as she'd planned. "Back off. Let him lose you at a red or something. We'll see where he goes, what he does next."

Leo started to say something, but she ended the call and stepped back into Jimmy's office.

"What's going on?" Jimmy called out.

The massage table was erected in the center of the room and Jimmy lay facedown on it, his hairy ass covered by a white towel. Puccini floated from the Echo on his desk. The air smelled of jojoba and sandalwood.

"He's on the move again," Blair said.

"On the move," Jimmy muttered. "Jesus, Blair, you better pray you don't lose him."

"We've been glued to this kid's ass for five months," Blair said. "Monitoring his cell phone, his email. We've got a tag on his car and Eddie the Smoke has been tailing him since he left Rebel Point. We won't lose him."

Today's masseuse was Celeste. Long eyelashes. Strong wrists. Oiled to the elbows.

"But you keep rolling the dice. You keep taking chances." Jimmy grunted as Celeste pressed knuckles into his sacrum. "I mean, why . . . *ungh* . . . why ambush the motel room?"

"To terrify the little fucker." A proverb occurred to Blair—the one about old dogs and new tricks. She couldn't help but smile. "We can't afford to let Brody relax. We're *herding* him, Jimmy. Not following him."

"Herding. Right . . ."

The Puccini encouraged a thoughtful, relaxing vibe, but the atmosphere in Jimmy's office was anything but. Physically, he was prone, glistening with essential oils. Energetically, he was like a shark in a tank, circling for the scent of blood.

"You need to be cool, Jimmy." Another proverb surfaced in Blair's mind, one she felt impelled to share: "Slow and steady wins the race."

"Not in my goddamn world," Jimmy snapped. "In my world, if you want something done, you've got to . . . *ungh* . . . grab it by the balls."

"But this isn't your world. It's mine." The smile left Blair's eyes, yet her lips crept higher, showing teeth. "This is my show, remember? I told you that I'd deliver Lola Bear, and that's exactly what I'm going to do."

...

Jimmy had trusted her with this, but it wasn't his style to play the long game. Direct force had always been his modus operandi. Blair was not opposed to violence—she'd employed it herself on many occasions—but was it effective when it came to procuring information? Jimmy certainly believed so, but the numbers suggested otherwise. In the twenty-plus years that he'd been searching for Lola Bear, his methods had netted only one crucial lead. A two-bit gun dealer out of Memphis had attempted to sell information—"Fifty Gs and I'll tell you what I know"—but had shown an eagerness to negotiate after Jimmy had taken a chainsaw to his left foot: *"Little Rock, Arkansas. Calls herself Jennifer— ARRGH CHRIST JESUS FUCK SHIT—Jennifer Ames."* Jimmy's top guy, Bruno Rossi, had gone to Little Rock and tracked "Jennifer Ames" down—sent Jimmy a photo of her buying groceries at a Harps Food Store. The next photo Jimmy received was of Bruno slumped in the corner of some brick room, a small, ragged bullet hole over his left eyebrow. It was accompanied by the message: *Back off Jimmy!* But Jimmy hadn't backed off. He sent more men to Little Rock, but Lola had blown town by the time they got there.

Other leads had gone nowhere, and then, nine months ago, one of Jimmy's lawyers, Aldo Perera, had tracked Lola's family to South Carolina. "By going back and cross-referencing old files, and with some black-hat-level hacking and old-fashioned cunning, I was able to link Vincent Petrescu's last will and testament to a general practice lawyer in Minnesota. Turns out Vince's sister, through her company, wired three payments of ten thousand dollars each to the Juniper Law Firm in Minneapolis—no doubt money that Vince had indirectly willed to Lola. From there, I joined the dots to a divorce lawyer in South Carolina. The details will numb the shit out of you, but the upshot—the divorcé: Ethan Ellis, a foreman at Blackridge Auto. Two kids. Brody and Molly. You'll find them in Rebel Point, a little shitburgh in the upstate region." So Jimmy had sent a team to Rebel Point and they watched the family for six weeks—too fucking long, by Jimmy's reckoning. There was no contact with Lola. Not even an email. Boiling with impatience, Jimmy had sojourned to Rebel Point with his direct-force strategy. A fruitless excursion, as it turned out; Ethan Ellis had no idea where Lola was, and in Jimmy's experience, people tend to speak truthfully when being dangled from the rooftop of a fourteen-story building.

Dropping the divorcé from the rooftop of a fourteen-story building hadn't worked, either. Jimmy had thought it would draw Lola—a vengeful cunt if ever there was one—out of hiding. But no beans.

"So we grab one of the kids." Jimmy's eyes had been wild and black in the scarred rag of his face. "Shit, *both* of them. Make the little fuckers talk."

At which point Blair had intervened.

"You think that'll work, Jimmy?"

"Sure. If they know something—"

"But they don't. You *know* they don't. Torturing them gets you nothing but a mess to clean up." Blair knew how to handle Jimmy—an intuitive understanding of his ugly, yet delicate, clockwork, and what it took to make him tick. "Maybe it's time for something other than brute force."

Jimmy's eyebrows had been burnt off in 1993 and the muscles across his brow were partially paralyzed. He conveyed many expressions, including doubt and consternation, by tilting his head and pressing his tongue to the inside of his cheek.

Blair said, "We need to use our brains, Jimmy."

His tongue had remained lodged in place for a full twenty seconds, then he retracted it and exhaled through his nose. "Brains, huh?" He struck a light to a cigar, reclined, and propped his expensive Italian shoes on his desk. "So tell me, Blair . . . you got any ideas?"

...

To begin with, she wasn't Jimmy's daughter.

The Strawberry Avenue Massacre, in which thirty-three rival gang members killed one another in a storm of semiautomatic gunfire, had been entirely Blair's doing. Unlike Jimmy, she saw value in the long game.

"You singlehandedly eliminated Swan Grove's gang problem," Jimmy had said to her. This had been several years later, after he'd taken Blair under his wing and spent tens of thousands of dollars training her to be a fighter as well as a thinker. "You did what the Feds couldn't. How?"

"Time and patience," Blair had replied.

She'd been born on a bed of damp cardboard, gasoline stench in the air, a bleak December wind howling through the broken windows of her momma's trailer. Momma was a tweaker and penniless. Daddy was gone, taken by a gator while harvesting hallucinogenic mushrooms in the Wasino Bayou. Daddy was a small man—not an inch over five-three—and the rumor went that the gator had swallowed him whole. He'd left Momma only a sack of burdens.

The trailer was run-down and let in the rain but had no lien against it. The same couldn't be said for Blair's momma, who owed more than she'd ever have. She chipped away at her debts, usually with her body, but it was all too little. By the age of eleven, Blair was earning, too. Typical of Blair, she used her wile, not her body. She rode the bus to New Orleans and petitioned tourists on Bourbon Street: *My granddaddy died and I'd so dearly like a rose for his grave. A yellow rose. Uncle Bloom's on Toulouse sell 'em for a dollar apiece.* She graduated from grade-six mooching to picking pockets, then to ferrying Class A narcotics for the Black Lizard Boys.

Swan Grove had none of NOLA's allure and all of its dirt. Located in the mire southeast of the city, it was sometimes referred to as the Big Easy's dim-witted stepchild. It had three sleazy blues bars, a strip joint, a riverboat burlesque. It also had two gangs: the Cajun Warlords and the Black Lizard Boys.

Dakota Mayo—Blair's momma—was in deep with the Lizards. She owed mainly for her meth addiction but had borrowed five thousand dollars over the years and, for all her whoring, had repaid only a touch of it. The Lizards' *veterano* was a hotheaded Mexican called Lupe "El Martillo" Paez. Lupe was unblessed in the smarts department, but commanded deference by way of his fists. Dakota was his plaything. His *perra.* "For as long as you owe me," he told her, "I keep the leash tight."

Employing Blair was part of the arrangement, but for how long would she remain a mule?

"How old are you, *chiquita*?"

"Twelve."

Blair was stringing washing in what passed for their yard. Lupe watched her from the hood of his Caddy, his legs spread, the tips of his Old Gringo boots flashing in the Louisiana sunlight. He rubbed his chin and nodded.

"*Sí . . . te veo pronto.*"

Blair was not yet a teenager but intelligent enough to know a couple of things: that the only way to slip El Martillo's leash was to cut off the hand holding it—an act that required considerable force. Also, the Lizards were not a one-man operation; Lupe had an army around him, and lieutenants who were more than ready to step into his Old Gringos.

Blair needed an army, too.

The Cajun Warlords ran the west side of the Grove. A rabble of rednecks, they'd had it all until the Lizards slithered in, and there was no love lost between the two gangs. There'd been bloodshed, and then compromise: the Lizards controlled hard drugs, firearms, and prostitution, and the Warlords controlled everything else. This included marijuana, moonshine, and gambling—primarily by way of underground fighting. Something else Blair knew, because she'd heard one of those clever women on *The View*—maybe it was Whoopi—say it once: A compromise is an agreement whereby both parties are equally dissatisfied.

Big Trapper Neal was boss of the Warlords. A former Creole State boxing champion, he conducted most of his business at his gym on Strawberry Avenue. The basement was one of several venues used for his lucrative Fight Nights. Upstairs, his spacious office (a rebel flag in one corner, a photo of Trapper meeting Sylvester Stallone on the wall) doubled as the Warlords' boardroom. This was where Blair first met Trapper. She just dropped by one day.

"Well, shit, girlie. Lookit you."

"I want to box," Blair said.

"I respect that, but I don't train girls."

"That's some bullshit, mister. Girls can box, too. You ever hear of Laila Ali?"

"I sure have. Heard of her daddy, too. But that don't change shit. You could tie the leather on, but the fact remains that I don't train girls. That means you ain't got no one to spar with."

"So?"

"No winner was ever made from just punching a bag."

"Do I look like I just want to punch a bag? Shit, mister, put me in with the boys."

Trapper was as wide as a truck's grille and when he laughed the floorboards trembled just a bit. He wiped eyes made bleary by years of taking leather, and even more years of guzzling his own hooch. "I tell you what." He slapped a hand on the table. A breeze from somewhere made the rebel flag shiver. "I could use some help around the place. Someone to drag a mop across the floors, to clean out the spit buckets. You do that, and maybe I'll show you a thing or two."

Going in, Blair had hoped things would move swiftly, but it soon became apparent this wouldn't be the case. She was still twelve when she first picked up a mop at Trapper's gym, and thirteen when she felt ready to plant the first seed. She'd been sparring with a knucklehead named Lorne Franco, four years older but built like a length of rope. She'd let Lorne knock her around, and between rounds the trainer, Ducky Rose, asked what was wrong.

"Nothing," Blair had responded. "Don't want to talk about it."

"You're getting schooled in there." Ducky was high up the Warlords' chain of command and Blair knew it. "Flash some goddamn leather. I got better things to do than watch this beanpole make a monkey out of you."

"I'm fine."

But she took a knee twice in the next round and the second time Ducky stopped it. "Left your pluck at the trailer park, kid," he said, snipping the tape off her fists. "That's not like you. Want to tell me what's wrong?"

"No."

"Drop the tough-girl act." Ducky stopped snipping and held her reddened hands firmly. "I'm talking to you as a friend now, not as a trainer."

At which point Blair dropped the tough-girl act and turned on the waterworks. It was easy to fake-cry with the sweat on her face and her eyes still puffy from Lorne's gloves.

"Come on, kid." Ducky handed her the same towel he'd tossed into the ring not five minutes before. "Don't let the boss see you crying. He'll get you back to dragging that mop around."

"Yeah. I know. Sorry." Blair ran the towel across her face. "It's just . . ." And she told Ducky the story she'd devised—how the Mexicans were tightening their stranglehold on Momma. "I guess she owes them big." And how, last night, eight of them had come over, stinking of tequila, and made her pay her dues. "I got the heck out of there. I couldn't—"

"Dirty goddamn spic assholes."

"Momma was still tweaking this morning. It's how she deals, you know?"

Ducky nodded.

"Bitch threw a glass at me. Just missed."

"Christ."

"And things'll only get worse." Blair wiped her eyes again and said, very clearly, so there was no way Ducky would misunderstand, "I overheard a couple of those beaners saying how more of them were coming to the Grove."

"More?"

"Lupe's cousins, I think. *Primos*. That's the Spanish word for cousins, right?"

"Fuck if I know."

"Some from New Mexico. Some from Veracruz."

"That so?" Ducky cleared his throat.

"Yeah. Something about Lupe wanting to expand his territory."

Seed planted. Blair stopped fake-crying and started counting. One-Mississippi. Two-Mississippi. She got only to forty-five-Mississippi before Ducky tromped his way upstairs to Trapper's office.

Blair let the seed gestate. She went about her business—just another luckless kid from Swan Grove—and on a warm September night, five weeks after her heart-to-heart with Ducky, she spray-painted WETBACK MO-FUCKS EAT SHIT!!! on the sidewalk outside the Lizards' clubhouse, and she was careful to leave the fat ass-end of a joint packed with Purple Widow—one of the Warlords' famed strains—in the gutter nearby.

Tensions between the gangs escalated. There was much crowing and flexing of muscle. Nothing more than that, but Blair knew it was just a matter of time. She watched and waited, occasionally fanning the flames. A whisper here. A comment there.

"Those damn Lizards really *are* cold-blooded," she said to Otto Dickinson during one of their morning training sessions. Otto wasn't as many rungs up the Warlords' ladder as Ducky, but he had a big mouth and he liked to run it. "Bunch of them at Shooter's last night saying how they'll soon be using rednecks for gator bait."

And to Héctor, her momma's meth dealer, she said, "Nope. No sparring today. Gym was closed." Héctor was a former student of the sweet science, before his life hit the shitter, and he regularly asked Blair how her training was coming along. "Trapper was at the range. Word is, some damn fool redneck shot his left foot clean off while trying out one of the Warlords' new guns."

Héctor and Lupe were very close. Héctor was a good earner. "Guns?" He pronounced it *gonz*. "What kinda *gonz*?"

"All kinds." Blair shrugged. "Whole crate of them came in last week."

Blair was careful how and when she leaked these deceptions. She understood that they needed to work their way beneath the skin. She also had to ensure nothing came back on her. Even the "innocent" observations of a teenage girl would arouse suspicion if divulged too frequently. What Blair never expected was for both gangs to own these fabrications with an odd kind of pride. Neither side denied anything, as if to do so would show weakness.

Her final move, and crowning achievement, was to deface Josephine Neal's grave. And Lord, how Trapper loved his momma! The Warlords' top dog visited Cedar Hill Cemetery three times a week and set a bouquet of lavenders—Momma's favorite—at the base of her stone, and he'd tell her that, by Christ, he missed her so, and that he was half the man without her (hard to imagine, considering he was pushing four hundred pounds). Sometimes he'd sing Jimmy C. Newman songs to her as the stone angels looked down. One night, Blair, now fourteen years old, left her trailer and walked the two and a half miles to Cedar Hill. She clambered over the wall, found Josephine Neal's grave, and went to work.

The cemetery caretaker cleaned up most of the mess, but he couldn't attach the heads back on the angels, and he was still scrubbing the word PUTA off the stone when Trapper showed up.

And so began the bloodshed.

Casper Morales—Lupe's primary link to La Eme at Orleans

Parish—was gunned down while gassing up his Grand Marquis at the Fuel King on Delray Avenue.

Little Rocky Carson—Trapper's second cousin on his daddy's side—was knifed to death in the entranceway of his apartment building. A six-year-old kid found the body.

Héctor Alonso—meth dealer and failed human being—had his throat cut on the 270 bus between Alligator Creek and the Grove. No witnesses.

Not that witnesses were necessary. The whole town knew what was going down. Drunk off his ass at Rooster Wilson's, even Swan Grove's chief of police was heard to remark, "Those god-damn assholes are going to wipe each other out, and I for one say let them get on with it."

The chief of police was a lazy slob who rarely did anything of note, but he was right on the money on this occasion. On October 5, 2008, fourteen months after Blair planted her first seed, five large sedans with blacked-out windows rumbled onto Strawberry Avenue. What followed could have been ripped from a Wild West movie, with store owners slamming their doors and rolling down their shutters, and parents dragging their kids in off the street. The Warlords opened fire first. Otto Dickinson had snuck onto the roof of Trapper's Gym with a Hi-Point carbine, and he ripped a .45 through Cristóbal Ayala's chest. A single, startling shot—*crack!*—and Cristóbal was dead before the echo faded.

The air filled, then, with the cacophony of gunfire, of dying men's screams, of the shattering of things. Blair heard the shots from her trailer two miles west. Her momma, roused from some meth-induced stupor, stepped from her bedroom and cocked her ear at the noise.

"What *is* that?"

"The sound of your debts being paid," Blair replied.

Once the bodies had been zipped into bags and the dust had settled, Blair tried to persuade her momma to sell the trailer and get the hell out of the Grove. "Let's go where nobody knows us. We can start again." But Momma's rut went deeper than her debt to the Black Lizard Boys. She found a new meth dealer in New Orleans and went right back to where she was before.

She was dead inside of two years, but Blair had already made plans of her own. She'd gone back to pickpocketing tourists on Bourbon Street and had saved enough coin for a bus to Philadelphia and a dirty room in the basement of an ex-boxer's house. Before long, she was back in the ring, fighting guys thirty pounds heavier than her in illegal bouts. She had nine fights and won four of them, using her smarts to wear her opponents down before blazing leather into their faces. Her longest fight went twenty-two rounds.

Jimmy discovered her after one of her losses. She'd taken a right hook from a lightning-fast welterweight that dropped her cold. She came to in the locker room with Jimmy's scarred face leering down at her.

"You were doing good," he said, "until he knocked you out."

"Shit happens." She touched the deep cut beneath her left eye. "Who the fuck are you?"

"A man who recognizes your talent. I'd like to train you to be a real fighter."

"I am a real fighter."

"I'm not talking about boxing . . . or whatever this is."

Blair didn't exactly jump at Jimmy's offer. She wanted to find out more about him first, which wasn't difficult, given his reputation. Two months later, he showed up at another fight (another loss). He offered her a job—his personal assistant, he said—and a room at his house in Carver City.

"Why me?" she asked. "I'm nothing special."

"I think you are," Jimmy said. "And I'm usually right about these things."

Two days later, she was in the back of a limo on her way to Carver City, her single bag of possessions on the seat beside her. Jimmy met her at the front door of his showy, modern residence, then led her to his office. It was large and clean, with an open fireplace and a cello in the corner that looked as if it had never been played. A forty-something male with muscles packed into a black T-shirt stood by the window. Jimmy nodded at him, then took a gun from the top drawer of his desk and placed it in Blair's hand.

"You know what that is?" he asked.

"A gun," Blair said. "A pistol."

"It's a Beretta M9. Italian, semiautomatic. This means the gun will reload itself, but pulling the trigger will only fire one bullet at a time. It's a fifteen-round mag, though, so you can do a lot of damage before you have to *stop* pulling the trigger. How does it feel?"

"Heavy."

"Won't feel that way for long. Howie is going to show you how to use it." Jimmy gestured toward the man with the muscles. "By the time he's finished with you, you'll be hitting targets from twenty yards with a blindfold on."

Blair looked from Jimmy to the pistol, turning it over in her hand, getting a feel for its weight. "You said I was going to be your personal assistant."

"And you are. I just didn't tell you what you'll be assisting me with." Jimmy smiled and clapped her on the shoulder. "Welcome to your first day on the job."

Howie was ex–Special Forces. He'd spent eleven years in the Middle East working counterinsurgency and counterterrorism operations, and another eight years training snipers at Fort Benning. As well as firearms, he was proficient in knife and weapons combat. It took time, but he taught Blair everything he knew. By the age of eighteen, she could field-strip an AR-15 in under thirty seconds and hit a moving target from sound alone. Jimmy was pleased with her progress, but it was not enough. He financed her intensive schooling in kendo, kung fu, and Krav Maga. *I'd like to train you to be a real fighter*, he'd said when they first met, but what he actually wanted was a killing machine.

And Blair knew why; Jimmy had told her all about Lola Bear, in painful and intimate detail.

"You were in awe of her," Blair said. She looked at Jimmy, seeing Lola in every scar, in the black torment of his expression. "Maybe you even loved her."

"No maybe about it."

"Is that what this is about? My training?" They were in Jimmy's orchard, Blair throwing knives at a series of targets she'd set up between the trees. "Are you trying to create a new Lola Bear?"

"No." Jimmy shook his head vehemently. "You're going to be better than her. Stronger than her. And you're going to help me bring her down."

"So this is a fight-fire-with-fire situation?"

"Exactly." Jimmy's chest swelled and his eyes glimmered in the hazy afternoon light. "Think you can handle that?"

Blair plucked a knife from her belt, threw it without looking, and struck a man-shaped target in the throat.

"I can handle anything," she said.

...

Blair had pointed out the obvious (although she couldn't be sure Jimmy had considered it): Brody and Molly Ellis were too valuable a bridge to burn. "We need to compromise them in some way," she'd said. "Make *them* do the work for us."

"Go on." Jimmy puffed his fat cigar.

"They need to feel threatened, scared, but with room to move—to *think*. If we play it right, they'll draw on contacts they wouldn't ordinarily consider. And maybe, just *maybe*, one of those contacts will lead them to Lola Bear."

Jimmy pushed his tongue to the inside of his cheek again, smoke leaking from the edges of his mouth. Then he shook his head. "No. Too much can go wrong."

"I think it'll work."

"Maybe." Jimmy shrugged. "But if they have information—contacts, addresses, phone numbers—it'll be quicker to beat it out of them. Shit, I'll take a tire iron to the cripple's leg, and you'll see how quickly the brother squawks."

"Brains, Jimmy, not brawn." Blair placed her fists on the desk and leaned toward him. "No one can think clearly while getting the shit kicked out of them, or while watching someone they love get hurt. It's not as effective as you like to believe. And twenty years of chasing Lola Bear, torturing her contacts, *still* not finding her, proves that."

Jimmy made a rumbling sound in his chest. Ash fell from the tip of his cigar and powdered his white shirt.

"Also," Blair continued, "they may not *have* those contacts yet. They may need to think laterally, ask around. It might require some footwork."

Jimmy considered this for a moment, then his eyes widened

and he snapped his fingers. "Well, shit, I can think laterally, too. Let's kidnap the sister. We'll put her on camera and send the video file to the kid."

"By email?"

"Shit, no. We'll put it on a flash drive and mail it anonymously. And we won't incriminate ourselves in the video. It'll just be the girl talking to the camera. She'll need to be beaten up a little—or a *lot*—but still able to deliver the message: *Find Lola Bear, dear brother of mine, or these very bad men will do very bad things.*"

"Okay." Blair nodded. "That's better, Jimmy. Smarter."

"You like that?"

"I do, and I'd say go for it, except . . ."

"Except?"

"The sister is the brains of the operation." Blair stood up straight and folded her muscular arms. It was often necessary to adopt such unwavering body language when dealing with Jimmy. "I don't think Brody can find Lola without her. Also, he might go to the police."

"Let him," Jimmy snorted. "They won't be able to link the video to us."

"You're missing the point." Blair said patiently. "For as long as Brody is relying on the police to find his sister, we can't rely on him to find Lola."

Jimmy took a long pull on his cigar. The tip bloomed and sizzled. "Okay, so we threaten to kill his sister if he goes to the cops. Problem solved."

"I don't think so. Brody will be too rattled. He'll still think he's got a better chance with the police." Blair relaxed her posture, but wrinkled her brow contemplatively. "I'd prefer to remove law enforcement from the equation. Then it's just him and us."

Jimmy made that rumbling sound again.

"I'll find a way to set Brody up," Blair insisted, and a word popped into her mind. She wasn't sure it was the correct word, but it had a wonderful, sinister ring. "*Artifice*. It's what I do best. Then we just sit back and wait."

"I'm not convinced."

"Give me this, Jimmy. Six months, that's all I ask. And if I can't deliver Lola Bear, *then* we kidnap the cripple. You can beat the shit out of her, put a bullet in her eye. Whatever you want."

Jimmy exhaled smoke and grinned.

"Six months," Blair said. "Then we do it your way."

...

Blair found out everything she could about Brody: where he'd lived, gone to school, his interests, favorite movies and music, his employment history, his friends and exes. Then she started watching him, day and night, assuming various disguises to avoid suspicion. She soon devised a scheme to enter his life, seduce him, then persuade him to steal her "stepmother's" diamonds and frame him for her murder. Jesus, didn't one of Jimmy's loaded poker buddies own a house in Freewood Valley? What a serendipitous fucking opportunity! They could use it to stage the crime, and Jimmy's accountant, Cynthia Gray, could play the part of the wicked stepmom. All she had to do was play dead for a few minutes. She even had one of those fucking hideous Warhol-style paintings of herself that they could hang on the wall for added effect.

Was it a shitfuck crazy plan? Well goddamn, yes it was. It *was*. But the craziest plans netted the biggest rewards, and framing Brody would keep him from going to the police.

"His old man is dead," Blair had said to Jimmy, having outlined her extravagant scheme. "We eliminated *that* source of support. The few friends he has are airheads and stoners—fucking useless, all of them. He has no immediate family, other than his sister. His landlord doesn't give a shit—"

"The kid has no one," Jimmy cut in.

"Right. At least not on the surface," Blair said. "But with his back against the wall, he's going to start digging."

Blair was about to make her move when a new development inspired a change of plan: Brody had started reconnoitering convenience stores in the early hours of the morning. With no job and barely a penny to his name (hacking his credit information and bank activity had confirmed this), it was obvious that he was going to rob one of them—probably Buddy's on Independence Avenue, which he'd cased three times.

Blair waited in the wings, recognizing how to use this development to her advantage, and relishing the opportunity to apply her pickpocketing skills once again.

"You're making this too easy, Brody."

After all, why fuck him when she could blackmail him?

...

Celeste had packed up and gone, leaving only a musk of sandalwood and jojoba. Jimmy sloped awkwardly across his chaise longue. The massage hadn't relaxed him at all.

"Alexa," he groaned. "Play Vivaldi."

Vivaldi's *The Four Seasons* floated from the Echo. Jimmy shifted stiffly, eyes closed. Blair stepped toward him and loomed until he cracked his eyelids and acknowledged her.

"I like how this is working out," she said, and displayed the same smile she'd used on Brody: coquettish, with a hint of devilry. Men, she'd learned, were a sucker for that smile.

"Good for you, but your six months is up at the end of October. That's . . ." Jimmy counted on his fingers. "Twenty-six days, then I'm pulling the plug on this goddamn cat-and-mouse and doing it my way."

"Chainsaw Jimmy. Always looking for blood."

"I prefer to be called the Italian Cat." Jimmy showed his teeth. "Nobody fucks with me. Even dogs run away."

Vivaldi stirred the room like a breeze. Dead leaves spiraled beyond the windows. Blair stooped, still smiling, and hooked a lock of silver hair behind Jimmy's ear.

"Bitch ruined me," he snarled. "All these years of searching, waiting for my moment—my revenge."

"You'll have it. Soon."

"I wish I had your confidence." Jimmy's fists trembled at his sides. "Goddamn it, Blair, this kid had better come through."

Blair dropped to one knee and leaned close to Jimmy. Her lips whispered against his cheek.

"Trust me," she said, and there was devilry in her voice, too. "A scared little boy will always find his mommy."

CHAPTER NINE

Faster, Brody. Go . . . *go*!"

Brody ripped through a four-way stop without slowing. A dusty old Buick puttered in front of him and he swerved right—drove fifteen yards with two wheels on the sidewalk, then swerved again to avoid a telephone booth. Molly took a sharp breath, her body pressed into the passenger seat.

"This is all a dream," she hissed. "A bad fucking dream."

Brody's eyes flicked to the mirror. The mobsters had fallen back. They negotiated the four-way stop more cautiously, then gunned it once they were through.

"I'll get us out of this," he said.

Another intersection loomed ahead. There was roadwork on the other side, traffic packed into a single lane. Brody touched the brake and turned left, timing his move to cut in front of a tractor-trailer. It howled at him, leaving rubber on the blacktop. Brody eased off the gas so that the truck flooded his rearview, then made an abrupt right turn, hoping the long trailer masked the maneuver. He jammed his foot to the floor again, blew a red light, then turned into the parking lot of a furniture store. Another glance in the mirror. No sign of Jimmy's guys. He zipped between rows of parked vehicles, then around the back of the store where the loading docks were. Brody considered tucking his car into one of the docks beside an empty trailer—hoping Leo and company wouldn't think to look back here—but noticed an access road leading across a patch of scrub, framed with chain-link. He took it at speed, came out on a quiet road that veered north out of town. Several tense glances into the mirrors showed nobody in pursuit. Brody took a series of arbitrary right and left turns before pulling into the gap behind an empty cattle shed.

"We lost them," he gasped. "Holy *shit.*"

Molly said nothing. She had her face buried in her hands, crying and trembling copiously. Brody cranked the window, took a deep breath. The air smelled of cow shit but it was still fresher than the stifling stench of fear inside the car.

His nostrils flared. He gripped the wheel to steady the earthquakes in his hands. *Lost them*, he thought, but something about that didn't seem right. He, Brody Ellis, had outmaneuvered Jimmy's goons in his crapped-out Pontiac. Even back at the motel, he'd outwitted them. It shouldn't have been that easy.

Molly lifted her face from her hands and looked at him. He didn't want to meet her gaze but, eventually, he did. He *had* to.

"What the fuck, Brody?"

"Give me your phone," he said.

...

He stepped out of the car with his own and Molly's cell phones in one hand, and the replica pistol in the other.

"What are you doing, Brody?" Molly struggled to get out on her side, clumsily gathering her crutches while pushing the door open. Brody had yanked the phone from her pocket when she refused to give it to him. Now he tossed it on the stony ground, dropped to one knee, and smashed the screen with the butt of the pistol.

"What the *fuck*?" Molly fell out of the car, picked herself up, and hobbled around to Brody. She hit him twice with one of her crutches, then lost balance and stumbled backward. By this time her cell phone was a mess of plastic and broken glass. Brody picked up the pieces and threw them into the trees behind the cattle shed.

"Brody?"

"This is how they found us. How they're tracking us." He waved his own phone at the satellites before dropping it at his feet. "Jesus, Moll, haven't you heard of geolocation?"

"Of course," she said. "It's a way of determining the location of any web-based device."

"It's . . . well, yeah." Five furious strikes with the pistol grip ended his cell phone's life. He flung the ruptured casing as far away as he could.

Molly sat on the hood of the car. Her eyes were heavy but she was out of tears. "Who are 'they,' Brody?" She was sad, angry, and scared, but Brody knew she was more disappointed than anything. "And why do you have a gun?"

Brody sighed. He aimed the pistol at the sky, pulled the trigger. Nothing happened.

"It's not real. It's a replica. I used it to rob a convenience store." He lowered the gun, then lowered his head, deeply ashamed. "That's where I got the money from."

He told her everything.

...

Brody's response to Molly getting bullied was to ask his dad if he could learn karate, and then to master the one-inch punch. Violence. His go-to solution, and one that mankind—with an emphasis on *man*—had favored since it dragged its knuckles along the ground. But Brody had bullies, too. Mainly on the inside. He'd had insecurity issues throughout his teens, which started when his mom hit the road, and manifested by way of nightmares, mood swings, and feelings of inadequacy. Molly had helped him through the worst of it, and while she occasionally expressed her frustrations by lashing out with her crutches, her default approach to problem solving was through conversation.

As it was now.

"There must be *something*," she said. She had calmed down, but there was still a flush of color on her cheeks. "A detail, a flaw in the plan—something that Blair forgot, and that we can use to prove your innocence."

"The police are not an option, Moll." They sat on the ground, their backs against the Pontiac's freshly dented fender. "Blair is smart on a different level. A *dangerous* level. Like a shark. She's thought of everything, and even if she hasn't—if there *is* a flaw in the plan—I don't fancy my public defender's chances against Jimmy Latzo's big city lawyers."

Molly sighed and rested her head on Brody's shoulder.

"And if, by some miracle, I *can* prove that I was framed," Brody continued, "I don't think Chainsaw Jimmy would let it lie. I broke into his house, after all. That's an irrefutable fact. Caught on tape. He'll kill me for that, if nothing else."

It was growing dark. The early October sun touched the horizon, pushing a rusty light through the trees and buildings. Power lines underscored the view. A breeze set everything flickering. It made the cattle shed creak and whistle.

"We need to run," Molly said. Even with her ability to strip a problem to its component parts and reassemble it into something hopeful, she still arrived at the same conclusion as Brody.

"To hide," he said.

"Not just hide. Disappear."

"Right."

"But we can't do that on our own. We need help."

Brody closed his eyes for a moment. She was still with him, at his side, despite everything. He wanted to throw his arms around her, drag her into the kind of hug that made small bones pop. He didn't, though; it seemed an incommensurate way of showing gratitude for such strength. So he exhaled from deep within his chest and blinked at tears and absorbed the delicate weight of her head on his shoulder.

"You mentioned Karl Janko earlier. Mom's friend." Molly lifted her head from Brody's shoulder and looked at him in the reddish light. "You think he can help?"

"It's worth a shot," Brody said. "I remember him more than I was letting on. And he was totally sketch. Someone like that might be able to help us . . . you know, disappear."

"He's probably in prison." Molly shook her head. "Or dead."

"Maybe. But it's somewhere to start."

"We know anybody else?"

"Johnny Frye—"

"The pest control guy?"

"He used to sell Ecstasy to high school kids."

"No. Absolutely not. Anybody else?"

"Christy Beale. She's cleaned up her act, but . . ." Brody shrugged, then started plucking clumps of yellow grass out of the dirt. "Kieran Houser. Franklin Ogg. Macy Zerilli—"

"The bartender at Rocky T's?" Molly rolled her eyes. "She wouldn't piss on you if you were on fire."

"This is true."

"These are shitty options, Brody. In fact, they're not options at all." Molly leaned to her stronger side, grabbed one of her crutches, and hoisted herself to her feet. The pain clearly bolted through her, because she grimaced, but nothing more than that. "So I guess we need to track down Karl Janko."

Brody nodded. "Like I said: a good place to start."

"The only place to start." Molly tapped the tip of one crutch against the Pontiac's buckled hood. "We also need to dump the car."

"Dump it? You're kidding, right?" Brody jumped to his feet, slapping dirt from the seat of his jeans. "I just spent five hundred bucks on a new fuel pump. And we might need to sleep—"

"Christ, Brody, do you really need me to spell this out for you? Jimmy Latzo's men are *looking* for this heap of shit." The way she squared her shoulders assured Brody this was not open to negotiation. "There aren't too many '99 Sunfires on the road today. It's distinctive, not to mention unreliable. We're dumping it."

A large bird signaled from somewhere. Smaller birds peppered the western sky, dark as drops of water on red cloth.

"Let's get out of here." Molly thrust her crutches into the dirt and started walking.

"Wait. Christ, Molly. *Wait.*" Brody loped toward her, gesturing inanely at his car. "We're *walking*?"

"Sure."

"But—"

"Grab our bags, and whatever else we need. I think"—she pointed one crutch at a sprinkle of lights to the north—"that's Elder. I saw it on Google maps coming in. About three miles away, I'd say. We'll leave the car here, cut across the fields. Should be there in a couple of hours."

"Molly, I really—"

"I'll be fine." She pulled Motrin and Lioresal from her jacket pocket, popped one of each into her palm, and swallowed them with a single, practiced click of her throat. "Let's go."

It was arduous going. The fields dipped and rose, in places marred with flints and potholes, and elsewhere with long, dry cogongrass that pulled at their heels. At one point they had to cut through a bedlam of leaning trees that conspired with the darkness, messed with their sense of direction. Molly fell twice. The first time she wouldn't accept Brody's help but the second time she did. They rested until they'd caught their breaths, pushed on, and eventually emerged on the edge of a stream with Elder's lights not quite where they thought they'd be.

They crossed the stream carefully, not bothering to take off their sneakers and socks. The landscape was easier on the other side and they pushed on eagerly. A skim of moon shone. Molly remained three or four paces ahead, digging her crutches into the dark ground.

Brody breathed hard and watched the accent of her back, the rhythmic tick of her legs. He shifted the weight of their bags from one shoulder to another.

"I'll say this just once." She stopped, turned to look at him. Elder's lights framed her. He could see a strip mall and an overpass and an illuminated billboard that promised the most competitive insurance rates in the Magnolia State. "This is on *you*, Brody. You own this shit. I don't ever want to hear—not fucking *once*— that you did this for me. You feed me that line of horseshit and I swear to God you'll never see me again."

BEFORE

(1992)
LOLA BEAR

Lola had wanted to make the room as comfortable as possible: fresh, colorful carnations, pictures of his wife and son—both long dead—on the bedside table, Tin Pan Alley music playing softly in the background. But Grandpa Bear was a stubborn old mule, even now, and all he insisted on was a glass of cold water and the TV tuned to CNN.

She watched him sleeping for a moment, supported by large pillows, his eyelids fluttering. All the muscle had been stripped from him. His body had been reshaped—the austere angles replaced by shadowy hollows and weak lines. To see him like this was unthinkable. This was the man who had taken care of her since she was fourteen, who'd taught her how to spot a concealed handgun, how to field dress a deer, how to tighten her shot groups at the range. And more, so much more. He was the beginning of everything she'd become.

Lola stepped farther into the room, suppressing her emotion, as she was inclined to do, but feeling that, at twenty-four years old, she was too young to lose the most important person in her life, and one of only two people that she actually cared about.

He opened his eyes suddenly, then turned toward her, noticing her there. His peripheral vision was still precise.

"Lola," he said warmly.

"Hey, Gramps." She found a smile, albeit a delicate one. "Just checking in. You need anything?"

He returned her smile—his a little stronger—and pondered the question for several seconds. "No," he croaked, and coughed, clearing his throat. "But *you* do." He drew one hand from beneath the sheets and pointed at the dresser against the far wall. "Bottom drawer."

Lola walked to the dresser and opened the bottom drawer. There were a few folded sweaters inside—clothes that Grandpa Bear would never wear again—and a brown faux-leather folder. She took it out.

"What is this?"

"Don't ask questions," Grandpa Bear said. "Just take it. Put it somewhere safe."

Lola opened the folder. Inside were driver's licenses, Social Security cards, and birth certificates. Three of each. Lola's photograph graced each driver's license. She looked at the one from North Dakota. The name stamped across the front read WARD, MARGARET NAOMI. The other names were Natalie Myles and Jennifer Ames.

"How can I not ask questions?" There was surprise in Lola's tone.

Grandpa Bear coughed again and adjusted his pillows—or *tried* to; he couldn't get the angle. Lola did it for him. He had been diagnosed with aggressive non-Hodgkin's lymphoma two and a half years earlier. Doctors gave him three to six months. He'd battled like he had in Europe, Korea, and Vietnam. Three wars' worth of toughness and experience. The fight was almost over, though.

"I know you work for Jimmy Latzo," he said, and coughed yet again. Lola handed him water and he sipped gratefully. "If I thought I could talk some sense into you, I would. But you are a stubborn young lady."

"That I am." She took the glass away. "Wonder where I get that from."

"Must be a Bear thing." The old man gave his head a little shake. "You could've been a cop, Lola. A damn good one."

"Sure, and get a psychiatric evaluation every time I fire my service pistol." Lola took out another driver's license. Same photograph. Different name. "Besides, all the sitting around, and all the paperwork, would drive me crazy."

"Like I said, there's no talking sense into you, so all I can do is protect you, give you an exit." Grandpa Bear tapped the folder. "Three exits, actually."

"Fake IDs?"

"No. Think of them as resets. New beginnings." Grandpa Bear coughed once again, fumbling for the glass. Lola held it to his lips and he took a long drink. He raised one finger when he'd had enough, then continued. "Working for Jimmy, there'll come a time when you have to run, either from the law or from Jimmy himself. That's the nature of the life you've chosen."

"Maybe."

"No maybe about it. This isn't a long-term career, and you'll make enemies. So I've given you three new starts. When the time comes, get as far away as you can, choose an identity, and live a different life. If you're ever compromised, ditch that identity, and move on to the next one." Grandpa Bear breathed deeply. His throat crackled. "Three should get you through, if you're careful."

Lola looked at Natalie Myles's Social Security card. "This is good work. Everything looks legit."

"I pulled a favor with an old friend, ex–Marshals Service. I saved his life in Iwo Jima. Just doing my job, but he promised to repay me somehow." Grandpa Bear tapped the folder again. "All these names are in the system. If you need to renew a driver's license, or apply for a passport, you can go through the legitimate channels. You can also vote, get a job, get married—"

"Married?" Lola smiled. "Vince will be happy."

"No. Not Vince. You'll be escaping your old life and everyone in it." Grandpa Bear settled back into his pillows. His chest pumped out another rotten cough. "The moment you assume one of those identities, you start living a lie. And it's a lie you can never *unlive*."

"Let's hope," Lola said, "it doesn't come to that."

"It almost certainly will." Grandpa Bear said nothing for a while. His chest climbed, then sagged. He looked unspeakably lovely, Lola thought. Large enough to have survived three wars, yet small enough to cradle.

"You should get some rest," she said.

"Soon. Listen . . ." He urged her closer. She smelled the medicines on his breath. "I want you to open bank accounts in all three names. Do it in the states the driver's licenses are issued in, so you don't raise any flags. And don't wait too long."

"I can do that," Lola said.

"Good. You'll come into your inheritance . . . any day now." Grandpa Bear allowed a tight, sad smile. "Divide it between your accounts. But launder it first, so there's no paper trail. And launder it again if and when you relocate. I have a contact who can help with that."

"Okay," Lola said.

His bleary eyes fluttered, rolled to the ceiling, then slowly closed. Sunlight fell through the window in an even yellow bar, while a TV in the corner silently relayed the news: riots in Los Angeles after four police officers were acquitted in the brutal beating of Rodney King.

"I said . . . get married, that you . . ." He mumbled, drifting into sleep. His lips made slight shapes. "But don't . . . don't . . ."

"It's okay, Gramps." Lola took his hand and squeezed gently. "Sleep now."

"Don't get married." He looked at her. There was something in his eyes. Pain or disappointment. It didn't matter which; both broke her heart. "Don't put down roots, or make anything that you can't leave behind."

Lola wondered what kind of life that would be, one without stability, without expectation or legacy. Was that really the track she was on? Or was there a brighter path ahead?

Grandpa Bear muttered something else—she didn't catch it—then drifted back off to sleep. Lola leaned over and kissed his forehead.

"I'll be okay," she whispered, more to herself than to Grandpa Bear, who'd given her so much, and had never let her down.

She tucked the folder beneath her arm and left the room.

CHAPTER TEN

Brody and Molly cut across farmland and entered Elder on its southwest side. The dark streets made surveying for suspicious vehicles and people difficult. When, after several minutes of walking, nobody had jumped them, Brody relaxed just a little.

"What's the plan, Moll?" He was content—relieved, even—to let his sister take the reins for a while.

"We're too close to where we lost them," Molly said. "They might have eyes on this place. So we need a ride somewhere else—forty, fifty miles away, at least. From there, we can catch a bus or train and go . . . shit, anywhere. As long as it has a motel and a library."

"A library," Brody repeated. "You plan on doing some reading?"

"Online reading, yes. Libraries have computers. I need to find Janko, remember, and I don't know how long that will take."

Molly approached a young woman outside a small theater, speaking slowly to make herself understood, this—quite deliberately—emphasizing her palsy. She explained that her phone was out of charge, and asked the woman if she would call a taxi for her.

"What's wrong with his phone?" The woman gestured at Brody, hovering just beyond the marquee's lights.

"Doesn't have one," Molly said, and shrugged. "Says he's a technophobe, but that doesn't stop him playing video games with his loser buddies."

"Uber's better. Cheaper," the woman said after a moment, accessing her app with impressive speed. "There are four in the area."

"Okay. Whatever. I can—"

"You can give me the cash."

"Yeah. Absolutely."

"Where are you going?"

Molly blanked, shook her head. "I don't . . ." She shifted her weight from one crutch to the other. "How far is Tupelo?"

The woman lowered her phone, her eyes floating between Molly and Brody. "Maybe a hundred miles."

"That's a little far," Molly said, thinking of the dwindling cash in Brody's brown paper bag. "Somewhere closer. But not *too* close. And big enough to have a bus or train terminal."

"Sparrow Hill is forty-five minutes north."

"Okay." Molly nodded. "Perfect."

The woman tapped her phone, stepped furtively toward Molly, showed her the screen. On it she'd written: *Want me to call the police??* Her eyebrows twitched in Brody's direction.

"No. He's my brother," Molly whispered. She touched the woman's elbow briefly, gently. "Thank you, though. We just need to get out of town."

"You sure?"

"Yeah."

The woman nodded stiffly and returned to her app. "Eighty bucks to Sparrow Hill. Driver will be here in three minutes."

"Thank you." Molly offered her a warm, grateful smile, then she added, not sure if she had to but wanting to be doubly careful, "And please, if anyone asks, you didn't see us."

...

Fifty miles to Sparrow Hill, I-55 most of the way, the highway like the blank, non-REM stages between dreams. Brody and

Molly sat in the back so they wouldn't have to talk to the driver. He was as chirpy as a bird to begin with, but took the hint after a string of uninterested, monosyllabic replies. He dropped them, as requested, at the bus depot on Burlington Avenue. The last thing he said was, "Going anywhere exciting?" To which Brody replied, "I hope not."

...

Brody counted his money in the bus depot's restroom, holding the bills the way he'd hold an injured mouse. $940. Bleak. Very bleak. At this rate, they'd be down to their last few dollars by the end of the week.

Six buses were leaving in the next hour. Molly wanted to go to New Mexico. Brody opted for Jefferson City, Missouri. A quicker, less expensive ride, and more central—potentially more convenient to wherever they had to travel next.

"It's still four hundred miles away," he said. "That's a good distance."

They paid cash for their tickets and were in Jefferson City by four P.M. the next day.

...

Brody had slept on the bus. Not well, but better than he expected to, and more than he *wanted* to. He'd planned to gaze meerkat-like out the rear window to remain certain they weren't being followed. There was no way, of course—they would have been jumped by now—but better to stay vigilant. It was too dark to see anything but headlights, though. Eventually he gave up. Sleep took him.

They found a motel called, laughably, Cozies, a step above

Motel 15, with its crack whores and gunshots, but not a broad step. Still, it was $48 a night, no credit card required. The beds were as hard as tortoiseshell.

...

They spent what remained of that day resting. Molly gulped meds. The bus journey, not to mention the miles they'd traveled on foot, had been hard on her. Brody massaged her legs and feet, circled a damp towel around her left thigh. She cried a little bit but tried to hide it.

They watched shit TV. Ordered Chinese food. Their new life.

...

And eventually they slept. Brody startled awake in the small hours when headlights swept across the thin curtains.

They're here. Oh my God. Jesus Christ—

He sprang out of bed, rushed to the window, peered between the wall and the curtain. But no, it was just a car turning around. Brody watched as it pulled out of the parking lot and drove away.

"Jesus."

He went to Molly, gazing at her while she slept. "I'm sorry." He cried, covering his eyes, even though she couldn't see, then dropped to his knees, placed his head in the nest between her arm and rib cage, and fell asleep.

He woke several hours later, his head now resting on a fold in the bedsheets. Molly had gone.

A note on the nightstand read: *At library.*

...

The paranoia was hard to shake. He sat in the gloom, curtains drawn, attuned to every sound. Cars hissed. Doors slammed. A couple in an upstairs room fought colorfully, then kissed and made up. Their bed thumped for thirty-seven tireless minutes.

Brody paced, counted stains on the walls, watched infomercials with the volume down. There were some leftover noodles and he ate them cold, grimacing at every soggy mouthful. He finally left the room and walked with his face turned to the sun, breathing the fumy air and sometimes flinching at the city's angry clatter.

...

How?

That was the question. He and Molly had destroyed their cell phones, ditched the car, paid for transport and accommodation with cash. No footprints. So how could Jimmy's men track them down?

"There's no way." Brody sat on the bleachers in an empty baseball park, the sun behind him now, throwing his shadow across the diamond. "We lost them in Mississippi. End of story."

Right. He'd outmaneuvered them, as improbable as that seemed, and had avoided them for forty-eight hours, 460 miles. With no way to follow, the mobsters had likely resorted to interrogating his and Molly's few acquaintances: Tyrese, Molly's colleagues at Arrow Dairy, their handful of friends—who'd hopefully diverted them to "Aunt Cherry" in Maine.

So . . .

"There's no way," Brody said again. He closed his eyes, though, considering every possibility, however unlikely.

How?

...

Brody walked back to Cozies in the near-dark, less wary of every sudden noise and shadow. The time to himself had been needed. He'd had space to think, and had subsequently started to believe they were in the clear.

At least for now. The moment they showed their faces, used their names, left a footprint, Jimmy's men would swoop. Maybe they weren't following, but they *were* looking.

Yet another "how" question surfaced when he returned to the motel room, recalling the paranoia like a foul taste: How long did it take Molly to search for someone online?

"You here, Moll?"

It was a boxy room with a cramped bathroom attached. He could *see* she wasn't there, but anxiety drew the question from him. A dusty alarm clock on the nightstand displayed 17:48 in faded numbers. She'd been gone all day. Brody ran a hand across his face, trying to convince himself that Jimmy's men were looking for *him*, not her, but paranoia was a slippery, wicked snake. He turned the TV on, hoping it would distract him, but it didn't. He imagined how Molly would scream when Jimmy pulled the starter rope on his favorite chainsaw.

"I can't stay here," he said, staggering from the room, slamming the door just as a taxi curved across the lot. It pulled into a space close to their door. Ranchera boomed from the driver's open window.

Then a rear window opened and Molly's face appeared. She looked tired, but never more beautiful. Relief crashed through Brody.

"Moll. Jesus. You were gone a long time."

"Yeah. Digging deep." She gestured at the empty seat beside her. "Get in. Let's grab a bite to eat. Talk."

"Did you—"

The window closed again, but before it did he heard her say, "I found Janko."

...

King Elvis was a themed burger joint on East High Street—more money than Brody wanted to spend, but Molly insisted. "I'm hungry, dammit, and I'm not going to Mickey-fucking-D's." Brody knew better than to argue. The closest he came to an objection was whistling through his teeth when Molly ordered an $18.99 Teddy Bear Burger.

"Karl Janko is dead," she said as soon as the waiter had left their table. She pulled several dog-eared sheets of paper, covered with her handwriting, from her purse, and shuffled through them. "Died twelve years ago. Murdered. Beaten up and drowned in a barrel."

"Christ," Brody said. He brought Janko to mind—had a clear memory of playing catch with him in their backyard in Minneapolis. "In a *barrel*? That's some medieval shit."

"No doubt. But he knew a lot of bad dudes. Shit, he *was* a bad dude. Some sources claim he was connected to the mob." Molly riffled through her notes and came up with the page she was looking for. "I started my search the same place everybody searches for people these days: social media. No luck there, so I Googled 'Karl Janko,' got half a million hits, then narrowed the field with key words and filters. That's when I found his obituary."

"That's good work, Moll," Brody said, and sighed. "Doesn't help us, though."

"The obit led me to other stories: sixteen months served in 1985 for grand theft auto; another stint in 1988 for aggravated assault. There were several charges he was acquitted of, or that were suddenly dropped, including criminal harassment, arson, and manslaughter in the first degree."

"What a swell guy," Brody said.

"I know, right? And he must have got in with some bad people. His murder was . . . *savage*. His thumbs had been cut off, his teeth were smashed in. There were abrasions around his wrists and ankles from where he'd been tied up—"

Molly stopped suddenly, lowering her notes into her lap. Their server had arrived with their drinks. He set them down mutely, then retreated to the bar. Molly sipped her vanilla milkshake with fluttering eyelids. "Oh wow. Yummy." She licked her lips, returned her notes to the tabletop, and continued:

"I read a few articles regarding the investigation. The police had very little evidence, followed a lot of dead ends. They believed—from the deliberate nature of Janko's injuries—that he'd been tortured for information."

Brody sighed again and shook his head. The only reply he could muster.

"I didn't dig too deeply," Molly went on, looking up from her notes. "I figured it was a waste of time. The dude's dead, right? But from what I could tell, his killer, or *killers*, were never found."

"Too many enemies," Brody muttered, thinking that he, unjustly, had an enemy, too, and one that was capable of something similar. Or worse.

"Janko was buried in his hometown of Cambridge, Massachusetts. No wife. No children." Molly sipped her milkshake, flipped through a few pages. "He was survived only by his step-brother, Wendell."

"Tragic," Brody said, running his hands through his hair. He wondered how many diners would vacate their tables if he pummeled the back of his skull and screamed his frustrations at the Elvis portraits on the walls. Instead he sipped his Pepsi and whispered, "So what do we do now?"

"Our options are . . . limited," Molly said. "And none of them are good."

"Tell me about it." Brody linked his fingers. "We need a miracle."

"Exactly. Which brings me to Wendell, the stepbrother. Something he said in one of the articles I read stayed with me—how he and Janko were thick as thieves when they were younger, but drifted apart in later life."

Molly sipped her milkshake again, making small delighted sounds. Those sounds alone were worth the price tag, Brody thought.

"I wondered if *he* might help us." Molly shrugged. "We knew his brother, right?"

"His *step*brother," Brody said. "And we *barely* knew him."

"Okay, but I figured Wendell doesn't need to know that. And if they were thick as thieves when they were younger, maybe they moved in similar circles."

"Had the same connections."

"Right. Someone who could help us disappear."

"Okay. A long shot, but worth exploring." Brody nodded. "Tell me about Wendell."

"He was tough to track down. He and Janko had different biological parents. Different surnames. Took a few hours, going through various genealogy and life-hacking sites. But I found him."

"And?"

"He's a Pentecostal minister."

"Aw, fuck."

"In Decatur, Illinois."

The tables around them had filled. King Elvis was in full swing. The air brimmed with dozens of voices, conversations, rich with aromas of barbecued animal and sarsaparilla. "Suspicious Minds" played through the speakers, just loud enough to hear. An Elvis impersonator sang "Happy Birthday" to a bucktoothed teen three tables away.

At some point their food arrived. Brody only noticed when Molly aimed ketchup at her fries, hit the table instead.

"Shit. Not even close."

"So what's Reverend Wendell going to do, Moll?" Brody smeared the ketchup away with a napkin. "Shelter us with angels?"

"First," Molly said, popping a fry into her mouth, "he was wrongly imprisoned in 1991, for murder, served eight years of a thirty-year sentence, so he may have some empathy for your—*our*—situation."

Brody looked at his meal—ribs, partly charred, glazed with sauce—with zero appetite.

"Second, we knew his stepbrother. There's a family connection. And he's close; Decatur is half a day's bus ride."

Brody said, "Feels like grasping at straws."

"We're lucky to have a straw to grasp." Molly went back to her milkshake but this time there were no delighted sounds. "Bottom line: the Reverend Wendell Mathias is duty-bound to provide guidance to those in need. And we are most certainly in need."

Brody yanked a rib, looked at it as he might a small, live fish, and dropped it back on the plate.

"And maybe he can't help us the way we *need* to be helped." Molly inhaled. Her thin chest trembled. "But he can at least pray for us."

...

Sleep didn't come quickly for Brody. It wasn't paranoia that kept him awake, but the Cadillac-sized concerns regarding their immediate future. The money was only part of it. More urgently, what would they do—where could they turn—after Janko's stepbrother offered prayer, then shooed them away?

What an ugly mess, he thought, wondering at which point his life had transitioned from generally shitty to totally fucked up. When he decided to rob Buddy's? When he—literally—bumped into Blair Latzo? Or maybe it was earlier . . . when his old man committed suicide, or when his mother . . .

"Mom . . ." he murmured.

Memories of her shimmered at the edges of his mind, and it occurred to him that maybe . . . he could find her . . .

"Mom."

. . . track her down. She was out there somewhere. She . . .

It took a long time, but when sleep came, it was as heavy as lead and just as gray.

...

They were on the road before ten, the first of two buses to Decatur. They faced a ninety-minute layover in Jacksonville, so wouldn't reach their destination until eight P.M.

"Prayer won't cut it," Brody said sharply.

They hadn't spoken much that morning—a few sentences

mumbled over breakfast, a couple of grunts and sighs while waiting to board the bus—so this statement rang like a ball-peen
hammer on steel.

"I know," Molly said.

Sunlight flashed across the windows, highlighting handprints
and grime. Two seats ahead, a little girl pulled bubble gum from
beneath the armrest while her mother slept. Somewhere behind,
an elderly fellow with an interdental lisp extolled Trump's quali-
ties in a loud, know-it-all tone of voice.

"We need money," Brody whispered. "And soon."

"You're not robbing anyone," Molly whispered in return.

"I was actually thinking," Brody began, "that I—*we*—could
get work on a farm. Picking apples or grapes or whatever. And
some farms offer basic lodging—you know, for illegals who don't
have anywhere else to live."

"And who work for next to nothing." Molly shook her head.
"It's a step up from slavery, I guess."

"It's somewhere to start." Brody shielded his eyes from the
sunlight. His forehead accommodated a low, dull ache. "We can
slowly get some money behind us. Maybe make new contacts."

"Something *I* considered," Molly said, and what she offered
next made Brody wonder if she'd read his mind as he drifted into
sleep the night before. "Wendell and Janko were thick as thieves
when they were younger."

"You mentioned that." Brody shrugged. "So?"

"So Wendell might know Mom."

CHAPTER ELEVEN

Eddie the Smoke was an independent. He had preferred clients, but allegiance to no one. *Like an assassin*, he often thought of himself. He went where the money was, and if this wasn't the first rule of business, it was certainly the most important one.

He began his tasteless professional life as a paparazzo (he took *the* notorious shot of a certain British rock star getting a blow job from a groupie in the parking lot behind the Viper Room), then moved from Hollywood to Philadelphia and became a private eye. It was dull, occasionally dangerous work. His clients were primarily insurance companies and lonely, suspicious wives (and in almost every case they had cause to be suspicious). "Cheats and pricks," he intoned of his job. "But Christ, they pay the bills." In 2006, he was approached by a well-known property magnate and hired to "tail" a competitor on a month-long tour of the Emirates. "I want to know where he stays, who he meets with, how often he takes a shit." Eddie the Smoke—then just Edwin Shaw—provided this information, and more besides, and at the end of the job was rewarded with a check for $30,000, plus expenses. At that point he determined that following people might be more lucrative than secretly taking photographs of them.

Over the years his clients included a former child star, a best-selling novelist, and more than one crooked politician. On official documents, under "occupation," Eddie usually wrote *tailer*, and nobody challenged him on the spelling.

...

He used technology, but didn't rely on it. Tracking devices were often lost or, worse, discovered. Geolocation was unreliable. Eddie favored the old-fashioned method of physically *following* his objective. He drove a dependable vehicle and carried a set of license plates from twenty-three states, magnetized for easy switching. He used multiple disguises, mainly hats and glasses. A baseball cap or pair of aviators altered not only his appearance but his character, too.

Eddie maintained a prudent distance when tailing, of course, but there were times when he couldn't help but get close. There were also occasions when it paid to get *very* close. He'd been an Uber driver since 2014, and in that time had given rides to twenty-nine of his targets. Uber was incredibly popular, and Eddie had the smarts to use it to his advantage.

"Going anywhere exciting?" he'd asked the kid, looking at his sad, purplish eyes in the rearview.

"I hope not," the kid had replied.

Eddie had worked for Jimmy Latzo several times. Knowing the way Jimmy operated, it was safe to assume that excitement was very much in this kid's future.

...

Followed State-Ways #1078 to Jacksonville, IL. Objective disembarked at 16:07. He and the cripple ate hoagies from Mac's on N. Main St. Boarded State-Ways #1211 to Decatur, IL. Disembarked at 20:04. Checked into Overnites on N. Water St. Room #17. Lights out at 23:02.

Text from Eddie the Smoke to Blair Mayo. 11:09 P.M. 10/08/19.

CHAPTER TWELVE

It was 10:10 on a Wednesday morning. Church was not in session, but the New Zion Gospel Choir was in full, rapturous swing.

...

They heard the singing from half a block away and looked at each other like thirsty travelers within earshot of running water. The corners of Brody's mouth lifted. Molly nodded and thonked ahead. She'd been dragging her crutches since they'd left the motel but now the rubber tips came down with a clear and determined rhythm. Brody followed. He walked not faster, but straighter, his energy like a brightening coil in his chest. They ascended broad steps outside the church. A sign above the doors declared WHERE GOD GUIDES HE PROVIDES. Molly threw her shoulder against the left door while Brody took the right. The doors swung inward. The singing cascaded.

It was rehearsal but the choir was nonetheless in its raiment of service: blue and white gowns, flashed with orange trim. Their voices boomed to the accompaniment of a slightly out-of-tune piano. A large and beautiful woman led them, one hand to the heavens, singing from the deep well of her solar plexus. "His divine *glory*, His *love*, His *mercy*," she bellowed. "Trust in the Lord and He *will* set you free." The New Zion Baptist Church was in a low-income neighborhood. Brody and Molly had passed boarded-over stores and crime scenes and thin, mistrustful children to get there, but there, throughout the choir, from baritone to soprano, every face was incandescent.

A cool tear tickled Brody's cheekbone. He scuffed it away, proceeded down the aisle on loose legs. He was not religious—God had not factored deeply in Brody's twenty-four years—but if nothing else came from this, then this moment, surrounded so profusely by song and faith, made the journey worthwhile.

The song ended in a crescendo of hallelujahs. A tall man with a smooth brown head stood up from the piano, took three strides toward his choir, then noticed the weeping white man and crippled woman standing wearily in the aisle.

"Brothers and sisters," he said, and even talking he had melody to his voice, "let your mercy fill this house like your song. Open your arms, your hearts, for the wretched are among us."

...

The hall was simple and elegant: white walls, plain doors. There was no stained glass or polychromed statues. The most elaborate aspect was the design: semicircular, with a sloping glass roof that shared views of the trees and sky from every angle. The pews faced a wide stage, a modest pulpit, and an altar overlooked by a thin, shimmering cross.

"We knew Karl," Molly said, then added, so there'd be no doubt which Karl she was referring to, "Your stepbrother."

"He was a friend of our mom's," Brody said.

The Reverend Wendell Mathias regarded them expressionlessly, as if waiting to hear more. Several seconds passed, then he pushed a hand across his shaved skull and flicked his eyes in a follow-me gesture.

"Florence," he called to the large woman on stage, "you'll have to do without my dazzling piano for a beat or two."

"A cappella for the Lord," Florence said, and chuckled. "Oh, we can do *that*."

Brody and Molly followed the reverend through a door behind the pulpit, into a windowless, utilitarian space annexed by a crowded office. There was a computer on the desk, files, papers, a stack of prayer books, a lamp that blinked and buzzed. A calendar pinned to the wall displayed Jesus, black and radiant, and a verse from Micah: *You will again have compassion on us; You will tread our sins underfoot and hurl all our iniquities into the depths of the sea.*

Reverend Mathias pushed aside paperwork and perched himself on the edge of the desk. Molly took the only chair. Brody leaned against the wall.

"You should know," the reverend said, "that I saw Karl only once in the years before his death. Our lives went in very different directions."

"We're aware of that," Molly said.

"So you'll excuse me for asking . . ." Reverend Mathias joined his hands, perhaps out of habit. "What exactly do you want from me?"

"To be a friend," Brody replied. "That may sound sad, or crazy, but you're about the closest thing we have."

"I don't even know you." A cry rose from the church proper: a holy high note. It was followed by baritone bass lines and percussive hand claps. Reverend Mathias listened for a moment, no doubt wishing he were out there, then looked at Brody and asked, "What kind of trouble are you in?"

Brody and Molly glanced at each other. Molly shifted uneasily. Brody ran a hand across the back of his neck.

"The long version," he said, "begins when our mother walked out on us. The short version begins when I decided to rob a convenience store."

It was the reverend's turn to shift uneasily. He separated his hands and raised one eyebrow.

"It wasn't even a real gun," Brody began in a dejected tone. "It was a replica. I bought it for sixty bucks."

...

The choir bounced joyously from "Break Every Chain" to "For Your Glory," then into something improvised and entirely sweet. Brody recounted the events that had spiraled them from Rebel Point to the New Zion Baptist Church. He spoke honestly and left nothing out. Reverend Mathias listened in silence, and Brody soon sensed a change in his demeanor, one of empathy. As such—and with the exception of his bald head—he looked hauntingly similar to October's depiction of Jesus Christ.

Molly swallowed a painkiller. The lamp hummed and flickered. Brody finished speaking, then joined his hands without thinking, as if in prayer.

"I know what you're thinking," he said after a moment. His tone was still miserable. "I'm the kind of bad news you could do without."

"I'm not thinking that at all," the reverend said. "And there's no such thing as *bad*, only misguided."

Brody nodded. "Even so, I'm sorry to drop this on your doorstep."

Molly said, "We had nowhere else to go."

...

The stack of prayer books had wobbled precariously as the reverend shifted his butt along the desk's edge. He took a few seconds to arrange them into stable piles, then turned again to Brody and Molly.

"My father married Karl's mother in 1977. Karl and I were the same age—eleven, only three weeks between our birthdays—but different in almost every other way." His eyes fogged as he regressed forty-two years. A smile touched his lips. "Heck, we shouldn't have gotten along as well as we did, but I think, in some ways, our differences made us closer."

"No sibling rivalry," Molly said. "Makes sense."

"Sure. Could be." The reverend nodded. "We grew up together. We went through a young man's rites of passage together. You know . . . bumbling into adolescence, discovering girls, dabbling in cigarettes and alcohol."

He blinked away the memories and smiled again. Molly looked at him with a fondness Brody recognized. Her posture, her body language, were at ease. She liked this guy. He was, in fairness, easy to like.

"I wanted to be a corporate accountant. Can you imagine?" The reverend looked to the low, dusty ceiling—what passed for heaven in this part of the church—as if to say, *What was I thinking?* "I got into Penn State and Karl followed me out a few months later. Not at the university; Karl wasn't of the academic persuasion. A job opportunity, he said. I welcomed having family so close, but it was clear our lives were bound for different points of the compass. Karl had started to get into trouble for petty crimes. Trespassing, disorderly conduct, possession of marijuana. I was concerned that his . . . misdemeanors might reflect negatively on my studies, so I put a little distance between us. He was my brother, though, and we still hung out from time to time. We watched the big college games together—Penn State all the way. We went to a few parties. We even went on a couple of double dates. But it wasn't like it used to be."

"Did you have mutual friends?" Molly asked.

"Sure," the reverend replied. "Not many, but yeah. Three or four."

Brody pushed off the wall, squaring his shoulders, like a man readying himself for a punch to the gut. "Did you know our mom?"

"What was her name?" the reverend asked.

"Natalie . . . Natalie Ellis."

"Her maiden name was Myles," Molly said.

"Natalie Myles?" Reverend Mathias cut a deep frown. "Doesn't ring any bells, and I'm pretty good with names. It's possible Karl met her while I was doing time."

The silence was awkward but blessedly brief, broken by the choir, all voices, full of glory.

"Karl was the problem child," the reverend said, feeling the need to clarify, "but the longest he served was twenty-six months for aggravated assault. I, on the other hand, served eight years for a murder I didn't commit."

Molly sat up in her seat, wincing as she shifted her weight. Brody looked from Reverend Mathias to October's Jesus, again struck by a likeness that went beyond the color of their skin.

The reverend continued, "The police picked me up three blocks from the scene of a fatal stabbing. A witness had seen a black man in a red jacket fleeing the area. Now, I wasn't wearing a jacket, but that was a minor consideration. Like the good officer said, it's easy to take a jacket off, even when running from the scene of a crime. Things went from bad to worse when the same witness IDed me in a lineup the following morning. And that, friends, was all it took. Thirty to life at SCI Graterford."

"Talk about wrong place at the wrong time," Brody said.

"That's some of it," the reverend agreed. "But *most* of it . . . well, let's just say that, for black Americans, it sometimes seems that the only place justice comes before prejudice is in the dictionary."

"I'm sorry you went through that," Molly said.

"Don't be sorry," the reverend said. "It's true what they say about God: He *is* everywhere, and I found him at Graterford Prison. He lifted me up—shone His light into some dark places. But God's tests are never easy. Faith, like everything, is worth more when you have to work for it."

Brody thought he'd give anything for a shot of faith. Faith that he and Molly would find a way through. Faith that the real killer—Blair—would be brought to justice. He didn't think it would come from God, though, but rather from an oversight on Blair's part. That, or a lightning strike of good fortune.

"I was pardoned by the governor of Pennsylvania in 1999, after the real murderer confessed, not only to the crime I was convicted of, but to several other serious misdeeds. He'd found God, too, apparently." The reverend's eyes rolled to the low ceiling again. Another smile touched his lips. *You sure work in mysterious ways.* "Anyway, I was out. I had nothing but a bachelor's degree I had no use for, and a few dollars in my pocket. By way of compensation, the state funded my re-education. I got my master of divinity degree, learned to play piano, and landed here in 2006."

"No looking back," Brody said.

"Oh, I look back often. And this may sound crazy, but I'd do it all again—"

"That *does* sound crazy," Molly blurted, then pressed her fingers to her lips. "Sorry. No offense meant."

The reverend waved it off. "I could have been an accountant working sixty-hour weeks, kissing corporate butt, never seeing my family. Now I live in God's light." He made a single gesture that encompassed his faith, his church, everything from the prayer books stacked behind him to the belief in his soul. "Furthermore, I know how it feels to be so low that you can taste the dirt when you breathe. And empathy is a valuable resource when it comes to forgiveness."

Silence from the hall as the choir closed out another timber-shaking number.

"What I don't know," Reverend Mathias said in that ominously still moment, "is how I can help you, other than through prayer."

Molly said, "That sounds like a good place to start."

"The man who's after me, Jimmy Latzo . . . he's well connected, merciless." Brody dragged a hand across his eyes. "I won't turn down the prayers, Reverend Mathias, but what I—*we*—really need is to get under the radar. To disappear. We were hoping you might still be in contact with some of your brother's acquaintances."

"His criminal friends?" The reverend pressed a thumb to his chin and frowned. "Someone who might provide you with forged paperwork?"

"Whatever it takes," Brody replied. "I'm not asking you to collude or break the law. Just point us in the right direction."

"The right direction is that way." The reverend pointed at the ceiling. "God is the answer."

Brody lowered his head despondently.

"He's the answer you need," the reverend said, and there was a different note in his voice, one of quiet resignation. "But I can see He's not the answer you want."

Brody lifted his eyes.

Reverend Mathias sighed. "I didn't know many of Karl's delinquent friends. Being in prison, ironically, distanced me from that side of his life. On the occasions he visited, I urged him to find distance, too. But he never did."

"Maybe he couldn't," Molly said.

"Maybe," the reverend said, nodding. "Some things have of a way of catching hold, and not letting go until they've dragged you all the way down."

"Tell me about it," Brody said wearily.

"Less chance of that happening"—the reverend dropped a wink—"when your focus is heavenward."

Brody realized there hadn't been any singing for a while, only muffled voices from the hall. The choir must have concluded their rehearsal, which made him wonder how much of the reverend's time they had used up. He was about to suggest to Molly that they hit the road, when the reverend stood up straighter. His expression cleared. He clapped his hands once, crisply.

"You look like you need a good meal. And Florence—my, she makes the most delicious soul-smothered chicken. Serves it with gravy and white rice. Mmm-mmm." All melancholy had left his voice. "I'll have her take you home, feed you up some—"

"Oh no," Molly said. "That's really not—"

"Hush, now. You're friends of the family. And you're not leaving here on empty bellies."

Brody and Molly displayed their identical smiles. Tired, but still lovely.

"That's very kind," Molly said. "Thank you."

"I can't help you beyond food and prayer," the reverend said.

"But I do have some of Karl's possessions—cleaned them out of his apartment after he died. A small boxful of things. Photographs, old vinyl records and mixtapes, letters to his ex-girlfriend. I'll bring it over to Florence's house later. You're welcome to look through, see if you find anything that . . . points you in the right direction."

"Thank you," Brody said. "I guess you never know."

"You're in a dark place. I know how that feels." The reverend's voice was somber, but kindness sparked in his eyes. "A little light goes a long way."

"I hope so." Brody indicated the door behind him, the indistinct voices beyond. "We can come back later, if you need to finish up with—"

"I do, but you're not going anywhere yet." The reverend pushed himself off the desk, took Molly's left hand and Brody's right. "Now we do what you should have been doing all along. Now we pray."

...

Florence lived with her sister and mother in a small two-bedroom house, which seemed larger on the inside, despite the clutter. It boomed with personality, like Florence herself, so that the walls, with all their pictures, and the surfaces, crowded with figurines and curios, drew the eye and expanded, like a broadly detailed painting.

Tamla Motown flowed from the kitchen. Florence browned chicken and sang along, matching the greats—Diana Ross, Marvin Gaye, Smokey Robinson—note for note. Crockery rattled as she danced. Every now and then, Florence's sister—younger, smaller, louder—dueted from elsewhere in the house. Conversely,

Florence's mother sat rocklike in the living room with Brody and Molly, watching them with a gaze that managed to be both discerning and comforting.

Brody ventured, "She may have smothered too much soul on the chicken." Molly cracked a smile, while Florence's mother retorted in a melodic voice, "Ain't no such thang as too much soul."

Family and friends joined them for dinner, a host of faces, all with cheerful voices. They filled their plates, found a spot at the table. They prayed, ate noisily, hummed along to the stereo still playing in the kitchen. Reverend Mathias arrived when a single piece of chicken and a spoonful of rice remained. He asked if everybody had eaten enough. Assured that they had, he gave thanks to his friends and to his God, then he ate.

When most of the company had left, and with Florence busying herself with the pots and pans, Reverend Mathias retired to the living room with Brody and Molly. He had the box of Karl's possessions in one arm—it was not a large box—and set it down on the coffee table, having to first clear a landslide of magazines and flyers from Kroger.

"I have memories," he said, pressing his finger to the side of his head. "But everything else is inside that box. Everything Karl left behind."

"Not much of a life," Molly observed.

Brody tightened inside, thinking that, if he were to die anytime soon, all he'd leave behind was a dusty leather jacket—one that had originally belonged to his old man. Twenty-four years of life, and all Brody had to show for it was a hand-me-down item of clothing. He sighed, dragged the box toward him, and fished out half a dozen vinyl albums and 45s—the kind of music college kids played while they smoked weed.

"I listened to Janet Jackson and Lionel Richie," the reverend said. "Karl listened to Pink Floyd and The 13th Floor Elevators. One of the many ways in which we were different."

Brody pushed aside dog-eared paperbacks, a signed baseball, a broken wristwatch. He found an old wallet with nothing inside.

"Already checked that," the reverend said.

There was an empty jewelry box, a martial arts magazine without a cover, a handful of mixtapes with faded cursive on their card inserts. Beneath these, a loose, creased photograph. Brody lifted it out carefully, turned it toward him. His heart plunged. Anger blew through him, unexpected and hot. He imagined it curling like woodsmoke from his skin.

"What is it?" Molly asked, seeing the change in his disposition.

"Mom."

She was young in the photograph. Early twenties. Sharp cheekbones. Light brown hair spilled across her shoulders. She stood next to Karl. They were in a bar or club, judging by the beer signs behind them. Both had their arms folded, their jaws firmed in a mock-intimidating expression, like a couple of linebackers posing for their TV shots. She was prettier than Brody remembered.

He passed the photo to Molly and forced several cooling breaths.

"That's really her." Molly shook her head. "Wow, Brody, she looks like you."

"Goddamn her," Brody said, then looked at the reverend. "Sorry."

Reverend Mathias cocked a disapproving eyebrow, then drew a pair of glasses from his breast pocket and slipped them on. They hid the creases around his eyes—made him look younger. "Let me see that." He held his hand out for the photograph. Molly handed it to him. "*This* is your mom?"

"Yeah." Brother and sister in unison.

"And what did you say her name was?"

"Natalie Ellis," Molly said. "Née Myles."

"Then I guess I *did* know her, but not well. Met her twice, maybe three times. I'm sure she said her name was Lola, though. You know, like that old song." The reverend sang a few bars of something neither Brody nor Molly had heard before. They regarded him with blank expressions. "I, uh . . . I guess you're too young. Anyway, yes, Lola Blythe. Or Byrd. Something like that."

Molly offered the slightest smile. "I thought you said you were good with names."

"Well, it was a long time ago," the reverend conceded, but looked at Brody and Molly through narrowed eyes, as if *they* might be wrong. "We were just kids. I was actually closer to your mom's cousin."

"Her cousin?" Molly said. She looked at Brody, who returned another blank stare.

"You didn't know she had a cousin?" the reverend asked.

"No." Brother and sister again.

The reverend gestured at the box. "Should be a photo in there."

Molly pulled the box toward her and swept through it. She lifted out the mixtapes and paperbacks, stacking them on top of the vinyls, clearing some space. "So much junk." She held up a Rhode Island fridge magnet, an empty video game case, a mini Rubik's Cube on a key chain. Two photographs followed. The first was a Polaroid of teenage Karl in a baseball uniform. The second was of a block-faced man with his stomach erupting from beneath a gray vest, probably Karl's father. Molly dug deeper into the box, uncovering more junk—a Michael Jordan bobblehead on a broken base, a VHS copy of *Top Gun*—before finding the photograph she sought. She studied it for several seconds, nodded, and handed it to Reverend Mathias.

"There she is," he said, and grinned. "Renée Giordano. Sweet as an apple."

Florence sang in the kitchen, occupying the pause as Reverend Mathias slipped away. His eyes were on the photo but his mind was in the past. Florence's mother slept in her armchair, a blanket across her knees. Her breathing was soft and sweet.

"We went on a few dates." The reverend broke out of his reverie. He sat upright, handed the photograph to Brody. "It looked, for a time, like it might develop into something good, something real. And then . . . well, then I took an eight-year vacation, courtesy of the state of Pennsylvania. Renée wrote me a few times, but the letters stopped after a year or so. I figured she'd found someone else. And so had I." He touched the crucifix around his neck. "We move on, you know."

The photograph was circa 1990, the colors mostly aged out of it. Karl sat at the head of a table loaded with barbecued meats. A young Wendell Mathias—with a high-top fade straight out of Kid 'n Play—sat to his right. The woman beside Wendell had a slender neck, coils of dark hair, eyes deep enough to demand gravity. She had one hand on Wendell's thigh.

"Renée Giovanni," Brody said.

"Gior*dano*," the reverend corrected.

The photograph was old, but the kindness hadn't seeped from Renée's face. It shone ahead of her beauty, in itself remarkable. But beauty fades, whereas kindness endures, and this—*this*—was what Brody homed in on, with the instinct of a butterfly to nectar.

He imagined her now. A successful crime novelist. A concert pianist. A senator. Did she live in a loft in Brooklyn Heights, or on a ranch in sunny Cali? Dreams hit his mind and rippled. He imagined Molly fanning shell grit from one hand, fowl squabbling around her ankles. He smelled morning coffee and freshly laundered towels. How would it feel to wake to a clean house, to the sound of livestock braying, or perhaps the Pacific roaring, before stepping down to breakfast with family? How would it feel to belong?

"Do you know where she is now?" Brody glanced at Reverend Mathias, but only for a second. Renée Giordano, even in an old photograph, was hard to look away from. "She's Mom's cousin, which makes her our, what . . . great-cousin?"

"Second cousin," Molly said.

"Right. She's family." Brody lifted his eyes again, rolled them toward Molly. "Blood?"

"Yeah," Molly replied, and then, "What's going through your mind, Brody? You think she can lead us to Mom?"

"I don't know." Brody shook his head. "I guess I'm thinking we can crash with her for a week or so, keep a low profile. We had no idea she existed, remember, so Jimmy Latzo won't, either."

"You can't be sure of that," Molly said.

"Where can we find her?" Brody asked the reverend.

He removed his glasses, slotted them back into his pocket. "I haven't heard from Renée in . . . more than twenty years. Heck, closer to thirty." Something flashed through his expression, maybe an alternate life, one where he hadn't been in the wrong place at the wrong time, and Renée's body had kept him warm at night, instead of God's light. "I looked her up a couple of times, out of curiosity, the way we do with the faces from our past. The internet makes that so much easier."

"That's how we found you," Molly said.

"I saw on Renée's Myspace page—that's how long ago this was—that she'd moved to Bloomington, Indiana, and landed a job with the Colts a short time later. Events coordinator, or some such. I wished her well, said a prayer for her, and moved on." The reverend angled his head to look at the photograph, still in Brody's hands. He inhaled sharply, then said, "Fast-forward a couple of years. Super Bowl Forty-One. Colts versus Bears."

"I remember it well," Brody said. "Manning was on fire."

"Don't I know it? We put up a big screen here in the hall, because you *can* follow God and the Bears. And then, after the game, with the Colts celebrating on the field, who should I see over Tony Dungy's shoulder but my old girlfriend, Renée Giordano."

Brody looked at Molly and nodded. He'd made up his mind.

"She looked happy," the reverend said. "Inside happy. Not just happy that the Colts had won. And I was happy for her."

He drifted again, eyes glazed. Brody drifted, too, imagining moonlight over the woodlands of Indiana, the silence of a safe neighborhood, drinking craft beers and playing Cards Against Humanity with family he never knew he had.

Florence clanged pots and pans. She sang along to The Temptations, "Ain't Too Proud to Beg," and her sister harmonized.

BEFORE

(2007)
AKA NATALIE ELLIS, NÉE MYLES

"Hey, Ethan—"

"Nat, Jesus, where—" His breath caught in his throat, an upsurge of emotion somewhere between relief and fear. "Where are you?"

She closed her eyes, the handset pressed to her ear. Traffic ripped by. A street she didn't know the name of. A city she was passing through. The phone booth smelled of cigarettes and plastic. There was a small bag at her feet.

"Natalie?"

"I'm not coming back, Ethan."

She had to be strong, and she had to sell her hardness. All those years of repressed emotions, of having sawdust in her heart, and these last thirteen, with Ethan and the kids, were an earthquake. She had laughed, cried, and dreamed with them. She had loved like a supernova, and been vital for every second.

"I'm leaving you," she said.

Her voice was a flatline. Not the merest blip, no hint of a heartbeat. It didn't matter; Ethan heard the words, not the deadness with which they were delivered. He started to contest, as she knew he would, to plead, like any person who faced the unknown, saying that things were great between them, that they had everything to look forward to, and couldn't . . . Jesus, Nat, couldn't they at least talk—

"Nothing to talk about," she cut in. Cold. Cold. Cold. And

then she told him a miserable lie, and prayed she'd never have to tell a worse one. "I don't love you anymore."

She hadn't thought it would come to this, because Jimmy—that reptile, that walking fucking *cancer*—was supposed to die. He'd been in a coma and on life support, yet he'd clawed his way out and continued to breathe—to get stronger, in fact. "You need a backup plan in case anything happens to me," Karl had advised her, and for all her caution and intelligence, this was the best she could do: to leave her family, assume a new identity, and hole up in a different part of the country.

She told Karl to make sure *nothing* happened to him. "Stay close to Jimmy. I need your eyes and ears. But be smart." The years ticked along. Did they erode Karl's vigilance, his cunning? He usually called her on the first of every month, but when August and September passed without contact, she started to worry.

She gave him another week, then hit the internet. A report from the *Altoona Mirror*—found only minutes into her search—confirmed her fears. The headline alone had been enough.

ALTOONA RESIDENT FOUND BEATEN, DROWNED

He didn't squawk. Of that Lola was sure. Not Karl. Not ever. He'd suffered at Jimmy's hands, like so many before him, but he never gave Lola up. If he had, Jimmy would have found her by now.

But how long before Jimmy made the right connections, received accurate intelligence, and came knocking? He cast a broad net, and without Karl to keep her informed, Lola felt exposed. Worse, she felt that her family was exposed.

Her other option was to go on the offensive, like she had in 1993. But she was too unpracticed for a close-quarters assault. She could hit Jimmy from long range with a high-power rifle, but that wasn't exactly straightforward. To begin with, it would take weeks to learn his routine, which in turn would require getting dangerously close. Also, Lola would probably have to position herself in a built-up location. This wasn't like shooting from the window of a book depository in 1963; modern police, with all their tech, would have her surrounded within minutes of her pulling the trigger.

Every offensive measure required a talent she no longer possessed, or a risk she wasn't willing to take. Of course, the surest way to keep her family safe was to give herself up. Failing that, she had to run.

It broke her heart, though. It broke everything.

"This can't be happening," Ethan said. Poor Ethan, who had no idea who she was, and how dark and deadly her past. She'd filled herself with lies and allowed them to leak out over the thirteen years of their marriage. "Please, Natalie. Come home. Whatever's wrong, we'll make it right."

Hard, she thought. *Be hard*.

"Nat . . ."

It was one word, and not even a full word. One syllable of her false name. Yet she heard the brokenness in it, like something made of sand, cracking, sifting between his fingers. She closed her eyes again and covered her mouth, because her own emotion wanted to spill from between her lips—the feelings that had reshaped her, that had moved like a plane over her rough edges. She could count on one hand the number of times she had cried: when Grandpa Bear had died, when Vince had died, when her children were born. Tears threatened now. Her chest bubbled and ached. She shook her head.

Hard.

She would not allow Ethan one iota of her heartbreak. She had to distance herself completely. No forwarding address. No weekend visits. It was a stony foundation upon which to rebuild—for all of them—but infinitely safer.

"Your things are here," Ethan said. "Clothes. Bathroom stuff. Books." He drew a damp breath. She imagined him smearing tears away with the heel of his hand. "Everything."

"Nothing I need," Lola said.

There were a few essentials in the bag at her feet, some of it taken from a safe-deposit box that Ethan didn't know about: her Baby Eagle and two boxes of ammo, a change of clothes, basic toiletries, $420 in cash, the faux-leather folder that Grandpa Bear had given her fifteen years ago containing two new identities (there *had* been three, but she'd just expired one of them). Lola had considered taking a few photographs of the children, but her heart would shatter every time she looked at them.

Life had been easier without emotion. As it would be again.

As if channeling her train of thought, Ethan said, "Your children are here."

Her chest throbbed. A hardy tear squeezed itself from her closed eye and raced along her cheekbone. She imagined Molly sleeping with her crutches beside the bed, and Brody, with his toys boxed away and his favorite rock band posters on the walls, yet still young enough to want the bedroom door ajar. They had closed their eyes on a normal world, and would open them to it being fractured.

Hard.

"I don't need them, either," Lola said, and there it was, only minutes later: a worse lie, still.

Two cruisers barreled down the street she didn't know the name of, all lights and sound. A digital billboard flashed hypnotically, selling first Taco Bell and then, ironically, cholesterol meds. Lola looked at her watch. The train to St. Louis left at 1:35. She didn't think she'd settle in St. Louis, but she could shed Natalie Ellis's skin there—become one of the two women she kept in the folder Grandpa Bear had given her.

"You can't do this over the phone, Natalie. A *goddamn* phone." This was the first time Ethan had raised his voice. In fact, he'd seldom shouted in all their years together. He was gentle and bighearted. "I'm worth more than that."

"No," she said. "You're not."

Lola ended the call before he could say anything else, and stood for several long seconds staring at the grime and cigarette burns on the pay phone's handset.

Cold. Cold. Cold.

She then picked up her bag, walked three blocks of whatever street this was to the train station, and boarded the 1:35 to St. Louis.

On to the next life.

CHAPTER THIRTEEN

Jimmy had twice-weekly massages, regular mani-pedis, fine whiskey tastings, and poker nights (quality cigars required) with his associates. But the hour he spent every day in the gym would always be his favorite time.

Music thumped from in-ceiling speakers, something loud and angry, to get the blood pounding. Jimmy applied ten-pound weights to each side of the barbell, bringing the total to seventy pounds. He curled eight reps, strict form, not swinging his back at all. He counted to twenty, then curled another five. Not bad for sixty-two.

He looked at his reflection in one of the many mirrors, enjoying the way his muscles moved beneath the embroidery of scar tissue.

"The Italian fucking Cat."

Jimmy was not a spiritual man, but he believed the universe followed certain lines. As he looked at his scarred body, he remembered the old neighborhood—Chase Street, specifically, behind Sicily Pizza. Mario Antonutti would sometimes bring out burned calzones or leftover slices, and there'd usually be a rabble of kids hanging around to intercept those scraps before they hit the dumpster. Only this one time, Jimmy, maybe seven years old, was out back all by himself when the door opened and Mario came out with three-quarters of a Sicilian pie—a solid rectangular base, topped with spicy sauce and singed, salty pepperoni—and there must have been *something* wrong with it, but to Jimmy it looked like the greatest pizza in all of history. He sat cross-legged on the ground and wolfed down the first slice.

Into his second slice, a cat leaped briskly onto a nearby trash can and watched him eat. Jimmy couldn't stop looking at the cat. Its left eye was sealed from fighting, it had half of one ear missing, and its calico fur was punctuated with scar tissue. "Nobody fucks with you," Jimmy said to the cat. "Even dogs run away." The cat responded with a hiss that sounded like paper tearing. Jimmy smiled and nudged the box—with more than half the pizza remaining—toward the cat and they ate it together.

...

Another eight reps at seventy pounds. Then five more. Jimmy dropped the barbell. It thudded at his feet with a forceful sound. The veins across his chest and in his throat bulged. He circled the gym and flexed.

"*Nobody* fucks with you."

He was not a big man, but he was strong. The son of an Italian steelworker, second-to-youngest in a household of twelve, he *had* to be strong. His old man would consistently drive him into the ground with the same force he'd use to shape steel, and Jimmy always popped back up. Sometimes he was hurt bad—a broken collarbone, six cracked ribs—but he rarely let it show and he never cried. Strength coursed through the Latzo DNA, as unequivocal as their olive coloring and brown eyes. "We were forged from the volcanic rock of Mount Etna," his Uncle Victor used to claim. Another family story recounted that, in 1878, while working on the Brooklyn Bridge, Luca Latzo—Jimmy's revered and respected *grande nonno*—threw four men to their deaths, reason unknown.

...

Lola Bear *had* fucked with him, however, and only the Latzo strength had kept his heart beating. Jimmy had no recollection of the three months he'd spent in a coma, or the sixteen months on life support. He didn't remember the trauma surgeon tweezering the 9mm round from his left kidney, or sawing a window into his skull to relieve the pressure on his swelling brain. His upper body had been slathered with silicone fluid, wrapped in gauze. Healthy skin had been removed from his legs and grafted to his face and shoulders. A machine had breathed for him. He had no memory of this.

The nightmares arrived soon after. Oil-like, narrow, confined. Lola Bear followed him. Sometimes she was a nimble panther that materialized out of the darkness and clawed. More often she spewed flames from her small ruby mouth and engulfed the world.

In one dream Jimmy caught the panther and slit its throat and pulled its surprised, beautiful head from its body.

It was three and a half years before he could speak, and the first words out of his cracked larynx were, "Where is she?"

He screamed the first time he looked in the mirror.

...

The doctors predicted a loss of motor coordination, impaired speech, and post-traumatic amnesia. Jimmy mixed gasoline with the nightmares and they fueled him. He hit the gym in 1997, four years after Lola tried to kill him. He curled three-pound wrist weights that first session—the kind of weights Beverly Hills housewives jogged with. After a month he was bench-pressing thirty pounds. After two months he was up to fifty. His arms and chest tightened with muscle.

Reinventing his body was one thing, but Lola had destroyed his reputation, too. Don Esposito had been good to Jimmy during his long convalescence. He supplied money, care, and protection in case that bitch returned to finish the job. He also provided a temporary residence when Jimmy got out of the hospital, seeing as Jimmy's house had been burned all the way to the fucking basement. But the Don giveth, and the Don taketh away, and he demoted Jimmy—fucking *excommunicated* him—when it became apparent that he was not going to die. From caporegime to civilian, just like that. Jimmy was pissed off, but he understood; Don Esposito was all about appearances, and Jimmy was weak back then, difficult to look at.

He was also a determined son of a bitch, and hell-bent on recuperating everything he'd lost. By the spring of 1998, he was able to form complete sentences and to speak without slurring too much. Duly emboldened, he donned three thousand dollars' worth of Italian finery and met with Hunch Calloway at the Tuscan Gourmet in Carver City—the clothes, the location, very much informing that it was business as usual.

Jimmy made no effort to hide his scars. A specialist in New York City had recommended a prosthetic mask that moved with his face, allowing some small expression. Jimmy declined. He despised his appearance, but the scars were a part of him, a reminder to everyone that it would take more than bullets and fire to put him in the ground. He thought regularly, fondly, of the cat he'd seen behind Sicily Pizza. *Nobody fucks with you. Even dogs run away.* This was precisely the message he wanted to present.

"What's the matter, Hunch? Can't look an old friend in the eye?"

"Jesus Christ, Jimmy. I *can*, it's just . . ."

"Look at me, Hunch."

"They said you were going to die."

"They were wrong."

Hunch Calloway had eyes and ears on every street corner from Pittsburgh to Providence. In the past, Jimmy had used him to procure the names of witnesses, jury members, and criminal informants. Hunch would turn CI himself ten months later, and would be executed for this foolish betrayal by Mykyta Dević, an enforcer for the Odessa Mafia.

"Where is she?" Jimmy asked.

"Lola?"

"Yes, Lola. Of course, fucking Lola."

"Nobody knows, Jimmy. She took off after . . . you know, after . . ."

"After she tried to kill me?"

"Right."

"And nobody knows nothing?"

"Right."

"What about Dane Greene, Johnny the Grease, Lucky Manzarek—those two-faced pricks she always kicked around with?"

"They've all gone, too. I heard Lucky went into witness protection, but I'm not sure." Hunch drank his water. He couldn't look at Jimmy for long. "Everything's changed, Jimmy. Guys are cutting deals and cutting loose. Don Esposito is keeping his head above water—he's got good people around him—but rumor is the sharks are circling. Not just the Feds. The fucking Ukrainians, the blacks, the spics. There's business to be done and they all want a piece."

Jimmy told Hunch to keep his ear close to the ground. "Catch a sniff of that cunt, and I want to be the first to know." He knew tracking Lola down wouldn't be quick or easy, but that was just as well; he needed time to prepare, physically and mentally.

Things were looking up, though. His lawyers had already secured investments with commercial real estate and land development companies in western Pennsylvania, with designs on obtaining majority ownership—by whatever means—within eighteen months. Jimmy was on his way to reestablishing ties with commerce and community: the foundation from which to expand.

At the gym, he was bench-pressing one hundred pounds, curling twenty-five. Kid weights, but it was a start.

"Nobody fucks with you."

The Italian Cat was coming back.

...

The criminal landscape changed over the next ten years. By 2008, Don Esposito had lost ground in western Pennsylvania, but remained a key player. He'd opened his doors to new enterprises, and maintained a profitable relationship with Jimmy, although the prospect of bringing him back into the family and reinstating him as caporegime was never considered. Don Esposito had his reasons for this, and had shared them with Jimmy during a golfing weekend at Mar-a-Lago.

"You're doing great, Jimmy. You don't make that disgusting rattling sound when you breathe anymore, and your hands don't tremble as much. You've come a long way." Don Esposito was seventy-three but could get around Trump's course in eighty or better. There was nothing wrong with his eye, or his judgment. "You've still got a long way to go, though. And times have changed. The glory days . . . fuck, they died when Little Nicky went down."

"I know that, Don."

"You don't know shit. You've been out of it too long." Don Esposito hit a fifty-yard pitch shot and landed inches from the pin. "Ow, sweet. You like that, Jimmy?"

"A great fucking shot, Don."

"You need to appreciate that everything is different now. We're dealing with multiple business interests. It's volatile as fuck." Unlike the late Hunch Calloway, Don Esposito had no problem looking Jimmy in the eye. "This is a time for politics, patience, and diplomacy. Your short fucking fuse could undo a lot of good work."

Jimmy tightened his jaw. A vein at the back of his skull ticked arythmically.

"And let's not forget the other thing," Don Esposito continued. "The *big* thing: You were taken down—almost taken *out*—by a woman. One fucking woman."

"No ordinary woman," Jimmy said.

"That may be so, but you can see how a detail like this could reflect badly on me."

"I'm going to find that bitch, Don, and I'm going to kill her." Jimmy said this, trying to keep his voice from shaking with rage. "In the meantime, I respect your decision."

"Of course you do. Now hand me my putter and shut the fuck up."

...

He dreamed about Lola every night. She was sinuous and rotten. He hated and loved her. "I'm coming for you, Lola. I'll catch you outside of a dream. I swear to you." And there were not many daylight hours when she didn't cross his mind. He might see her in the black reflection of his TV or cell phone, or in the heat haze above Donegal Steelworks. She fueled every dollar he earned, every soldier he hired. "You've become my ambition. My purpose. And I will give you the glorious death you deserve. I'll catch every slow drop of blood in my mouth, and let the birds take your skin."

...

Jimmy finished his workout the same as always: with a line of Peruvian flake, snorted off the seat of his weight bench. He prowled the gym until his eyes grew as large as tulips.

The door opened. Blair stepped in.

"You can't fucking knock?" Jimmy snapped.

"I *did* knock." Blair pointed at the ceiling. "The goddamn music's too loud."

Jimmy turned down the volume and wiped his nose with the back of his hand, removing any excess coke. "What do you want?"

"I have news."

Blair had surpassed his expectations regarding adeptness and cold-bloodedness. He once saw her kill a man with a nail file after he'd roofied her margarita. It happened in a moment. He, the man, was surprised to find himself bleeding so magnificently. Blair also enjoyed chess, world cinema, and Filipino knife fighting.

"News?"

"Actually, it can wait until you've come down."

"Tell me now."

"No."

Men underestimated her. They disarmed themselves. Blair

used this to her advantage. Lola had been the same. How many of their victims had fallen because they had surrendered the first—and only—shot? Jimmy maintained that Blair wasn't a replacement for Lola, but they were the same in so many ways.

Blair was more ruthless, however. More patient. This patience infuriated Jimmy sometimes. He needed it, though. It was the white to his black.

She caught up with him later, after he'd showered and his eyes were back to normal size.

"The latest from Eddie the Smoke," she said. "Brody and Molly have arrived in Bloomington, Indiana."

"Bloomington . . . ?"

"It's where Renée Giordano lives."

Jimmy pressed his tongue to the inside of his cheek and searched his memory, running through countless faces and acquaintances. People he'd worked with. People he'd hurt. The name was familiar, but he couldn't place it.

"Renée Gior—"

"I asked around," Blair cut in, seeing him struggle. "Drew blanks, until Joey Cabrini told me that she's Lola Bear's cousin."

"Her cousin?" Jimmy narrowed his eyes. "And did we get to her?" Then he shrugged, as if the question required no response. "I mean, of *course* we got to her."

"You had Karl Janko rough her up back in '97," Blair said dryly. "You were recovering at the time. Still too frail to do it yourself."

"Karl fucking *Janko*?" Jimmy's eyes went from squinted pencil lines to wide, bright circles. "But he was working *with* Lola."

"You didn't know that then."

Jimmy blinked. He looked like he'd been slapped. "And have we got to the cousin since?"

Blair shook her head. "You crossed her off the list."

"Jesus Christ."

"It's an oversight, Jimmy, but put it out of your head. It's history." Blair paused, allowing Jimmy a moment to refocus. "Something we need to consider, though: Renée Giordano knows who you are, and almost certainly knows your history with Lola. The fact that you're now hunting Brody will seem like too great a coincidence."

"She'll know it's a setup." The glimmer in Jimmy's eyes shifted from ire to hunger. "So is it time to do it my way?"

"No. We hang tight." Blair stood rock-still and held Jimmy's gaze with impressive confidence. "If the cousin knows where Lola is, there's every chance she'll share that information with Brody."

"She won't share a damn thing," Jimmy snapped, "if she suspects it's a setup."

"I think she will," Blair said. "She has Brody and Molly to consider now. How else will she get them out of your crosshairs?"

Jimmy had been opposed to this bullshit cat-and-mouse since the moment Blair had proposed it. He'd acquiesced, though— soft touch that he was—and had spent six months on the sidelines with nothing to get excited about. He was ready to go back to doing it old school, but Blair's last two sentences had stirred something inside him. A maybe. A hopefulness. A morsel of enthusiasm no larger than a berry.

He didn't realize how tense he was until the muscles across his shoulders dropped a full two inches.

"Okay," he said. "How do you see this playing out?"

"The only way it *can* play out." Blair linked her fingers. Her nails were still streaked with the pink varnish she'd applied on the night she met Brody at Rocky T's. "Brody is about to realize he's been drawn into a war. He knows the cops can't help him—not that he'd risk turning himself in. Running is not a long-term solution. Leading you to his badass mom—who brought you down once before—is his only hope of survival."

Jimmy considered the likelihood of this. He paced his office, tongue lodged into his cheek. His heart fluttered, but that might have been the last of the cocaine.

"How—" he began, then that morsel of enthusiasm expanded greatly. It surged from his chest into his throat, tasting both vinegary and delightful. "How do you know the way things will play out? The way people will act?"

"It's human instinct, Jimmy." Blair spoke with the same detachment she'd adopted when opening Mr. Roofie's throat with a nail file. "In the face of an insurmountable threat, we seek security."

"Even so . . . you're exceptional."

Blair nodded. Her patience was only outgunned by her confidence.

Jimmy stopped pacing. He sat on the couch and dared a tiny smile.

"I think we're close," Blair said. "I really do."

"Maybe," Jimmy allowed.

"After so long . . . how does it feel?"

Jimmy closed his eyes to better isolate the feeling, but slipped instead into a post-cocaine, post-workout sleep, where many fires burned but their flames were lighter, comforting.

CHAPTER FOURTEEN

Brody had indulged in fantasy, knowing it would lead to disappointment, but unable to help himself. After scuttling from one flea-pit motel to the next, and living with Tyrese before that, he needed to believe that some degree of comfort was forthcoming. He'd imagined fragrant, bouncy towels, a bed with a memory-foam mattress, drinking freshly ground coffee, and watching Netflix originals with newly discovered family. Wonderful, nourishing things, when really, a comfortable sofa in a warm, safe home would have sufficed.

Renée Giordano's home was comfortable, in a way, and welcoming. Brody got the sofa, the freshly ground coffee, but he also got more.

He got truths, understanding, despair.

More than he could ever have imagined.

...

The bus rides from Decatur to Bloomington consumed thirteen long hours, including a four-hour layover in Indianapolis. Brody reflected that it would have taken three and a half in a car, and thought wistfully of his little Pontiac Shitbox, wondering if it was still parked behind the cattle shed on the outskirts of Bayonet. He liked to think it had been put to good use. Maybe a family of red wolves had appropriated it, a mother on the backseat nursing her litter. Or maybe some dusty vagrant had made it his own, the contents of his shopping cart distributed across the front seats and dash. One man's shitbox is another man's palace.

They arrived in Bloomington at 12:20 P.M. Molly immediately went to work. Brody went to Starbucks. He ordered a grande latte, dropped into one of the lounge-style chairs, and sipped it while flipping through the *Indy Star*'s sports pages. He then ordered a chai tea to go—for Molly—and by the time he'd walked to the public library downtown, she had located their second cousin.

"Not that it matters," she said, "but to give you a heads-up, Renée became a wheelchair user five years ago."

"Oh shit. What happened?"

"Motorcycle accident." Molly had her notes in one hand and her chai tea in the other. "Hit some wet leaves, lost control, got smoked by a Chevy Tahoe."

"Christ," Brody said, and swallowed a sour lump in his throat. "So how did you find her?"

"She's unlisted, of course, because nothing is easy."

"Right."

Molly sipped her tea. "I tried the usual social media suspects first. Nothing. Then I Googled 'Renée Giordano Indianapolis Colts.' It brought up, among other things, a newspaper article from 2014, about a charity fun run to raise money for Renée. It was organized by her friend, a woman named"—Molly consulted her notes—"Beth Livingstone. They'd worked together at the Colts. The run raised forty-six thousand dollars. Tony Dungy took part."

"Way to go, Tony."

"Now, Renée doesn't have a Facebook page, because, as you know, nothing is easy, but Beth Livingstone *does*. So I checked it out." Molly swept hair from her brow and took another sip of tea. "It's the usual shitshow of dog photos and Bible quotes, but I scrolled back to 2014 and found photos of the charity run. Renée is in quite a few of them. Then I jumped forward a few months and found a photograph of Renée behind the wheel of her new custom disability van, paid for, in part, with money from the run."

"Okay," Brody said.

"It's a red Honda Odyssey, a little Colts pennant in the rear window. But the most telling thing about the photo is the street sign in the background." Molly looked at her notes again. "Terracotta Avenue. So then I jumped onto Google Maps, took a virtual stroll down Terracotta Avenue, and there's the red Honda Odyssey with the Colts pennant in the back, parked in the driveway of number 1516."

"You should have been a private detective," Brody said, looking at his sister with something close to awe. "You're amazing."

Molly smiled sweetly. "Only on days that end with a *y*."

The library hummed around them, the sound of whispering, footsteps, pages turning. Children laughed in an adjacent room, full of color.

"Terracotta Avenue is a twenty-five-minute walk from here. So . . ." Molly finished her tea and grabbed her crutches. "Do you want to go meet our second cousin?"

Brody said, "Let's go."

...

The midafternoon sun broke through a webbing of cloud. It never got summer-day hot, but Brody's shoulders slumped and Molly pushed out every breath. Her crutches dragged.

It took forty minutes, not twenty-five, to reach Terracotta Avenue. There was a silver Toyota Sienna in the driveway of 1516—no Colts pennant in the window—and a Smart car parked behind this.

"You think she still lives here?" Brody asked.

Molly nodded, using her crutch to point at the ramp leading to the front door. "I guess she bought another minivan since the Google car zipped through the neighborhood."

A Hispanic man with deep eye makeup answered the door. He looked Brody up and down, and regarded Molly with a softer expression.

"Is Renée home?" Brody asked.

"Who are you?"

"Family."

He looked doubtful, but flitted away. Moments later, Renée rolled into the hallway. She didn't get far before stopping, tires squeaking on the hardwood. Her jaw dropped an inch.

"Brody," she said, and he detected the tightness in her voice. "I've only ever seen you in photographs, and the last one I saw was nearly thirteen years ago."

Brody had nothing. He opened his mouth, but . . . silence.

"And Molly," Renée said. "Your mother lost sleep for you, praying for you. And look at you now. So beautiful."

"Hello, Renée," Molly said.

Renée smiled, and Brody saw what Reverend Mathias must have all those years ago, and what had shone through in those old photographs. An unassailable beauty. A deep and penetrating kindness.

"Come in," she said. "Come in, come in."

...

Renée's caregiver, Manuel, he with the eye makeup, brought them sodas, then left them alone. Renée led them onto the rear deck. "You can never get too much fresh air." A wonderful old maple provided shelter from the afternoon sun.

Molly sat with a sigh. She dropped one of her crutches. It clattered to the deck and she left it there—flapped a weary hand at it—then plucked a near-empty strip of pills from her purse.

"Baclofen?" Renée asked.

"Yeah." Molly popped two into her palm and gulped them. "Lioresal."

"Me, too," Renée said. "I can't wilfully move anything south of my boobies, but sometimes my legs do the funky chicken. It's the darnedest thing."

"God bless pharmaceuticals."

"Amen."

"I'm on antidepressants, too. Lexapro. And Motrin for the pain."

"Celebrex here, and Prozac. Also, stool softeners and anticonvulsants."

"Where," Molly said dryly, "would we be without the miracles of modern science?"

"And how are you paying for these miracles?" Renée's gaze switched between Brody and Molly. "Excuse my bluntness, but you look like you just hopped out of a garbage can. I assume you don't have insurance."

Brody squirmed in his seat. "I, um . . . we . . ." He looked at the maple, leaves peeling from it in the breeze.

"I had a part-time job," Molly said. "In Rebel Point. It wasn't much money, but it helped."

"Right, and we had savings," Brody added. "Dad's savings, mostly. And we sold his car—"

"Which didn't cover the lien. Upside down, they call it in the car business. But we sold some of his other possessions—power tools, his vinyl collection, his stereo—and when the money ran out, Brody robbed a convenience store."

A crow called from the maple's high branches, accenting its pitch as if to question Molly's statement, if not her audacity. It was met with a silence that begged for someone to fill it. At length, Renée did.

"I guessed you were in trouble. Why else would you come here? But back up a moment." Renée made a rewind gesture with the forefinger of her right hand. "Your dad's savings? His possessions? Did something happen to him?"

"He died," Molly said.

"Oh my." Renée pressed the same forefinger to her lips. "He wouldn't have been very old."

"Fifty-four."

"I'm so sorry. That's just . . ." Renée shook her head. "Cancer?"

"Suicide," Molly said.

"Really?"

Something in the way Renée said this—a bleakly curious tone, rather than one of surprise—triggered an uneasy feeling within Brody. He might have dismissed it, but her further questioning didn't help.

She asked, "Do you mind if I ask how?"

"He jumped off a building," Molly replied.

"He jumped?" It was doubt, not curiosity, in Renée's voice now, and Brody didn't like it, not one little bit.

The crow called again and the maple's branches clattered as it flew away. That uneasy feeling settled close to Brody's heart. Renée gripped her armrests—clearly bracing herself—and asked the same question as Reverend Mathias.

"What kind of trouble are you in?"

...

Molly had told Brody on their short hike from Bayonet to Elder
that this was on him. *You own this shit*, she'd stormed, and Brody
intended to. It would have been easy to paint himself in a less
damning light while relating events to Reverend Mathias, but he
hadn't. He'd recounted his sorry tale with candor, shouldering
the responsibility for his errant actions. He did the same with
Renée. "I fucked up," he began, and started to tell her how he'd
tipped his and Molly's precariously balanced world into the shitter. He added no filler, no shine, and paused only twice—once
to take a long drink of soda, and again after mentioning Jimmy
Latzo for the first time.

"I knew it," Renée said.

"What?" Brody asked.

The kindness in Renée's eyes faded, replaced with a knot of
deep thought. Dark lines crossed her brow. Her irises flicked
from side to side, as if she were viewing many things—incidents
from her past, perhaps, replayed in clear and startling snapshots.

"Are you okay?" Molly asked.

"Yes, I . . ." Renée exhaled from the depths of her lungs. She
blinked twice—coming back to herself—and looked at Brody.
"Carry on."

Brody did, hesitantly to begin with, and with a set of questions
tumbling through his mind. They tailed a notion that there was
more to this, and that his part in it was relatively minor. Distracted, he stumbled through, still with candor, describing the
fear and anxiety—looking over their shoulders every mile of the
way, outrunning Jimmy's goons in Bayonet, dumping his old shit-
banger and riding bus after stinking bus across the Midwest—
before finishing on a sweeter note: their meeting the Reverend
Wendell Mathias.

"He sends his fondest wishes," Molly said to Renée. "I think he still misses you."

"Wendell," Renée said. The kindness returned, not just to her eyes, but to her entire body. She sighed wistfully and appeared to expand in her chair. "Reverend?"

"He was pardoned in 1999," Brody said. "Found his calling with the church."

"He's the reason we're here," Molly said. "In fact, we didn't know you existed until he told us."

"Right," Brody said. He took another sip of his soda and leaned forward. "Why wouldn't our mom tell us about you?"

Renée hesitated, then shrugged and looked down at her hands. "I was a part of her old life. The life she ran away from."

"We *are* the life she ran away from," Molly said.

"No, sweetie." Renée shook her head. "This was before you came along."

"Before?" A shallow crease appeared in the center of Molly's forehead; she was lost in thought, but not for long. "Her name was Lola," she said suddenly. Her eyes brightened and she sat up straight. "Byrd or Blythe. Right?"

"Did Wendell tell you that?"

"Kind of. He thought he had Mom mixed up with someone else. It was a long time ago, but he said he was usually good with names."

Renée offered a small smile. "Bear, not Byrd. Her name was Lola Bear." She sat back in her chair and spoke her next sentence with an icy suddenness: "You may have been followed here."

The notion that there was more to this deepened, but it was too big for Brody to grasp. He pushed against it. "That's not possible. Jimmy's guys jumped us in Mississippi but we lost them. I told you that. Then we dumped my car, dumped our phones. We rode buses and used cash. We've been careful."

Molly must also have sensed something bigger at play, but didn't push against it. She asked, "What's going on, Renée?"

Renée's jaw tightened. She drew her shoulders in again and watched a leaf skate across the deck. "How much do you know about your mother?"

The sunlight shone through the rustling leaves of the old maple. Renée started talking, and by the time she stopped, it was close to dark.

CHAPTER FIFTEEN

At the height of his influence and infamy, Jimmy Latzo had twenty-six people on his payroll. They ranged from personal assistants, lawyers, and crooked cops to soldiers and enforcers. When a "situation" needed attention, Jimmy liked to go in strong, and he only hired the best: the most accurate shooters, the smartest negotiators, the deadliest fighters. Lola Bear ticked every box, and a few boxes that Jimmy hadn't considered. She joined his ranks in 1991.

"It was highly irregular—hell, totally *unheard*-of—for a woman to be on the front line," Renée said, adjusting her position in the wheelchair. "But your mom was special."

"She *worked* for Jimmy Latzo?" Brody's voice hit a rare pitch, reserved for his most disbelieving of statements. "She was a . . . a fucking *mobster*?"

"No," Renée replied. "Jimmy was the mobster. Lola worked *for* Jimmy. There's a difference."

"One degree of separation," Molly noted. "How did she get involved in that?"

"She fell in love," Renée said. A faint smile pinched the corners of her mouth. "His name was Vincent Petrescu, and he was everything to your mom. Her world entire, as the poets might say. She met him at the Western Penn 3-Gun, and it was Vincent who introduced her to Jimmy."

"I've got so many questions," Brody said. The uneasy feeling in his chest had turned into a cold hand. It squeezed and let go, squeezed and let go. "I don't know where to begin, but . . .

who is Vincent Petrescu, and what the hell is the Western Penn 3-Gun?"

"It's a shooting tournament. Three different types of firearms. Rifle, pistol, and shotgun. Whoever hits the most targets in the shortest time is the winner." Renée spread her hands, as if the outcome of this competition were never in question. "Lola won by a considerable margin. Vincent finished second."

"Who was he?" Molly asked.

"One of Jimmy's most trusted soldiers," Renée said. "He was capable, strong, and he respected your mom. A lot of guys in the life treated their women like shit. But not Vincent. He was a gentleman."

Renée cleared her throat. She sipped from her glass and breathed the air for a moment. Her dark hair, shimmering white at the roots, moved lazily in the breeze. Brody and Molly looked at each other deeply, if only to see something familiar, something they knew to be true.

"Your mom started running errands for Jimmy," Renée continued. "She told me, on one of the few occasions she talked to me about that part of her life, that she only did it for the money. That may have been true, but there was more to it. Lola had a solemnness about her, a certain . . . *coldness*. I think working for Jimmy warmed her in some way."

"A coldness?" Molly frowned. "What do you mean?"

"She rarely showed emotion," Renée said. "She hardly ever laughed, and I never saw her cry. Everything was repressed, pushed down deep. Any psychologist in the world would point to her childhood, which was extremely tough."

"How so?" This was Brody.

"Lonely. Lacking. Abusive." Renée shrugged. A sad light

touched her eyes. "Lola's father was killed in Vietnam, three months before she was born. Chloe—Lola's mom—struggled in every way imaginable. She took handouts, worked multiple jobs, sometimes leaving Lola at home—six, seven years old—so that she could earn enough money to put food in their bellies and clothes on their backs. They were hard times. Then Chloe met Mav Hamm, and they only got harder."

Molly glanced at Brody, all this information—these truths—passing across her face, evoking an expression he'd never seen before and couldn't quite name. A reddish leaf tumbled from the maple, landed in her hair, where it fluttered for a second, then blew away.

"Lola's stepdaddy, Mav Hamm." Renée lifted one eyebrow, as if the name alone were cause for mistrust. "Or Maverick Cooper Hamm, if you want to be formal about it. He was a nasty piece of work—a mean, *shitty* human being—and he shut down everything worth nurturing inside Lola. He may have even killed some vital part of her. But he brought something to life, too. Something dangerous."

More leaves swirled across the deck, brushing over the tops of Brody's sneakers and against Renée's legs. One caught beneath the hem of her jeans and tapped uselessly against her ankle.

"I mentioned that your mom rarely showed emotion," Renée continued. "That's true, but I don't want you thinking that she was emotion*less*. Believe me, she had everything inside her. It just took a long time to come out. But when it did, *when* she felt something, she felt it furiously. That worked for love—Vincent Petrescu is proof of that—but it also worked for hate. For rage."

The cold hand inside Brody's chest squeezed tightly, and didn't let go for a long time.

"What did she do?" he asked.

"She beat Mav half to death," Renée replied. "Put him into a coma."

"A *coma*?" Molly repeated, her voice reaching a higher octave than usual. "Jesus Christ."

"He came out of it eventually, but . . ." Renée shook her head, as if to suggest that things were never quite the same for Maverick Cooper Hamm. "The crazy thing is, Lola was only eleven years old at the time."

Molly sat back with such force that her chair nearly tipped over. Brody had to reach to steady it.

Renée finished her drink and said, "It happened like this."

...

Chloe met Mav at the Lycoming County Fair. She'd taken Lola, then nine, because it had been months since they'd spent any real time together, and she had a few dollars in her pocket from the extra shifts she'd pulled at the car wash. Mav had been shoeing a pony, and afterward had handed Lola a brush and invited her to groom the pony's mane. She did, working carefully, with smooth, gentle strokes. "Nice and easy, girl, that's the way," Mav had said. "Say, Mom, I think you got a natural here." He'd looked at Chloe and winked and something inside her had fluttered in a way it hadn't for many years. He was not all the way handsome, Chloe thought. He had a chipped front tooth and a squint in one eye, but his voice was barrel-deep and his chest looked large enough to curl up on. Chloe made a point of passing by the pony pen later that day. She got talking to Mav. He was funny and charming. She saw depth in his eyes. He took her for dinner at Bello Italiano three nights later.

It was all peaches and cream for the first few months—holding hands, tender promises, long walks in the park. The warning signs only appeared after Chloe had confessed her love for him, although she didn't view them as warning signs at the time. They were more like . . . *mannerisms*, the curious traits of the Y chromosome. He had started to pinch the tender skin at the back of Chloe's arm to get her attention, and to switch the TV show she was watching over to whatever sport was playing. Yes, these boorish quirks were frustrating, and yes, Chloe believed she deserved more respect. But Mav was good to her in other ways. He put new brakes on her car, always paid when they went to the movies or to dinner, and bought Chloe her very own Steelers jersey to wear on Sundays.

Besides, Chloe mused, no relationship was perfect. No *honest* relationship, at any rate.

Mav hit her once before they were married, but only because she'd stepped out of line. They'd been drinking at their local bar with Mav's friends, and Chloe had suggested Mav slow down just a bit—jeez, did he want to spend the night sleeping on the bathroom floor again? Just a joke, was all, and they all laughed, Mav hardest of all, but when they got back to Chloe's place, he socked her cleanly in the eye. Chloe sagged against the wall, holding her face in her hands. "Don't ever disrespect me in front of my friends," he'd snarled. "Take heed, Chlo, that gun was about one-quarter cocked. Next time, I'll take your fucking head off."

Chloe nodded and cried, partly at the pain, mostly at the miserable *surprise* of it all. That was the first time she'd been hit by a man that wasn't her daddy, and it was *scary*. She slept on the sofa that night—except she didn't sleep, of course; she lay awake with a bag of frozen peas pressed to her left eye, thinking it all through, and with a little perspective she concluded that she *had* disrespected Mav, and that was silly of her. Mav came down the following morning and she pushed a stack of strawberry banana pancakes in front of him—his favorite—and kissed his forehead and told him she was sorry.

Meanwhile, Lola drifted in the background, silently registering every degree of abuse. She was always a quiet girl—*contained*, Chloe often thought of her—but had become particularly subdued since Mav arrived on the scene. This didn't change, even when they moved into Mav's ranch house in Salladasburg. It was a nice place, if a little run-down, with a huge yard for Lola to run around in, and sometimes the cows would dawdle down from Clemons Farm, lift their big heads over the fence, and chew the tall grass on Mav's land.

"Isn't this a wonderful place to live?" Chloe asked her daughter, which was her way of skirting around the *real* question: *Do you like Mav?* Lola didn't reply, but the stillness that came over her, and the ice in her eyes, was all the answer Chloe needed.

She and Mav were married in July 1978. Things were better for a while—Mav showed flashes of his old charming self—but by Thanksgiving the bloom was truly off the rose. The little pinches that Mav administered to get Chloe's attention became harder and meaner, and left welts that didn't fade for days. On the plus side, the cold weather allowed Chloe to wear clothing that hid the bruising on her legs and throat, and when friends saw the broken arm that Mav had given her for Christmas, she explained in her best oh-silly-me voice that she'd slipped on the ice.

"He hurts you," Lola had said, which surprised Chloe, because her daughter rarely acknowledged Mav, let alone spoke about him. This had been on the afternoon of Lola's eleventh birthday. She and Chloe were eating chocolate cake in the kitchen. Mav was in the yard, changing the exhaust on his Ford truck.

Chloe had covered her mouth and felt a pang of hurt deep inside. Hurt and shame. She managed to say, "He does a lot of good things for us."

"Can he do those things without hurting you?"

"Everybody's different, Lola." This wasn't an answer. Not even close. "Eat your cake."

Lola did, and said no more. She went about her day-to-day in her usual solemn manner, but over the next couple of months Chloe logged a certain change. Her daughter would sporadically emerge from her containment, and always with unwavering focus. She read novels in a single sitting, smashed rocks, climbed tall trees. She spent all of one Sunday afternoon chopping wood, and didn't stop until both hands were blistered and bleeding. Lola even started a conversation with Mav—a rare phenomenon, indeed. "Do you know," she said across the dinner table, looking him in the eye, "that the human skull is made up of twenty-two pieces? It's like some crazy jigsaw puzzle." And Mav had wiped gravy off his chin and said, "That a fact?"

The snow melted. The trees wore pale green at the tips of their branches. Mav watched the Pirates play their preseason games and swore at the TV a lot. One night in late March, Lola walked out to Mav's toolshed and selected a hammer from its place on the rack. It was the one he'd used to shoe the pony that day at the county fair. It wasn't too heavy—about the right weight for a purposeful eleven-year-old—with a blunt, square face and a squat claw. Mav called it his spanging hammer. Lola held it at her side and walked out of the toolshed, across the yard, and into the house. She went through the side door so she wouldn't have to pass through the kitchen, where Chloe was making corned beef sandwiches for Mav's lunch the next day—because how could she know that his days of eating solid food were behind him?

Lola walked into the living room and crossed to Mav's armchair. He was too absorbed in the baseball game to notice her. Without breaking stride, she raised the spanging hammer and rang the blunt, square face off the side of Mav's skull. "Christ *that*?" he blurted. His muddy eyes rolled and a rivulet of blood raced from his hairline. He looked giddily at Lola and she spanged him with the hammer again, this time impacting his right cheekbone so deeply that his eye sagged in its socket. He sneered and tried getting to his feet but his legs noodled beneath him. "Oooh," he said, and dropped to one knee. Lola rapped the hammer off the top of his skull—right in the middle of the jigsaw puzzle—and she felt some of the pieces separate. Mav's entire right side started to jitter. The blood didn't trickle, it poured. The last coherent words he ever spoke were "Willie Stargell at the plate," then Lola whopped him again and this was lights-out.

...

Birds called across the neighborhood, the first verses of evening song, and the sunlight had deepened to a coppery pink belt in the west. It was reflected in Brody's eyes.

"How do you know all this?" he asked.

"Chloe died at forty-eight. Breast cancer. She spent the last five weeks of her life with her sister—my mom—and I visited most days. I'd take her her meds, read to her, puff up her pillows, and in return she shared her story." Renée blinked and wiped her eyes. "I learned a lot about my Aunt Chloe during that time, and even more about Lola."

A stillness fell between them, with each lost to their own complicated emotions. It continued until Manuel brought out Renée's meds in a small plastic cup, along with a glass of water.

"Five minutes," he said, and wagged his finger theatrically. "Then you come inside; it's getting cold."

"Yes, thank you, Manuel," Renée said, spilling the meds into her palm. "We're nearly finished here."

He nodded and clicked his Fitbit. "It's five twenty-seven. I leave soon."

"Okay." Renée smiled. "I'll see you tomorrow."

"Ten A.M." Manuel turned and headed toward the house, but before going inside he called over his shoulder, "Five minutes. *Cinco.*" He flashed five fingers and closed the slider behind him.

Renée downed her prescriptions and sipped her water. Molly, in camaraderie, dug Motrin from her purse and took it dry. Their eyes met. They shared a smile.

"I wish we could have met under happier circumstances," Renée said, looking from Molly to Brody. "But I'm so happy you're here."

Molly reached across, clasped Renée's hand, and held it with a meaningfulness Brody couldn't remember seeing before. He knew then that he would continue this wild journey—wherever it took him—on his own.

He needed more information, though. *We're nearly finished here*, Renée had said to Manuel, but Brody thought they were just getting started. There were so many questions left unanswered, so many blanks to fill in. He looked at the darkening sky and wondered where to begin, and it was Molly—always Molly—who led the way. How would he manage without her?

"What happened to Mom?" she asked, still holding Renée's hand. "You know . . . after Mav?"

"Cormorant Place happened," Renée replied, turning her face to the colorful old maple. "It's still there, right in the heart of Lycoming County, and if you visit their website it still professes to be a juvenile care facility. But it is now and has always been a psychiatric hospital for children."

Brody had an image of doped-up kids playing Connect 4, eating mashed potatoes with plastic spoons, watching non-stimulating TV—*Little House on the Prairie*, maybe—on a small set bolted high on the wall.

"How long was she there?" he asked.

"Just over three years," Renée said. She slipped her hand from Molly's and eased back into her seat. "She was discharged in August of 1982. That was when I first met her. We'd been living in Oregon, but moved back to Pennsylvania when my dad lost his job. I was thirteen at the time, crushing on Simon Le Bon and playing Atari. Lola was only a year older, but you'd think she came from a different planet. Her hair was short and scruffy, her skin was pale. She'd never heard of *Magnum, P.I.* or Duran Duran or *Pac-Man*. I'd talk to her but . . . there was nothing."

"Poor girl." Molly winced and stretched out her left leg, kneading the muscles in her thigh. "But things got better, right? *She* got better."

"Eventually," Renée said. "I like to think I had something to do with that. I saw her all the time—we lived twenty miles from each other—and it was good for her to be around a regular, happy kid. That was Grandpa Bear's idea. He was a smart old fella, and he was the real reason Lola . . . *developed* the way she did."

"Grandpa Bear." Brody dragged a palm across the stubble on his jaw. He might have laughed if he wasn't so tired. "Sounds like something from a fairy tale."

"It does. And he *was* kind of mythical." Renée took another sip of water. The glass flashed in the evening sunlight. "Frankie Bear. Lola's grandfather on her daddy's side. He used his influence to get Lola out of Cormorant Place."

"His influence?" Brody frowned. "Was he a mobster, too?"

"He was in the military," Renée said. "A decorated war veteran. *Wars*, actually—one of the very rare individuals to have served in World War Two, Korea, and Vietnam."

"He saw combat in 'Nam?" Brody asked.

"Not directly. He was a general, one of Westmoreland's crew, then he stuck around to help train the ARVN. He came home in '72 and opened a shooting range in Altoona."

"You think he'd be sick of the sound of gunfire," Molly said.

Brody said, "Maybe it gets comforting after a while."

"Maybe," Renée said. She looked at the old maple again, then continued. "Chloe went off the rails after what happened with Mav. Alcohol. Antidepressants. She declared herself unfit to be a parent and Frankie took guardianship, then pulled the strings to get Lola out of that god-awful hospital. Good for Lola, but good for Frankie, too. He'd lost his wife in a traffic accident in the late fifties, and his only son was killed in Vietnam. Lola was all the family he had, and he cared for that little girl with every piece of his heart."

"Why didn't he help before?" Brody asked. "When Mom was a little kid, and Chloe most needed help?"

"He *did*," Renée said. "He sent money on occasion, and dropped off a bag of groceries whenever he was in the neighborhood. It was never much, but Frankie was a hard-nosed old dog, and he believed that Chloe fending for herself would make her stronger. He was the same with Lola. To say he raised her tough is the understatement of the century."

Brody thought of the spanging hammer looping down on the jigsaw puzzle of Mav's skull and said, "I think she was already tough."

"She was tough inside," Renée said. "But she had no skills.

Frankie changed that. Now, a cynical person might say that Frankie turned Lola into the ultimate trophy kid. I prefer to believe he was preparing her for all the harshness and mean-spiritedness in the world. He knew that he wouldn't be around forever, and that Lola would have to be tough to make it alone."

Renée yawned, then finished her water. A breeze knifed across the deck, much colder than it had been.

"So he gave Lola the benefit of his wisdom," she said. "And Lola—machinelike, unaffected by her emotions—learned extremely quickly. Frankie taught her how to survive in the wild. They'd go off for weeks and live in the mountains, with nothing but a sharp knife and the clothes on their backs. He taught her how to make smoke bombs and booby traps, how to camouflage herself, how to hunt with a bow. He shared his knowledge of firearms and close-quarters combat. He also introduced Lola to Benjamin Chen, one of the most renowned Xing Yi instructors in America."

"Xing Yi?" Molly asked.

"One of the martial arts," Renée responded. "Xing Yi Quan. It focuses on swift, direct movements with explosive power. Your mom held a third-degree black sash by the time she was seventeen—a rank that can take the serious student seven years to achieve. She did it in three."

Brody's upper lip twitched, the closest he'd come to smiling since arriving at Renée's house. A memory had floated into his mind: his mom steering him toward a particular YouTube video, and the subsequent hours he'd spent striking a pillow duct-taped to a fence post in their backyard.

"Additionally," Renée continued, "and off her own back, Lola learned kendo, judo, and kickboxing."

"Holy shit," Brody said. "It's like *The Matrix*."

"There was nothing Hollywood about it," Renée said. "It was bare-bones and ugly. She used to get up at four o'clock every morning and grind."

"That's unbelievable," Molly said, shaking her head.

"And then there was *me,* providing some degree of ordinariness by pinning John Stamos posters to Lola's bedroom wall and introducing her to the new Culture Club record." Renée drifted for a few seconds, her eyes shining in the early evening light. "We had some fun. It was nice to see her emerge. But she was more interested in becoming an elite warrior than she was in being a teenage girl."

A fire truck howled a few blocks west and faded somewhere toward downtown. Brody thought of Tank Hill, his neighborhood in Rebel Point, where the sirens were so commonplace he failed to hear them after a while, but the gunshots always woke him at night. *We'll get out of here,* he'd promised Molly—a promise, by pure bad luck, he'd managed to keep. But maybe this tranquil neighborhood, with its hushing trees and occasional sirens, might be the beginning of something, if only for Molly.

"Lola blew the roof off everything she did. The martial arts, the shooting, the weapons combat. I thought she was some kind of superhero." Renée brushed a fallen leaf from her lap and adjusted her position in the wheelchair again. "Then she met Vincent Petrescu, and if the first electrical storm of emotion she displayed was rage, at eleven, then the next was love, at twenty-two. My God, she was besotted."

Another breeze scraped across the deck. Brody cupped his elbows and shivered.

"Yes, it's cold, it's getting late, and I've talked for too long." Renée eased the brake off her wheelchair. "I'll say one more thing before we go inside. Vincent introduced Lola to Jimmy Latzo. I told you that. And it was Jimmy—twisted with jealousy—who took everything away from her."

"He killed Vincent," Molly said.

Renée nodded. "Not a smart move."

Brody's palms moved from his elbows to his forehead. Scraps of information flickered through his mind: Karl Janko beaten up and drowned in a barrel; his father plummeting to his death from the roof of the Folgt Building; Jimmy Latzo's fiery collapse in 1993. The authorities suspected gang warfare, according to the numerous articles Brody had read, but there was another theory: that an anonymous soldier had been responsible. The work of one vengeful man.

Or one woman, Brody thought.

"I saw Lola briefly before she left," Renée said, grasping the hand rims on her chair and wheeling smoothly toward the house. "That was the last time I saw her. I could still smell the smoke."

BEFORE

(2010–2019)
AKA JENNIFER AMES/MARGARET WARD

Jennifer Ames had lived for two years, seven months.

She was a librarian in Little Rock, Arkansas. She had shorter, darker hair than Lola Bear, and was about fifteen pounds heavier. She wore different clothes, too. Frumpy sweaters and leggings, and cheap jewelry from Banana Republic.

This invention of Lola's—this middle-American calendar girl—had been at the range, and had noticed some jackass checking her out. Because of her shooting, or because he wanted to jump her bones. Lola didn't know. But there was another possibility. Maybe he recognized her. Lola subtly pointed him out to Arlen Stoat, whom she'd known since arriving in Little Rock. "Steer clear, Jen," Arlen warned her. "Jason Kazarian. Fancies himself a gangsta. You know, with an *a*. Sells shooters to street kids in Memphis." Lola remembered that Jimmy Latzo had associates in Memphis. He was part-owner of a restaurant on Beale Street. He'd likely circulated her photograph among the criminal element. Alarm bells chimed loudly. Lola spent the next week in a state of hypervigilance—making note of suspicious persons and vehicles with out-of-state plates, and checking the backseat of her car before getting in—and just when she began to believe that she was being paranoid, Bruno Rossi came to town.

Karl had warned her about Bruno in their final communication. "Jimmy's new guy," he'd said. "Fucking man-ape." A brief but fair description. Bruno was *big*—six-four, packed with gym muscle that would slow him down and expose weaknesses. Lola didn't want a fistfight, though. One bullet to center mass would do it.

She had led Bruno to a quiet industrial street in East Little Rock, with enough distance between them that she could park up and quickly hide behind a storage crate. He'd just exited his car when Lola jumped out, leveled her Baby Eagle, and took the shot. Bruno staggered back several feet and hit the blacktop. He shrieked, clutching his midsection, or so Lola thought. In fact, he was removing his .45 from where it was secured between his jacket and ballistic vest. As Lola approached to finish the job, he sat up and fired five times at her legs (he didn't want to kill her—oh no, that was Jimmy's privilege). Lola anticipated the move. She rolled to her right, feeling the rounds cut through the air only inches away. In a previous life, she would have completed the move by popping to one knee, aiming on instinct, and blowing a hole through Bruno's skull. In this life, she lacked that Jedi-like prowess. She *did* pop to one knee, but overbalanced, staggered, and had to plant one hand to steady herself. Another bullet rippled the air—Bruno firing behind him as he took up a better position. He got behind his car and kept low. He'd moved slowly, though. The ballistic vest had saved his life, but the impact of a 9mm round would have bruised or broken several ribs. Coupled with the fact that he couldn't kill Lola, this gave her a distinct advantage.

She zigzagged toward his car, giving him nothing to aim at, then slid across the hood in one slick movement. Bruno anticipated the maneuver, but she was too fast for him to guarantee a nonlethal shot. He used muscle instead, throwing himself at her, wrapping his thick arms around hers so that she couldn't raise her gun. The trauma to his central mass had upset his power, though, and Lola made room to move. She simultaneously head-butted his chest and drove her knee into his groin, then freed her non-shooting hand and elbowed him in the throat. He spluttered and stepped away, sweeping his left arm downward, knocking the gun from her hand. They traded blows. Lola connected with his solar plexus and ribs, feeling the tight bind of the bulletproof vest. He answered with a punch that she blocked but that knocked her back anyway. It gave him the space he needed. Grimacing, clearly in pain, he raised his .45 and fired twice.

The first bullet fizzed between Lola's legs. If Bruno's aim had been steadier, he would have shattered her left kneecap and everything behind it. The second bullet ripped across her calf. She felt the burn of it, then the warmth of her blood. It dropped her to one knee.

"You're not so tough," Bruno gasped. He stepped closer, aimed at her other leg, pulled the trigger.

Click.

An eight-round mag. Bruno stared at his gun stupidly. Lola picked up hers. She thrust forward, close enough to plant a kiss on Bruno's surprised mouth, and shot him point-blank in the stomach—the ballistic equivalent of a one-inch punch (she thought, dazedly, of her son, from a lifetime ago, striking a post in their backyard). Every one of Bruno's two hundred and thirty pounds was raised off the ground. He flew backward and landed hard. Lola stepped over him and shot him in the head. His blood made a satisfying pattern on the sidewalk.

...

She dragged Bruno's corpse into one of the warehouses, propped him in a corner, then used his phone to take a photo. The flash overexposed the shot and made the hole above Bruno's left eyebrow appear quite small. It also drew the last hint of color from his face and made his teeth shine. It was a grim arrangement, and told a certain truth: that Bruno Rossi had died in pain.

She sent it to Jimmy.

Lola pocketed the phone. It would be full of contacts, messages, web-browsing history, perhaps strategies. Information was power. She ripped the sleeve from Bruno's suit jacket and used it to bandage her bleeding calf. Her DNA was all over the scene—Lola's first public appearance since 1993, and hopefully her last.

She limped back to her car.

The first sirens howled as she pulled away.

...

She was on a bus to Austin three hours later, drowsy with painkillers. She'd left behind the frumpy sweaters, the cheap jewelry, the librarian's job. The small bag on the rack above her seat—the same bag she'd used when she left Ethan and the kids—contained a pair of jeans, a first-aid kit, her Baby Eagle with half a box of ammo, $216 in cash, and the faux-leather folder that Grandpa Bear had given her in 1992.

One identity remaining. One life. One more chance.

The bus moved southwest. Lola listened to the thrum of the wheels on the highway. A strange comfort. She slept beneath a shell-thin layer and dreamed angrily.

A ninety-minute layover in Dallas. This gave her the opportunity to change the dressing on her calf. She then limped to the nearest drugstore and bought hydrogen peroxide and a pair of scissors.

Later that morning, at a dusty motel in Austin, Lola burned Jennifer Ames's documents in the bathroom sink.

Dead. Done.

She cut and dyed her hair, and became Margaret Ward.

...

All but $118 of Jennifer Ames's money disappeared from her Chase Bank account. It was filtered through various businesses both at home and overseas, and gradually integrated (minus a five percent fee) into Margaret Ward's Bank of America account.

There was no link from Jennifer Ames to Margaret Ward, thanks to Grandpa Bear's money-laundering contact.

He'd thought of everything. Good old Grandpa Bear.

Lola didn't stay in Austin. It didn't feel like a good fit for Margaret. She moved to Oklahoma, then Colorado, and finally settled in Lone Arrow, Nebraska.

The years passed. She worked as a waitress, a farmhand, a builder's laborer, a store clerk. She watched her children grow via the marvel of social media. Neither Brody nor Molly were active Facebookers, but their occasional posts opened bittersweet windows into their lives. Lola missed them so much.

There were men. Two of them. She used the first for sex, an arrangement that suited them both. He was younger than her, as fit as a thoroughbred. It was easy breaking it off. The second relationship was deeper. Christian Mellor. A fifty-three-year-old English teacher. Smart, generous, and patient.

Lola recalled what Grandpa Bear had said to her—his final lesson: *Don't put down roots, or make anything that you can't leave behind.*

She cut Christian loose when she started to fall in love.

This hurt. Not as much as losing Vince, or breaking away from Ethan and the kids, but enough to question the point of it all. Was her life merely an exercise in survival? Was she allowed nothing to nurture and live for? Thoughts like these chipped at her soul. She felt haunted by her own ghost.

Owlfeather Farm—purchased eight years and two months into Margaret Ward's existence—was her rebellion against the emptiness, and against everything that had her in chains. Yes, it was another example of putting down roots, but they weren't *human* roots. Nothing could be scarred by her having to run. Besides, it was a prime location, with good visibility all around. It would be her stronghold.

If she needed it to be.

Fifty-seven acres, bordered on either side by farmland, to the north by a small but dense patch of forest, and to the south by Big Crow Road. Lola farmed beans and alfalfa. She had chickens, goats, cows, and horses. It was small, and lean in terms of profit, but it was hers, and she threw herself into it completely.

The days turned into weeks, the weeks into months. Margaret Ward's skin grew comfortable. She loved her work, played pinochle with the old folks every Thursday, and sometimes shot skeet with Butch Morgan. Her favorite thing, though, was to ride Poe, her horse, across her acreage, with the sun melting in the west—to inhale the endless sky and feel the wind ripple her hair. In those moments, she never felt freer, and it was possible to believe.

She never let her guard down, though.

Nine and a half years since she'd pulled a trigger in anger.

CHAPTER SIXTEEN

Despite everything they had learned, Brody slept deeply that first night at Renée's. Molly had the spare room. He took the sofa. It was long and soft and unfathomably comfortable. He sank into plush pillows, and though his mind reeled with information—everything from his mother's real name to her working for Jimmy Latzo—his exhaustion won out. A great gray cloud consumed him and he sank helplessly.

"How long do we stay here?" Molly asked the following morning. She had woken him with a mug of freshly ground coffee—the kind he'd been fantasizing about. It smelled rich and delicious and it lifted him, wide-eyed, into a sitting position. He took the mug, sipped from it, savored the taste.

"We need more information," he said. It wasn't an answer, but it concealed what he was thinking: that he planned to continue without her.

He showered for a long time and it was the greatest shower of his life. Pink steam ghosted around him, scented with lilac. He breathed it into his lungs and exhaled, like a man who has been trapped in a mine, stepping into fresh air for the first time in weeks. His skin prickled with cleanliness. Afterward, he used one of Renée's razors to shave. He had lost weight, there were shadowy crescents beneath his eyes, but he looked more like himself than he had in a long time.

His thoughts were still a knife-fight of words and images, though—glimpses of his mother's past and his own potential future. But out of the clash of everything in his head, he kept returning to two things. The first was how Jimmy Latzo had been taken down in 1993, his empire reduced to ashes. The second was Renée saying that she thought Lola was some kind of superhero.

Not *everything* in his mind clashed. Some of the pieces clicked. They had synergy.

For better or worse, Brody sensed the end was in sight.

...

Later that day, he went to Bryan Park with Molly and Renée. He pushed Renée's chair at an easy pace. Molly walked beside them, thumping along on her crutches. There were plenty of people around, walking through the rich fall scenery, running the loop, throwing footballs, and shooting hoops. The trees were alive with color, shimmering in the afternoon light. It was, by any measure, a picture-book October scene, but Brody was too distracted to enjoy it. He had taken to looking regularly over his shoulder.

"You can relax, Brody," Renée said. She'd noticed his agitation, even though he was behind her. "They're not going to jump us."

His arms were rigid, his hands clamped around the push handles. He wondered if Renée could feel the tension through the chair. "You still think we were followed here?"

"I think you should assume as much," Renée replied after a moment. "And proceed accordingly."

"But we were so careful."

"You're dealing with professionals."

They strolled for another minute or so, then Brody looked over his shoulder again. Molly did the same.

"Anybody look suspicious to you?" she asked.

Renée was right; Jimmy worked with professionals, people who could blend in, make themselves invisible. The woman walking her dog, her phone welded to one ear, might be talking directly to Jimmy, or perhaps to another contact elsewhere in the park. *The target is approaching the basketball courts, heading your way.* Maybe one of the elderly men playing dominoes was Jimmy's uncle, still on the payroll. The guy taking pictures of trees might also be taking pictures of Brody. Or how about the hipster chick with the skateboard, the dude taking shots from the free-throw line, the crane-like woman doing tai chi?

"Everybody looks suspicious," he said.

There were fewer people farther along the path, and Renée took that opportunity to share what Brody already suspected: that Lola had singlehandedly dismantled Jimmy's empire back in 1993. She'd killed sixteen men and seven attack dogs, and had fled the scene with Jimmy's mansion engulfed in flames. Intent on revenge, Jimmy had spent the last twenty-plus years hunting Lola, tracking down and questioning—in many cases torturing—anybody who knew her.

"And I guess," Molly said, "that's how Karl Janko ended up in a barrel."

"You guess right," Renée said.

Now Jimmy was after Brody, and no, this wasn't a coincidence. It *had* to be a setup. Brody contemplated this, putting together an unlikely puzzle in his mind, but some of the pieces didn't fit.

"How would he know?" he asked. They had paused to watch two squirrels chase one another around the trunk of an elm tree. Both Molly and Renée giggled at their antics, then Molly turned to Brody and frowned.

"Say what?"

"I put myself in this position," Brody replied. "Jimmy didn't *make* me rob a convenience store. He didn't *make* me drop my wallet at the scene. So how can I have been set up when it was *my* actions that started this whole thing?"

"I wondered that, too," Renée said. "Everything with Blair's stepmom—the diamonds, the so-called murder, *that* was a trap, but the convenience store wasn't."

"Right," Brody said. "It doesn't make sense."

"It does, though," Molly said. "Because it *was* a trap, only one that you made and walked into yourself. You put yourself on a plate for them, Brody."

The squirrels had clambered into the higher branches, out of sight. Molly walked on. Brody was lost in thought for a few seconds—lost in space, Molly always said—then Renée snapped, "Giddyap!" and he blinked hard, pushed on.

"What do you mean?" he asked, drawing level with Molly.

"They were watching you," Molly said, and shrugged as if this were obvious. "How many times did you survey Buddy's Convenience Store before you finally robbed it?"

"Three, four times, maybe," Brody replied. "I wanted to make sure I had all my ducks in a row."

"I'm glad you put some thought into your stupidity," Molly said, and Renée snorted laughter, then clapped a hand over her mouth. "Meanwhile, this girl Blair—who clearly works for Jimmy—saw what you were planning. I mean, it's obvious, right? So she just sat in the wings, waiting for you to make your move."

Brody winced. Yeah, that logic held.

"Okay," he said, seizing something else. "But that doesn't explain . . ."

He was going to say, *that doesn't explain the wallet*, but the words faded as a memory swam to the front of his mind. Atlantic City, New Jersey, three years ago. He'd gone for a boys' weekend with his buddy Kieran. They'd been drinking in a bar on the boardwalk. It was a good time. No luck with the ladies, but they hadn't landed in any trouble, either. As they left for the night, stepping out onto the boardwalk, some snot-faced kid ran into Kieran, caromed off him, and kept running. No excuse me. No apology. It was only when they got back to their hotel that Kieran noticed his phone was missing. He placed his hand on his empty front pocket, looked back in the direction of the boardwalk, and said, "That little motherfucker—"

"Pickpocketed me," Brody finished out loud. He stopped pushing Renée, and his eyes glazed with the same abashed, slightly hurt expression that Kieran's had on that night in Atlantic City.

"What?" Molly asked.

"Blair," Brody said distantly. He remembered reeling from Buddy's Convenience Store with the replica gun in one hand, the bag of cash in the other, and bumping into Blair. Or, more accurately, she—appearing from nowhere—had bumped into *him*. Brody had reached to steady her and they did a clumsy kind of two-step before she pulled away from him. "That bitch *pickpocketed* me."

He explained, again, how it went down to Molly and Renée. They agreed that Blair lifting his wallet from his jacket pocket was the most likely explanation. Really, the *only* explanation. Along with many other emotions, Brody felt a splash of vindication. He'd been carrying the weight of dropping his wallet at the scene of the robbery all this time. Apparently he hadn't been *that* stupid.

They started moving again and Molly said, "It was a setup, Brody. Jimmy is using you to find Mom."

Brody nodded. This knowledge offered small relief. Okay, so he was not the primary target, but he was still in Jimmy's crosshairs, and very much in danger. They both were.

"This explains why the stepmother's murder didn't make the news. Jimmy staged the whole thing." Brody recalled the blood—so much blood—and the body, sprawled with one arm behind her head and a huge knife implanted in her chest. "He did a *very* convincing job. Him and Blair."

"From what I know of Jimmy," Renée said, "I'd say Blair is masterminding this whole thing."

Brody flashed back to their meeting at Rocky T's. Punky, colorful Blair, with a cool cunning in her eyes and a sharpness he knew could slice to the bone. Blair, with her Valentino Garavani boots and $1,700 jacket, and hadn't he wondered then what a spoiled brat from the Laurels was doing alone at Buddy's at 4:55 in the morning?

Jesus, he'd been played like a hillbilly's banjo.

"It's all so elaborate, though," he said. He'd fallen behind Molly again in his deep thought, and put on a burst of speed to catch up. "If they think I have information, why *not* jump us? Why not beat it out of me?"

"Do you, though?" Renée asked.

"Do I what?"

"Have information," Renée replied. "Specifically, do you know where your mother is?"

"No," Brody answered curtly. "Of course I don't."

"And Jimmy knows that. So beating and torturing you is a waste of time. But if you're scared enough, and if you have nowhere else to run, maybe you'll look for her."

"Maybe," Brody said.

"You have a better chance of tracking her down than he does," Renée said. "At least, that's what he's counting on."

"Right," Molly agreed. "And all Jimmy has to do is follow."

Brody scratched the back of his head. It was a desperate strategy, yes, but more than twenty years of searching for Lola Bear, drawing blanks, had no doubt made Jimmy a desperate man.

"That whole thing in Bayonet," he said. "Getting jumped by Jimmy's boys, us getting away, them giving chase . . . that was just an act to . . . to *scare* us—get us to run in the right direction?"

"I don't know for sure, but . . ." The inflection in Renée's voice suggested she *did* know for sure, and now so did Brody.

A kid blazed across their path to catch an overthrown pass. He leaped theatrically, tipped the football, and it sprang away from him. His buddies jeered. Elsewhere, parents scanned their phones while their toddlers let loose in the playground, and a squat, bearded dude wrestled his French bulldog playfully.

Clouds had gathered in the north. They had bruised edges. Rain, for sure. Somewhere out there, Jimmy Latzo licked his wounds and hated, scouring the Lower 48 for a woman named Lola Bear.

"All of this," Brody said. "The pain, the fear, the running. It's all because of our mom."

"They're watching you," Renée said, gesturing not at the wide autumn sprawl of Bryan Park, but at the northern clouds, portending some doom. "The question is, how do you want to play it?"

...

"We need to talk about the elephant in the room," Brody said to Renée later that evening. "Or rather, the elephant in Spring Grove Cemetery."

Renée frowned and wheeled a little closer to Brody. It was just the two of them. Molly—complaining of hip pain after their walk in the park—had dosed up on Motrin and retired to bed. This presented the perfect opportunity to talk to Renée one-on-one, and to learn some harder, necessary truths.

"Did Jimmy Latzo kill my father?"

For all the hardship Brody had endured recently, none of it compared to the bleakest moment of his life—a sliver of time that he relived often, and never *more* often than on that day with Renée.

It happened on the evening of February 26, 2019, when a dour-faced police officer capsized his and Molly's life with two short, knife-like sentences. The first was, "I'd like you to steel yourselves." *Steel.* What a fabulous choice of word, Brody thought, and wondered if this cop wrote crime novels in his spare time. Brody nodded but didn't steel himself. He perched on the arm of the sofa and looked at the police officer as the second sentence was delivered: "I'm afraid your father is dead." There. Precise terminology. No vagueness. *Dead*—the most unambiguous word in the English language. Brody responded pathetically, by saying, "No, he isn't," as if "dead" could be disputed, after all, and he'd pointed at the latest edition of *Rolling Stone*, still open on the coffee table where his father had been reading it the night before.

In the weeks and months that followed, Molly asked questions like, *Why?* and *What now?* Brody's inner dialogue was one of denial, not that his father was dead—Brody had identified the body via photograph; Dad's face was covered on one side, but there was no mistaking his patchy beard, his Greek nose—but rather the manner of his death. Ethan Ellis had been a man of boundless love, encouragement, and optimism. Jesus, he'd held on to a biker jacket from his teens because he intended to one day buy the Harley to go with it.

He would never take his own life. *Never.*

That Jimmy had killed him had been on Brody's mind since learning about his mother's connection to the mobster, but the notion was so terrible that he kept pushing it away, focusing on other things. It was barbed, though, and would snag him. It would draw blood. He knew Molly had considered it, too. She hadn't spoken to him about it yet, because to face it would be to accept it, but it was only a matter of time.

Brody needed to face it, though. *The question is, how do you want to play it?* Renée had asked in regard to everything he'd learned, and getting closer to the truth about his father's death would factor heavily in his decision.

Now Renée lowered the armrest on her chair and transferred to the sofa. A smile touched her lips and eyes. That kindness again, never far away, and she patted the seat beside her, inviting Brody to sit. He did, and he held his breath.

"I can't say for sure," she said. "But taking everything into account, I'd say the probability is high."

Something inside Brody rattled with a cold, heavy sound. It felt like a chain strung through several of his ribs. He breathed around it with tremendous effort, then looked at Renée and nodded. She hadn't told him anything he didn't already suspect, but to hear her say it out loud was harder than he had anticipated. The first of his tears came. Renée rubbed his back and said nothing until he did.

"I'll be okay. It's . . ."

"Take your time."

Brody remembered his dad's smile, as welcoming as blue water, and the sturdiness of his arms. He'd had tough mechanic's hands, but a deft touch, so he could apply a Band-Aid, or wipe the goop from beneath Brody's nose, with a fabulous tenderness.

A kind man, a hopeful man, and Brody's favorite place, as a child, had been in his arms, enjoying the warmth of him, listening to the blood rush through his kingly body.

"After the funeral, I went to the Rebel Point Police Department and asked them to launch a murder investigation. I had no evidence other than my absolute conviction that my father would never commit suicide." Brody took a Kleenex from the box Renée offered and dragged it across his cheeks. "The sergeant I spoke to told me that mental health issues present in many forms, and not all of them are obvious. He gave me the number for a bereavement counselor and sent me on my way."

Renée rubbed his back again. A small gesture, but it felt wonderful. He didn't think it possible to miss something he'd never had, but he missed extended family. How much fuller would his life have been with a host of aunts, uncles, and cousins?

"I went in for justice, but all I got was a business card." Brody wiped his damp eyelashes, then balled the Kleenex and tossed it on the side table. "I knew it, though. I fucking *knew* Dad was murdered. And now I know who did it."

Had Dad been accosted in the street, Brody wondered, dragged into an alleyway and sedated? Or maybe one of Jimmy's boys had hidden in the back of his Malibu, and as soon as Dad got behind the wheel: *Drive, motherfucker.* A northeastern accent. A .45 locked to his temple. *Do exactly what I tell you, and don't try anything stupid.* Brody pressed the heel of his hand to his forehead, trying to urge the images to the rear of his mind. What good would it do, to imagine Dad's fear, his consternation? How could it help, to envision Jimmy's goons balancing Dad at the edge of the Folgt Building's rooftop, with Jimmy snarling in his face? *Where is she, Ethan?* And Dad desperately holding on with those tough, deft hands—the same hands that had applied

Band-Aids to Brody's knees and wiped his nose. *You tell me what you know, or by God it's the express way down for you.*

"He must have been so scared," Brody said. "And confused. He died . . . confused. That's . . . I almost can't bear to think of that. Poor Dad. Poor, sweet Dad."

Renée handed him another Kleenex and he took it. He didn't want to use it, but to think of his dad in the closing moments of his life . . . Jesus, how many stunned, panicked thoughts had he processed in the three seconds it took to plummet fourteen stories?

He used that Kleenex and another two besides.

"Jimmy," he said, except he growled it, a sound like rocks tumbling down the chute of his throat. "Jimmy fucking Latzo. But this isn't just about him, is it? My mom has a lot to answer for."

"Brody—"

"She's caused so much pain. How could she do this to us?"

"She loved you, Brody." Renée adjusted her position on the sofa, tilting her upper body so that she could look Brody in the eye. "You and Molly. From the few notes and photographs she sent me, it's clear how much she loved you. It would have broken her heart to run away. But she did it to keep you safe—to move the target away from you."

"If she loved us," Brody said, "she would have given herself up. Or *fought* Jimmy. If she's such a badass, why didn't she fight him again?"

"Your mom did what she thought was best," Renée said. The kindness in her voice was laced with seriousness. "And she was careful. There was no way Jimmy should have tracked you down."

"I guess she wasn't careful enough."

"You were three random people with no connection to Lola Bear," Renée said. "I don't know how Jimmy found you."

"And you?" Brody broke her gaze for a second. He gestured at Renée's empty wheelchair. "Was it really a motorcycle accident, or did Jimmy get to you, too?"

"It *was* an accident," Renée said. "And it was entirely my fault; I was going too fast, and riding conditions were not good. But my lack of judgment, my fate . . . it does play a part in this. I appreciate now how breakable we all are, and how valuable life is. And knowing what had happened to Karl Janko, I made the decision that if Jimmy came for me, I'd tell him everything I know."

The chain strung through Brody's rib cage snapped tight. He managed a shallow breath and said, "You know where my mother is, don't you?"

And Renée said, "I have a pretty good idea."

...

Brody took Tylenol to manage the ache in his chest. Despite downing her own medication after dinner, Renée selected a bottle of Merlot—"For special occasions or maudlin moments"— and poured herself a glass.

"Jimmy spent two years in the hospital, and another two years convalescing. During this time, Lola Bear disappeared. *Poof!* Gone, baby." Renée snapped her fingers and sipped her wine. "With you and Molly filling in the blanks, I now know that she changed her name to Natalie Myles and moved to Minneapolis."

"Uh-huh." Brody nodded. "Nokomis East, close to the lake."

"I also know that she met and fell in love with a young mechanic named Ethan Ellis."

"And I was born in August of '95, twenty-three months after she tried to kill Jimmy." Brody lifted one side of his mouth, closer to a sneer than a smile. "She didn't waste any time, did she?"

"A family is the perfect cover," Renée said. "She threw herself into being a wife and mother just like she had everything else: quickly, and with passion."

"So we were . . . what? Camouflage?"

"Don't go down that road, Brody. Just because she fast-tracked the family life doesn't mean she loved you any less."

"I'll have to take your word for it."

Renée gave him a sideways glance, then continued, "Other than the occasional cryptic note and a few photographs of you and Molly, I never heard from your mom. She had severed all ties with her old life, except for one."

Brody recalled the visits from the tall guy with the tight T-shirts and Boston accent. "Karl Janko."

"Right. She and Karl were close, but Jimmy never knew that. They had kept their alliance under the radar—smart practice in an environment where so many people want to put a bullet in your back."

"It couldn't have been *that* under the radar," Brody remarked. "I saw a photo of them together, standing shoulder to shoulder, like a couple of old *hermanos*. Not exactly covert."

"It was normal to fraternize; they were colleagues, not enemies. But Jimmy had no idea how close they really were. I guess he was more focused on Lola's relationship with Vince, and how he might worm his way between them." Renée swirled the wine in her glass, then took a deep drink. "Lola stayed in touch with Karl after she blew the scene. He was her link to the western Pennsylvania crime scene, and, more importantly, to Jimmy. Karl informed her of Jimmy's every move. Where he went. Who he questioned. Lola was able to stay one move ahead."

"And Jimmy never questioned you?" Brody asked.

"He did, but not in person. This was twenty-two years ago,

when he was still too weak. So get this: he sent Karl." Renée snickered, one hand over her glass to keep the wine from spilling. "I remember that day. Karl and I watched *Friends* and ate banana bread. I think he told Jimmy that he broke both my legs, and Jimmy was satisfied with that."

"You were lucky," Brody said. He thought of his dad again, dropping to his death, and Karl, upended into a barrelful of water with his arms tied behind his back. "He could easily have sent another of his guys."

"True, but even if he had, and even if that guy *had* broken my legs, or worse, I wouldn't have told him where your mother was, because I didn't *know* where she was." Renée shrugged, finished her wine. "Not *then*, anyway."

She set her empty glass down, then transferred back to her chair and wheeled over to a display case with a drawer in the bottom. With a little effort—and refusing Brody's offer to help—she opened the drawer and pulled out a folded manila envelope. She placed this in her lap, rolled back to the sofa, and eased into the seat beside Brody.

"I destroyed most of the notes your mom sent." Renée opened the envelope and withdrew a handful of photographs. She flipped through them while she talked. "They were veiled enough that I probably didn't have to—there was no name on them, certainly no return address—but I didn't want to take any chances. I liked receiving them, though. They offered a tiny window into your mom's new life, and let me know she was still alive."

Brody glimpsed some of the photographs as Renée flipped through them. Many were of her—a younger Renée, standing next to her date on prom night, sitting on the hood of an old Dodge with a beer in her hand, straddling a custom chopper with ridiculous ape hanger handlebars. There were tourist shots—Niagara Falls, Machu Picchu, the Eiffel Tower—along with snaps of pets and flowers and some well-known faces from her time with the Colts. A more recent photograph showed Renée with her arm around a man with close-set eyes and babyish curls.

"Boyfriend?" Brody asked.

"Fiancé," Renée said, and rolled her eyes. "He called the engagement off after my accident. I guess he couldn't deal with the wheelchair."

"Some kind of guy, huh?" Brody said. "I think maybe you dodged a bullet."

"No maybe about it."

She flipped through a few more shots, pausing to look at one of her and Lola in their teens—Renée was holding a copy of *Bop* magazine, Lola had a hunting knife strapped to her thigh—before handing Brody a photograph of a baby swaddled in a *Sesame Street* blanket.

"Who's this?" he asked.

"It's you," Renée replied. "Four weeks old."

"Oh." A new pain rose in his chest. It hit his throat and dissolved, leaving a vapor of melancholy. The baby in the photograph was cradled in female arms. Her face was out of shot, but these were his mother's arms. Over the last couple of days, he'd learned that Lola Bear seldom showed emotion, but he saw only love in the way she held him, one hand tenderly supporting his tiny head.

To mask his own emotion, he said, "I was an ugly little bugger."

"You were beautiful. Here." Renée handed him another photograph, this one of Molly. She was maybe three years old—all curls and smiles—leaning on her walker.

"I remember that walker," Brody said. He blinked at tears. "Molly hated it."

"One more."

This final photograph was of Brody and Molly together, Christmas morning of 2006—their last Christmas with Mom. They wore matching sweaters and outstanding grins, surrounded by gifts and torn wrapping paper. Brody's melancholy deepened. He'd been happy once. He had a mom and a dad. Life was easy. It was good.

"Why are you showing me these?" he asked.

"You have a lot of anger toward your mom, and that's justified. But you need to know that she was proud of you. Of Molly, too. And she loved you very much. She wouldn't have sent me these photographs if she didn't."

"Maybe, but it changes nothing." Brody handed the photos back. "This is her war. She's been running for too long."

"I agree." Renée nodded and touched his knee gently. "You know I do. But without the truth, it's hard to make a decision that you can live with."

"What's hard is feeling like a pawn on somebody else's chessboard," Brody said. "I'm tired of being moved around. I need to take control."

Renée held up both hands, perhaps to illustrate that she was not controlling him at all, merely passing along information. She poured another glass of wine.

"This is going to my head. I should slow down." She took a big glug anyway. "Your mom sent a photo, or a note, every eighteen months or so. They stopped completely after Karl was killed: 2007. That's when she left you, right?"

Brody nodded.

"She must have felt that, without Karl, she couldn't keep her family safe. So she ran away, taking the target with her." Renée swigged wine and started flipping through the photographs again.

"I heard nothing. For years. I thought she was dead. And then, last summer . . ."

She passed him a photo of a beautiful black horse with a splash of white on its nose. It stood in a field. There was a fence in the background, and what looked like the edge of a red barn, or maybe a silo. Brody flipped the photo over. A short message had been printed on the back.

I found Little Moon
Miss you, Pickle

"I don't understand," Brody said.

"You're not supposed to. It's *veiled*. Like all of your mom's messages." Renée took the photo back and looked at it fondly. "We'd spend hours watching TV, your mom and I. Eating popcorn, huddled beneath a comforter. *The A-Team*, *Three's Company*, *Scarecrow and Mrs. King*. My favorite was *The Facts of Life*. Your mom really liked *Little Moon Farm*."

Brody stared at Renée vaguely.

"*Little Moon Farm*," Renée continued after another hit of wine, "was about two teenage sisters—Sage and Pickle Moon—who moved away from the city to run a farm they'd inherited. It was nonsense. The kind of schlock that was everywhere on TV back then. But, you know, we kind of loved it."

"A guilty pleasure," Brody said.

"Yes, but without the guilt." Renée smiled, turning the photo over to read the message on the back. "We always said we'd buy a farm one day. It was our dream for a while."

"I found Little Moon," Brody mumbled, reading the first part of the message. "So she lives on a farm? Well, that's narrowed it down to, what, two million possibilities?"

234 I Rio Youers

"Silly boy," Renée said playfully. The wine was definitely going to her head. "This photo was sent in an envelope with a postmark from Lenora, Kansas. Now, your mom is too smart to mail anything from the town she's hiding in, but I figured she wouldn't travel *too* far to mail one photograph."

"Okay." Brody leaned a little closer.

"It was a long shot, but I had a realtor friend of mine search for all the farms in a seventy-five-mile radius of Lenora that had sold within the previous year." Renée sipped her wine and winked. "I told him I was thinking of writing a book about agricultural buying trends."

"Riveting," Brody said. "And?"

"I'd hoped to whittle it down to maybe a dozen properties," Renée said. "But he came back with a hundred and eighteen hits, everything from tiny chicken shacks to multimillion-dollar farms that had sold to huge corporations."

"That doesn't help much," Brody said.

"Right. I went through them, eliminating anything too rickety or expensive, but that still left me with forty or so, spread across northwest Kansas and into Nebraska. I didn't know how to narrow them down further, other than fly out there and wheel myself door-to-door. It all seemed too much, and I'd started to question why her location was so important to me." Renée sighed, and after a solemn pause added, "I knew why, of course. I just didn't want to admit it."

"You wanted that information," Brody said, "in case Jimmy came knocking."

"It's like I said . . ." Renée gestured at her ragdoll legs. "I appreciate how valuable life is, and how easily we break."

"I get it," Brody said.

"Anyway, I got lucky," Renée said. "I was idly going through the listings, looking at the photographs, when something caught my attention: a red barn. Well, not the *barn*, exactly, but the word 'Owlfeather' painted across the front in big yellow letters."

Renée showed Brody the photo again, pointing out the barn that had sneaked into the right side of the frame. He hadn't noticed before, but now saw the beginning of a letter that had been painted across the front. An *O*, yes, or maybe a *C*. Whichever, it was bright yellow.

"It's the same barn," Renée said. "I put the two photographs side by side. And it's not just the yellow lettering. The trees behind, the wooden fence . . . it's all the same."

"Okay," Brody said, and sat up in his seat. "That's good."

"Owlfeather Farm, two miles west of Lone Arrow, Nebraska. It was purchased in June of 2018 by a lone female buyer. I couldn't find any information about her, other than her name: Margaret Ward."

"At the risk of sounding like a misogynist dick," Brody said, "is it unusual for lone females to buy farms?"

"I asked my realtor friend the same question," Renée said. "And get this: only eight percent of farms in Nebraska have a principal female operator. So while it's not unheard of, it *is* unusual. This information, together with the photo . . . I'd say there's a good chance Margaret Ward used to be known as Natalie Ellis, and Lola Bear before that."

Questions elbowed and pushed in Brody's mind, all wanting to be heard first. How could his mom afford to buy a farm? How far away was Lone Arrow, Nebraska? How long would it take to get there on a bus? Brody placed a hand on either side of his head and squeezed, narrowing his focus.

"No guarantees," Renée said, going back to her wine. "She may have moved on since then, or maybe she sent a photo of somebody else's farm. But my gut tells me this is where you'll find your mom."

They sat in silence for several minutes. Brody mapped scenarios in his mind, trying to define the clearest, safest way through for him and Molly. Renée finished her wine, then pressed the cork into the bottle and took it, and her empty glass, into the kitchen. While she was gone, Brody grabbed Renée's iPad from where it was charging next to the TV and started to gather information. Lone Arrow was 810 miles from Bloomington. The nearest major bus line served Kearney, Nebraska, thirty-five miles north. It was a nineteen-hour ride from Bloomington to Kearney, with changes in Indianapolis, Chicago, and Omaha. A long, ugly journey, and the thought of trading the comfort of Renée's house for a showdown with Jimmy Latzo was stomach-turning. On the flip side, to deliver this war to the woman who *should* be fighting it was his best—and perhaps his only—shot at getting free.

"Given what we know," he said when Renée returned to the room, "and what I'm potentially walking into, do you agree that Molly is safer here with you?"

"I do," Renée said. "I was actually going to suggest it. Not least because she's almost out of her prescriptions; I can share mine as required."

"You're an angel," Brody said.

"A tipsy angel."

"And there's no chance Jimmy will come here?"

Renée considered this for a few seconds, then shook her head. "Wherever *you* go, he'll follow. You're his focus. But if he comes here—which I doubt—I'll tell him what I told you."

"Then I'm leaving tonight," Brody said.

"Tonight?" Renée said, surprised. "Nebraska is a long way,

Brody. Wouldn't it be better to get some rest, have a decent breakfast—"

"No, I want to do this quietly, while Molly's asleep."

"You're not going to say goodbye?"

"I'll look in, but I won't wake her. She'll want to come with me, and I won't be strong enough to say no. Nor would I have the right." Brody swiped the iPad's screen and accessed the timetable. "There's a bus to Indy at ten, and I can make the eleven-fifty connection to Chicago. With everything running on time, I'll be in Iowa by the time she wakes up."

...

Within minutes, Brody had his things packed and was ready to hit the road. A life on the run called for few possessions, he reflected, and there wasn't much more to say for it. At least Molly didn't have to run anymore.

He crept into the spare room. A night-light threw a purplish glow across the bed. Molly slept with her hair fanned across the pillow, the quilt pulled high and gathered beneath her chin. Her face was smooth and peaceful, in contrast to her waking face, which was tight and worked. She looked ten years younger.

Brody whispered goodbye and kissed the top of her head. That was when the magnitude, and the emotional gravity, of what he was about to do hit home. He went downstairs in a haze, put on his dad's leather jacket, and couldn't keep the tears from falling.

Renée saw him and wheeled to his side. She reached out of her chair to wipe his eyes with her fingers, and he let her, feeling childlike and cared-for.

"You don't have to do this," she said. "We can wait for Jimmy to come knocking—which he will if you're still here—and we'll tell him what we know. This doesn't have to be your fight."

"It does," Brody said, thinking of his dad. "It already is. But thank you, Renée. Thank you so much for everything."

"Be careful, Brody. Come back to us."

"Don't tell Molly," he said, indicating his tears and wildly trembling hands. "Tell her I was strong."

"I will."

"If she knows how scared I am, she'll follow." He glanced at his reflection in the hallway mirror. He looked so small in his dad's jacket. "It won't matter how many states she has to cross."

CHAPTER SEVENTEEN

Rain fell in drab lines. It might have been revitalizing in the early morning, with the stained hue of the leaves and the silvery gleam off the blacktop, but by night it was spiritless. It slanted through the streetlights and droned, caring nothing for the long, warm days it had left behind. Moreover, it felt ominous, like a warning.

Renée had offered to call him a cab. Brody had refused, wanting the mile-long walk to invigorate him and clear his head of lingering doubts. He wished, now, that he'd taken her offer. The rain had really picked up since he'd left the house. He was shivering and miserable, and the night was unaccountably darker without Molly beside him.

She would wake in the morning to find him gone. Would she follow? Brody didn't think so. Molly would be hurt and angry, but Renée—who'd taken to Molly as if she were a long-lost kid sister—would convince her that this was the best way.

...

He heard a car behind him and turned, but the street was empty. The rain was haze-like in the distance. It swelled around the streetlights in heavy orange bags. A wet flag rippled outside an office building.

Renée's warning echoed in his mind: *You may have been followed here.* That had seemed implausible at the time, but now, having spoken more with Renée, and alone on these dismal streets, he knew it was true.

Brody wiped rain from his eyes and peered through the murk. A truck rumbled across the intersection two blocks west, spraying fans of water from its tires. Brody continued on. The bus depot was at the intersection of South Walnut and East Third Street, half a mile away. On the next block, a homeless kid mumbled for spare change from a barely lit doorway. Brody flipped him a quarter. A car appeared on the street behind them, moving slowly. "God's blessing," the kid said. Brody wondered if he worked for Jimmy, one of his many spies dotted around the city. Would he send a text after Brody had gone? TARGET HEADING EAST ON W. KIRKWOOD AVE. Brody kept walking. The car crept closer, its headlights working through the rain. Brody imagined it stopping beside him, one of the rear doors banging open, being grabbed and dragged inside. A pistol would be slotted beneath the shelf of his jaw. *We can take you any time we want, kid, put a bullet in your throat.* The car pulled alongside Brody and he flinched, but it kept going and soon its taillights faded.

...

Brody picked up the pace and eventually turned onto South Walnut Street. He saw the lights from the bus depot two blocks away. They offered no comfort, looking cold and clinical in the rain. Walnut was one way, three lanes flowing north. Vehicles crawled behind their headlights. Traffic signals blinked like robotic eyes. The sidewalks were empty, save for a single dim figure huddled beneath an umbrella, and a young couple tucked inside a doorway, waiting for the rain to let up.

Brody regarded them suspiciously, then noticed the SUV parked across the street. The side windows were tinted, but there was enough streetlight to determine movement in the driver and passenger seats. Two people. Brody imagined Blair to be one of them, smiling through her wagon-red lipstick, knowing that *he* knew it was a setup—that he'd put it all together.

No more games, he thought. *All cards on the table.*

Blair, with her designer boots propped on the dash, daring him with her eyes. Another ultimatum.

So what are you going to do, Bro?

He stared at the SUV for fully two minutes before the driver's window buzzed down and some blaze-eyed dude leaned his head out.

"The fuck you staring at, friend?"

A middle-aged woman in the passenger seat. Platinum hair and a missing front tooth. Not Blair. She blew a kiss, then flipped him off. Brody turned and took dizzy steps toward the bus depot. How close had he been to approaching the SUV and rapping on the window, telling the occupants everything he knew? *You don't have to do this,* Renée had said, and she was right. He could spill the beans and take a backseat.

But no. Things had changed. The game was different. There was more to this than just getting Jimmy off his back. *Much* more.

Brody had a new motivation: revenge.

He owed his mom nothing, but revealing her location would stack the odds in Jimmy's favor. His most ruthless enforcers would take Lola by surprise—probably at night, while she was asleep. They would overwhelm her, put a bullet in her knee, then tie her up and hand her to Jimmy. Brody couldn't let that happen. His mom's long and miserable death was not part of the game plan, and he for damn sure wasn't going to give Jimmy the win.

Brody needed to confront Lola Bear. But this was no mawkish family reunion. It was a battle strategy, to ready and deploy her.

He thought of his dad holding on to everything with those tough, deft hands, begging for his life, and the last face he saw was Jimmy Latzo's.

Brody crossed the road toward the bus depot. The hard rain pattered off his leather jacket.

"Now," he said.

Now was the time to steel himself.

PART II
NEBRASKA

CHAPTER EIGHTEEN

The hands of time have no bias. They will deteriorate every-thing, and without mercy. From the sweetest fruit to the toughest mountain. Emotion, too. Some say that time heals, but it doesn't. It gradually degrades feeling and sense. The very opposite of healing.

Time is the great enemy of all, and cannot be defeated. Inactivity, Lola knew, was a lesser foe, but more quickly damaging. She had softened during her twenty-six years on the run, having traded hours in the dojo, and on the range, for numerous day jobs. A barista, a librarian, a waitress, a farmer. She had even been a mother, albeit a poor one.

I am an ordinary woman, Lola often thought, looking in the mirror at her softer stomach and looser arms—this fifty-one-year-old Pinocchio, who could be cut where once she was wooden.

Yes, she still trained, but not with the same discipline. She was still quick, but no longer breathtaking. She still had power, but her days as a force were behind her.

Benjamin Chen's voice ghosted to her from back in the day: "We are nothing without motion, Lola. Even the sharpest knife will rust."

...

Lola had just finished loading hay bales when her phone vibrated. Three quick thumps. *Brrrz-brrrz-brrrz.* She looked across the riding arena to the 175-yard driveway that stitched her property to Big Crow Road. The infrared sensor at the entranceway had been activated. Inside her comfortable little farmhouse, an alarm would have sounded. A single, high-pitched note. The sensor was also linked to her cell phone, for when she was outside the house. A different signal, but the same message: *You have a visitor.*

Unexpected visits were rare. Almost everything was by schedule or appointment, and that's exactly how Lola wanted it. Every now and then her veterinarian, Coot Birnie, would drop by to shoot the breeze, usually with a hot coffee and a boxful of pastries from Find's, because this was the country, and that's how country folk do. And canvassers approached on occasion, although most were deterred by the sign Lola had attached to her fencepost: I BELIEVE IN THE 2ND AMENDMENT TO PROTECT THE OTHER 26.

Lola might be a rusty knife, but she hadn't evaded Jimmy all these years by taking chances. She bolted from the trailer she'd just loaded, past the chicken coops and goat pen, to the back door of her house. She moved well, although she felt that rust, mainly in her knees and ankles. Adrenaline provided the oil. Her lungs ballooned, her eyes dilated. There was no fear. Only focus.

She burst through the back door and into the kitchen, whacked her hip on the table on her way to the hallway—she would have glided past not so many years ago—and took the stairs two at a time. The guest bedroom faced south, offering views of the horse barn, the riding arena, and the long, curved driveway. This room hadn't seen a guest since the previous owner had lived here. Lola had an exercise bike in one corner and a Weatherby Mark V bolt-action rifle in the window. She got behind the scope and sighted down the driveway.

...

She had been hiding from Jimmy, but he hadn't been hiding from her. He was not the high-profile player he used to be, but he still had influence and he liked to be heard. As such, it wasn't hard to track his business dealings and identify key employees. She had pinned the most recent photographs she could find to a bulletin board beside the window. Eight of them, including Joey Cabrini, son of Marco Cabrini, who'd shot Lola in the shoulder during her raid on Jimmy's house. Joey had his old man's curly black hair, as well as a small birthmark on his throat that would be visible through a rifle scope. There was Eddie "the Smoke" Shaw, a professional stalker, whose disguises included a variety of baseball caps and glasses, and false goatees in carrot and white. Lola was confident she could place and eliminate these men, along with other faces on her wall of fame. But Blair Mayo was a different story. Young, lethal in a way Lola used to be, Blair would require additional strategy, and would make nothing simple.

Lola glanced at the photographs now, noting distinguishing features: Joey's birthmark, the scar beneath Blair's left eye, Jared Conte's missing earlobe, Leo Rossi's crooked nose. She returned to the scope, looped her finger around the Mark V's trigger, and waited for her visitor to step into the reticle.

...

Would they advance down the driveway in broad daylight? Probably not, but they might think it was a crazy enough move to catch Lola off guard. The front of her property was a better option than the back, which was exposed between the woodland and her house, even more so after she'd hayed the long grass. Approaching under cover of darkness was smarter, of course (she had a Sightmark Night Raider scope for such an eventuality) but bringing the fight to her would always be a gamble, at any time. Jimmy didn't know what home security measures she'd taken. He was hotheaded enough to risk going in blind, but after all these years, would he take that chance?

Movement through the foliage. Lola held her breath, steadying the scope. The leaves winked yellow and gold, so magnified she could count their veins. She glimpsed blue jeans. Jimmy had always insisted his crew dress to impress. They represented him, and he was unconscionably vain. Perhaps having his face burned off had changed that.

The Mark V's muzzle inched right, mirroring her visitor's progress. Lola saw the collar of a black leather jacket, light brown hair, the flash of an ear, pink in the cold.

"Who are you?" she whispered on the exhale, then held her breath again. *And what do you want?*

She'd always believed that *if* they came, they would do so away from her property, negating any advantage she might have—alarms, vantage points, access to greater firepower, knowledge of the environment. They would ambush her on the way back from the Grocery King, perhaps, or on one of Lone Arrow's many quiet streets. It would be difficult for Lola to anticipate such an attack, but she was always prepared; she never left the house without a Glock 42 in her bra holster and a fixed-blade knife strapped to her strong side. Nebraska state law prohibited carrying a loaded shotgun in a vehicle, but she didn't drive anywhere without a sawed-off concealed beneath the dash, both barrels occupied. Would all this be enough? Lola had no idea. She knew only two things for certain: that Jimmy's crew would not kill her quickly (the boss would want to have his fun), and that they would come in numbers.

So who was this lone visitor? Not a canvasser; they only ever approached by vehicle, because her farm was so remote. Not someone looking for work, not when the ground was about to freeze. Whoever it was, he or she was nearing the apex of her driveway, and would soon come fully into view. And *if* his or her face matched one of those on the bulletin board, Lola would pull the trigger. Butch Morgan, who owned the property nearest hers, might hear the report, but gunshots weren't uncommon in the country. Butch would likely think Lola was firing a warning shot to scare off a—

All thought flew from her mind. It was as if her brain had been instantly detached and locked in a tight black box. She gasped and stepped away from the window.

"No," she said. "It can't be."

She reached for something—a scenario where this was possible, or at least made a modicum of sense—but her brain only produced small puffs of air. So she returned to the scope and watched numbly as her son, her beautiful son, advanced into the crosshairs, and back into her life.

...

There followed five slow seconds in which Lola felt Margaret Ward's comfortable existence slip from her shoulders like a borrowed cloak. Then she jumped into action.

She grabbed her Baby Eagle from the top drawer of her dresser, chambering a round as she broke downstairs, then through the kitchen (she didn't bang her hip on the table this time), and out the back door. Questions raised a racket in her skull. Lola ignored them—focused on the objective.

Brody.

Around the back of the farmhouse, using available cover: her pickup truck, a heap of firewood, the toolshed. She sprinted from there to the barn, cutting through so that she could approach the driveway from the side and hopefully reach Brody without being seen. Lola had to assume Jimmy was hot on his heels. She wanted her son under cover before the bullets started to fly.

Sweat ran from her hairline. It latched her denim shirt to her back. The rust had slowed her down and set an ache in her joints, but the adrenaline was still there, producing responses that had been dormant for years. Lola felt freest when bringing her horse to gallop, but she felt fully alive in this moment. It was a familiar rush. Later, she would admit to having missed it.

She ran across the horse arena, exposed now but keeping low. The fence would mostly cover her at eye level. Brody continued toward the house, moving slowly, as if unsure. He hadn't seen her yet, but he would soon. One hell of a reunion.

Something caught her eye as she approached the driveway. A flash, quick as a blink, maybe a mile to the south. It might be sunlight winking off the windshield of a parked vehicle. Then again, it might be one of Jimmy's guys watching the farm through binoculars. She also considered the possibility of it being a tactical scope, although she didn't think so; they'd have to be quite the marksperson to guarantee nonlethal from a mile away.

They were looking for positive ID, then Jimmy's army would roll in. And she couldn't run—not with her son on the battlefield.

...

Lola leaped the fence, took cover behind one of the ash trees, then broke and ran at Brody from the side. She hit him like a linebacker, carrying him across the driveway, to the cover of a tree on the other side. It happened too quickly for him to struggle. She held him down with her knee to his chest and placed the barrel of her handgun to her lips.

Mama says shhhh.

...

No vehicle sounds. She waited. Brody started to squirm and she shot him a warning glance, the gun still pressed to her lips. Her other hand was on her phone, waiting for it to vibrate.

Nothing.

"Don't move, baby boy." She lifted her knee from Brody's chest and dashed to the other side of the driveway. From here, through the trees, she could see a section of Big Crow Road as it approached her property. She counted to sixty. Still nothing. Brody clambered to his feet. She held up one hand: *Wait*. Another count. She heard the murmur of traffic on Highway 183, but that was all.

Might they advance from the north, having used Brody as a decoy? Unlikely. They would come from the front, probably in armored SUVs. They would come in force.

So where were they?

Lola moved back to Brody. He brushed dirt from his jacket (not *his* jacket—it was Ethan's; Lola recognized it immediately) and for a moment wouldn't, or couldn't, look at her. His teeth were clenched. Maybe he hadn't been followed.

"Talk to me," she said.

His eyes flashed across hers, then fixed on the branches above. His hands trembled. There were too many emotions for her to read. Just when she thought he wouldn't say anything—that she would have to do the talking, at least to begin with—he found his voice and blew her world apart.

"Jimmy Latzo found us. He killed Dad and I'm next."

He cracked, then. The strength went out of his legs and he sagged. He might have fallen if Lola hadn't caught him. She gathered him close, as she had a thousand times. He placed his head on her shoulder. A tired, scared boy.

"I need your help," he said.

CHAPTER NINETEEN

Jimmy had offered her a room at his house rent-free—she was his *numero uno* and he wanted her close, he liked the extra security—but Blair insisted on her own space. Not just a room, but an apartment, a place she could kick off her boots and distance herself from work. She was a twenty-five-year-old woman, after all. Somewhere inside, behind the cunning and the knives, that twenty-five-year-old woman wanted to burn toast and sleep on the sofa and listen to her neighbors fuck, and it was important she had the opportunity to do just that.

More than anything, she needed time away from Jimmy. She was his power source, his battery. Just being close to him was draining.

Her phone buzzed at 11:48 A.M. A message from Jimmy: GET UR ASS HERE NOW!!! Uppercase. Three exclamation marks. There were rarely fewer than two, whatever the message. Such was his nature.

Blair waited a couple of minutes, then texted back: on my way
All lowercase. Not even a period.

She poured two half-empty glasses of wine down the sink, picked her clothes up off the floor. Memories of last night—or early this morning, to be more accurate—flickered through her mind. He said his name was Gary but she checked his wallet when he used the bathroom and it was actually Peter. He lived in Seven Springs, not Manhattan (liar), he was forty-one years old, not thirty-five (liar), and his business card revealed that he was an insurance broker, not a literary agent (liar). Peter was a competent lover, though, and he'd made her laugh more than once. A sense of humor was not as important as honesty, but it was a good quality, nonetheless.

"Should I call you?" he'd asked spiritlessly, rooting around for his socks at 6:03.

"No."

Blair often felt that these intimacies were as close as she'd ever get to feeling normal.

...

12:17 P.M.

WHERE THE FUCK R U!!!
the traffic sucks today
U DIDN'T TAKE THE EXPRESSWAY??
no. stopped at rite-aid. needed eyeliner
FUCKING EYELINE I TOLD U 2 GET UR ASS HETE!!!
be there in 15
FUUUUUCCCCCKK!!!

Blair turned off her phone, cranked the radio, and made her way to Jimmy's. The traffic flowed smoothly and she hadn't stopped at Rite-Aid for eyeliner. These deceptions weren't in Gary the Literary Agent's league, but they were plausible, and necessary. When the boss was three-exclamation-marks excited, it was often prudent to vent him before getting too close.

...

His cigar was as fat as a table leg. Bluish brown smoke wreathed his head. Blair approached coolly. There was a smile inside the smoke—or what passed for a smile on Jimmy's damaged face.

"Here she is. At long last."

"What's going on, Jimmy?"

A smile, yes, but he wasn't fully vented. She could tell from the tension in his voice, and by the way the tip of his cigar jittered ever so slightly. Brad Lemke stood to his right. Lorne Dupont towered on the left. Six hundred pounds of muscle between them. *Maybe* enough IQ to fill an inkwell.

There was a stack of $2,000 straps on the desk in front of Jimmy. Fifteen of them. He gestured at the cash with an appraising nod.

"Yours," he said.

"Why?"

"It's a thank-you." Jimmy drew on his cigar and his smile lengthened. "We used to call it a 'bonus' back in the day. But whatever, you've earned it."

The penny dropped—the reason for Jimmy's excitement. Not anger, but elation. Blair looked at the money but didn't touch it. She hadn't earned it yet.

"Eddie should have contacted *me* first," she said, and curled her lip. Eddie the fucking Smoke, stealing her thunder. "I engineered this. It's my job."

"The fuck it is," Jimmy said. "You work for me, so it's *my* job."

Blair rolled her eyes. As if Jimmy—who had all the deftness of a land mine—could ever finagle something so intricate.

"Fine," she said.

Jimmy knocked ash from his cigar, grabbed his phone, swiped through a couple of screens. "Eddie sent me these an hour ago. They were taken this morning, between nine-fifty and ten o'clock central time."

Eleven photographs, crisp quality. The first five showed a middle-aged woman with bleached blond hair bucking hay onto a flatbed trailer. She wore black jeans, a blue denim shirt. Eddie's zoom was powerful enough to pick up the red Levi's tag stitched to the front pocket. The next three photographs were close-ups of her face, one of them in profile. The final three were of her running across a field, keeping low. White fencing provided some cover, but Eddie was elevated enough—probably positioned on the roof of his car—to see the pistol in her right hand.

"She dyed her hair, and her ass is a little rounder than it used to be." Jimmy puffed smoke and pointed at the phone in Blair's hand. "But that's her, all right. Lola Bear. We found the bitch."

"We?"

"Yeah, well . . . thanks to your crazy-ass plan." He pointed at her with the soggy end of his cigar. "But shit, Blair, it *worked*. The kid led us directly to his mommy."

"He did it knowingly," Blair said. "He's prepping her for a fight."

"And I'm going to oblige."

A distracted smile touched Blair's face. She wanted to revel in the satisfaction of having located Lola Bear, but the job was only ninety percent complete. Jimmy didn't appear to comprehend this. He pushed the money toward her—$30,000 in total—and said something about her spending it when they got back, then he laughed maniacally and banged the desk with his fist. Brad and Lorne laughed, too, with all the character of rocks in a sack. Blair looked from one face to the next. She didn't want to dampen the mood, but felt it important to point out that there was still work to do, and didn't they—

"Whoa, hold on just a second." Blair cut through her own train of thought. Jimmy's words had finally sunk in. "When we get *back*? Back from where?"

"Nebraska," Jimmy replied. His smile faltered. He flicked ash and nodded at the phone. "Lone Pine, or some shitkicking town like that—"

"Lone Arrow," Blair corrected him. She'd already scrolled to Eddie's message and clicked on the address. It brought up a satellite image of Owlfeather Farm. Blair zoomed in.

"*Arrow.* Yeah. Whatever." Jimmy's cigar sizzled as he pulled on it. "Leo and his boys are already in place. That's five. You three make eight. Jared Conte and the Tucson Tank are meeting us at the airport. Ten will be enough. I've chartered a jet that will have us touching down at four-oh-five central."

"Jimmy, listen to me—"

"If all goes to plan, I'll be spilling Lola's blood—and plenty of it—before nightfall. I'm going to kill the kid, too. While she watches."

"*Jimmy.*" Blair didn't raise her voice, but she gave it a keen edge, and it sliced through the room like a guillotine. Jimmy sat back in his seat, the cigar parked between two fingers. The tip still jittered.

"What's the problem?" he asked.

"We're not going to Nebraska."

"Oh, but we are." He pressed his tongue against the inside of his cheek. This looked like so many of his expressions, but she'd been with him long enough to know it was frustration, bordering on anger. "We are going, we will make misery, and we will sing 'Beautiful *fucking* Nebraska' while we do."

"You're emotional. That's understandable." Blair took a deep breath, trying to control her own emotion. She hadn't orchestrated this whole maneuver for it to collapse now. "But you're not thinking clearly."

The tip of Jimmy's cigar crackled, or it might have been the fire in his eyes. "I have dreamed about Lola every night since dragging myself off life support. Vivid, beautiful dreams. I have developed strength and endurance, and rebuilt my empire, for the sole purpose of making her pay for what she took from me. Now I know where she is."

"I know that, Jimmy, but—"

"Trust me, Blair, I have never thought clearer than I'm thinking right now."

"She'll kill us all," Blair said. She spoke softly, but her words chimed with a certainty that was hard to ignore. Even Lorne, who likely wouldn't feel a pool cue broken across his shoulders, looked uncomfortable.

Jimmy stubbed out his cigar with angry little jabs.

"Fuck you," he said.

"Look at this satellite image," Blair urged, holding his phone so he could see. She centered on Owlfeather Farm, then pinched and zoomed out. "A farmhouse, a barn, a couple of small buildings— all of it surrounded by open land. She'll see us coming and pick us off. One. By. One."

"Then we'll attack at night, while she's asleep." Jimmy looked at Brad and Lorne for support and they nodded hesitantly.

"We don't know her defenses. She's probably rigged the land with alarms and motion sensors. Jesus, she might have a bunch of redneck security guards armed with AKs." Blair kept the incredulity from her tone. It wouldn't do to make Jimmy feel as stupid as he actually was. "Of course, the biggest problem with infiltrating at night is that *we* won't be able to see her."

"We'll use night-vision equipment," Jimmy said. He banged his fist on the desk again, not elatedly this time. "We'll recon the property. Drive a fucking AFV through her front door. Whatever it takes."

"She'll kill us all."

Jimmy stood up quickly, sending his chair skating backward. It thumped against the wall hard enough to leave a mark. He balled his fists and discharged a broad variety of expletives. Lorne Dupont wisely shuffled several feet to the left, removing himself from Jimmy's radius.

Blair said nothing. She stood with her eyes to the front and waited for the flames to die. Eventually, they did. Jimmy dragged his hands through his hair, then stepped to the window and looked out.

"That oak has always been tenacious," he said plaintively. "Some of its leaves are still green."

It might have been the silvery light against his skin, or the set of his shoulders as he expanded his chest and breathed, but in that moment Blair thought she saw the man he used to be, before Lola Bear, before the scars. She tried to envision a different life for him, as a doctor or teacher, but such imaginings were beyond her. Jimmy embodied infamy and vice like a Maserati embodied speed. It was in the slope of his neck, in the bumps of his knuckles, in every motor neuron and sensory receptor. His destiny had been rifled like a gun barrel.

"What's the point of all this?" he said a moment later. He had relaxed his body but his voice was still tight and high. "What's the point of *you*, Blair? Or Leo, or Jared, or any one of the others? Why spend so much time and money on finding Lola Bear, if all we're going to do is stand back and see what happens next?"

"We're not going to stand back," Blair said, measuring not only her words, but the spaces between them. "This is when we make our next move."

"Oh right. *Another* move. You see, Blair, I think you're taking this 'patient approach' thing too far." He turned away from the window. The light, now, made him appear agitated and savage. "I say we go in full force and we get that bitch."

"It's your call, Jimmy," Blair said. Her voice fluttered—a touch of emotion sneaking through. "But if you do that, you can count me out."

"Fuck you, Blair. This is what I *trained* you for. The weapons combat. The Krav fucking Maga." He blustered toward her, wringing his fists again. "What are you, *scared?*"

"I am *not* scared of Lola Bear. I will dismantle that bitch. But taking the fight to her, on her turf, is suicide." Blair tapped two fingers off the side of her skull. "*Brains*, Jimmy."

"Fuck brains, and fuck you." Jimmy snatched his cell phone from her hand and looked at Lola's photograph. "We finally have her in our sights. This is the time for brawn."

He scrolled to another photograph and stared at it for a long time. The years passed across his face like silhouettes on a screen. The dreams he'd mentioned flickered in his eyes. "Lola," he breathed, then said it again, and again. His mouth glistened. Eventually, he turned off his phone, then pulled up his chair and dropped into it.

Blair steadied herself and tried once again to reason with him. "You *will* need your army, Jimmy. Every man you've got. You'll need me, too. But we have to stack the advantages in our favor." She leaned across his desk, her fists knotted on the polished wood. "We have to bring the fight here."

Jimmy looked at her. He'd come a long way, but he was still wrecked inside. Too many open wounds. Only Lola could heal him completely.

"I appreciate the bonus, but the job isn't finished." Blair pushed the money toward him. "I didn't say I'd find Lola Bear, I said I'd *deliver* her."

Jimmy smiled humorlessly and shook his head. "And how are you going to do that?"

There. She had him. Sweet relief. There'd been some tricky pieces, but they clicked into place, the same way they had when she got to Brody at Rocky T's. The feel-good chemicals— dopamine, serotonin—flooded her. This was why she lived. The mastery, the control, the breathtaking rush of it all. She tingled to the tips of her fingers and smiled. If only Gary the Literary Agent could see her now.

"You still want to go after the cripple?" she asked.

CHAPTER TWENTY

All kinds of things were happening inside him. Fireworks. Meteor storms. Earthquakes. He was in his mother's arms. She held him like she used to, one hand just above his left hip, the other cupping the back of his neck. Beneath the hay and sweat, she even smelled the same. This should have induced a flood of memories, but there was nothing beyond the meteor storms and earthquakes. It lasted only seconds, perhaps, but it felt longer, and just when he started to get a sense of himself, she turned him around and planted her palm between his shoulder blades.

"Move your ass."

They dashed toward the house, Brody in front, Lola right behind. She glanced over her shoulder several times, pistol at the ready. In the aftermath of the fireworks, a curious concern surfaced in Brody's mind: What kind of life must his mother live, to be perpetually prepared for a situation like this? Her heart would be like a paperweight, he thought, keeping everything in order but essentially dead. Could she even dream when she slept with one eye open?

They went in through the back door. Lola locked and bolted it behind her, then took the lead. Pistol in hand, she checked the downstairs rooms and made certain the front door was locked (Brody had a feeling it was *always* locked) before going upstairs. She paused on the landing, attentive to every small sound, then opened the door to her bedroom. After checking the closet and en suite, she motioned to Brody.

"In here."

He nodded from a thousand miles away and entered the room.

His mom glanced out the window, her gaze sweeping the land at the rear of her property.

"I need you to focus," she said, touching one shoulder and turning him toward her. "Can you do that for me?"

"Sure," he said with a cracked voice. He didn't think he could, though. His focus was still on the driveway, having been knocked from his body when she tackled him broadside.

"Okay. Good." She looked into his eyes. "You're here, Brody, with me, but do I need to worry about your sister?"

"No."

"You're sure? Where is she?"

"Safe," he replied. It seemed he could only manage one word at a time.

Lola stared at him a second longer—stared *hard*—then nodded and clapped him on the shoulder. "Stay here. I'll be right back."

She left the bedroom, still behind her pistol. Brody heard doors opening. He dropped his bag, sat on the edge of her bed, and looked numbly around. It was an unloved space, appropriate for an unloved person. There was no softness or delicacy. The walls were painted sunflower yellow (many years ago, judging by the water marks and discoloration), and were bare except for a small painting of a horse. The dresser housed no perfumes or makeup, only an iPad and a stack of magazines. Clothes were draped over the back of a chair. There was a paperback on the floor next to the bed. No nightstands. Brody felt an odd grief for her, then realized this wasn't his mother's room—his mother, Natalie Ellis née Myles, who'd laughed with him and loved him and sat him on the throne of her world. This was Lola Bear's room, and Lola was an obdurate killer with a paperweight for a heart.

"Killer," he mumbled through dry lips. And yes, that was why he was here, the *only* reason. This wasn't about reuniting with his mom like some desperate cub. It was about getting Jimmy Latzo off his back and avenging his father's death.

I need you to focus. Can you do that for me?

Brody stood up, blinked several times, breathed in through his nose and out through his mouth. Gooseflesh rippled his arms.

"I've got this," he said to himself, then Lola came back into the room and thrust a semiautomatic rifle into his hands.

...

She opened the window. A cold breeze lifted the curtains and puffed the hair from Brody's brow. It felt wonderful. Unlike the rifle he held—the very real, very lethal gun, which had never top-fired blanks, and couldn't be bought for sixty bucks and a baseball cap. A metallic taste flooded Brody's mouth. He pined for his replica.

Lola registered the dumbfounded expression on his face (he thought it must be hard to miss). "That's an MMR Carbine," she said. "Built on the AR-15 platform."

"It's a fucking *assault* rifle."

"Technically, it's not, because it's semi, not fully automatic. A bullshit distinction, if you ask me, because it'll still fire as fast as you can cycle the trigger." Lola swept the magazines onto the floor, spun the iPad onto the bed, and dragged the dresser over to the window. "It's designed to perform devastating damage, very quickly. So yeah, it's a fucking assault rifle."

Brody looked from the MMR, to his mom, then back again. "What do you expect *me* to do with it?"

"Do you know that one in five guns bought legally in this country is an AR-15, or variant? It's the nation's number-one choice for home defense." She gestured out the window. "So . . . defend."

Brody didn't move. The rifle wasn't heavy—it was surprisingly light, in fact—but lifting it was another matter.

"Listen to me," Lola said, stepping toward him. He edged backward, as if she were an animal with a tendency to bite. "Everything between the tree line and the house is my land. It's wide open. No cover. I don't think you'll have to pull the trigger. But if you *do*, don't worry about accuracy, just aim toward the assailant. Get anywhere close and they'll retreat or go prone. If there's more than one, alternate between them. I'll assist from the room next door, and I'll also cover the front in case they come from both directions."

"I don't know if I can shoot *at* someone," Brody said, but recalled that he *could*, if sufficiently pushed. The incident in Bayonet dashed across his mind, and he remembered the hard shift he'd felt inside—the sudden and unnerving coldness in his veins. A little something he'd inherited from his mom, as it turned out. "I just . . . I . . ."

"It's time to snap into survival mode. Now watch." Lola knelt in front of the dresser, her arms poised, demonstrating position. "Four points of contact: shooting hand, supporting hand, shoulder, and cheek. Bring the sights to your eye, not the other way around. Use the dresser for stability, and don't grip the gun too tightly."

"This can't be happening," Brody whispered.

"Oh, it's happening," Lola assured him. "And if you need extra motivation: just know that anybody who approaches from that direction likely had a hand in killing your father, and that they're coming here to kill us both."

A blank expression from Brody. His mind was anything but;

he imagined gray-faced mobsters accosting his old man, dragging him into the service elevator of the Folgt Building, then dangling him from the rooftop while Jimmy fired questions.

He imagined those same mobsters emerging from the woods at the back of his mom's land, weapons strapped to their bodies.

Lola grasped his shoulder—man, she was *strong*—positioned him in front of the dresser, kicked the back of his right leg so he dropped to one knee. "Supporting hand here, on the handguard." She moved his left hand into position, palm beneath and thumb over the barrel. "Shooting hand here, on the pistol grip." Same again, placing his right hand where it needed to be. "All fingers stay clear of the trigger guard until you have a target. Understand?"

"Yes," he said, and here came the adrenaline—bouncing and tumbling, like barrels going downhill.

"Now pull the buttstock into your shoulder. Here." She showed him, placing her hands over his and drawing back until the stock was tucked into the pocket of his right shoulder. "That's good. Keep it on the inside. Nice and secure. Remember: bring the sights toward you, don't hunker over the gun."

"Like this?"

"Yes, but you're twisting your body. Square your shoulders as much as you can, tuck your elbows in. That'll help with recoil and shot recovery—that's the adjustment your body and the rifle need to make between shots. The smaller the adjustment, the better."

"It's a lot to remember," Brody gasped. The window might be open, but there was less oxygen in the room, he was sure of it.

"The safety selector is here, just north of the pistol grip. You don't have to hunt for it; inch your right thumb up and you'll find it."

"This thing?"

"Yes. Thumb the switch down when you're ready to fire—
ready being the operative word. Do *not* engage the safety until
you have mounted the rifle and acquired a target."

"Which won't happen," Brody said. He glanced at his mom
with big eyes. "They won't come this way, right?"

"I doubt it," Lola said. "But we need to be ready, just in case.
Now, this is a semiautomatic rifle, which means—"

"I know what it means. One bullet for every trigger pull.
There's been enough on TV about guns lately." He palmed sweat
from his brow, then got back into position. "None of it good."

"When fatigue sets in—and it will, into your arms and legs—
get up and shake it out. Stretch. Take five. But keep your eye on
that window. If you see movement at the tree line, it's probably
a deer. Use the optic if you want to make sure." She tapped a
knurled wheel on the riflescope. "This adjusts the magnification.
Play around with it a little. Get comfortable."

Brody nodded, swallowed awkwardly. Lola stared at him for
a second, then—unbelievably—kissed the top of his head and
swept from the room.

"We need to talk," she called from the hallway. "We'll do it
later. For now, I need your help to keep us alive."

...

His mom never asked if he'd been followed. Quite aside from it
being an inane question, it was, in this instance, entirely redundant. His very presence had put her on high alert. Being holed
up, scoping her acreage for threats, was not the retaliatory response he'd hoped for, but did he honestly expect her to smear
greasepaint across her face, strap an RPG to her back, and take

the fight to Jimmy? Okay, so he'd fantasized as much on the journey here, but the reality was different. They would need to withstand the impending assault, then pick up the pieces—hopefully Jimmy's—after the smoke had cleared.

The minutes stretched out. Twenty . . . forty-five . . . eighty. Lola called to him every so often. "Give me a status report," and, less militarily, "Anything, Brody?" This was obviously to keep him on his toes. On one occasion she asked, with a note of concern, "How are you holding up?"

"Been better," he called back.

More than once, he told himself that it had been a good decision to leave Molly with Renée. If he'd done anything right during this whole nightmare, it was that.

His adrenaline evaporated deep into the second hour. Brody set the rifle down, stood up, and stretched. His arms were on fire. Pain lanced from his knees to his hips. He paced the breadth of the room, working out the discomfort. Time trickled steadily by. Brody didn't know how long, but at some point he noticed the light had changed.

He mounted the rifle again, scoping from northeast to northwest and back again. How many times? Fifty? One hundred? All emotion drained from him, then exhaustion moved in. Brody stretched again, easing the stiffness from his arms and legs. Take five, his mom had said, so he did. The next thing he knew, he was climbing out of a light doze, his forehead resting on top of the dresser.

"Oh shit."

He snapped upright, looked out the window, certain he would see a troop of Jimmy's boys within twenty yards of the house. The sun had dipped westward, pushing its light into a pillow of cloud. It was murky out there, but he was able to see that his mom's acreage was as empty and featureless as it had been all day.

"Okay." Brody breathed, one hand on his chest. "No one there."

His mom came in several minutes later with packaged food. Potato chips, a Snickers, a can of Welch's Grape Soda. "It's not healthy, but the sugar should pep you up." Brody tore into the Snickers bar, nodding gratefully. He took a bite, swallowed, then pointed out the window.

"It's getting too dark to see."

Lola nodded, then left the room. She returned a moment later with a new scope, which she fitted to the MMR.

"That's a thermal scope," she said. Her hair was tied back, and the pistol she'd been carrying was now holstered to her right hip. "The clarity and magnification aren't as good, but you can pick up a heat signature at sixteen hundred yards. You'll see anything— or anybody—coming out of those woods."

"Right," Brody mumbled around a mouthful of his candy bar.

"A lot of wildlife here, especially at night. Deer and coyote, mostly." Lola cracked a tired smile. "Those coyotes are a pain in the ass. Feel free to get some target practice in."

The next few hours moved languidly. It was dark, cold, and uncomfortable. The sugar *did* lift him, but not for long. His exhaustion was as lumbering, yet oddly attractive, as a sea turtle, and it flopped across him by inches. He wondered how his mom was doing. Was she equally exhausted, or had she trained herself to operate without sleep, like an elite sniper? *Not this kid*, Brody thought, and closed his eyes for a second—maybe a couple of minutes, ten at the most—before returning to the scope.

He saw deer, or *thought* he did, a dozen of them, highlighted a hot white though the thermal optic—his tiredness underscored when they separated into a thousand brilliant particles and drifted across the darkness like dandelion seeds.

...

Brody slept, properly and deeply. He stirred in the early hours to find himself in his mom's bed, the covers pulled up to his chest. *She tucked me in*, he thought blearily. It was dark but he saw her outline at the window, scanning her property through the riflescope.

CHAPTER TWENTY-ONE

"Tell me about Molly. Where is she?"

His mom stood in the space previously occupied by the dresser. She *was* tired, despite whatever training she'd had. Not even the vivid morning light could lift the pallor from her skin. Her eyes, though, sparkled with something Brody couldn't read, and didn't like.

"With Renée." He stepped out of the en suite, having just brushed his teeth and splashed his armpits with cold water. In terms of his morning ablutions, this would have to do.

"You didn't think," Lola said, "that she'd be safer here?"

"What? No. Jesus, no." Brody shook his head. He gestured at the gun in her holster, then at the bigger gun on the dresser. "Are you serious? This is a fucking war zone."

Lola narrowed her eyes, hands on her hips. Silence fell between them. Somewhere, a bird called.

"Listen," Brody began, as if this needed further justification. "I'm running short on cash. Molly was almost out of meds. All things considered, Renée is in a much better position to take care of her."

Lola pondered this for a moment, then nodded. "Okay," she said. It was the response Brody wanted, but he still didn't care for that look in her eye.

She left the room, heading back to her window. Brody started to follow—he wanted to dig into her odd curiosity; Jesus, shouldn't *he* be the one asking questions?—when an alarm sounded. A single high note.

...

Lola got into position: behind a rifle in the front window. A shooter's rifle, Brody thought, designed for power, distance, and accuracy. He stood numbly on the landing. Without breaking her sight picture, she said to him, "It's probably farm business, but if I give the go, grab the MMR and start laying down suppressive fire from the next room."

"Suppressive fire," Brody repeated. Four weeks ago, he'd been sprawled across Tyrese's sofa, watching *The People's Court* on Channel 62. He tried drawing a neat line from there to here, but couldn't. That line made no sense.

He moved, though, and with purpose. He grabbed the MMR from the dresser. It already felt familiar—comfortable, even. Engaging in any kind of conflict would knock that familiarity into a different time zone, but he didn't have to worry about that for now; his mom met him on the landing. She'd taken off her holster and tucked the pistol into the back of her jeans.

"Stand down, soldier," she said. "It's just Hudson."

"Hudson?"

"From the Country Market. He's here to pick up the eggs."

...

The window in the spare room was open and Brody caught snatches of his mom's conversation with Hudson. Her tone was convivial, and he detected a subtle change in her accent—a shift in her vowels—that deepened the Midwest connection. It was convincing, and Brody was impressed with how smoothly she'd switched from gun-savvy mom to happy-go-lucky cowgirl. Must be some kind of survival mechanism, he thought. Serial killers probably had the same chameleonic trait.

This show had drawn him into the spare room. He watched from the window for a moment, making sure he wasn't seen. Hudson had a ruddy face and Paul Newman eyes, and his posturing suggested he might have a soft spot for Lola—or Margaret, as he knew her. He licked his lips frequently, thumbs hooked into the belt loops of his jeans. It was an interesting display on both parts, but Brody didn't watch for long; his attention was claimed first by the bolt-action rifle set up in front of the window— it looked powerful enough to drop a charging rhino—and then by the bulletin board on the wall. Specifically, the photographs pinned to it.

"No fucking way."

Eight headshots, cropped and enlarged. Three of the faces were familiar: Jimmy Latzo's, with his Gotti hairdo and unmistakable scarring. This was the same photograph that accompanied the article in *The Mighty Penn Online*, reporting that Jimmy was being questioned in connection with the murder of Art Binkle, whose severed head was discovered spinning on a turntable at 45 rpm. There were photographs of Leo and Joey, too—Brody's nemeses from the motel in Bayonet.

Three familiar faces, and one other that was *very* familiar.

"Hello, Blair."

Hers was in the middle. A candid shot, no doubt lifted from some online source. Her hair was brown, sensibly pulled back from her face, not purple and punky. Without the wild makeup, she looked both older than the girl who'd sat across from him at Rocky T's, and younger. Brody might not have recognized her at all, but the cunning in her eyes was one hundred percent Blair.

He recalled how she'd drawn him in—her clever fabrications, the sexually loaded body language—only to tear his world apart.

Hudson rolled out a big old country laugh. It was a pleasing sound, if not entirely genuine. Brody dragged his eyes from Blair's headshot and approached the window again. His mom appeared relaxed—just another Wednesday morning in Lone Arrow, Nebraska. He could see the shape of the pistol beneath her shirt, though. A suitable metaphor for the margin between lives.

"Say, Huddy," she said, stepping a little closer to him. "You get any out-of-towners through the store yesterday?"

"I'd say likely. We're right off the 183. See a strange face or two most days." Hudson tucked his hands into his back pockets. "Why'd you ask?"

"Had a fella come by here," Lola replied. "Pencil-pusher. From the Federal Highway Administration, he said."

"That so?"

"Asking questions about the land." Pronounced *lend* with the accent. "Boundaries and such. Says not to be surprised if I see surveyor types in the area. You see anybody like that on the way out here?"

Hudson removed one hand from his back pocket to rub his chin. "Hmm, can't say that I did."

"Likely parked up in SUVs, or some other corporate vehicle?"

Hudson snapped his fingers. "Shoot, Maggie, I *did* see a car parked out by Crandall's place. Not an SUV. A Nissan, or some other Jap model." He took a step back and peered from east to west, as if checking for traffic. "You think they're looking to buy you out, run a highway through here?"

"They'll do it over my bones," Lola said, and that earned another big old laugh from Hudson. Lola laughed, too—she was very convincing—and led Hudson around the side of the farmhouse, but not before casting a deep, searching stare at the driveway.

Brody stepped away from the window, thinking that Lola's performance as Nebraskan Farmer was second only to her performance as Loving Mother, which she'd kept up for twelve years. Anger flashed through him. A feeling of betrayal, too, and disjunction. He wanted to hold on to those negative emotions; to relinquish them would be to allow room for forgiveness, and he wasn't ready for that. Or so he believed. He looked at the bulletin board again—all those people who wanted her dead—then at the rifle. It was fixed to a hunting tripod, and it was this, the permanence of it, that struck him inside. This woman lived in fear, and had since Jimmy Latzo stepped onto the warpath. She'd spent most of her life looking over her shoulder.

She loved you, Brody, Renée had said. The kindness in her eyes had been deep. As had the honesty. *It would have broken her heart to run away. But she did it to keep you safe—to move the target away from you.*

Sympathy rose above all other emotions. It was unexpected, and disconcerting. Brody ran his hands through his hair and tried to recall the anger. A cold and dependable sentiment. But it had diminished. The size of a coin.

...

He checked the back window, scoped the tree line. His mom joined him minutes later.

"There's a car out near Crandall's place," she said. "About a mile from here. I think it's Eddie the Smoke."

"Is he dangerous?"

"Not directly. He used to be a paparazzo. Now he's a cross between a private eye and a stalker. He follows people, and watches them."

"And he's got eyes on us?" Brody asked.

"Right. And if we move, he'll follow."

"So we just stay here?"

"You got it." Lola managed a dry smile. "If you weren't here, I'd take Eddie out, then hit the road. I'm not sure where I'd go; I've run out of lives. But I'd find a way . . . somehow."

"Am I complicating your plans?" Brody cocked an eyebrow.

"If I run," Lola explained, "Jimmy will come after you, and I can't allow that to happen."

"Then take us with you," Brody said. "Me and Molly. We'll all start again—look out for one another."

"I care too much to subject you to this life." Lola shook her head. "That's the reason I ran away last time."

"You care?"

Lola didn't reply, but she lowered her eyes. A glimmer of emotion.

"So what do we do?" Brody asked, letting it go.

"The only thing we *can* do," Lola replied. "We wait."

She returned to her station. Brody crouched in front of the window and looked across her acreage. He saw movement, but didn't panic this time. It was more deer, at the edge of the tree line, a mother and her fawn. Brody studied them through the scope. They made him smile.

Satisfied the coast was clear, he left his window to join Lola in the spare room. She was curling twenty-five-pound dumbbells. Three sets of ten. Her biceps rolled behind her shirtsleeves, straining at the fabric. She was a year older than Renée, which put her at a spirited fifty-one. Brody watched her, feeling a jab of pride—this accompanied by the now-familiar sting of having been deceived.

"Hey," she said, setting the dumbbells down beside her exercise bike. Brody thought she might drop into a plank position, or start doing push-ups, but she stayed on her feet.

"Hey," Brody said. His gaze shifted around the room. Another unloved space. He lingered for a moment on Blair's photograph, then looked at the rifle in the window. "All clear out back. I think you're right; no one's coming that way."

"Probably not."

He took in the view: one hundred yards of open driveway, flanked by ash trees, curving east for another seventy yards or so toward the road. The horse arena was to the right of the drive-way, and the barn—OWLFEATHER FARM painted above the doors in yellow letters—was to the right of this. He saw a strip of Big Crow Road, and then it was flat country all the way to the horizon.

"You think they'll come in cars?" Brody asked. "Or on foot, using the trees for cover?"

"Cars, I think," Lola said, joining him at the window. "At least until I hit their tires. Or take out the drivers, if they're not behind bullet-resistant glass. They'll get as close as they can, though, then they'll use cover."

"It'll happen quickly."

"Yeah, and it'll be over quickly." Lola sighed. "One way or another."

"At least you won't have to hide anymore." Brody ran his finger along the buttstock of the rifle. His other hand was clenched, drumming lightly against his thigh. "I had to come. You know that, right?"

"I know that."

"I knew I was bringing a war."

"You didn't bring anything that wasn't already here," Lola said. "Why do you think I have all this hardware?"

Brody nodded and looked down at the rifle between them. "What kind of gun is this?"

"It's a Mark V DGR," Lola replied. "DGR stands for danger-ous game rifle."

"Dangerous? That's perfect for Jimmy."

"It's bolt-action, so it's slower than the MMR, and it only holds four rounds—one in the chamber, three in the drop box." Lola reached beneath the rifle and ejected a compact magazine. Car-tridges glittered inside. "I can switch this out quickly, though, and the .300 Weatherby mag will stop anything that comes down the driveway."

"I remember when you used to bake muffins," Brody said.

"Yeah?" Lola clicked the drop box back into place. "I still bake muffins."

"Chocolate chip?"

"You know it."

They both smiled. It was strained, but mostly pleasant. Brody turned his attention back to the window. The ash trees shook their beautiful yellow leaves in the clear morning light. The goats bleated in their pen.

"You have an alarm?" he asked, remembering the shrill tone that had filled the house prior to Hudson's arrival.

"My early warning system," Lola said. "It's rigged to a sensor at the bottom of the driveway."

"So why bother watching the front?" Brody asked. "Why not just get into position when you hear the alarm?"

"If Jimmy attacks, he's going to come hard and fast. Every second is critical. I want to be behind that rifle, and ready." She drew an invisible line from her right eye to the point where the driveway curved. "And for your information, I've also been watching both sides—"

"If?" Brody cut in.

Lola stumbled on her words and looked at him. "Huh?"

"You said if Jimmy comes. *If.*" Brody frowned. "You think he's had a change of heart?"

"No, I don't. It's just . . ." More stumbling. Her eyes danced left and right, then settled on her boot tops. A wisp of hair had worked itself loose and fluttered across her brow.

"You're not telling me something," Brody said.

"Okay." She nodded, folded her arms. "But before I say anything, you have to understand that I'm hardwired to analyze a situation and consider all possible outcomes. This means looking seriously at worst-case scenarios."

"And?"

"Jimmy's a goddamn pit bull. He has a small brain and a short fuse. Which makes me wonder why he hasn't attacked already."

"He's putting his pieces into place," Brody said.

"Even that's too smart for him," Lola said. "But yes, he's making moves, somehow, some way. He's waited a long time to get his hands on me, and he won't want to screw it up."

"What are you thinking?"

"Best-case scenario: he comes here hotheaded—hoping to take me by surprise—and I shoot him dead." She patted the top of the rifle as she might a dog. "*Real* dead this time. Then you and Molly can live here with me. You can feed the chickens, ride the horses. We all live happily ever after."

"Worst-case?"

Her eyes dipped again. "Jimmy gets smart, and he uses Molly to bait me out."

A cold feeling flooded from the pit of Brody's stomach. It went down his legs first, then it hit his heart, his throat, his brain. He gasped—every breath was a thin effort. Frost flowers bloomed across his mind. His mom reached for him but he knocked her hand away.

"That can't happen," he hissed. Their earlier conversation recurred—Lola asking where Molly was, and if he'd considered that she might be safer here, with them. Was this *his* fault? In his endeavor to do something absolutely right, had he in fact done something terribly wrong? He shook his head and pointed a trembling finger at his mom. "That *cannot* happen."

"Take a breath, Brody. Calm down."

He nodded. His gasps lengthened into short breaths. The cold feeling was replaced by a dull nausea.

"Listen to me," Lola continued. She reached for him again, this time taking his hand and squeezing reassuringly. "It probably *won't* happen. Jimmy has always been predictable, and holding Molly hostage doesn't fit his MO. He has the cruelty, but not the cunning."

On this last word, Brody's eyes snapped to the bulletin board. He shook off his mom's hand, stepped around the rifle, and tapped Blair's headshot.

"*She* has the cunning," he said. "And I think she might be running the show."

"You know her?"

"Yeah, that's Blair. She was the one who suckered me into this whole thing." He spoke through clenched teeth. "She's . . . slippery."

"And deadly," Lola said, looking at the photograph. "Blair Mayo. She's a two-time state boxing champion. She also has distinctions in kung fu and Krav Maga—"

"Krav what?"

"Maga. It's an Israeli self-defense system. Incredibly brutal. As if that wasn't enough, she's the first female to win the Western Penn 3-Gun since I won it in 1990."

"Jesus," Brody said. He recalled her coquettishness, the way she'd sucked on her straw—*Dee-fucking-lish*—and batted her eyelashes. A masquerade, obviously, but it was still a stretch to connect that Miley Cyrus version of Blair to the John Wick version his mom had unveiled. "I can't even . . ."

Lola pulled her cell phone from her pocket, opened her browser, then tapped on a series of links she'd bookmarked—stories from *The MMA Report, East Coast Boxing, The 48 Gun Club.* They featured various action shots of Blair: firing a semi-automatic pistol; throwing leather in the ring; hoisting a trophy after winning a kung fu tournament. The last link brought up a story about Blair putting an opponent—a fierce rival—into a coma with a roundhouse kick.

"Holy shit," Brody said. His nausea had abated, replaced by a fluttering that filled his rib cage like spooked birds. He wanted to run, to scream, to reach inside the photographs of Blair and Jimmy, and twist their necks until something broke.

Leo and Joey looked tame in comparison. He bounced the side of his fist off their faces.

"I know these motherfuckers, too."

"Leo Rossi and Joey Cabrini," his mom said.

"They jumped us in Mississippi, then let us go." He recalled the misery of seeing Molly with a gun locked to her head, and the hard shift this had encouraged inside him. "They were herding us toward you."

"We need to talk," Lola said, putting her phone away. "I want to know everything that happened. I *do*. But I have too many other things to think about right now."

Brody sagged against the wall. He hurt throughout. "Molly. Jesus, we . . . we need to warn her somehow. We can contact Renée—"

"Brody—"

"Or call the police—"

"Brody, *listen*." There was a snap to her voice that he recognized from when he was a kid—when he liberated brownies from the Tupperware on top of the fridge, or watched R-rated comedy skits on YouTube. "You've been here nearly twenty-four hours. If Jimmy wants to go after Molly, he'll have her already."

"And this worst-case scenario didn't occur to you yesterday?"

"I expected an immediate attack," Lola said. "When it didn't happen, I started to run through alternative strategies. Everything from his assembling a battalion to air-dropping teargas on the house. The Molly scenario occurred to me late last night."

"Jesus *Christ*."

"The best thing we can do right now is stay focused. Stay strong." Lola's voice was taut, but not without compassion. "Jimmy will show his hand soon enough, and I *will* respond."

Brody nodded meekly, head low. She was a warrior—could hit without aiming, kill without qualm, dismantle armies. He wasn't going to cry in front of her, but he wanted to. And she must have sensed this, because she took him into her arms and held him until the spooked birds quieted.

"I'm not going to let anything happen to Molly," she assured him. "And I'm not going to let anything happen to you."

Brody nodded, feeling small and young.

"Do you hear me?"

"Yes," he croaked.

"Do you *hear* me?"

"Yes."

She continued to hold him—one hand just above his left hip, the other cupping the back of his neck—and he found comfort in her strength, her protection, while bleakly aware of the imagery: a deer and her fawn, viewed through a riflescope.

CHAPTER TWENTY-TWO

Brody cooked breakfast while his mom kept a lookout. This was her suggestion, and although he didn't have much of an appetite, he obliged; he was happy to escape that upstairs room for a while and apply his mind to something normal. He fried bacon and scrambled eggs, trying not to think about Molly. The view from the kitchen window helped: a scratch of dusty yard, the chicken coops, the edge of a field where cows cropped grass and jostled their big, beautiful bodies against the fence. Once or twice, Brody imagined living here—in a more peaceful time—waking early to feed the chickens and muck out the stables, then sitting down to a hearty breakfast while cows lowed in the background. It was a simple, pleasing fantasy, but broken every time his mom's footfalls thudded from one room to the next.

They ate in the spare room, the photos of Jimmy, Blair, et al., staring down at them, the rifle hoisted on its tripod, sentinel-like. Lola wolfed her food and left not a morsel. Brody nudged his with a fork.

"Good," she said, wiping Tabasco from her chin.

"You learn to cook in a hurry," Brody said, "when your mom runs away and your dad has to pull double shifts to keep the roof over your head."

Lola ignored this. She pointed her fork at his plate. "You need to eat."

"Not hungry."

"Don't care. Eat. Keep your strength up."

He ate, but listlessly, and didn't enjoy it. Afterward, he washed the dishes—laughably normal behavior, and he reveled in it—

then returned to his post. He scoped the back of her property for three hours, stopping only to use the bathroom and stretch when fatigue set in.

"I thought it would be over by now," he said to his mom. He'd walked to the guest room to work the tiredness from his legs. "I should be either dead or free."

"Stay alert," Lola said. She sat cross-legged on the floor, weapons and paraphernalia arranged around her. There were three different pistols, a KA-BAR knife, a stun gun that looked like a cell phone, two cans of pepper spray. "Jimmy won't be able to hold out much longer. Here, load this." She tossed him an empty magazine and a box of 9mm rounds.

"I . . . what?" He looked at her. "I don't . . ."

"Let me show you." She stood and demonstrated. "This is the back of the mag. The flat end of the round goes against this. Now take your round, use it to push down on the follower— that's this spring-loaded plate—then slide it all the way back. These little lips will keep it from popping out. Use your second round to push down on the first, slide it back. Then repeat with the third round, the fourth, and so on."

Lola handed the magazine back to him. He sat on the floor, the box of ammo beside him, and started to slide the rounds in one after the other. It was tricky to begin with—a couple of the cartridges slipped between his fingers and pinged across the floor—but he soon got the hang of it. Once the mag was full, he handed it back to Lola.

"Thank you. Good job."

"You have any other guns?"

"A shotgun in the barn," she said. "I use that for shooting skeet with the neighbors. And I have a sawed-off in the truck, beneath the dash."

"No grenade launchers or RPGs?"

"Wouldn't that be nice?" Lola picked up her KA-BAR knife and started sliding it across a whetstone. "You can only buy that kind of firepower illegally, and I've been keeping off the criminal grid."

"So that you don't alert Jimmy?"

"Exactly." She looked, for a beat, quietly impressed, then went back to the whetstone. "The black market is big, but Jimmy has a lot of contacts. It's best not to take any chances."

Brody watched Lola sharpen her knife—noting her technique—and was about to ask if he could try when her early warning system sounded. They sprang to their feet. Brody started for the bedroom to grab the MMR, but Lola held him with a raised hand. She stood in front of her rifle, looking at her cell phone.

"Five of two," she said, coolly sliding the phone into her pocket. "It's probably Janey. She comes Wednesdays and Fridays to help with the horses."

Brody stood, locked in place. He felt his heartbeat in the balls of his feet. His mom scoped the driveway for what seemed an incredibly long time, then nodded and stepped away from the rifle.

"Yeah, it's Janey." She scooted around Brody, onto the landing. "I'll send her away. But listen, I'm going to need you to pull a few shifts around the place. These animals want looking after."

Brody smirked and shook his head. "You got me loading ammo and shoveling shit," he said.

"Welcome to my world," Lola said.

...

Janey was in her early twenties, dressed in old clothes, not a spot of makeup, and disarmingly attractive. Under different circumstances, Brody would have liked her to stick around—maybe she could show him how to groom and feed the horses—but this was certainly not the time and his mom was right to send her away. Brody watched Janey's truck rumble back down the driveway, around the curve, and out of sight. Not shy of fantasy, he imagined being in her passenger seat, the radio tuned to some country-and-western station, nothing but open road ahead.

"So," Lola said, joining him again. "About that horseshit."

He spent the next two hours mucking out the stables (the shit—and there was a lot of it—was wheelbarrowed to a dry stack behind the barn), then watering and feeding the horses and other animals. His mom gave him her cell phone with the instruction to return to the house, on the double, if it buzzed three times. "That's my early warning system for when I'm working outside." It *did* buzz, while he was feeding the chickens, and he tossed the sack of scratch down and bolted for the house. This time it was the vet, who'd come—a week early, apparently—to administer biannual cattle vaccinations. Again, Lola sent him on his way.

Brody finished his chores, then showered and took up his post. He scoped the rear of the property until sundown.

...

It had been a warm day, but by six-thirty P.M. the temperature had dropped to the midthirties, and with the window open (for optimum visibility), Brody was forced to put on his dad's motorcycle jacket. He studied the cold twilight through the thermal scope—which he had switched himself—but a heavy layer of disquietude had obscured his concentration. Brody tried to shake it off. He paced, stretched, and splashed his face with icy water, but his unease only deepened. So he wrapped the jacket tighter around his body and went to see his mom in the spare room. She was alert, as ever, not behind the rifle but sitting against the wall, rolling a quarter across her knuckles. It glinted in the subdued lamplight.

Brody stared at her, his arms folded.

"What is it?" Lola asked.

"I don't like doing nothing," he said. "Molly might be in danger, and we're sitting here with our thumbs up our asses."

She stopped rolling the coin, flipped it, snatched it out of the air. "Okay. So what do you propose?"

"Maybe we should take the fight to Jimmy."

No response. No expression, even. Brody sat against the adjacent wall, one knee drawn to his chest. They looked at each other, their breaths visible in the cold air.

"I know you're frustrated," Lola said at last. There was thoughtfulness in her tone, but her eyes were still blank. "And angry—"

"Yes, I'm angry," Brody snapped. "I'm fucking furious. And I'm still grieving my father—the kindest, best man I've ever known."

"I know."

"No, you *don't*. You ran away. You don't know shit." Brody sighed and said under his breath, "This is all your fault."

She heard him, at least he thought she did, but she showed no sign of objection. She slipped the coin into her pocket and watched her breath flower in the air.

"I'm sorry, I just . . ." He ran one hand along his stubbly jaw. "I'm scared for Molly."

"I understand," Lola said. "And believe me, I want us all to walk away from this, alive and together. But that won't happen if we take the fight to Jimmy."

"Why not? It worked last time."

"Last time was twenty-six years ago. I was reckless then. And talented." She lowered her head. "Things have changed."

"But we have to do something."

"We're outgunned, Brody, and outnumbered. This house, with its open land and good visibility, is the only advantage we have, and I don't want to give it up." Lola gestured at the rifle in the window—the defensive center of her operation. It appeared, at that moment, quite inadequate. "Jimmy is too impatient to hold out much longer. So we're going to sit tight and see what we're dealing with."

"If he was going to attack," Brody said, "he would have done it already."

"Maybe. Probably." She blew into her hands and rubbed them together. "But not definitely. We hold our ground, maintain our advantage. At least until we get more information."

The next few minutes passed without a word between them. Brody listened to the chickens bristling, the cows mooing, the evening breeze whispering through the ash trees. A truck bounced and rumbled along Big Crow Road. He returned to his window, but only for a moment. The scene out back was dark and empty.

"Nothing," he reported.

His mom nodded, then looked at him—a double take, of sorts. A small, knowing smile touched her lips.

"What?" Brody asked.

"That jacket," she replied. "It was your dad's."

"Oh. Yeah."

"Jacket first, motorcycle later. Am I right?"

"That was the plan."

She stared for a long time, not at him, he realized, but at some memory induced by the jacket. This angered him a little, although he didn't know why. Perhaps because, until now, she'd barely mentioned his father, and had shown no remorse.

"You have my eyes," she said, coming out of her reverie with a long blink. "My mouth. But you have his profile. I look at you in that jacket and keep thinking it's him."

"Don't," Brody said.

"Don't what?"

"Talk about him." He shook his head. "You don't deserve that."

This drew a rare beat of emotion: *hurt.* Brody saw it in her eyes. Just a flash, then gone.

"Okay," she said. She took a breath that filled her chest and let it out slowly. "Then let's talk about you."

"You're suddenly interested?" Brody spread his hands. "You want me to summarize twelve years in . . . what, five minutes? Ten?"

"That's not what I meant," Lola said patiently. "I know what you've been up to. You took drumming lessons when you were fourteen and started a band called Righteous Mojo, but then broke your ankle wakeboarding on Lake Murray and never drummed again. You had a dog-sitting job for three days, but got fired after you lost the dog. You sold your PlayStation to buy Molly a ticket to see Lady Gaga. Your first car was a 1999 Pontiac Sunfire—"

"First and last."

"You dropped out of high school when you were seventeen—a year from graduation. And oh, Brody, I was heartbroken, but I *get* it, and I have no right to be mad."

"No right at all."

"You got a job bussing tables at Angel's Diner, then working the drive-through at the McDonald's on Aqua Street. You dated Emily Knowles for four months, and Bianca Ciaramella for—"

"Okay, okay, I get it." Brody held up his hands. "So you've been stalking my Facebook."

"Your Instagram, too," Lola said. "And your Myspace, when that was a thing."

"Doesn't make you Mom of the Year." Brody leaned against the wall, then dropped into a sitting position. He was still mad, but it was oddly comforting to know that his mom had been watching him from afar. *She loved you, Brody*, Renée spoke up in his mind again. *It would have broken her heart to run away.* He looked at her and shrugged. "Is this it? Are we talking now?"

"Yeah," Lola said. She checked the time on her cell: 19:46. "You can tell me the fun stuff later. Right now I want to know what happened to you, and how you found me."

...

The story itself didn't take long—he'd become adept at telling it—but he paused twice to scope the back of the farm (while Lola checked east and west), and again to fetch provisions from downstairs. By the time he'd finished, it was almost ten. The floor of the spare room was littered with empty juice boxes and assorted wrappers.

Lola sat pensively. Every now and then she blinked slowly, or creased her brow. Otherwise, she was still.

"Not one part of this has been easy, Mom," Brody said. "It's been a long, hard road. And scary. But here I am."

It occurred to him that this was the first time he'd called her "Mom" since arriving. There'd been no hesitation, no stuttering. The word had popped from his mouth with surprising ease, leaving a trail of odd feelings. Lola registered it, too; her eyes glistened with an ambivalent light, somewhere between happy and sad. She opened her mouth to say something, then closed it again.

"You," Brody added quickly, not wanting to dwell on these feelings, "are either my savior or my sacrifice. I had no choice but to find you."

The lamp hummed. A candy wrapper skittered across the floorboards, prompted by a breeze through the window. Lola stood, worked a kink out of her lower back, and walked slowly to the bulletin board. From the position of her head, Brody thought she was looking at Blair, not Jimmy.

"You did the right thing," she said.

Brody hadn't felt the cold for some time. The atmosphere in the room was not warm, but it had a blanket-like weight that covered every molecule of air. The same could be said of Lola's emotion. It couldn't be seen, but it was there—a heavy, volatile energy.

"I'm sorry for everything you've been through," she said. "And I'm sorry for what happened to your father. I did everything I could to avoid that."

"I believe you," Brody said.

She turned around and looked at him for a long time, or at his jacket, perhaps—his father, the memories dry but still bright, like drifts of dead leaves beneath the porch. He thought for one moment that she was going to hug him, cry on his shoulder, but she only nodded and turned back to the photographs of her enemies.

"Get a couple of hours' rest," she said. "If they come, it'll be between midnight and dawn. I want you alert and at that rifle-scope."

"Right," Brody said. He stood up, shuffled to his mom's room, and shaved the edge off his tiredness with a thin sleep. He then rolled out of bed and looked through the riflescope until a tangerine light edged into the east.

Nobody came.

...

They breakfasted, after which Brody collected the eggs, watered the animals, and shoveled more shit. Lola told him to expect the alarm to sound at nine A.M., and again at nine forty-five. It did. Farm business on both occasions. He kept working.

"It'll be today," Lola said when he came back in.

"Today what?"

"Whatever Jimmy is planning." Her face was gray. She looked so tired. "We'll find out today."

"How do you know?"

"Experience."

The UPS truck arrived that afternoon.

...

Brody assumed Lola had slept in increments—ten minutes here and there, just enough to recoup some drive. When he got out of the shower, he found her curled up on her bed. If this was a nap, it had gotten out of control; she was deep, and would likely sleep the entire day if he didn't wake her.

He couldn't bring himself to do it, though. Not yet. The early warning system would snap her out of her dreams—within seconds—if it went off. Her resting was to their advantage. He could hold the fort for now.

He managed eighty minutes; Lola had unnerved him when

she'd predicted that Jimmy would play his hand that day, and Brody felt safer with her awake. So he brought soup and toast to her room, and gently woke her. She cracked one eyelid, looked at him, then jerked awake.

"How long was I asleep?"

"Not long enough." He placed the tray down on the edge of her bed. "I made you soup, inasmuch as I poured it from a can and heated it on the stove."

"Thank you." She smiled, but there was more to it—a softness in her gaze, a delicate hitch in her breath. She was *touched*, and in a way she hadn't been, perhaps, for some time. "Thank you, Brody."

"Okay."

He went to check the side and front windows, but before he left the room she said to him, "You were always a good kid, with a big and genuine heart. I'm so proud of you."

...

In the hour before the UPS truck rumbled onto the property, delivering the item that would incite a desperate and terrifying course of action, Lola and Brody sat together in the spare room. They talked. Not easy conversations, but a distance was narrowed as Brody began to determine the overlap between Lola Bear and her other personas.

He said, "There's so much about you I don't know, and may never know, but the one question I keep coming back to is, why? If your life is so dangerous, why did you get married and start a family?"

"The simple answer is because I chose to," Lola replied. "I

didn't want to deny myself happiness, or the chance of a normal life. If I'd done that, Jimmy would have won. He would have killed me inside."

"That's a selfish answer," Brody said honestly.

"Your great-grandfather would agree," Lola said. "He warned me about putting down roots, but you have to remember that I thought I was in the clear. I met and fell in love with your father quickly. *Too* quickly. Jimmy was on life support at the time. Karl told me that his family—his brothers and sisters, there were eight or nine of them, I think, a big family . . . Karl told me that they considered pulling the plug, because even if Jimmy survived he would have no quality of life. He'd be brain-damaged—you know, eating baby food, buzzing around in a motorized chair."

"Jimmy wasn't ready to die, though," Brody said. "He had unfinished business."

"Don't I know it."

"Jesus, you should've put a pillow over his face while he was in the hospital. Gone back and finished the job." Brody looked at her, his expression puzzled. "Why didn't you?"

"There's more than one answer to that question," Lola said. There was a weariness to her voice, as if she'd had this conversation with herself on numerous occasions. "Firstly, sneaking into a hospital to kill someone isn't as easy as the movies would have you believe. There are people everywhere. Not just nurses and doctors, but orderlies, security personnel, other patients, visitors. *Witnesses*, in other words. There are also security cameras on every floor, in the stairwells and elevators. Additionally, Jimmy had people around him all the time—that big family I mentioned, and his other family, too. La Cosa Nostra. He was still a made man at the time, and the big boss—Don Esposito—made sure he was protected."

"Even so," Brody said, "a few security cameras and mobsters should've been no problem for Lola Bear."

"If he was at home, I would have risked it," Lola said, looking stormily at Jimmy's photograph on the bulletin board. "Soldiers or not. Shit, I'd done it before. But he was under constant surveillance in the hospital—first in Pittsburgh, then New York City. There was no way I could get in and out cleanly."

"Makes sense, I guess," Brody said, and shrugged. "Sometimes, being tough is not enough."

"It's never about being tough, Brody. It's *always* about being smart." Lola turned her gaze back to him, still stormy. "Which brings me to the final answer to your question: I didn't think I *had* to finish Jimmy off, because Jimmy was going to do that all by himself. Jesus, he had his last rites administered twice—*twice*! And when it became apparent that he wasn't going to die, I figured him being a vegetable for the rest of his life was a reasonable punishment. Perhaps even a *better* punishment."

"That didn't happen, either."

"Right. The Italian goddamn Cat." Lola breathed deeply through her nose. A muscle in her jaw twitched. "So he's back on his feet, making moves, building a crew. No longer with Don Esposito, but forging deals of his own. *That* would've been the perfect time to go back and finish the job, but I had you at my knee and Molly in my belly. I was in a different place—a different *world*—slowed down by two pregnancies, mentally and physically. I simply wasn't ready."

Lola rolled her eyes to the ceiling, remembering. It might have been the cold, but Brody noticed her hands were trembling.

"I used to go behind your dad's back," she continued after a brief but heavy pause. "Sneak off to the range every couple of weeks, try to stay sharp. But it wasn't enough, and I was terrified,

Brody, for the first time in my life . . . terrified that Jimmy would not only come after me, but after my family, too."

"Yeah," Brody said. "That's a tough scene."

"I had Karl, though." A fragile smile touched Lola's lips. "We'd looked out for each other since day one. He was a good friend to have."

"Renée told me how close you were," Brody said. "She said you kept your alliance on the down-low."

"In that line of work, it helps to know if someone is whispering behind your back."

"Was he there the night you went after Jimmy?"

"No," Lola replied. "Him and a couple of other guys were in New Mexico, some counterfeit money thing that Jimmy was trying to get off the ground. Jimmy called them back—he wanted boots on the ground—but it was all over before their plane touched down in Pittsburgh."

"One of Jimmy's few surviving soldiers," Brody noted. "And close enough to keep you in the loop."

"I called him twice a day to begin with, fully expecting him to tell me that Jimmy was dead." Lola blinked brightly, dazedly, as if she still couldn't believe that Jimmy had pulled through. "That didn't happen, obviously, but Karl and I kept in touch—usually by phone, sometimes in person."

Brody nodded. "I remember him coming to the house."

"A few times, yeah. He'd play catch with you, have a beer with your dad, then he'd quietly tell me what was going on with Jimmy." Lola drew her knees up, looped her arms around them. "That's why we moved from Minneapolis to South Carolina. We said goodbye to a comfortable life—a nice house, a safe community, good jobs. But Karl told me that Jimmy had invested in a payday loan company in the Twin Cities, so that was it. We had to relocate."

"How did you swing that with Dad?" Brody asked.

"I didn't swing it. I told him I wanted to leave and he agreed." Lola smiled. "He was a good man. He loved me."

A horse whinnied, probably wanting to escape the stall; they'd all been stabled since Brody arrived. Crows called from the trees. Every now and then one would swoop past the window. The sky beyond was gray and carried rain. It all looked and sounded so ordinary out there that Brody couldn't imagine it changing.

"And there was Vince," Lola said. "It's probably not appropriate to talk about my first boyfriend with you, but he's important, because he awoke so many feelings inside me. I would not have fallen so hard and fast for your father if not for Vince."

"I get it," Brody said. "He taught you how to love."

"Yes, but that sounds so cliché." Lola paused, trying to find the words. Brody waited silently, watching the first raindrops streak the window, until she nodded and placed one hand against her chest. "*Balance*. That's what Vince gave me. You hear martial artists talk about balance all the time, but it applies to everything—to every pursuit. Talent, achievement, love . . . they represent the balance of heart and ability. When one aspect falters, you draw on the other."

"But you had talent," Brody said. "All those trophies you won. The shooting tournaments, the Xing Yi—"

"I had ability," Lola said. "*So* much ability. But without the heart, I was little more than a machine. I functioned, but didn't feel. Vince brought that part of me to life."

Brody said, "Something else that Jimmy crushed."

A dark look from Lola. "Yes. And his timing was . . . well,

heartbreaking. Vince and I had hatched a plan to escape the life—to get away from Jimmy once and for all. We were going to move to Northern California. A brand-new start. No gunrunning, burying bodies, or trading bullets with drug dealers. We had it all worked out."

"And Jimmy found out you were leaving?"

"No, I don't think so," Lola said. "We didn't tell anybody. We were smart. But Jimmy had been pursuing me for years. I spurned his advances, of course, but jealousy got the better of him."

"Son of a bitch didn't like to lose," Brody said, paraphrasing a quote from one of the articles he'd read.

"We were *this* close to getting out." Lola sighed and held her thumb and forefinger an inch apart. "Vince and I had purchased one-way tickets on a flight to San Francisco. Adios, Carver City. Adios, Jimmy. Three days before our departure, Vince got called on a job to Philly. Not our territory, but you do what the boss says. This was at ten-forty A.M. By seven P.M. that evening, I was identifying photographs of Vince's body."

Other than lowering her eyes, she showed no sadness. It was there, though—a shadow on her aura. Brody never knew Vincent Petrescu. He didn't really know Lola Bear, either. This was, for all intents and purposes, a stranger's account, yet it was all he could do to keep from crossing the room and hugging her.

"Jimmy tried to make it look like a rival gang hit. The Badland Brothers used to cut the ears off their victims, and that's what Jimmy did to Vince." Lola nodded and looked at Brody, her eyes cold and certain. "I would always have *suspected* that Jimmy was behind it, because of who and what he is: a goddamn psychotic lunatic. But I had conclusive proof that removed all doubt."

"And then you went on the warpath."

"I did. I went through attack dogs, bullets, and flamethrowers to get to Jimmy. Nothing was going to stop me." Lola drew a deep breath into her lungs. "Although not a day goes by when I don't wish I'd stopped myself . . . just walked away."

The breeze whipped rain through the open window. It hit the wall in tiny droplets and shone in the pale light. Swallows and wrens had joined the crows' cawing. A peculiar discussion.

"I miss Vince. I miss your father, oh, so much. And I miss you and Molly." Lola wiped a speck of rain from the back of her hand. "I often think about the mess I've made, and how I didn't do anything right. But I look at you now and know that I did."

Brody scooted along the floor, took her hand. She squeezed firmly, as if to assure herself that he was actually here. Words drifted across his mind. He reached, found the right ones—*I don't fully understand, but I don't blame you, either*—but before he could open his mouth, the alarm system sounded throughout the house.

Lola removed her hand from his and got to her feet.

"I think this is it," she said.

...

Brody grabbed the MMR and took up position in the room next to Lola's. He didn't need the scope to see the large brown vehicle flashing between the trees.

"I see a truck," he called out.

"A UPS delivery truck," his mom called back.

"What should I do?"

"Hold position. Do *not* open fire unless I say."

He opened the window, mounted the rifle, watched the UPS truck round the curve in the driveway and rumble into view. Brody scoped. A male driver, in his forties. Nobody else up front.

He wondered if Jimmy's boys were packed into the back. A kind of Trojan horse.

Thumb on the safety, ready. He felt his heartbeat through the rifle's stock, all the way to the handguard.

The driveway ended in a broad turning circle sixty feet from the front door. The driver steered through most of it, then stopped his truck with its rear doors facing the house. Brody imagined them banging open and Jimmy's army spilling out. Twelve, fifteen, twenty guys packing muscle and heat. And Brody would open fire—on impulse, if nothing else—and wouldn't stop pulling the trigger until the magazine was spent.

"Hold steady," his mom called. Maybe she'd read his mind.

He couldn't see the driver because of the angle he'd parked at, but the truck wobbled as he made his way from the front seat into the back. One of the two rear doors opened a few seconds later. The driver stepped out, on his own. He carried a small box beneath one arm. Brody watched him walk down the pathway that linked the turning circle to the front door. Three thuds as he mounted the porch steps—out of view now—and then the doorbell chimed.

His delivery made, the driver returned to his big brown truck and drove away.

...

"Is it a bomb?"

"No. It's not heavy enough to be a bomb. And Jimmy won't blow me up." Lola gave Brody a wry smile. "He wants to kill me slowly."

"Maybe a chemical device?" Brody ventured. "You know, like fentanyl, or some kind of knockout gas?"

The package sat on the kitchen table. A plain brown box, twelve inches long, seven inches wide. It was addressed, not to Margaret Ward, but to Lola Bear.

"Doubtful," Lola said, lifting one side of the box to look underneath it. "There's no crystallization at the edges, no oily marks or strange odor. The return address is bogus, though."

She pointed at the smaller label in the top corner. It read: IC INDUSTRIES, PHOENIX, 54558.

"Phoenix, Arizona?" Brody asked.

"It's a reference to the mythical bird that rose from the ashes. The zip is standard letter mapping, like you'd find on a phone keypad. It spells KILL U. The IC in IC Industries stands for Italian Cat."

"Jesus Christ." Brody took a step back. "It's from him. It's really from him."

"Yes, it is." Lola pulled a knife from the block on the counter behind her. "It's a message."

She carefully cut the packing tape and lifted the box's flaps. Inside, beneath a cushion of bubble wrap, was a dirty white sneaker with a crust of blood on the toe.

The ground opened beneath Brody. He swayed, clasped the edge of the table. Everything dimmed for the first—but not the last—time that day.

"Oh my God," he moaned. "That's Molly's shoe."

"No," Lola said. She took the sneaker out and turned it slowly in her hands. "It's a love letter."

CHAPTER TWENTY-THREE

Lola had seen both sides of Vincent Petrescu. There was the enforcer, who would snap the fingers of drugs and weapons dealers who were short in their earnings. Then there was the *man*, intelligent, loyal, a son and brother who made regular donations to the children's hospital in Reflection Park, and called his *bunica* in Romania every other Sunday. Lola would never deny her attraction to the bad boy with the .45 at his side, but it was the *man* that she fell in love with.

The man who uncovered a warmth inside her she hadn't known existed.

The man who put her first, in everything.

The man who wrote her love letters.

It would brighten her day when she found them, and encourage that new and wonderful feeling inside. *It's all better with you here*—written on a scrap of paper tucked between the pages of a magazine. *Addicted to what you give me*—on a Post-it note inside a CD case. *Thanks for being my Happy Place*—folded and tucked beneath the insole of her left shoe. This last was a favorite hiding place for his sweet nothings, and indeed the spot where he'd secreted his final note to her: one word—*JIMMY*—written in his own blood.

Jimmy knew this story. Lola had told him as he lay dying in the hallway of his burning mansion. And now he'd borrowed Vince's idea to send a note of his own.

Lola placed Molly's sneaker on the kitchen table. It was her left sneaker, of course—closer to her heart, as Vince would say—and when Lola lifted the tongue and looked inside, she noticed the insole sticking up at the back, eerily similar to how Vince's insole had been sticking up when she'd looked inside his shoe twenty-six years before.

Deep breathing sounds from behind her. Brody was doubled over, leaning against the wall. Lola glanced at him, then turned back to Molly's sneaker.

She lifted the insole, expecting to find a folded piece of paper, probably with an address written on it, almost certainly written in Molly's blood (Jimmy wouldn't miss *that* trick). Instead she saw that a rectangle of the cushioning had been cut out, and neatly filled with a USB flash drive.

Lola took the drive out and held it up, like an appraiser holding up a diamond.

"What . . . the fuck?" Brody gasped.

"You probably don't want to see what's on this," she said.

...

A single MP4 video file. Run time: 03:31. It opened on a shot of an oil-stained floor and scrolled slowly up to reveal a bare concrete wall. An abandoned factory or warehouse, Lola thought. The camera jigged left, lost focus, came back in. The same shot, except now she saw a man-shaped shadow against the wall.

Mumbling in the background: "Please . . . let us go . . . please." This was followed by a distinct, violent thud and then screaming. Both sounds cut through Lola. Next to her, Brody flinched. He'd chosen to watch. "I need to know," he'd said. Now he covered his ears and took a broad step back. "That's Molly," he said.

More screaming, followed by a muffled whimpering, closer to the camera. Two people, Lola thought, one of them gagged.

The shadow moved. Lola heard footsteps (she imagined expensive Italian heels clicking off the floor). A man stepped into the shot. It was Jimmy. Lola knew this, even though he wore a black hood over his head, eyeholes cut into it. She could tell from the way he walked, the cant of his back, his narrow, almost boyish hips. He wore leather gloves to hide the scarring on his hands.

"Hello, Lola." Even his voice was disguised, pushed through a filter, almost robotic.

"Is that Jimmy?" Brody asked.

"Yes, but there's no way of proving it."

"Why's he hiding?"

"To keep us from going to the police."

The camera followed Jimmy as he stepped left past two empty racks and a fire door and an old blue machine that probably hadn't worked for a long time.

"Hit that bitch again."

The same meaty thud and Molly screamed again—a hurt, hopeless wail, then tears and tears.

"Again."

Jimmy flicked his hand, suggesting the camera follow the action. It did. A quick snap left. A different scene: red-painted cinder block, heating ducts, a low yellow light. Molly was chained at the wrists to an overhead crossbar that sagged a little with her weight. Her weaker left leg was drawn inward, like a cowering animal.

"Don't watch," Lola said.

"I'm going to kill him."

Lola paused the video at 01:21. Still two minutes and ten seconds of this nightmare to go. She turned to Brody.

"Get the hell out of here."

"No. I need to see."

"You don't."

He said, "This is a goddamn *war*. I don't want to second-guess myself on the battlefield. I want every reason to put a bullet in Jimmy's brain."

"Brody—"

"Hit play."

She hit play. The camera jerked away from Molly, lost focus for a second, swam back, and here was the second person: Renée, strapped into her wheelchair, sobbing through the wad of flannel stuffed into her mouth. Blood flowed from her hairline and from a deep cut that looped from her left ear to her cheekbone.

Back to Molly. The camera zoomed in on her face. She had a broken lip and bruising around her eye. The camera jerked again, zoomed out. Another hooded person stepped into the shot, smaller in frame. No gloves. He or she carried a heavy-duty pipe wrench in one hand. *She*, definitely a she; Brody noticed the bright pink varnish on her fingernails and flashed back to Rocky T's.

"Blair," he said.

Blair raised the wrench and brought it down in a blur, smashing it against Molly's left leg, just above the knee. Molly screamed and thrashed, swinging from the chain. Blair hit her in the same place again.

Brody groaned, covered his eyes, staggered away.

Pause at 01:56.

"Get out of here, Brody," Lola insisted. "Please."

He cried out—a hurting, furious explosion of sound—and threw his fist against the wall, two solid thuds that made the window tremble in its frame. "I'm not going anywhere," he said. "This is on me. I won't back away."

306 | Rio Youers

"But you *can*."

"I'm the reason Molly and Renée are there."

"No, Brody. *I* am."

"I guess we're both to blame, which means we're in this together." He flexed his right hand, examined the grazed skin on his knuckles, then nodded at the screen. "If I'm soldier enough to fire an assault rifle from your bedroom window, then I'm soldier enough to watch this."

Lola lowered her eyes, recognizing the thick cord of resolve—stubbornness, Grandpa Bear would've called it—that ran through him. He truly was her son. Reinforcing this, their thoughts ran parallel; she had seen enough of the video, but for what she had to do, she needed to see more.

She turned back to her laptop and clicked play.

Molly drooped from the chain, turning a slow circle. A long thread of saliva hung from her mouth. The shot switched back to Jimmy. He stared at the camera for a long time.

"I need you, Lola," he said. "I need you very badly."

He took half a dozen slow steps to his right and stopped a yard or so from Renée's chair. He touched her hair and she shrank away from him. The camera operator adjusted his or her position to get all four of them in the shot: Jimmy and Renée in the foreground, Blair and Molly behind. Molly lifted her head and moaned. The chain rattled. "*Pleeeeeease*," she wailed. Jimmy reached behind him and pulled a semiautomatic pistol from the waistband of his pants. He pointed it at Renée's head.

"*No*," Molly screamed. "*Please, Pleeee—*"

Blair silenced her: one deft punch to the jaw. Molly went limp and spun on her chain.

"You know where to find me," Jimmy said to the camera. It looked for a moment like he was going to lower the gun but he pulled the trigger instead. The report was dull and shocking. Renée's head snapped backward and the right side of her skull opened in a hail of bone and matter. The force lifted her chair onto one wheel. It almost tipped, then it settled and rolled a few inches. The movement caused Renée's head to flop forward. Blood spouted from the entry wound and gushed from the exit.

Jimmy tucked the pistol into the back of his pants and stepped close to the camera. His eyes blazed through the jagged holes cut into the hood.

"Come get me, you bitch," he said.

End of video.

...

Ten seconds of painful, disbelieving silence, then Lola closed the laptop's lid with a loud snap. She turned toward Brody. His eyes were big and wet.

"We've got work to do," she said.

CHAPTER TWENTY-FOUR

The message from Jimmy—the brutal, inhuman hand he had played—meant that Brody and Lola no longer had to scope the property. Nobody was coming, at any time of the day or night. Jimmy had been clear: he wanted Lola to go to him. This was hardly a source of relief, but they were at least free to suffer in their own way. Lola fell into an exhausted sleep. Brody was tired, too, but sleep wasn't in the cards. He wandered the farm, drifting in and out of himself, the most hopeless of ghosts. He'd find himself in the barn or the basement with no memory of how he got there. He fed the chickens at midnight.

The world returned, gradually. It felt like a wound both opening and closing. At 6:50 A.M., with a scratch of light in the east, Brody stripped off his shirt and ran. He bolted across the yellowing land to the north—the very land he'd watched over since his arrival—and into the woods. He didn't feel the cold or the sting of the branches as they whipped against his skin. Deer sprang ahead of him in beautiful shapes.

The light climbed. A saffron mist clung to the understory. Brody broke from the woods and stumbled back to the house, bleeding and bruised. His mom was still asleep, curled up in an armchair in the living room. Brody draped a thick blanket over her and found one for himself. He sat in front of the empty fireplace and remembered Molly, age two, lying in a hospital bed, her legs in twin casts. He had cupped her hand and silently promised to be there if she needed him. *If*. She was such a determined girl.

Brody eventually succumbed to sleep, but his dreams were like the mist in the woods: thin and crowded by darkness.

...

On any normal day—or as normal as her life ever got under a constant threat—Lola would wake at five A.M., shower, eat breakfast, then go to work. Hers was a small farm but there was always plenty to do, and an early start occasionally meant that she could dedicate her afternoon to other pursuits, like riding her horse or getting off a few shots at the range.

Brody's arrival had derailed Margaret Ward's existence—ended it, in fact—but Lola woke late that Friday morning determined to play the role one last time. So she pulled on her dirty old denims and made her rounds. She groomed the horses and let them run in the arena. She cleaned and hosed the stables, mucked out the chicken coops, refreshed all the feeders and troughs. Hudson came at eleven and she gave him a vibrant, nothing-wrong-here smile, then handed him sixty fresh eggs stacked into two trays, just like she always did.

"Missed you at pinochle last night," he said as he climbed back into his truck, and she told him that she'd be there next week, even though she knew that her days of playing pinochle were well and truly behind her.

She spent some time with her cattle, looking for signs of disease: scours, coughing, nasal discharge. Maybe it was pointless, given what she was about to do, but doing something normal—even checking a calf for diarrhea—helped her cope with the many things that were *not* normal.

Brody was awake when she returned to the house, but not exactly alert. He sat on the floor in the living room, huddled in a blanket, rocking back and forth.

"I'll make us something to eat," Lola said.

"Not hungry."

"The worst thing we can do right now is deteriorate. We need to stay strong."

She went to the kitchen and started pulling eggs, meats, and vegetables out of the fridge. Brody joined her after a moment. He sat at the table, stared at the closed laptop for a second or two, then pushed it away from him.

"Is there any point," he said, "in going to the police?"

"No," Lola said.

"But if you show them that . . . that *video*"—he sneered when he said it, his hateful eyes directed at the laptop—"they'll have to do something. They'll at least investigate."

"You're right." Lola lifted a skillet out of the cupboard and dropped it on the stove with a bang. "But there's no way to prove it's Jimmy in the video. Investigators might question him, on suspicion, probably at his home while sipping cognac—he has friends on the force—but no arrest will be made without evidence."

"There has to be something in that video," Brody said. "Some small clue that—"

"Involving the authorities is a dangerous move, with little chance of success. It will only frustrate Jimmy, and then he'll do something worse to Molly."

"Kill her?"

"Not right away. She's his bargaining chip, but there's still lots he can do." Lola sprayed oil into the skillet and cranked the heat. "Eventually he'll tire of hurting her. *Then* he'll kill her. And then he'll come at me the old-fashioned way."

Brody stared at her, dark pouches beneath his eyes, his mouth slightly open. He had the hollow, dead look of a prisoner of war: a boy whose world has been upended, the few good things he had known tipped out.

Lola went to him, one hand on his face—which was cold, so cold—her forehead touching his.

"I'm going to take care of this," she promised him.

"Okay." A weak, cracked word.

"I told you," she said, "that when Jimmy played his hand, I would respond. And that's exactly what I'm going to do."

"I'm coming with you."

"I know."

"I'm going to kill that son of a bitch." Brody started to cry and she lifted him into her arms and held on tight. She felt a fluttering in her own chest but pushed it away.

"Listen to me, Brody—"

"*Kill* him."

"Listen: I have a plan, and it *has* to go off without a hitch." She held him at arm's length and drove her gaze deep into his. "I need you to do exactly what I say, when I say. Do you understand?"

A vague response.

"Do you *understand*?"

"Yes."

"Good." Lola lowered him onto his seat and returned to the skillet. "We leave in a few hours."

...

They drove into Lone Arrow proper. Population 5,100. Main Street was narrow, three stoplights, lined with the usual crop of small-town stores and eateries. There were no McDonald's or

Starbucks. Savior came by way of the First United Methodist Church and the Bald Eagle Shooting Range.

Lola pulled her pickup into one of the spaces in the range's lot. It was a low-key establishment, with neat white lettering across the brickwork and two signs in the glass door. One read: NO MINORS UNLESS ACCOMPANIED BY AN ADULT, and the other: NO ALCOHOLIC BEVERAGES OR DRUGS PERMITTED ON THIS PROPERTY.

She said, "I'm going to do everything I can to keep you from pulling a trigger. You might have to, though. It's a good idea for you to know how."

Brody nodded, staring straight ahead.

"This place is better equipped than it looks. Fourteen lanes, good ventilation. Best of all, it has a tactical area, with cover and moving targets. The local police use it for training."

"Okay," he mumbled.

"I can't teach you much in the time we have." Lola shook her head. "You'll be as green when you come out as when you go in. Just a different shade of green. That's about the best I can do."

They got out of the truck. Lola lifted a carryall of firearms from the backseat: the MMR, her Baby Eagle, the Glock 42. She glanced across the street and saw a silver Nissan Maxima pull up outside Bricker's Hardware, a single male occupant, red goatee and a ball cap.

"Just put Jimmy in front of me," Brody mumbled. "I only need one shot."

"If only it were that simple," Lola said. "Come on."

...

They started on the lanes. A crash course in pistol shooting. Lola showed him arm and hand position. "Push out with your shooting hand, pull back with your support hand. Same mechanic as with the rifle; think of your right arm as the buttstock . . ." She helped with his trigger control. "Don't jerk the trigger. That will upset your aim. You want a nice, smooth motion. That gun should surprise you a little every time it goes off . . ." She explained the importance of sight alignment. "See the target, but focus on the front sight. I mean *really* focus. There's a magic point where everything on the periphery melts away, then you'll keyhole every shot . . ." Brody put round after round down the range, and Lola helped him make adjustments until his groups came back tight.

"Good," she said, showing him a target where every hit but one was within the inner ring. "I guess the apple doesn't fall far from the tree."

This earned a thin, wavering smile.

They proceeded to the tactical area, where Lola showed Brody cover techniques, how to shoot from prone and kneeling positions, and how to quickly transition from pistol to rifle and back again. Man-shaped targets swooped and popped up. "Same basics as stationary shooting," Lola instructed. "Focus on that front sight post. Smooth trigger pulls. But track the target through the shot, even after you pull the trigger." Brody missed and missed again. "You need to adjust your lead," Lola said. "Your shots are late. Think about angle, distance, and speed. That's a calculation you need to make instantly, and no two shots are the same."

Brody missed.

"Sight alignment. Smooth tracking."

He missed.

"You're jerking the trigger."

Brody clipped targets. He hit shoulders and thighs.

"Better. Try again, starting from cover. And think about your lead."

Six hits to center mass. Two to the head.

"Attaboy."

The hours ticked by. Two and then three. They took a short break, then headed back to the lanes.

"I don't know," Brody said, flexing his right hand, rolling his shoulder. "My fingers are killing me. And my *arm* . . ."

"What are you going to do if you take a bullet to the shoulder?" Lola asked. "Give up? Curl into a ball and hope the enemy doesn't see you?"

"No, I . . ."

Lola popped the top two buttons of her shirt and pulled it open enough to expose a knot of scar tissue on her left shoulder.

"Little present from Marco Cabrini," she said. "Joey's old man."

"You told me you got that scar falling out of a tree."

"Something else I lied about." She shrugged and buttoned up. "Let's keep going."

...

They shot side by side for fifteen minutes, then Lola handed Brody the MMR and two boxes of ammo.

"Switch it up," she said, removing her ear protectors. "Apply everything I've shown you. I want to see some tight groups when I get back."

"Where are you going?"

"I've got a little business to take care of."

She left the Bald Eagle via the back door and cut across the Dollar Tree lot to Station Road, which she followed north for two blocks, then took Main west, then Vincent Street south, approaching Bricker's Hardware from the other direction. The silver Nissan was still parked outside. Lola crept up on the passenger side, opened the door, and jumped in.

"Hello, Eddie."

Within one second she had the muzzle of her Baby Eagle tucked beneath his rib cage and she pressed hard.

"Oh fuck," he gasped, and then, thinking clearly, "I call Jimmy every hour. If he doesn't hear from me, he'll hurt the girl."

"Hurt her, yes. But he's not going to kill her. Not yet." She pressed even harder with the gun and he winced and shrank against the driver's door. "I think a little more pain is an acceptable trade for running a bullet through your internals."

"Fuck."

"I don't *want* to shoot you, though. Because you're a goddamn chickenshit asshole, and I derive no pleasure from shooting goddamn chickenshit assholes." She started to twist the pistol. He groaned and dribbled. "But, you know, if I *have* to . . ."

"Chrissakes," Eddie snorted. "What's this about?"

Lola smiled. "It's about you giving me what I want."

He breathed hard and a section of his false goatee came unglued. Sweat ran from beneath his ball cap.

"What *do* you want?" he hissed. "Just fucking tell me."

She told him.

...

Lola returned to the range to find Brody stripping the MMR and returning it to the carryall.

"Ran out of ammo," he said.

"Good." She nodded. "Any kills?"

"Just the same one," he said. "Over and over."

...

It was almost six P.M. by the time they got back to the farm. Brody took Advil for his shoulder and for everything else that ached.

"Grab whatever you need," Lola said.

They loaded up the truck and headed east.

CHAPTER TWENTY-FIVE

They drove more than two hundred miles that evening, listening to the drone of the engine and nothing else. They were trapped with their imaginations. And maybe they deserved that, Brody mused. They had each played a part in putting Molly where she was. They should each conceptualize what she might be going through.

Brody distilled every harrowing thought into gasoline and dripped it into a bottle inside him. By the time they reached the Omaha city limits, that bottle was three-quarters full. He didn't know if he had the ability to do what needed to be done, but he for damn sure had the fuel.

...

An imperfect moon watched them over the Missouri River, into Iowa, then shut its eye behind a lid of soft cloud. Soon after, Lola exited the interstate and pulled up outside a hotel. It wasn't much, but it was multiple stars better than anything Brody had stayed in with Molly.

"I'm not tired," he said. "We should keep going. I'll drive."

"We've got nine hundred miles of interstate ahead of us," Lola said. "We need to rest."

She got out of the truck, stretched, grabbed her bags from the backseat—including the carryall filled with weapons. They were all in there: the pistols, the rifles, even the shotgun from the barn. Along with the sawed-off strapped beneath the dash, they were considerably armed.

Brody grabbed his own bag—he'd ditched the replica; the time for nonlethal had passed—and walked with his mom toward the hotel entrance.

"What do you need me to do?" he asked.

"Huh?" Lola rubbed her eyes.

"You said you had a plan, and that you need me to do exactly what you say, when you say." Brody winced as he heaved his bag onto his right shoulder. "What is it?"

"Right." She lowered her gaze and stepped ahead of him. "I'll tell you when we get there."

...

Despite the world and all its cruelty, and the bleak industry of his imagination, Brody fell asleep within seconds of his head touching the pillow. His dreams were as deep and quiet as the ocean floor.

They were on the road by six, after removing a skin of ice from the truck's windshield. One quick stop for gas, another for breakfast—McDonald's drive-through, convenience over nutrition. Brody's appetite was surprisingly lively. He wolfed all of his and finished what his mom couldn't.

"Still hungry?" she asked. "We can hit another drive-through."

"I'm good for now," Brody said. "Let's keep going."

They rolled east, into the new day, watching the red seam ahead of them first crack, then bleed, then spread into a dramatic apricot sunrise. Lola flicked the radio on, skipping through stations until she found something that rocked.

"That's some sunrise," she said.

With no delays, they would roll into Pennsylvania, and onto Jimmy's turf, sometime around eight P.M. If his mom's mysterious plan didn't work, he might be sleeping with the fishes by eight-thirty, making this the last sunrise he'd ever see.

"It's beautiful," he said.

"I watch the sun come up most mornings," Lola said. "I always take a moment, you know, just to breathe it in. And I still can't look at a sunrise without thinking about your dad. It was his favorite time of the day."

"I didn't know that."

"It's true." Lola nodded and cracked a faint smile. "Every two or three weeks we'd wake early, drive to the High Bridge in St. Paul, and watch the sun come up over the city. My memory is that it was always spectacular—the way it reflected off the high-rises downtown and shimmered on the Mississippi—but that might just be the way I choose to remember it. We sometimes skew our memories to suit us, right?"

"I guess so," Brody said.

"It was probably cloudy and cold, and I was probably cranky, pregnant, and desperate to pee. But in my mind"—Lola tapped her right temple—"it was always perfect."

Brody settled back in his seat, momentarily at peace. Maybe it was the sunrise coupled with the music, or the knowledge that they were on their way to ending this, whatever "the end" might mean. But he thought it had more to do with Lola—this new glimpse of her spirit and tenderheartedness. For the first time in years, he was beginning to feel like he had a mom.

"I have a lot of good memories," he said. "I don't think any of them are skewed."

"Like?"

"Like our camping vacation at Crow Wing Lake—"

"When your dad went fishing and capsized the kayak."

"Oh God, and that *storm*." Brody puffed out his cheeks. "That shit was biblical. Then there was the Christmas we all went carol-singing dressed as snowmen—"

"And snow*women*."

"Right, and nobody knew who we were. I don't think we got through one carol without laughing our asses off."

"Yeah, that was a good time."

"And remember when our TV broke, and we put on our own production of *The Simpsons*?"

"You stole the show," Lola said. "You were a great Bart."

"We were all great."

Lola smiled, tapping her thumbs on the wheel as the radio played. Brody looked out the window and lost himself to the past—to good memories and bad. He indulged them all, though; he wasn't running from anything today. The scenery flashed by. Flat farmland. A river. A water tower. More and more farmland. Brody finally snapped back to the present when a fleet of hot-air balloons drifted over the interstate, low enough to hear the roar of their burners.

Lola must have snapped out of her memories, too.

"That was the happiest I've ever been," she said.

Brody turned to her, expecting to see her usual noncommittal expression, but there was more now: a depth to her eyes, a trembling in her jaw, a crimping of her brow. It was as if her tough exterior layers were peeling away, revealing the hesitant, more tender person beneath.

"If I could go back to any time in my life," she continued, "it would be then, with you, Molly, and your dad."

"Really?"

"No doubt about it." She gripped the wheel firmly. Maybe her hands were trembling, too. "I had a difficult childhood. It was better with Grandpa Bear, but it wasn't normal. And Vince . . .

I was happy with him, but we were working for Jimmy, and that was not a good scene. The last twelve years have been lonely, sometimes fulfilling, but rarely happy. And then there was Natalie Ellis, the opposite of Lola Bear, with her reusable grocery bags and rusty minivan, the years of changing diapers, baking muffins, the PTA meetings, the Little League baseball games and swimming lessons. Of all the lives I've lived, that was by far the happiest."

Brody said, "If this ends well, maybe we can start again. The three of us."

Lola nodded, but flinched at the same time. Perhaps it was the sunlight in her eyes.

"I've endured some terrible things," she said. "I've encountered very bad people, lived through years of isolation, been pushed beyond my endurance. But leaving my family was the hardest thing I've ever had to do. That night, when I kissed you and Molly goodbye, thinking I would never see you again . . . I can't even put into words how much that broke me inside. And I've never been *un*broken since."

Another layer lifted away and now Brody thought she might cry (a phenomenon he'd never seen, not even when she was Natalie Ellis). She held the tears back, though. Her eyes were fixed dead ahead, unblinking.

"I thought about you all the time. Not just big stuff like school and relationships, but the little things, too: what time you got up in the morning, which superheroes were your favorites, if Molly still liked chocolate milk on her Cheerios." She pressed her lips together and drifted into the past again, but only for a moment. "I contemplated going home to you—three, four times a day I'd think about it. I even packed a bag on one occasion. I couldn't do it, though. I just couldn't put you into that kind of danger. If I'd known, of course, that Jimmy would find you anyhow . . ."

The interstate got tighter as they approached Des Moines. The landscape barely changed, though: a deep rolling green on both sides, punctuated by blue road signs and off-white buildings. The radio signal swam in and out. Lola hit scan a couple of times, found nothing to her taste, so shut it off.

"I was always a quiet kid. Not much of an ego, never really open with my emotions." Lola shook her head. "That changed, somewhere around ten or eleven years old."

Brody thought of Mav Hamm, the first to be introduced to Lola's ego.

"I developed strength, determination, and feelings," she said. "But I always felt divided—*torn*—between that sad, emotionally repressed little girl and the fierce, ambitious woman she became. This is how I've lived, and how I've made decisions. I didn't always make the right ones, but when it came to my family, I always tried."

A hawk circled above the interstate, then cut away to the north, where heavier clouds had gathered. It would rain before long. Lola looked in that direction, drumming one hand lightly on the wheel. Brody heard the quiver on her breath.

"I'm sorry, Brody, for bringing you into a life you don't deserve, and then running away from you. I'm sorry that all my shadows found Molly and your dad. And Renée. Poor, sweet Renée." A hitch in her breath. She blinked her cold, dry eyes. "I can't undo the suffering or make anything right. All I can do is stop the shadows, put an end to the pain."

"We'll get Jimmy," Brody said. "He'll pay for every horrible thing he's ever done, not just to you and me, but to everybody."

A shallow smile from Lola. "You've got some grit, son. I'll give you that."

"It's mostly rage," Brody said. "If this truck breaks down, I'll grab the guns and *run* to Carver City, and nothing will stop me."

The truck didn't break down. It rolled smoothly east, through Iowa and into Illinois, where they stopped to refuel and grab a bite to eat. Brody reflected on his recent trip to the Prairie State with Molly, how they'd staggered through the doors of the New Zion Baptist Church with gospel music ringing, and the Reverend Wendell Mathias had offered his hand.

It had been a hard journey, and it was about to get harder, but there'd been hope along the way, and kindness. Rare points of light in a cripplingly dark tunnel.

A hard rain followed them into Indiana. Lola worked the wipers. She didn't slow down. Understandably, their conversation got thinner as they chalked up the miles and the reality of what they were driving toward took hold. Brody closed his eyes and found a point in his rage—a bright, burning coal—that he could hold on to. He imagined that coal igniting a fire that started out small, but soon spread and set everything burning. With this in his mind—and with the lulling rhythm of the truck—he fell asleep.

It must have been a deep sleep, because it was dusk when he stirred and a nearby road sign revealed they were forty miles from Cleveland, Ohio, which put them about two hundred miles— and three hours—from Carver City.

Also, they'd parked, and Lola wasn't in the truck.

Brody sat up, wiping his eyes. He looked blearily through the fading light and saw they were in a rest area. His mom sat on a bench facing the interstate. He couldn't be sure, but it looked like she was crying.

...

She pulled a shirtsleeve across her cheeks. Her rounded back bobbed and trembled. Brody approached slowly, knowing she wouldn't want him to see, but wanting her to know that he cared. He got to within fifteen feet and was about to speak when she beat him to it; she knew he was there, even without turning around.

"This was supposed to take two minutes," she said, watching the traffic rush by. "Just a brief spell, alone, with my thoughts. But it's been ten minutes and I'm *still* having that spell."

Brody pulled level with the bench. Even in the dull light he saw that her eyes were red and wet.

"I don't cry," she said, giving her head a little shake. "This is . . ."

"It's okay," Brody said. He sat beside her and looped an arm over her back. Such a simple thing, really—the act of reaching out and offering comfort. She had comforted him so often over the past few days. Now it was his turn, and it felt big and wonderful and not simple at all.

She leaned into him, her head on his shoulder. Cars and trucks zipped along the eastbound lane, a thousand lives moving at sixty miles an hour, each multifaceted, with challenges, burdens, and travails. Although none, Brody surmised, were quite like theirs.

Lola wiped her face, studied the tears on her fingers, as if evaluating their rarity. The trees around them rattled their naked branches.

"I'm not going to make it out of there," she said.

Brody considered her skill with firearms. He'd watched her at the range as she racked up headshots on moving targets—with zero effort, it seemed. He recalled how she'd tackled him on her driveway. One moment he was staring at the farmhouse, wondering if he had the right place, and the next he was flat on his back with her knee planted on his chest.

"You will," he said, and he believed it.

"I'm not what I used to be. Nothing like. I'm older. Slower." She wiped more tears away. "And I'm scared."

"I know. And that's okay."

Lola sat up, her eyelashes heavy and dark, her shoulders low. Brody rubbed her back and she looked at him gratefully.

"I can't say I'm glad you came, Brody," she said, and a sad smile played across her face. "Except I *am*. I wish the situation had been different, of course, but seeing you again has lifted my lonely old heart."

They embraced warmly and with meaning. Lola sighed, kissed the top of his head, and stood up.

"Okay," she said. "Let's go end this."

...

They crossed into Pennsylvania a few minutes shy of seven P.M., Lola's home state and the one place in America she had vowed never to return to. She followed the turnpike to Interstate 79, then cut south toward Pittsburgh. The darkness felt different here, she thought. The open skies of Nebraska allowed for a nighttime that breathed. Here, it felt crowded and ugly, or maybe that had more to do with the individual she was going to see.

An hour outside Carver City, Lola veered off-route and pulled into a hotel parking lot.

"We're not stopping, are we?" Brody asked.

"No," Lola said. "I need to do something."

"Here?" Brody shook his head. "Can I help?"

"It's a female thing," Lola said.

She got out of the truck, walked across the parking lot, and into the hotel. It was not grand, but it had a waiting area with comfortable seats and reasonable privacy. She sat down, took out her cell phone, and brought up the information that Eddie the Smoke had provided while she had the muzzle of her pistol pressed into his ribs.

A telephone number with a western Pennsylvania code.

She started dialing but hit the wrong digit and had to restart, not once but three times. Deep breaths. Composure. She tried again and completed the number. A chill laddered her spine as she brought the phone to her ear.

He answered on the second ring. His voice was as stale and suffocating as the air from an old grave.

"I've been expecting you," he said.

"Hello, Jimmy," she said.

...

The final hour of their long drive passed in silence. The tension was too thick for conversation. Even breathing was difficult. Brody focused on that single burning coal, and the fact that, within hours, this would all be over. All the running. All the bloodshed. Lola reflected on her childhood, and how wonderful it had sometimes been to feel nothing.

The miles ticked by. The guns rattled on the backseat.

They soon saw the burnt fog of light pollution hanging over Carver City.

CHAPTER TWENTY-SIX

Thousands of dreams. Thousands of miles. Hundreds of thousands of dollars. And blood, of course. Gallons of blood. This was what had filled the valley between him and Lola Bear. A broad valley, but he had built his bridge one piece at a time. He had persevered when the wind howled and the storm raged. And he had crossed.

Jimmy sat in the front office of his Carver City warehouse. He'd owned this place for thirty-three years. Its location—behind the rail yard, and away from the other warehouses and units in the industrial zone—made it the perfect site to conduct business. Most of that business was legitimate, but it had stored and shipped out plenty of contraband over the years, and any number of corpses packed into barrels of sodium hydroxide—the last being Renée Giordano's. He sat with his right leg twitching, his jaw anxiously clenched. The only light came from the warehouse floor, and it shone through the office glass, just enough for Jimmy to see the scars on his hands. If he were to strip naked, he'd see the other scars—these disfigurements he'd carried. An indignity, but a mere gloss over the real wound, the one inside, the one that still bled.

"Even dogs run away," he whispered.

The clock on his cell phone read 20:11. Forty-seven minutes since Lola had called. Forty-seven minutes of nervous excitement and deep distrust. He'd vented and preened. He'd shadow-boxed and prayed. A pinkie nail of coke—just a little bump—had aligned his self-control.

The bitch was coming.

328 | Rio Youers

All quiet on the warehouse floor. It ordinarily functioned around the clock but there were no employees tonight. Only soldiers, eleven of them (he'd drafted some extra muscle for this—he wasn't going to fuck it up), armed with machine pistols and AR-15s. There were more outside, some equipped with riot gear. He felt a strong sense of déjà vu, but the outcome would be different this time around.

The quiet lasted a moment longer, then Jimmy heard the hectic approach of a vehicle. Headlights splashed through the open bay door as Blair's SUV pulled to a hard stop outside. She cut the engine and got out. Remarkable Blair, who'd delivered on her promise. Implacable Blair, who wouldn't stop until the job was done. She entered the warehouse, passing in and out of the shadows. Her expression was harsh and focused. She had a .45 on each hip and a bandolier across her chest loaded with throwing knives.

Jimmy relaxed in his seat as she entered the office, to give the impression of cool. Everything inside him jumped, though.

"Got a call from Jared: a half-ton Sierra with Nebraska plates was just spotted on Corporation Boulevard. Eddie the Smoke confirmed it's her." There was no air of smugness about Blair. She was all business. "ETA is ten minutes, maybe fifteen if she catches all those red lights on Franklin."

Jimmy linked his fingers—cool, oh so cool—and asked, "Are you ready?"

"The guys are taking up position now: ten flanking the approach, four on the roof. There'll be two on you, and I'll fill in any gaps." She looked at him carefully. "Are *you* ready?"

"Nobody kills her," Jimmy said. It was an answer of sorts.

"Everything south of the knees," Blair agreed. "If that's what it comes to."

Jimmy licked his lips. Snapshots from a hundred dreams flooded his mind, all violent, all beautiful. "I'll take her hands tonight. Tomorrow I'll take her feet."

"You can take whatever you want."

He stood up, feeling a hundred feet tall, as if he might smash through the office ceiling, up through the warehouse roof, and stand like a giant over Carver City.

"Get the cripple," he said.

...

Carver City had been a benign commuter town until the western Pennsylvania mob gave it a face-lift. Rudy Tucoletti—who controlled the city until his death in 1989—encouraged multi-family housing and retail development, which escalated industry of a different nature. "Americans love waffles," Rudy used to say. "But we also love drugs and guns." Rudy had a lock on these, too (always kicking up to Don Esposito), and the inevitable rise in crime offered lucrative extortion opportunities.

Jimmy built on this during his brief tenure, and twenty-six years later—like Jimmy himself—the scars remained. Carver City held the dubious distinction of being the second most dangerous city in Pennsylvania, with a violent crime rate of 1,622 per 100,000 residents.

"You used to live here?" Brody asked, looking at the gray brick buildings and boarded-over windows, the overpasses sprayed with graffiti, the trash-lined streets. "Jesus, it makes Rebel Point look like Disney World."

"I *operated* here," Lola said. "I lived in Greensburg. A much nicer city."

They drove through the downtown core, where Brody saw

the hunched shape of what might once have been a picturesque neighborhood. There was a colonial-style post office, an old movie house called the Fortuna, a broad park with two base-ball diamonds and a water fountain. It was all run-down now. The cheerless streets were peppered with FOR LEASE signs, dive bars, and pawnbrokers. Call girls paraded beneath the Fortuna's cracked marquee.

"How far is Jimmy's house from here?" Brody asked.

"We're not going to his house," Lola said.

East off Main Street, and here were the fruits of Rudy Tuco-letti's labors: strip malls, fast food joints, motels, and apartment buildings. Police cruisers prowled like sharks in shallow water. The industrial zone was beyond this, a nest of factories and ware-houses, with a four-track railway running in and out, and smoke-stacks pumping refuse into the night sky.

"Where the hell are we going?" Brody asked.

Lola didn't respond. She bounced the truck across a scrub lot and veered onto a road with flex units on one side and loading docks on the other. This intersected a narrow lane that paralleled the length of a rumbling, smoky factory. Lola followed it around the back, then turned onto a gravel track marked EMPLOYEE AND DELIVERY ENTRANCE ONLY. There was a deserted rail yard to the left, enclosed by a sagging chain-link fence. Empty boxcars sat in the darkness. To the right, a posse of transmission towers stood protectively around a bleak, humming substation.

Lola drove slowly down the middle of the track. Vehicles had been parked along both sides. Halfway down, she brought the truck to a stop but kept the engine running. The headlights picked out the exterior of an isolated warehouse fifty yards away.

"Mom?" Brody asked, his voice cracking. "What's going on?"

She looked at him through a mask of fear and sadness—the

face of a woman who has resolved to take a long, hot bath with a razor blade. "You said it yourself," she said. "I'm either your savior or your sacrifice. And I'm too old to be your savior." She grabbed her phone from where she'd slotted it in the cupholder, pulled up her recent calls, and tapped the number at the top of the list.

Brody heard the ringing tone through the phone's earpiece. It was picked up quickly, although the person at the other end was content to let Lola speak first.

"I'm here," she said.

"I know," came the reply.

Floodlights flared above the warehouse's bay door. A second later, a battalion of Jimmy's goons emerged from behind their parked vehicles and surrounded the truck with weapons raised.

...

Brody counted ten mean-looking guys, with ten very serious guns. Joey—the meathead he'd one-inch punched in Bayonet— was on the left side, staring at him down the barrel of an AR-15. He was not acting this time.

"Jesus Christ." Brody's skin crawled, his muscles contracted. He was vaguely aware of the guns on the backseat, but knew if he lunged for one of them, Jimmy's guys would turn his mom's truck into a cheese grater.

What was the point of those guns if *this* was the plan? Or the time he'd spent at the range? *I'm going to do everything I can to keep you from pulling a trigger*, Lola had said. *You might have to, though. It's a good idea for you to know how.*

But a better idea, apparently, to just give up.

The bay door rolled open, spilling more light into the loading area. Molly limped onto the dock. She was being bolstered from behind by Blair, who held a pistol to her head. Seeing Blair again triggered a fresh rage inside Brody. It was like a shock wave, starting in his gut and radiating outward. Molly was the nullifier; if she hadn't been here, Brody would have erupted.

Two armed thugs followed. Leo—the other bozo from Bayonet—was one of them. Then came the star of the show. Jimmy Latzo, dressed in a sharp suit, his hair immaculately combed. He had a cell phone pressed to his ear.

"Welcome home, Lola," he hissed.

...

Lola tapped the mute button on her phone and turned to Brody.

"I told you," she said, "that I have a plan, and that I need you to do exactly what I say, when I say."

"I remember," Brody murmured.

"So here's what I need you to do." The humanness she'd displayed earlier was absent now. This was cold Lola. Machinelike Lola. "I need you to get Molly, and then get the hell out of here. Don't look back. Do *not* go to the police. There's not a cop in Carver City who'll come out here tonight, anyway. And you'll only put yourself back on Jimmy's shit list."

"You're giving up?" Brody said.

"You're free now," Lola said. "Both of you. Go back to Nebraska. The farm is willed to you, Brody. You and Molly. Look after it."

"I don't want the farm, I want . . ." He had no words. The air had been robbed from his lungs. He screwed his eyes closed and managed, "I want the three of us. *Together*. Riding the horses. Feeding the goddamn chickens."

"That's not going to happen."

Jimmy's voice came through the earpiece. "Get out of the truck, Lola. Hands in the air. Try anything stupid and I'll have Blair put a bullet in this little cunt's ear."

Lola unmuted the phone and spoke into it. "I'm not moving until my daughter is sitting in the backseat. You want to try shooting me out of here, go ahead."

Jimmy lowered the phone and said something to Blair. After a moment, she nodded, said something back. Her gun never left Molly's temple.

"This is how it's going to work," Jimmy returned, his voice clear in the stillness. "You're going to send your boy out to get her. While he's doing that, my men will remove any guns you're carrying from the equation. It's better for everyone that we don't have any nasty surprises."

"I agree," Lola said.

"Then your kids *slowly* get into the truck, while you *slowly* get out. My men will pat you down—again, no surprises—and the little tots drive away." Jimmy growled contentedly. Even this came through the earpiece. "Everybody's happy. Except you, Lola. You most certainly will *not* be happy. But you know that, don't you?"

"Let's do this," Lola said, her voice remarkably calm. She killed the call and tossed her phone into the cupholder.

Blair started to walk Molly toward the truck.

"Go get your sister," Lola said.

"Mom, I—"

"*Now*, Brody. You said you'd do exactly what I need you to do. This is what I need. So *do* it."

Brody felt something tear inside him. It was small, but vital. A connection between his heart and brain. Or his body and soul. It spilled emotion instead of blood: anger, grief, fear, sadness, confusion, relief, disappointment. A copious flow. He reflected on his mom's rare show of emotion—how she'd cried at the side of the road. And *this* was the reason why: because she was quitting, throwing in the towel, giving up.

"You can't do this," Brody whispered. "You can't let Jimmy win."

"Jimmy always wins."

"He killed Dad. You remember him, right? Ethan Anthony Ellis. You had two kids with him. Used to watch the sunrise together."

"Brody—"

"And Renée. Oh Jesus, she was so sweet and kind. And Jimmy killed her—just fucking *killed* her."

"Right, and I am not going to let him kill you." Lola's voice remained calm but there were sparks in her eyes. "This is the only way, Brody. Look out the window: sixteen armed guys *plus* Blair, who equals at least another five—"

"Sixteen?" Brody frowned.

"Ten surrounding the truck. Four on the roof. Two with Jimmy."

Brody looked at the warehouse roof and saw the outlines of four gunmen.

"We can't beat them all," Lola said.

"But if we'd planned something, hit them by surprise—"

"You're inexperienced," Lola said. "I'm old and slow. This was never a fight we could win."

"But I was willing to die trying."

"Right. You'd be dead, then Jimmy would kill Molly, too. And I can't let that happen." She took a deep breath—as steady as her voice—and placed one cool hand on his face. "I left you twelve years ago to get you out of danger. I'm doing the same thing now."

Blair had walked Molly one-third of the way toward the truck and stopped. Her eyes—they were different shades of brown, Brody remembered—were narrowed, ready for anything.

"Go get your sister," Lola said again.

Brody nodded, and memories skated briefly through his mind: the old days with Mom, Dad, and Molly—magical Christmas mornings, camping at Crow Wing Lake, carol-singing dressed as snowmen. And more recent times, from their long conversations in the spare room to her teaching him how to load a fifteen-round mag.

He looked at her, his mouth open, and he was about to say that he didn't want to lose her again, then he bled out. No memories. No emotions. Only numbness.

He opened the passenger door and stepped outside.

...

Two armed goons advanced on him. One wore a bulletproof vest and a riot helmet. "Hands in the air," he shouted. Brody did as he was ordered. The other gunman turned Brody around and pushed him against the truck. His hands were everywhere: in Brody's crotch, around his ankles, down both sides of his rib cage. He turned Brody again and frisked his front.

"Clear."

The goon in the riot helmet shoved Brody ahead of the truck. "Get moving." Brody reeled and fell to one knee. "Up. Get up." Brody got up. He started walking toward Blair and Molly. The goon followed, urging Brody along with the muzzle of his AR-15.

Blair gave a signal. Three more gunmen moved on the truck. They checked the cargo bed—empty—and opened the rear doors. One of them lifted the carryall of weapons from the backseat. Lola sat behind the wheel and didn't move. Jimmy's boys emptied their bags, spilling clothes everywhere. They checked beneath the seats, the center console, the glove compartment.

"Clear."

Brody had almost reached Molly by this point. Her clothes were dirty and bloodstained, and she wore only one sneaker. A heartbreaking detail, Brody thought. She looked at him through one eye—the other was bruised closed—and spoke his name softly.

Blair said his name, too. "Heya, Bro." She pushed Molly toward him, and Brody lunged to catch her.

"Molly," he said, lifting her, holding her. "Molly, I'm sorry. I'm so sorry."

"Oh, Brody," she said, placing her hand on his face where their mom had. "None of this is your fault."

They held each other a moment longer, then Blair sneered, "So sweet," and Brody looked at her. There was no anger in his expression, only that numbness—an empty, spiritless stare. This appeared to unnerve Blair just a touch. That wily glint in her eye faded and she pressed her lips together.

Brody had no words for her, either. No breath. He simply gathered Molly closer and turned back to the truck.

"Wait," Blair said.

He stopped, looked over his shoulder. Molly stumbled against him. He propped her up as gently as he could, fixing Blair with that same numb gaze.

"You did everything I wanted you to. You've earned this . . ." Blair reached into her back pocket, took out a worn black wallet, and offered it to him. "I told you I'd destroyed it. That was a lie. One of many, as it turns out."

This earned the slightest reaction; his left eyebrow twitched. He took the wallet, let it fall open. The face on the South Carolina driver's license was his. The name on the Social Security card, and on the numerous maxed-out store and credit cards, was his.

"This isn't your problem anymore," Blair said. "Get out of here. And don't even *think* about going to the cops, or you'll be in a whole new kind of shitstorm—one even I couldn't dream up."

Brody said nothing. He pushed his wallet into his pocket, then he and Molly staggered back to the truck, stepping into the glare of the headlights like two broken characters walking into the sunset. The goon in the riot helmet followed them the whole way, his rifle unnecessarily poised.

As Brody helped Molly onto the backseat, Blair shouted, *"Okay, bitch. Out of the truck. And remember, there are seventeen guns pointed at your kids."* Brody climbed in on the passenger side as his mom stepped out on the driver's. *"Slowly. Hands where I can see them."* She didn't get the chance to raise her hands; four bruisers—two in riot gear—jumped forward. They threw her over the hood, her arms and legs spread. One of them cracked her head against the hard steel. The sound was loud inside the truck—a dull, metallic *thonk*. They frisked her forcefully, their monstrous hands probing, grabbing. As they lifted her, turned her around, Brody saw a shallow cut over her eye. Blood trickled from it, down her face, around her jawline. A single drop fell and splashed on the hood. It stood out on the silver paint with shocking clarity.

They searched her from the front, taking every opportunity to express their ugliness. One of them forced her mouth open and ran his finger around her gums, checking for a cyanide pill, Brody thought.

"Clear."

Lola was turned around and marched toward the warehouse. She had a gunman on each arm, one in front—walking backward with his rifle in her face—and one behind. In the second before being led away, she had looked at Brody through the truck's windshield.

I love you, she had mouthed.

The other gunmen fell in behind. Two of them kept their sights locked on the truck. This didn't surprise Brody; the entire switch had been executed with military precision. Except for one small detail: they'd neglected to check under the dashboard.

"Brody . . ." Molly groaned from the backseat.

"I'm here, Moll," he said. But he wasn't. Not really.

He slid behind the wheel, started the ignition, and backed away.

...

He got as far as the lane that ran beside the rumbling factory, then stepped on the brake. It was the blood—that single drop of blood on the hood. Brody couldn't take his eye off it, the way it spread as the truck picked up speed. It looked like . . . like . . .

"Brody?" Molly said. "What are you doing?"

"Can you drive?" he asked.

"Can I . . ." Molly groaned. "Jesus, Brody. My left leg's messed up and I can only see out of one eye."

That drop of blood. It looked like the bright, burning coal that Brody had forged earlier—a symbol of his rage and resolve. With this association, the coal reignited. A spark, a flame. It melted his numbness.

"You work the gas and brake with your right foot," he said, looking at Molly in the rearview. "And you only need one eye to see."

"See? Brody, let's *go*." Molly lowered her head. "Can we . . . let's please . . . let's just go."

"I can't turn away from this, Moll," he said. "It's too big. I'll never be able to live with myself."

"I don't know what you're saying," she mumbled. "I just . . . I don't."

He pulled a thin wrap of notes from his pocket, turned in his seat, and handed it to her. "Two hundred and eighty-four dollars. That's all the money we have left. It'll cover some of your meds and a new pair of sneakers. Then get yourself a bus ticket."

"Brody—"

"Go to Nebraska," he said. "Owlfeather Farm. It's just outside a small town called Lone Arrow. Will you remember that?"

"Mom's farm," Molly said. Renée had obviously told her what she'd found, probably right before Jimmy came knocking.

"It's your farm now," Brody said. He clasped her hand and smiled weakly. "You'll love it. You have horses."

"I'm not going on my own."

His eye drifted back to the drop of blood on the hood. It had lost it shape, but not its color—its *redness*. And it was no longer just his mom's blood. It was his dad's, and Renée's, and Karl Janko's. It was every drop of blood that Jimmy had ever spilled. It was every vile thing he'd done.

"You have to," he said.

"I don't know what you're planning," Molly said, grasping as he pulled his hand from hers. "But I know it's something stupid."

"Yeah, it is." He reached beneath the dashboard. "This whole thing started when I did something stupid. I guess that's how it should end."

"Please, Brody . . . don't do this."

He grabbed the sawed-off shotgun and freed it from the clips holding it in place. The weight of it in his palm, its cold metalwork and the smooth wood of its stock, stirred the newly realized hardness in his veins.

"Jesus Christ, Brody," Molly grabbed the shoulder of his leather jacket. "This isn't just stupid. It's *suicide*."

Brody shook her off, opened the door, and hopped down from the truck. The night was icy and smelled sour. Smoke from the factory billowed overhead, a dirty shade of orange.

"*Brody*."

"I love you, Molly. You're the best thing in my life by a thousand miles." Brody bypassed all the combative emotion—all the rage and grief—and gave her the biggest smile he could. "Now get out of here."

He started toward the warehouse, the shotgun clasped in one hand. Only two cartridges in the side-by-side barrels, but he only needed to kill two people.

...

Jimmy walked down to meet her, taking his sweet time, savoring every moment. His hair was now completely silver. The expensive oils he'd applied made it shine. No wrinkles across his brow or around his eyes, though. The scarring had kept his face from aging.

He stopped, looked her in the eye. They were the same height, five-foot-six. *Good for fucking*, he'd once snarled at her, laughing it off as flirtation when she knew he was being horribly serious. He didn't have fucking on his mind now, though. He curled the hard ridge of tissue that passed for his upper lip and spat in her face. His saliva was warm and it smelled and Lola didn't flinch.

"I was beginning to wonder if this day would ever come." His voice was raspier. He'd lost that Italian smoothness. Maybe his vocal cords had been damaged in the fire. "But here you are."

She said nothing.

"You have Blair to thank." He nodded toward Blair, who stood with her hands on her hips, close to her .45s—two of the many guns brought to the party. Lola thought that, if she moved suddenly, the jumpier soldiers would pull their triggers. There might even be some friendly fire. A small consolation, particularly if Jimmy got caught in the crossfire. At the very least, Lola would bleed out before he could have his fun.

"Go ahead," Blair said. "Thank me."

Lola looked at Jimmy and remained silent.

"She's like you, only better, stronger, faster." He pressed his tongue to the inside of his cheek. His eyes glowed, all but crackling. "And smarter. *Much* smarter. I'd put you in a cage with her, a fight to the death, for the sheer spectacle, but I fear it'd be over too soon."

"Oh, it would," Blair said.

Jimmy ran his palm across Lola's face, smearing the blood and spit away. "I want this to last a long, long time." He held his hand up for her to see, then licked the blood clean, not to shock her—he couldn't do that—but because he was thirsty.

"I've dreamed you," he said simply, sadly, then balled the hand he'd just licked and struck her across the jaw. He had terrific power for a man in his sixties—for a man who should have died twenty-six years ago, who'd breathed through a machine and navigated a coma. *I could never beat you,* she thought with bitterness and consternation. *I was foolish to ever think I could.*

She tried to stay upright but couldn't. The pain mapped a route from her jaw, to her spine, to her hips, then down her legs. She dropped heavily, blood leaking from her mouth onto the gravel.

This was just the beginning. There would be weeks of this. Maybe months. Lola spat more blood and sought out that desolate place inside her—that detached, solemn box she had lived in as a child—but instead found herself peering longingly down the gravel track. She frowned, then sighed. Her ground-level perspective showed her a pair of blue and white sneakers advancing behind the parked vehicles on the right-hand side of the track, moving stealthily from one to the next. Brody's sneakers, of course, because the goddamn kid didn't know when to quit.

"Fuck," she said.

No desolate place, no box. Not yet. Now she had to protect her child.

Now she had to fight.

CHAPTER TWENTY-SEVEN

Brody expected to infiltrate the warehouse, sneak between crates and boxes, avoiding surveillance, until he found Blair and Jimmy. He'd envisioned a scenario where they were in a room together, unarmed, with no means of egress. Sitting ducks. Two shots. *Boom boom*, as John Lee Hooker famously sang.

Not the case. Blair, Jimmy, and his band of soldiers were still outside, forming a loose circle around Lola. Their weapons were lowered, but that didn't mean they weren't on high alert. One small sound—a sniff, a broken twig—and those barrels would be raised. The gunmen on the warehouse roof were a bigger problem. Their vantage point offered a greater probability of Brody being spotted as he closed in. For now, all eyes were on Jimmy.

Brody's were, too. He watched as Jimmy hit his mom—a bone-jarring right hook that dropped her to the ground. The coal inside Brody flared, its heat rising. He crept forward, using the parked vehicles for cover. He'd never fired a shotgun. The one thing he knew was that closer equaled deadlier. This was likely even truer with eighteen inches lopped off the barrels.

Gravel crunched beneath his sneakers. He stopped, held his breath, counted to ten. Nobody had heard; their attention was on the boss, holding court with his cruelty. Keeping low, Brody moved to the next vehicle—close enough now to hear Jimmy's voice.

". . . if you'll scream as loud as Vincent screamed. You know, Lola, for all his toughness . . ."

There were two more vehicles parked along this side, which would bring Brody to within range of his targets—lethal range, hopefully, depending on the shotgun's spread. He had a decision to make, though. Should he use the vehicles to get closer and risk being spotted? Or break cover and take the shot now, guaranteeing the element of surprise, but sacrificing the shotgun's effectiveness?

Closer, he thought. If this was his last act on this godforsaken earth, he'd for damn sure make it count. He wanted Blair—wanted to blast the cunningness out of her eyes. But what he *really* wanted was the man who had killed his father.

". . . and I will enjoy every moment, every drop of blood . . ."

The coal burned. Brody felt it in his fingertips, in the soles of his feet. It blazed through his heart. He shifted to the next vehicle. The nearest gunman stood with his back to Brody, maybe eight feet away. Brody could lift him out of his boots with one trigger pull.

Tempting, but no . . .

Jimmy kicked Lola in the ribs—a savage, eye-watering strike—and Brody used the distraction to move up to the final parked vehicle. This was it—as close as he could get. He took a moment to visualize what he had to do.

Two shots: Jimmy and Blair.

He brought his father's face to mind, then popped up from behind the hood, raising the shotgun. Lola moved at the same time. So did one of the gunmen on the roof.

The gunman fired first. The shot was desperate and missed Brody by a few inches, but it was close enough to stagger him. He jerked the front trigger and sent a comet of lead shot into the night sky. The report was formidable. The recoil more so. It knocked Brody backward and he sat down with a thud, behind the car and out of sight.

Another round zipped through the air where he'd been standing only a second before.

"Jesus," he gasped.

All hell broke loose.

...

In surrendering, Lola's only strategy was to exhibit no emotion, show no pain, and deny Jimmy as much satisfaction as possible. It was a disappointing end for a woman once revered for her mettle, but to fight would be to lose, and the only thing worse than dying would be to award Jimmy the glory of her defeat.

This was the plan, and she'd made her peace with it. Ever since viewing the three-and-a-half-minute video that Jimmy had sent, she knew that she had to bargain for her children's safety. And what else did she have to offer? Taking Brody to the range, packing all the guns and ammo, had been a precaution. Both Grandpa Bear and Shifu Chen had taught her to always be prepared, but she didn't think a single bullet would fly.

Her thinking changed when Brody reentered the fray.

She made her move only moments after Jimmy had kicked her in the ribs. It was not the optimum time in which to initiate an attack—by God, that kick had *hurt*—but Brody had provided a distraction, a tiny window in which to operate. He emerged from behind the nearest vehicle with her sawed-off twelve-gauge in his hands, raising it to shoulder-level. One of the gunmen on the roof registered the movement and reacted quickly, getting off a shot before Brody could adequately position the shotgun. Every set of eyes turned away from Lola and toward Brody, who'd fired a shot of his own—a wild effort that threatened no one, but caused Jimmy, Blair, and a few of the soldiers to scatter. Brody teetered and dropped. Had he been hit? Lola didn't think so, and she couldn't contemplate the possibility. She had to abandon any thought or action not directly connected to amassing a body count.

Step one in that thought process was to get a gun.

In the three-second window created by Brody's distraction, she had regained her feet and scanned the environment for opportunities. The gunman to her right had curled over when the shots were fired, making his rifle difficult to appropriate. The big bruiser to her left—Scott Hauer, aka the Tucson Tank; she recognized his face from the photo on her bulletin board—had dropped to one knee. He had an M4 carbine at the ready position and a Glock 19 in an open holster. He also wore a ballistic vest, making him the perfect shield.

Lola ducked behind him, lifted the Glock from his holster. Ideally, she would take out Jimmy and Blair first, but the gunman on the roof had fired at Brody again, and three more were closing in on his position. He only had one shell left in that twelve-gauge. If they flanked him—which they would—he'd be dead for sure.

She took out the gunman on the roof. One accurate shot. The way his forehead lifted indicated hollow points in the mag. A second later, one of the soldiers advancing on Brody's position was facedown with a bullet between his shoulder blades. Two dead before they realized what was happening—before the Tucson Tank realized that his gun was being used.

Lola took aim at the next gunman approaching Brody's position. The first shot hit his shoulder. It staggered but didn't drop him. He shrieked and turned sideways. Lola fired again and the left side of his face disappeared.

Three down.

Blair—so sharp—assessed the threat and rounded on Lola, both .45s engaged, looking for a nonlethal shot. She took it: a bullet to the kneecap. Bone and cartilage exploded. Blood flew. But not Lola's blood; Blair had shot the Tucson Tank—Lola's shield—in the knee. It had the desired effect. He howled and writhed and Lola had to fight to keep him in position. Blair fired again, missing her gun hand by an inch.

Only one option: Lola put the Glock to the Tucson Tank's cheekbone and pulled the trigger. She turned her face away just in time. Blood and bone fragments sprayed her hair and the side of her throat. The Tank flopped against her, one leg twitching.

Lola heaved the corpse to its feet as Blair fired between and through its legs. Another gunman had opened fire, thudding bullets into the ground. Lola squeezed off shots of her own— two of them at Blair, who deftly rolled and found cover beside the warehouse steps. The other gunman came up on Lola's side. In his panic, or inexperience, he chose the side with the gun. She halted him with a bullet to the chest.

Lola assessed the scene, peering from behind the shattered remains of the Tank's skull. Jimmy—the sly cat—had evidently ducked into cover. Five gunmen were dead. Others were scrambling or prone. If they all shot at once, they'd tear her apart. They'd been given a nonlethal directive, though, which made them hesitate.

Her shield was a heavy son of a bitch, and slick with blood. She would have to dump it and find cover. She looked first toward the row of parked cars where Brody had toppled from sight. As she watched, the last advancing gunman—it was Joey Cabrini, she saw now—slipped behind the back of an SUV. He'd reached his target.

Back-to-back shots rang out. One of them—the first, thankfully—was a shotgun.

Cover, Lola thought. She blind-fired the Glock until it clicked empty, seven erratic shots that bought her the time she needed. She retrieved the Tank's M4 from the ground, dragged his corpse several feet, dropped it, and broke for the vehicles parked on the near side of the gravel track. Bullets followed her, chipping at the ground around her boots. She lunged for the cover of the nearest car, and that was when she was hit. Not a bullet, a blade—one of the throwing knives from Blair's bandolier. It struck her left forearm with the power and suddenness of a scorpion's sting. That little bitch really was dangerous.

Lola scuttled behind the wheel and took a moment to center herself. Bullets splashed the car and blew out the glass. She looked at the knife in her arm but didn't remove it—let it stem the blood flow. Keeping low, she scurried farther along the rank of vehicles, and blended with the shadows.

...

Gunfire cracked against the night sky and blurred the few stars. Brody's first thought was to hide beneath the SUV he'd taken cover behind. A more compelling thought—in keeping with the coal that burned inside him, and the hard DNA passed down from Lola—was to use the one shell remaining in the shotgun. Remembering his crash course at the range, he maintained a short distance from cover to increase his movement and visibility. A peek over the hood confirmed Blair was too far away and Jimmy was out of sight. Several bodies were scattered across the warehouse's frontage. He couldn't see his mom at all, then realized—to his awe—that she was using one of Jimmy's guys as a shield. All the attention was on her.

Almost all. A familiar gunman marched toward the SUV: Joey from Bayonet. His directive then had been to intimidate—to terrify. Now his intent was to kill.

Brody recalled another lesson from the range. "Keep low," his mom had said. "Make yourself a smaller target. If you can go prone, do it." Brody dropped to his knees, then slowly to his stomach. The SUV's shadow fell over him like a blanket. He brought the shotgun to his shoulder and held it firmly, remembering its bright kick.

Joey advanced. Brody tracked his position from beneath the SUV. He shut out everything else—the gunshots, the screams—and focused on Joey's combat boots, getting steadily closer. He exhaled a jerky breath and curled his finger around the rear trigger.

It happened quickly. Joey slunk around the back of the SUV, paused for a second, then jumped out. He was crouched, looking down the barrel of his AR-15, its muzzle aimed several inches too high. Brody didn't hesitate. He pulled the trigger an instant before Joey pulled his.

Joey's shot missed. Brody's didn't.

The sawed-off hammered against his shoulder and voiced a devastating report. A cloud of shot erupted from the left barrel. It severed one of Joey's legs at the knee and left the other hanging from a thick cord of fat and muscle. Joey dropped as if someone had yanked a rug from behind him. He didn't scream—he grunted, shocked and pig-like, rocking on his belly with his eyes rolled to whites.

Brody repelled all emotion: horror, guilt, disgust. This moment was about survival. Later—if there *was* a later—he could anatomize the shooting and everything associated with it. He could be human again, but right now he needed his blood to run cold.

He got to his knees, turned the shotgun around, and cracked the butt against Joey's forehead. It took three swift, fierce strikes to knock him unconscious.

Brody yanked the AR-15 from Joey's limp grasp and soldiered on.

...

Lola flared inside. She tasted the fight, the thrill, the heat. A sound like ringing crystal flooded her mind. She hadn't planned on going to war, but here she was.

The unstoppable Lola Bear, locked and loaded once again.

The three remaining gunmen on the roof were open targets. All, to their credit, had gone prone, but their little pale faces still peeked up over the edge, and that was enough. Lola squeezed the M4's trigger twice and took two of them out. She moved to another vehicle—to get a better angle, but also to create confusion as to where the shots were coming from—and took out the third.

The rooftop threat had been eliminated. The ground threat remained: at least seven soldiers. And Blair. And Jimmy. They were scattered. Some were in cover. Shots rang from multiple directions. Bullets struck the parked vehicles with hammer-like sounds. Glass exploded. Tires hissed. Lola blind-fired toward the warehouse, then moved again. She peered through the tinted window of a Chevy Suburban and noticed muzzle flash from behind the vehicles parked on the other side of the gravel track. Staccato shots, directed at the warehouse.

Brody.

"*Keep moving*," Lola shouted between shots. He was in the shadows, but if she had noticed his muzzle flash, Jimmy's guys had, too. Underscoring this logic, bullets rattled the hood and windshield of the car closest to Brody's position. Lola located the shooter. He was tucked into the deep shadow around the loading dock. She switched the M4 to three-round burst, rolled from cover, and squeezed the trigger twice. One of the six bullets found its mark. The shooter staggered from the shadows, clutching his bleeding gut. Lola switched back to semiauto, aimed, and removed a piece of his skull.

Back into cover. She moved.

Bullets continued to sting the air. The vehicles rocked on their flats, their paint jobs perforated. Another gunman broke from the shadows and charged Lola's side of the track, firing on the run. He'd clearly abandoned the nonlethal objective. Lola timed her move. She aimed through the broken windows of what had once been a Lexus and squeezed off a shot.

Nowhere near. Her support hand was weakening—that goddamn knife in her forearm, affecting her aim. She fired twice more, missed both times. Now the charging gunman—it was Jared Conte, another face from her wall of fame—had seen *her* muzzle flash and swung his rifle toward her.

She dropped just in time. Bullets sizzled over her head.

"*I've got you, bitch*," he screamed.

Lola rolled to the next vehicle along and took up a new position. Grimacing, she mounted the M4 and popped up over the hood.

Jared was no slouch. He was ready for her.

Lola's luck, her talent, whatever it was, had run out. The barrel of Jared's rifle looked enormous.

He was beaten to the trigger, though. Not by Lola, but by

Brody, who'd broken cover on his side of the track. He fired once, hitting Jared in the back. A ballistic vest stopped the bullet, but the force of it knocked him to his knees. Lola finished the job. Her left hand trembled but she was close enough that it didn't matter.

She aimed for the middle of Jared's face but got his throat. Six or seven inches low, but the result was the same.

Another dead soldier.

Lola moved into deeper cover, clutching her wounded forearm. She didn't know how many of Jimmy's guys were still in the fight, or how many rounds were in the M4's mag—assuming there had been thirty to begin with. It was not like her to lose count. Another sign of getting old.

"Head in the game," she berated herself, wiping grime and blood from her face. She needed a pistol, that much was certain, so that she could aim and fire one-handed. Maybe then—

She felt that scorpion sting again, in her right thigh this time. It rocked her on her feet, and as she tried to back away another perfectly weighted blade plunged into her right hip, deep enough to chip bone.

"Shit," Lola whispered.

Blair crouched beside the foremost vehicle, an alligator grin on her face. She'd used Jared as a distraction—hell, as a *sacrifice*— and it had worked. As Lola watched, she plucked another knife from her bandolier and flashed it through the smoky air. Lola twisted sideways and avoided it by an inch. She raised the M4 one-handed and sprayed off a few hopeful rounds. Blair rolled to her right with a nimbleness that Lola hadn't had for twenty years. She came up with both .45s in her hands but wouldn't chance the lethal shot. Instead, she weaved toward Lola, closing the distance between them with daunting speed. Lola managed to squeeze off another round—it went well wide—then Blair knocked the M4 out of her grasp. It bounced off the hood of a nearby car and dropped out of sight. Lola threw an elbow and a knee, but Blair blocked both with no real effort, countering with a front kick to Lola's right thigh. It was a deliberate, exact strike that drove the knife there deeper into the muscle.

Lola folded at the knees and tumbled down a shallow embankment, stopping at the chain-link fence that separated the warehouse grounds from the rail yard. The night took a slow, frightening loop. Gunfire boomed and echoed.

Blair's outline floated on the bank above her, framed by dirty light.

"Jimmy wants you alive," she said. "But I want to give him your fucking head."

CHAPTER TWENTY-EIGHT

The caustic odor of propellant choked the air, and gun smoke drifted in white rags. Jimmy Latzo had reappeared. He stepped around the bodies of his fallen soldiers, picked up a rifle, and fired into the sky until the mag was dry.

"*Motherfuckers!*" he screamed. His eyes were broad circles, and even from a distance Brody could see the damnation in them. "*You fucking fucks. I'll fucking kill you fuckers!*"

He threw the empty rifle away, picked up another, and pumped rounds into the line of vehicles behind which Brody had taken cover.

"*Motherfuckers!*"

Brody scrambled to a different position. The visibility wasn't as good but the cover was better. Until that point, he'd primarily been laying down suppressive fire, letting his mom do the heavy lifting, but seeing Jimmy set a rock tumbling through him. Everything shook. His blood chilled. It was all he could do to keep from leaping over the cars and running at him with his gun blazing.

Jimmy emptied this second rifle, picked up another. The remaining soldiers rallied to his side—five of them in a ragged line. Two had lower body wounds. One had blood pouring down his face. They still packed firepower, though, and they could still use it. Leo Rossi—Brody's other friend from Bayonet, who'd held a gun to Molly's head—stood at the far end of the line.

Brody blind-fired to set them on their toes. They retaliated, all weapons smoking, spent shells helicoptering to the ground. Brody moved to yet a new position and braved a glance. The shooting stopped. The smoke lifted. Jimmy motioned his guys to flank the vehicles while he held the front. Brody halted them with a splash of gunfire. He hit one of them, a lucky shot, and the thug dropped, screaming, clutching his knee. It wasn't all luck, though. Leo Rossi had fired a couple of reflex shots. One went wide. The other punched through Brody's leather jacket and ripped through his side.

Shot I've been shot I've been—

The pain was like a forest fire in miniature. A raging, wicked thing. Brody hit the ground in a heap, then pushed himself against the wheel of the car. He clutched his side. Blood seeped through his fingers.

"Come on, you motherfucker," Jimmy yelled.

Brody looked at the blood on his hand, then at the AR-15. He didn't know where his mom was, and couldn't depend on her now. This was down to him. One bullet. That was all he needed. One sweet, precise shot to blow the life out of Jimmy's body.

He nodded. This was it.

Fuck you, Jimmy, he thought, and broke from cover, bringing the gun to his shoulder. He rose through a haze of pain and anger. He even *heard* it. A wild engine sound. A kamikaze cry. Leo and the other thugs faded from view. The bodies, the blood, the warehouse . . . it all faded. Only Jimmy remained.

He expanded in Brody's eye. In that second, he was the entire world.

This was Jimmy Latzo. Mobster. Torturer. The Italian Cat.

This was the man who had killed his father.

Brody locked him in his sights and pulled the trigger.

Nothing.

He pulled the trigger a second time. And a third.

Zilch. Zip. The gun was spent.

Brody sagged. His heart curled up and died. The rest of his body would follow, he thought, although he could still hear that wild engine sound, that kamikaze cry. Jimmy's guys mounted their rifles and prepared to shoot, but Jimmy raised one hand and held them.

"No," he growled. Craziness spilled from his eyes. His scars were flushed and glowing. "This motherfucker is mine."

He lifted his rifle and took aim, then a bright white light covered everything.

...

Headlights—high beam—raced toward them. The police, Brody assumed, even though he couldn't see the splashy beat of their reds and blues. His mom had suggested they wouldn't venture out here, but this much gunfire, even in Carver City, surely couldn't be ignored.

Jimmy and his goons squinted, throwing up their hands to deflect the light. Brody did, too, but not before he saw that this wasn't the arrival of Carver City's finest. It was a pickup truck. A silver Sierra 1500. His mom's truck, no less.

Molly behind the wheel.

She took the gravel track at startled-cat speed, grit flying from the rear tires, the engine—that kamikaze cry—filling the night. She didn't stop. She didn't touch the brake. Brody caught a glimpse of her—or *imagined* he did: grinning deliriously, hair hanging across the bruised side of her face, hands gripping the wheel.

Leo was the first to be hit. The grille snapped him. His face met and collapsed the windshield and he spun away over the roof—launched so high that he was the last to touch down. The next three thugs were thrown to the sides, bouncing and breaking over the gravel. One of them hit the car Brody stood behind with fatal force. The unfortunate chump that Brody had shot in the kneecap—already on the ground—was pulled into the wheel arch and dragged along until Molly had concluded her brief terror drive.

The truck jounced and slowed, its momentum influenced by these external forces. It struck Jimmy at half the speed. He rolled over the hood and along the driver's side, coming to rest several feet away. The side mirror had ripped the jacket from his body.

Molly came to rest, too. The truck slewed, coughing up a curtain of dust, and crashed into the warehouse's metal siding. Smoke boiled from beneath the crimped hood.

Brody stood for too long with his jaw hanging, blinking his wide, wondering eyes. "Molly," he finally whispered, and started toward the truck, forgetting the bullet hole in his side—remembering when the pain speared through his body.

His legs betrayed him. He dropped.

"Molly," he said again.

He started to crawl.

...

It was all sound and haze. Lola breathed gunpowder and coughed. Stars winked through the smoke, or maybe that was the pain—fierce points of light mottling her vision.

Blair placed her boot on Lola's throat and pressed down.

"I thought you were special."

Lola twisted and struck with her stronger right hand, but could get no leverage, no power. Blair smiled and held her in place.

"I was in awe of you, even though I'd never met you. I revered your talent, and urged Jimmy—who *can* be a little hotheaded at times—to tread carefully. That all seems excessive, now that I've met you." Blair exerted more pressure, grinding at the heel. "You're really quite disappointing."

The knives in Lola's forearm and hip had come out when she'd toppled down the embankment. The one in her thigh was still there, driven deep by Blair's front kick. Lola gasped, eyes bulging, and dug her fingers into the wound. She plucked at the slick handle, working it loose by fractions. Pain bolted down her right side. It took everything she had to shut it out.

"I have this clear picture of walking back to Jimmy, carrying your head by the hair." Blair grinned and held up this imaginary trophy, rolling her wrist to mimic swinging it like some gruesome pendulum. "It's such a warrior-like image, isn't it? The kind of thing that inspires myths and legends."

Lola's vision grayed, but more stars appeared. The brightest, biggest stars yet. Her chest locked, needing oxygen that wasn't there. She teased the knife out another quarter of an inch.

"I mean," Blair continued, "Jimmy would be *pissed*, and I can understand that—he's waited a long time to kill you. But oh, that *image*."

Lola pinched at the knife handle, wiggling it inside the wound. Another fraction of an inch. She almost had it in her grasp.

"I'm torn, Ms. Bear." Blair pressed with her heel, harder still. A muscle in her jaw flexed. "Although I'm glory-bound either way."

There was a rush of insistent light somewhere behind Blair, an emphatic engine sound. It was all very dreamlike . . . confusing.

Lola wondered if it was death, its brightness and roar. *Not yet*, she thought. She hadn't expected to win this war, but she still had one move left. With every scrap of spirit left in her soul, she pulled the throwing knife from her thigh, and plunged it into Blair's left calf.

Blair never saw it coming. She didn't scream or hiss, but she *did* lift her boot from Lola's throat and stagger backward, and that was all Lola needed—to be able to move, to *breathe*. If she could get to her feet, or even to one knee, she had a chance. Blair was wounded now. The playing field was about twenty years from being level, but this fight wasn't over.

Become the storm, she thought, summoning the long-ago wisdom of Benjamin Chen. But a storm would not be enough here. She needed to engulf and destroy. *Become the fire*. She needed to burn.

Lola rolled over, got her hands beneath her, and pushed herself up—first to one knee, then to her feet. Blair immediately attacked, and she was still strong. A forceful punch, a looping elbow. Lola dodged the first, half blocked the second. She was able to counter, throwing a fist into Blair's rib cage, applying everything Shifu Chen had taught her: generating power through her body, letting it amass, then directing it into the final few inches of her strike. It was not the punch she hoped for—she lacked the strength for that—but it buckled Blair nonetheless, and broke ribs. Two, maybe three.

Blair twisted away from her, dragging in hurt breaths. She held her side and snarled. Lola put the fire into her feet and kicked. Once to Blair's upper arm, again to her injured leg. Neither kick landed cleanly. The women exchanged a clumsy fusillade of fists, knees, and elbows. Blair got the better of it. She blocked two high punches, set her feet, and threw a fist of her own. It cut through Lola's defense, smashed into her sternum, and sent her staggering backward.

Stars again, bright and piercing. Lola fell against the sagging chain-link fence—it bowed beneath her weight—and barked a jagged, burning breath. With room to move, Blair seized her opportunity. She drew her .45s and aimed.

Lola leaned backward, pushed with the balls of her feet, and flipped over the fence. Bullets whizzed beneath her; Blair was still going for leg shots. What little tension remained in the fence buoyed Lola's weight and she landed on her feet in the rail yard. She turned immediately and staggered away, melting into the shadows.

The yard was dark, full of cover. Boxcars hulked in silhouette. A cold locomotive stared blindly. Lola ducked behind a concrete buffer stop, covered her mouth, and stifled a scream.

Her head cleared. Not by much, but enough to focus on her objective: add to the body count, whatever it took. The rail yard had leveled the playing field a few more degrees. Lola could use the shadows. Use her experience.

Be the fire.

She watched as Blair hopped the chain-link fence and wiped something—blood, probably—from her mouth. She still held her guns.

"Okay, you tired old bitch." Her voice carried to Lola, laced with mania. "Now we've got a fight."

CHAPTER TWENTY-NINE

Not again, Jimmy thought. *No fucking way.*

There was a bleak, watery pain in his hip. Something in there was cracked or dislocated. His left knee had been rearranged and his foot pointed at two o'clock rather than twelve. He was no stranger to pain, though. Oh no, he and pain were old compadres. Thick and thin. Ben and fucking Jerry. He dragged himself to one of the parked cars—which were supposed to provide cover for *his* fucking guys—and used it to get upright. Blood ran into his eyes. He gingerly touched his scalp and felt not hair but the top of his skull.

Not good. Not fucking good at *all*.

His left foot stabilized him, but couldn't bear his weight. He could limp, though, and did so, moving from the car to where Brad Lemke lay mumbling on the ground. Brad's legs were a mess of odd angles and sticking-out bones. One side of his face had met the gravel and been planed to a smooth red surface. His pistol was on the ground, out of reach.

"Glab-glab," Brad said. His eye locked on Jimmy, then flashed open and closed. "Glab-glab. Glab-glab."

"Yeah," Jimmy said. He bent his right knee—managed to reach down and hook Brad's pistol up off the ground. "It's all fucking bullshit."

He aimed unsteadily and shot Brad, twice, because the first bullet only clipped off one of his ears. The second was truer, though, upsetting the smooth red half of his face.

No more glab-glab for Brad.

Or for *any* of them. Jimmy looked around. Corpses everywhere.

Corpses wearing riot shields and bullet-resistant vests, carrying semiautomatic rifles. How much goddamn protection did they *need*? And yet . . . corpses. He saw Scott Hauer—the Tucson Tank himself—with one side of his skull blown away. Jared Conte was facedown in a lake of blood. Leo Rossi's spine was L-shaped and his brains were waterfalling out of his open head.

No sign of Blair. She'd gone after Lola. There'd been gunshots from that direction but Jimmy had no idea which of them was still standing. Probably Lola, given the way this whole shitshow had gone down.

This was all horribly familiar.

"Not again," Jimmy insisted, and shook his head. This wasn't over. *He* was still standing, after all, and *he* was the only one that mattered.

He could still spill some blood, and dammit, he was going to.

Right on cue: the pickup truck's door clunked open and the cripple dropped out. She stood for a moment, then collapsed to her knees. Jimmy looked at her through the blood-mask of his face, thinking that a little eye-for-an-eye action was appropriate here. He checked the pistol. Eight rounds in the magazine and one in the chamber. He could kill the bitch nine times.

Jimmy shunted the mag home and wavered toward the truck. Pain rolled through him. He'd known, and survived, worse. It wouldn't stop him now. Still some distance away, he lifted the pistol and squeezed off a shot. The bullet punched a hole through the truck's fender. The girl screamed. She tried getting to her feet, but floundered and sprawled. Jimmy fired again and lifted a cloud of grit three inches from her left hand.

"*Bitch*," he screamed. His damaged hip, and the blood in his eyes, had affected his aim. He gritted his teeth and labored closer, stomping one foot, dragging the other. Five feet from the girl—

close enough, goddammit—he took aim again, and was about to pull the trigger when two words flared at the back of his mind.

Bargaining chip.

He blinked. This was a Blair-like moment of ingenuity. If Lola was still alive, she'd likely be open to renegotiation. It was the reason this crippled little bitch was brought in to begin with. If Lola was dead, and Blair came back . . . well, shit, he would pull the trigger then. And happily.

"Get up," Jimmy sneered. He hopped the last few feet and pressed the gun to the back of her head. "Now. Right fucking now. Get up."

She didn't move. He rapped the barrel against her skull, hard enough to draw blood, and that did the trick. The girl whimpered, lifting one hand over her head, pushing herself up with the other. Jimmy helped, insomuch as he grabbed a fistful of her collar and pulled.

"Let's go. Fucking move it."

They started toward the warehouse, the girl in front, Jimmy behind. They stumbled and limped in peculiar unison.

"Look at us," he observed wryly. "Couple of hop-along assholes."

He eased her toward the loading dock steps and they struggled up slowly. Jimmy wiped blood from his eyes and fought a wave of wooziness. He could *do* this, by Christ. Just a little longer.

"Lola," he shouted, or *tried* to. His voice cracked—barely a sound came out. He moved the girl in front of the warehouse's open bay door and stepped behind her, the gun placed to her head. She gasped and squirmed.

"*Lola.*" That was better. Much louder. He spat blood, took a breath, and shouted, "*Lola Bear. I have your daughter. Come and get her.*"

His voice carried across the lot.

He'd win this war yet.

...

Brody had the perfect shot—the center of Jimmy Latzo's spine—but didn't have a gun. By the time he'd acquired one (and checked to make sure it was loaded), Jimmy had scaled the loading dock steps and positioned himself behind Molly.

Jimmy called out to Lola—a desperate, frenzied cry. Or perhaps he always sounded that way.

Raising the gun—another AR-15 variant—Brody hobbled in front of the warehouse and faced Jimmy.

"Let her go," he groaned.

Jimmy looked at him. His face was a red horror mask. A flap of skin drooped across his brow. "Get the fuck out of here, kid," he snarled, "while you still can."

"Let her *go*." Brody staggered closer, tightening his grip on the rifle. He didn't have a shot, though. Jimmy was behind Molly, with only his bloody face exposed over her shoulder. And while it temptingly resembled the center of a target, Brody's hands trembled too much to risk pulling the trigger.

"Fuck you," Jimmy hissed. He extended the pistol and fired twice in Brody's direction. Neither bullet came close. He appeared to consider another shot—his gun hand shook as much as Brody's—then thought better of it, obviously deciding it was wiser to conserve ammo.

Brody stood his ground. He had hoped to appear stronger than he was, but his trembling hands betrayed him, as did his ashen face and the blood trickling from beneath his jacket. He wouldn't pull the trigger and Jimmy knew it.

Molly squirmed and Jimmy settled her again with another dull crack from the pistol barrel. Brody's finger hovered close to the trigger.

"You want this bitch," Jimmy said. "Go put a bullet in your mommy's back. Then I'll consider it."

"Only person I'm shooting is you," Brody said.

Jimmy snorted laughter. A wet, mad sound. Blood dripped from his jaw, onto Molly's shoulder.

"Go get your mom," he said. "Tell her I'm waiting."

He ushered Molly backward, through the open bay door, and slowly into the shadows. Brody watched them disappear. He waited for a moment, trying to smother his pain and fear, then he followed.

...

Lola's experience was offset by Blair's youth, and the fact that she wasn't as badly injured. She was wily, too; Lola listened for her footfalls through the rail yard, maybe a couple of hurt, rasping breaths. Blair made no sound at all, though. She was a ghost.

Lola waited, studying the darkness. She reached and grabbed the most basic, primitive weapon: a rock. It was the size of her fist, easy to grip and swing. Blair—with her .45s—had the advantage here, too, but up close it would all be the same.

...

The front of the warehouse was bathed in light. There was some deep shadow cast by the raised loading dock, but Brody couldn't enter the bay or side doors without being seen. Jimmy was always dangerous. He might have positioned himself behind a crate, using the top of it to stabilize his aim, ready to pull the trigger the moment Brody hobbled into view.

Needing another way in, Brody moved away from the open bay door, then around the crumpled truck and along the side of the warehouse. It was darker here, but he found what he wanted soon enough: an office window. Brody tried opening it. Locked, of course. He shook off his dad's leather jacket—not without discomfort—and balled it like a mitten around his right fist. As he struck the window, he fired the rifle with his left hand, the stock tucked against his ribs—six loud shots that enveloped the sound of breaking glass.

Brody reached through the window, flipped the catch, lifted it open. He pulled his jacket on again—it was black; a good color for sneaking through the shadows—then leaned across the sill and let forward momentum carry him over, into the office. He landed on the tiles and broken glass with a crunch, clutching his side as the pain bloomed.

Getting to his feet was hard. He brought Molly to mind. And his dad. Renée, too. He held them there, poised above the burning coal like a ridge he could grasp on the updraft.

Sweat coated his body. The office rolled once—a gloomy, boxlike space with an uneven floor. Brody caught hold of the desk, steadied himself, then made his way into the warehouse proper. He heard Jimmy immediately, gasping and cursing.

Brody hugged the shadows and advanced from behind a row of crates stacked along one side, knowing he couldn't approach from the front or let Jimmy see him at all.

He needed to go past Jimmy, attack from behind.

...

Blair played the stealth game for a while, then switched her strategy, opting to draw Lola out.

"You can't beat me, Ms. Bear," she goaded, and brayed laughter—a sound full of color and confidence. "You're too slow. Too worn out. Too old."

There was a time for caution, and a time to throw down. Clearly, Lola had given her no reason to be afraid.

"Come on, bitch. Let's do this."

Lola moved, making no sound at all, relying on her experience; impetuousness was for the young. Every step was painstaking, lifting and softly placing her boots, taking an indirect route, but one that kept her hidden. She slipped between two buffer stops, crept into the shadow of a maintenance shed, crossed the tracks behind a rusty locomotive. As ever, she focused on one objective: increasing the body count. She'd lost blood. The pain was a blizzard. She still burned, though.

She saw Blair, mostly in shadow, standing on the tracks between two boxcars.

"I'm right here, Lola. Let's see what you've got."

Keep running your mouth, little girl, Lola thought. She edged closer, approaching on Blair's blind side. Fifteen yards away, she grabbed a handful of dirt and stones and threw it, not aiming for Blair, but for the boxcar beside her.

The debris struck with a rattling sound, diverting Blair's attention. Lola sprang from the shadows and attacked with the rock in her hand. She envisioned bringing it down on the top of Blair's skull and dividing it into three, drawing on an old memory featuring her stepdaddy and his spanging hammer.

Not this time. Blair heard—or maybe sensed—Lola's approach. She swiveled, avoided the downward swoop of the rock, countered with a humming fist that caught Lola square and dropped her.

"Like I said: Too slow. Too worn out. Too old."

Blair pulled her guns.

...

It wasn't all crates, shadow, and cover. There were walkways, doorways, broad lanes for forklift trucks to maneuver. Jimmy had retreated down the center gangway, shambling backward with the gun still rooted to Molly's skull. He wasn't hard to track.

"Nobody *fuuuuucks* with me," he bellowed. He'd lost his mind as well as the top of his scalp. "Dogs run the fuck away."

Brody timed his moves, shuffling across the exposed areas, crawling from one crate to the next. He dragged his feet and breathed hard. Jimmy would have heard him if he hadn't been making so much noise himself.

"Nobody. *No-fucking-body.*"

Jimmy stopped walking. There was a row of forklift trucks behind him, open walkway to his left and right. Brody didn't think he could cross that space without being seen. Molly, however, provided a distraction. She pushed against Jimmy, rolling her head from side to side, flicking her hair into his face. While Jimmy dealt with her—a third sickening pistol whip—Brody crossed the walkway and snuck in behind the forklifts. He paused to let a wagon train of hurt pass through his upper body, then limped into position, rifle raised, eight feet from Jimmy's back.

A dark thought struck him, though, and he lifted his finger from the trigger. What if he shot Molly, too? With this caliber, at this range, it was entirely possible the bullet would tear through Jimmy and hit Molly's spine, or her lung, or her heart. Even a headshot, point-blank, could deflect badly. He had to get Molly away from him before pulling the trigger.

"Nobody . . . fucking dogs."

Brody flipped the rifle around, buttstock forward. One good strike to the back of Jimmy's sick, bleeding skull would do it. He gasped and blinked through the pain, tightened his grip on the gun.

"Dogs fucking run."

Brody edged closer.

...

Lola still had the rock in her hand. She threw it without thinking, without aiming, a hopeful pitch from the ground. It had little power, but devilish accuracy, hitting Blair beneath the jaw. Blair's head snapped backward. She reeled—almost tripped over one of the rails. Lola swept with her stronger left leg. Her boot met Blair's right ankle with a vicious thud.

She swept again . . . and again.

This third strike did it. Blair gave at the knee, then hit the ground. She fired both pistols and sent two bullets to the stars. Lola scrambled to her feet and pounced. She kicked one of the guns from Blair's grasp—it spun away into the darkness—then dropped a knee onto the damaged side of her rib cage. Blair screamed. It was the first time Lola had heard that sound, and it was wonderful.

Blood trickled from the knife wounds in Lola's left forearm, her right thigh and hip. There was nothing wrong with her right fist, though. She rained two full-blooded blows into Blair's face, smashing her cheekbone, breaking her nose. Blair's mouth gaped for air. She swung the other pistol toward Lola, but Lola batted it away. It toppled from Blair's hand and rang off the rail.

"Who's worn out now?" Lola sneered. "Who's slow?"

Blair twisted and struggled, trying to regain her feet. Lola scooped up a handful of gravel from between the crossties, rammed it into Blair's open mouth, and looped a punch to the underside of her jaw. Small stones and broken teeth flew.

"Who's fucking *old*?"

Lola reached for the gun. Blair—desperately, impossibly—saw an opening. She threw a punch of her own, connecting with Lola's left forearm. It jarred the wound there, causing Lola to sprawl. Her hand came down several inches from the gun. Blair spat a cloud of grit and got to one knee. She launched a volley of blows born out of pain and the unthinkable notion of defeat. Some connected. Others glanced off Lola's arms and face. The two women fought their way to their feet, lifted on an upsurge of adrenaline and defiance.

They rose together. They fell together.

Exhausted, hurting . . . Lola dropped to her knees and Blair fell against her. She rolled away, still coughing stones—snatched the last knife from her bandolier and threw it. Lola felt the blade bite through her jacket, into her upper arm, but it didn't have the velocity to stick. It fell to the ground, small and shiny against the black crosstie.

Lola picked it up.

There wasn't much on Blair's face besides blood and pain, but Lola thought, for just a second, she saw something that might be respect. It floated out of Blair's eyes, a haunted, somewhat childlike expression. Her mouth opened soundlessly. Blood and grayish saliva drizzled down her chin.

Lola threw the knife.

She threw it from her broken childhood, from a box of muted emotions, from twenty-six years of running. She threw it for all of Jimmy's victims, who were *her* victims, too. She threw it for her children, and for the uncompromising strip of fire that best defined her soul.

The knife hit Blair in the center of her forehead and plunged to the midpoint of the handle. It went through her skull and into her frontal lobe. Blair first squinted, then opened her eyes as wide as they would go. A rill of blood trickled down the middle of her nose.

"Mizzy Bear," she said, and almost smiled.

Lola wiped her face and breathed painfully. It took several efforts, but she eventually got to her feet. She looked toward the warehouse—it was eerily still over there—then back at Blair. Such an impressive woman, but too young, too dangerous.

"You gave me one hell of a fight," Lola said.

"Mizzy Bear."

A cold breeze howled between the boxcars. The nearby factory clashed and clanged. Blair's left eye spasmed to one side and she held out her hand. Lola didn't know what to do with this gesture, and it didn't matter anyway. Blair dropped her hand a second later and fell down dead.

Lola stepped around her and picked up the .45. She knew what dead was. She'd also known the dead to come back.

"You were the best I ever beat," she said.

Lola aimed the gun, pulled the trigger once, and blew Blair's skull wide open.

...

Jimmy gesticulated as he made his deranged announcements about dogs running away, waving the pistol between Molly's skull and anywhere else. A sudden knock to the back of the head could cause him to yank the trigger. Brody had to strike at the right time.

He wasn't quiet—he wheezed with pain and nervous energy, dragging his body like a heavy sack—but it didn't matter; Jimmy was lost in his own world, waiting for his nemesis to appear so that he could exact his long-awaited revenge. His white shirt was mapped with blood—continents separated by small bodies of water. He was canted to the right, his weight almost entirely on his good leg.

"Nobody *fucks*. Dogs *run*."

Brody got to within a foot of him. Close enough to smell the blood, the heat, the madness. Tendrils of steam danced from the gap in Jimmy's scalp.

"They fucking *run*."

Not this dog, Brody thought. He waited for Jimmy to lift the pistol from Molly's head, then he struck. It was a crisp, direct hit. The buttstock met the rear of Jimmy's skull with a force that sent a recoil-like vibration through Brody's arms. The sound was appalling—a damp, toe-curling crack. Jimmy wobbled. He fired two shots. Bullets pinged off the warehouse roof.

He was a tough old cat, though, and he didn't go down. He half turned and Brody hit him again, not as hard, but it was enough. Jimmy fell but took Molly with him.

They landed in a tangle. Molly tried to separate herself, but Jimmy held tight. His eyes were mad fog lights. They flicked every which way, then found Brody and swelled. He aimed the gun and pulled the trigger.

Too close; the bullet scuffed the shoulder of Brody's jacket. He flinched, then winced—the hole in his side protested at the sudden movement. There was no chance of returning fire, not until Molly was in the clear. She shimmied and fought. Jimmy struggled to hold on to her, still waving the gun in Brody's direction. Brody took a chance. He lurched forward and smashed the rifle's buttstock against Jimmy's injured knee.

Jimmy wailed. His arms flew out to the sides and his body jumped. Another bullet sizzled from his pistol. It skimmed harmlessly away, across the concrete floor. Molly scrambled out of his orbit.

Brody flipped the rifle back around, pulling the buttstock into his shoulder and peering down sights that doubled and swam. Jimmy—the solid old bastard—rose unsteadily to one knee. He leered through his red mask and took two more shots at Brody. The first flashed past Brody's right ear, hot and loud. The second did nothing. Just a gutless click. The gun was empty.

Brody made a sound deep in his chest—a relieved sob. He limped closer to compensate for his uncertain aim. He didn't want to miss.

"You killed my dad," he whispered.

"Dogs run away," Jimmy replied with the matter-of-factness of a four-year-old. His wide, mad eyes flashed.

Brody hooked his finger around the trigger, exerted the slightest pressure, then eased off. Did he really want to kill this man? Jimmy had nothing left, after all. No gun. No mind. Furthermore, did Brody want Molly to witness it—to *see* him take a life? Something like that would leave a constant shadow. It would scar and harm, and undoubtedly cause a rift in their relationship.

He looked at her. His beautiful, strong sister, always the voice of reason and wisdom. Always his hero.

"Do it," she said.

Brody did it.

...

Three shots, to remove all doubt. The same number of bullets his mom had fired into Jimmy. Brody's were more decisive, though. One to the center of Jimmy's chest. One to his throat. One to his head.

Jimmy went down, and down Jimmy stayed.

"No more lives for you," Brody said.

The Italian Cat was dead.

Brody dropped the rifle and went to Molly. She threw her arms around him and they cried together. He didn't know if the fight was over, if their mom was still alive, or how they'd deal with the aftermath. The only certainty was that he was in his sister's arms, and in that moment, that was all he wanted.

CHAPTER THIRTY

Lola still burned, and would until she knew this was over.

She moved as stealthily as she was able, through the rail yard, then along the bullet-ridden line of vehicles on the left side of the gravel track. The only sounds came from elsewhere: the whirr of heavy-duty machinery, a loaded semi bouncing over a potholed road, the bangs and clonks from the factory. She had heard gunshots from the warehouse—and thought she'd heard Jimmy's voice at one point—but now the silence was complete.

The dead were scattered. Some lay in simple puddles of blood. Others were tangled and broken. Lola had readied herself to find Brody dead—an outcome she'd tried so hard to avoid, even to the point of sacrificing herself. When she saw her truck, though, crumpled against the warehouse's siding, her apprehension took an even darker turn: not one dead child, but two.

She looked at a row of broken bodies, including the one still under the truck. It wasn't difficult to piece together what had happened. Molly had returned, fast and furious, and taken out four, maybe five of Jimmy's guys. Lola recalled the rush of light she'd seen when Blair was standing on her throat, accompanied by a shrill engine sound. She'd wondered if it was death, and it *was*, but not for her.

Lola checked the truck. Empty. She shifted along the front of the warehouse, and here, tucked into the shadows, was her carry-all of guns. She discarded Blair's .45 and grabbed her Baby Eagle. The fire spread inside her. She thought of the last few shots she'd heard from the warehouse and imagined Jimmy standing over the bodies of her dead children.

She ascended the loading dock steps and slipped through the side door. Silence at first, and then, proceeding toward the main throughway, she heard crying. It sounded like a child.

Not Jimmy.

Lola peeked around the side of a cramped storage rack. Overhead lighting illuminated the front third of the center aisle, and there, huddled where the light ran out, were Brody and Molly.

Jimmy lay several feet away, perfectly still and unquestionably dead.

Lola had never been quick to feel emotion, but she felt something then: a thrilling and immediate jolt to her heart. It staggered and invigorated her. It extinguished the flame. She dropped her gun and moaned, took a dazed step, then broke into a weary, shambling run.

Tears flowed from her eyes. They felt good.

She stopped a little short, thinking she should give them space, give them time. They had been through so much together. They had supported one another, warred, and ultimately triumphed. This was about them, and Lola wasn't sure that she belonged. She hovered close by, shuffling her feet and blinking the tears away.

Then Molly looked at her through broken eyes. She held out her hand, much like Blair had, but Lola understood this gesture.

A different fire kindled inside her.

Lola went to her children.

...

Carver City police were no strangers to violent crime. They put their lives at risk every day, but they knew where to draw the line.

The first reports of "multiple gunshots" at Dynasty Warehousing came in at 21:01. Average police response time in

Carver City was sixteen minutes (a skewed average; it was only seven in the white neighborhoods). The first unit could have arrived on scene within this time frame, but was advised to wait for backup; Dynasty Warehousing was Latzo territory. This was gang-related, no doubt about it. Let the bullets fly, then go clean up.

At 21:29, six CCPD patrol cars and two special service vehicles rolled toward Jimmy's warehouse. A police chopper looped overhead. The news teams would undoubtedly follow.

Sergeant Maya Cornell drove the lead car. She stopped midway along the gravel track, tires throwing up dust. The cruiser's headlights illuminated the carnage.

"Jesus fucking Christ," her partner said.

Cornell nodded. "Tell the coroner he's going to need a bigger boat."

...

Fifteen minutes, give or take, since the final gunshot. Quicker than Lola expected.

"*This is the Carver City Police Department. We have all exits covered and eyes in the sky. Lay down your weapons and come out with your hands nice and high.*"

"Can you walk?" Lola asked.

"Think so," Brody replied. "Slowly."

"I'll need help," Molly said. "And I can maybe put *one* hand nice and high."

"Good enough," Lola said. She pushed herself to her feet, took several steps toward the bay door, and called out as clearly as she could: "*We hear you and we're coming out. Two females, one male. We are unarmed and in need of medical attention.*"

She helped Brody and Molly to their feet, and the three of them made their way toward the exit, each depending on the other. The light outside was hot and fierce. Lola saw the outlines of multiple police vehicles and officers with assault rifles.

"Think we can take 'em," Brody whispered.

Lola managed a tired smile. She separated herself from Brody and Molly as they emerged through the exit, raising both hands.

Six officers approached. Two held position in the loading area. Four proceeded up the steps. One of them—Cornell on her name tag, three stripes on her arm—looked at Lola and said, "What the hell happened here?"

"I'll tell you everything," Lola said, "from the comfort of my hospital bed."

Molly stumbled. Brody tried to keep her up, but they both fell to their knees. Cornell nodded. Two of the officers lowered their weapons and stepped forward to help.

A news chopper had joined the CCPD air unit. They thundered overhead. More headlights—more news crews—bounced down the gravel track. One of the cops had broken position to head them off.

Sergeant Cornell looked from the choppers, to the bodies strewn in front of the warehouse, then back to Lola.

"Who are you?" she asked.

Lola shook her head. Too many answers to that question, and they reeled through her mind, each bringing its own flame, its own strength. A lover. A mother. A wife. A granddaughter. A student. A cousin. A friend. A killer. A warrior.

She was all of them. She was every woman.

"My name is Lola Bear," she said.

EPILOGUE

MAGGIE'S FARM

(2020)

Poe was eight years old, a coal-black American saddlebred with a white brushstroke down his nose. He could rack at twenty-four miles an hour but preferred to canter, and that was fine with Molly. She guided him out of the arena, around the chicken coop and goat pen, then onto the field. A dry, used path ran toward the woods. Molly clicked her tongue, applied a brief squeeze with her legs, and Poe took his signal. He strode smoothly, his hooves tapping off a three-beat rhythm. Molly moved with him, always in control.

Alfalfa grew on both sides, knee-high and deep green. To the east, beyond Butch Morgan's fields of swaying corn, three new wind turbines reached into the Nebraska sky. They were a source of excitement and controversy among local famers; one of the first things Molly was asked to do on her arrival at Owlfeather—she was still bandaged and sore—was sign a petition against them. Her signature made no difference. The turbines were installed, and Molly didn't mind at all. She liked them, in fact, admired their quiet power and majesty. She sometimes rode Poe out there and sat listening to the lazy whoosh of their blades turning. It had a certain calm.

Today, though, she rode west, around the three-acre splash of woodland, to Assumption Creek, where Poe drank noisily. Deer watched from the opposite bank with their ears twitching. Molly kicked her heels and got moving again. She followed the creek to the ruins of the Church of the Resurrection, struck by a tornado in 2007 and yet to be resurrected. Old timbers angled toward the sky. Musk thistle grew among the pews. Beyond this the land rose modestly, then dropped away, and here the view was complete. No wind turbines or tumbledown churches. Nothing man-made for miles. Only green, steady earth and a broad strip of river, almost gold in the late sunlight.

...

She patted Poe's crest. "Good boy." He snorted appreciatively and switched his tail. Crickets hummed in the long grass, and that, for a time, was the only sound. Molly watched the river roll and lost herself to thought. She remembered Rebel Point, the police sirens, the neighbors constantly at odds, the thin curtain that separated her private space from Brody's.

She was so far from that now, literally and figuratively. Sometimes that distance took her breath away.

Poe's ears flicked, alerted to a sound from behind them that Molly, in her reverie, heard late. She turned and watched another horse canter around the church ruins. Autumn, a bay Arabian, and frequently feisty. Her rider was broad in the shoulders, wore a short beard and a white cowboy hat—a visual change indicative of the great distance that he, too, had traveled.

He pulled up beside Molly and worked the reins. Autumn flared her nostrils and champed, bumping against placid Poe.

"Whoa, girl."

Molly grinned as Brody walked a few figure eights and hushed his horse, finally getting her under control.

"What took you so long?" she said.

...

The river turned from gold to bronze, capped with silver where rocks broke the surface. The sun dropped slowly, like a hand bearing weight. A different light lined the horizon. It was beautiful. All of it.

"I was talking to Mom," Brody said.

"Yeah? How's she doing?"

"She's a little . . . *emotional*." Brody couldn't help but smile; this was not a word that had been used to describe their mom very often. "But she'll be okay."

"We'll *all* be okay." Molly gazed across the open land. "We've got this."

Brody nodded. "We'll one-inch punch it, right?"

"Always."

Their credo, still, and they embodied it, appearing basic and harmless, but packed with interior power. The press, following the shoot-out at Dynasty Warehousing (the "Second Carver City Massacre," some news outlets called it—the first being from 1993, also starring Jimmy Latzo) jumped on this: the David and Goliath angle. They knew only what Lola, Molly, and Brody had told the authorities, though, and Lola had insisted they keep everything low-key. Their line: they were victims and had acted in self-defense.

This was corroborated by the 03:31 video in which Molly was tortured, and Renée Giordano shot to death. The assailants were masked, but there was enough evidence to damn them. Molly's statement, for one. But also: the victims' hair and blood was discovered in a basement room of Dynasty Warehousing, owned and operated by Jimmy Latzo; the original MP4 video file was dug out of the hard drive of Jimmy's personal computer; forensic voice analysis matched Jimmy's voice, despite his efforts to disguise it. As if this wasn't enough, Renée's partially dissolved remains were discovered in a barrel of sodium hydroxide at a hazardous waste facility (also owned by Jimmy Latzo) two miles from the warehouse.

"Why you?" the FBI agent asked Molly after she had given her statement.

"Jimmy Latzo was after my mom," Molly replied truthfully. "I guess they've got history."

Lola downplayed this history, as well as any act of heroism.

She said: "Jimmy was convinced I had something to do with what happened in 1993. I *didn't*, of course, but I was forced into hiding—I changed my identity, my backstory. Jimmy is resourceful, though. He tracked my kids down, and after he sent that video . . . well, I went there to reason with him. Things turned bad."

"Eighteen dead?" the FBI agent said. "That's not *bad*. That's apocalyptic."

"They turned on each other," Lola said. "Some of them wanted to let us go. Some of them didn't. We did what we had to. No more. No less."

Certain evidence—a sawed-off shotgun with Brody's prints all over it; Blair Mayo's grisly corpse—invited further questioning, but the authorities were content not to dig too deeply. Some very bad people were dead. The victim's accounts held up. File under "closed" and move on.

There were no objections, no impassioned pursuit of the truth. A few of Jimmy's high-rolling "friends," business associates, and siblings came out of the woodwork, but they knew what Jimmy was about and were not at all surprised that his death came in a barrage of gunfire. They paid their respects and carried on as before.

The press kept him alive, though, for as long as they were

able. They glorified the information they'd been given and disinterred old stories and legends. Jimmy's ignominy spread beyond the northeastern states. He had his fans, like any mobster or mass murderer (his subreddit had 32.6k subscribers) but the popular opinion was that the world was better off without him.

At the opposite end of the good-and-evil spectrum, a service was held for Renée Giordano in her hometown of Bloomington, Indiana. It was gloriously attended.

The Indianapolis Colts wore black armbands and observed a minute's silence at their next home game.

...

In January 2020, a donation of $2,800 was made to the pediatric ward of Freewood Valley Hospital, under the name of Buddy's Convenience Store. This was, give or take a few dollars, the amount Brody had stolen from Buddy's cash register. He had hoped this act of goodwill would appease the universe and lessen the frequency of his nightmares. It didn't.

"How do you manage?" he'd asked his mom. This was shortly after getting out of the hospital, when he was still too sore for farmwork, and trapped with his thoughts for most of the day. "Do you shut yourself down and pretend it didn't happen?"

"It all comes down to balance," Lola had replied, and made weights out of her hands. "You can't let the darkness consume you. And you can't smile stupidly and pretend everything is A-okay. You shoulder the bad, you draw on the good. That's the only way to walk straight."

Janey had said something similar. "Make peace with what happened. You're a good man, and you protect what you love." Their relationship was one of the new lights in Brody's life, and had come out of nowhere. Brody had been grooming Autumn, who was unsettled, stomping her hooves, when Janey—who still came Wednesdays and Fridays to help with the horses—stepped beside him, placed her hand over his, and gently guided the brush. "Long, easy strokes. That's how she likes it." Autumn settled, but Brody ran hot. It was the best he'd felt in quite some time.

He didn't tell Janey everything. There were details she didn't need to know, and that he was doing his best to forget. They were like bugs, though. They got into small places. They buzzed and scratched. And they were always busier at night.

There was blood in his dreams. Sometimes it was Jimmy's, or Joey Cabrini's (always accompanied by that pig-like grunting). Most of the time, though, it was Brody's blood. In the worst of his nightmares, he kept getting back up. He'd be shot through the leg or chest, and up he'd pop. He'd take a bullet to the head and keep on ticking, fueled by something inside that refused to die.

"I can't stay down," he'd said to Janey. She was curled into him, one hand on his chest. Three A.M. moonlight bled through a gap in the curtains. "I don't know if it will ever end."

"It will," Janey had replied, "if you get up stronger."

This brief and brilliant wisdom—get up stronger—complemented the "one-inch punch" philosophy. He carried both into his everyday and worked hard. The farm cradled him. It felt secure, a place from which to feed and grow. His days were spent spreading fertilizer, irrigating crops, spraying pesticides, tending the livestock. The work packed muscle onto his shoulders and arms.

He frequented the Bald Eagle Shooting Range. His mom's idea. "You won't control your fear," she'd said, "until you've bridled it." She was right. Brody had hammered rounds into waves of gunmen, goons, and mobsters, until gradually they morphed into twelve-by-twelve targets. Paper squares with a series of concentric circles and a bright dot at the center.

His arm got steadier, his aim truer.

The nightmares dulled but didn't stop.

Evenings were spent with family, or with Janey. Sometimes the four of them would ride across the fading countryside, the wind chasing through their hair, until even their horses were breathless. They cooked together, streamed movies, cheered for the local baseball team. They slept on bedrolls beneath the endless sky, with coyotes prowling nearby and bull snakes hissing in the grass.

Molly remained his light, without her having to shine it. She tackled her own nightmares with a fierce tenacity. Working on the farm helped (Molly loved those horses). She saw a therapist once a week. "Benign discussion," she called it. Also, Butch Morgan's son was tall and understanding, and in him she'd found a companion. They weren't as far along the romance trail as Brody and Janey, but the look in Molly's eye suggested she hoped they soon would be.

She and Brody had the same ghost. Not the bleeding, dripping characters that rattled their dreams, but a silent, forceful woman who haunted their waking hours.

Blair.

She lived in the corner of Molly's eye. Molly would be in the barn, or maybe the kitchen, and would turn quickly, certain she'd seen Blair standing in the doorway with a pipe wrench in her hand. Other times, she lingered in the darkness beside Molly's bed, only to disappear the moment Molly rolled over to look.

Blair haunted Brody in a different way. She lived in his wallet.

Her returning it had been an odd, unexpected gesture, and

Brody thought about it often. Was it a genuine attempt at decency, or had she been mocking him—flaunting her absolute control? It was probably the latter, but Brody couldn't shake the notion that Blair had wanted to show him something beyond her cunning and cruelty: a redemptive quality that so rarely surfaced. He had searched though the wallet while lying in his hospital bed, expecting to find a note folded to fingernail size and tucked deep into one of the pockets. It would read, *Forgive me*, or maybe even, *Help me*.

There was no note.

Brody searched for her online, looking for a history of neglect or humanity—a skeleton for his ghost. He found nothing beyond the marksperson and martial arts accolades. No mention of a family. No social media presence. The press made no special mention of her in the aftermath of the shooting. She was just another redshirt in the Jimmy Latzo script.

Brody bought a new wallet. He filled it with a Nebraska driver's license, a concealed handgun permit, a credit card with a manageable APR, and with money that he'd earned through hard work. He kept his old wallet, though, and looked through it every now and then, remembering the girl with the purple hair and $1,500 boots, who had blazed through his life like a rocket.

...

Renée had said that she believed Lola was some kind of superhero, and she *was*, in many ways, but at her core she was fractured and wonderful and wholly normal. She was also, perhaps, the last person to realize this.

Lola held her children when they needed holding. She encouraged, comforted, and reassured them with a tenderness that was undeniably close to the surface. In these moments, it would be easy to believe she didn't have traumas of her own, but Brody recognized the ghosts behind her eyes.

She had told Brody that balance was the only way to walk straight, but sometimes she wavered, too.

"Is everything okay?"

Before riding out to meet Molly, Brody had walked into the kitchen to find Lola sitting at the table. Her cheeks were damp and she had a Kleenex balled in her fist.

"Oh hey, sweetie." She blinked her wet eyes. "I thought you were out."

"Leaving now." He and Molly were meeting at the place they called Resurrection Lookout. A serene, untouched stretch of acreage, where it was natural to reflect on what was, and what might be. "You didn't answer my question."

"I know you think I'm crying . . . and yes, I *am*, but . . ." She sighed, then managed a shaky smile. "Jesus, who am I kidding? I've actually cried a lot lately."

"I know."

"I think it's a sign I'm turning into a normal person."

"You've always been a normal person." Brody grabbed his hat from the kitchen countertop and placed it on his head. He hesitated for a moment—sometimes it was better to give his mom some space—but then took the seat opposite her at the table. "It's just that everything else around you was messed up."

"I suppose that's true." She wiped her cheeks and looked at him. He saw no ghosts in her eyes now, only honesty and trust.

"I know it's true," he said.

The clock in the hallway ticked dutifully into the early evening, emphasizing the Nebraska quiet. Even the animals had settled. Lola breathed over her upper lip and glanced at her hands.

Her knuckles were callused from her training (or was it her therapy?): striking a solid wooden post in the barn until it bowed and had to be supported.

"I don't ever want you to think I'm not happy," she said, "or that I don't want you and Molly here. It's just . . . everything with Jimmy. I carried that weight for a long time, and now that it's gone, it feels like a part of me has been chipped away. That's a good thing, I know, but I still feel . . . *less*, somehow. Does that make any sense?"

"I guess so," Brody said. "You have a lot to unpack. We all do."

"It's complicated, huh?"

He reached across the table, took her callused hand, and squeezed. She looked at him gratefully and another tear flashed down her cheek.

"To complicate matters further, I also feel . . . well, *more*. More fulfilled. More complete. I'm a full-time mom again, which is the best feeling in the world. But it comes with its own perils, because now I'm worried about you. *Mom* things. Are you going to fall off that horse and break your neck? Are you going to get Janey pregnant—"

"Aw, Mom—"

"Is Cal Morgan going to look after Molly, because if he doesn't . . ." She trailed off, offering another weak smile. "I sometimes think it was easier being shot at. I know what to do about that, at least."

"Molly can look after herself." Brody grinned, his eyes glimmering beneath the brim of his cowboy hat. "And me? Well, I think I got all of the stupid out of my system."

"You better have."

"And these things you're feeling . . . yeah, they're scary. But they're healthy, Mom. They're *normal*."

"Normal," Lola repeated. "That word again. You know, this is the first time I've ever had a normal life. I didn't have one as a kid. I didn't have one when I was working for Jimmy. And I didn't have one when you were younger, because the threat was still out there. But here I am, in my early fifties, and my life is finally my own."

"It's daunting," Brody said.

"It's breathtaking."

The kitchen brightened as the late sun touched the window and ran across the floor.

They said nothing else but held hands a moment longer.

...

Autumn bristled again but Brody gave the reins a tug and she settled quickly. He looked at Molly with one eyebrow raised: *Not bad for a city boy.*

Molly winked. Her smile was as curved and radiant as the river.

The minutes rolled by, and beautifully. They watched from their saddles as the sun splashed the horizon with warm paints and a thin moon appeared. Birds whistled. The crickets droned.

"Sure beats the smokestacks in Tank Hill," Molly said.

"Beats everything," Brody said.

Raw, deeper color, and then it all began to ebb. Molly opened her arms as if to embrace it, keep a piece of it for herself. Brody did the same.

"We're almost there, sis," he said.

Their shadows were long and blended with the land.

ACKNOWLEDGMENTS

Writing *Lola on Fire* was a rush, a wild ride. I traveled solo for the first few drafts, which is just the way I like it, then brought in a host of friends and good people for subsequent drafts. They each played a part and helped make the journey more enriching and fulfilling. *Lola on Fire* is the result of the miles we clocked together.

To begin with, I had the best beta readers a novelist could hope for: Chris Ryall of IDW Publishing, and *New York Times* bestselling authors Christopher Golden and Tim Lebbon. They offered their enthusiasm, as well as suggestions and constructive criticism. I'm so lucky to have had their knowledge and expertise to draw on, and even luckier to have them as friends.

Joe Hill has supported my work in the past, and he was in my corner for *Lola on Fire*, too. Joe read a later (fourth or fifth) draft, then sent me a long email detailing the parts he liked, and the parts that still required a little TLC. It was exactly the email I needed. Applying Joe's suggestions made *Lola on Fire* a stronger, better novel, and I'm incredibly grateful to him for it.

Okay, I've name-checked three *New York Times* bestsellers so far. May as well make it four: Michael Koryta read *Lola on Fire* while delayed at an airport, then announced on Twitter how much he enjoyed the book. That may seem like a relatively small thing, but that Tweet grabbed my future editor's attention . . . and *that*, friends, is a big reason why this book is in your hands today. Thanks, Michael!

I have one of the best agents in the business in Howard Morhaim, who took me under his wing when I didn't have much to offer, and whose belief in me has never faltered. He cares about my work, he cares about my career, he cares about *me*. I consider him to be more than my agent. He's also my friend. Thank you, Howard, for everything. *Lola on Fire* is as much your book as it is mine. We did this together.

Also in the Morhaim Literary camp, my thanks to Megan Gelement, who makes everything so easy by being great at what she does, and a huge thank-you to Michael Prevett, who is representing *Lola*'s further fortunes in the sunny climes of Los Angeles.

And, of course, *Lola on Fire* would be nothing without my brilliant editor, Jennifer Brehl, who brought this book to life with unwavering excitement and endless faith. Working with her has been every bit the rewarding, educational, and wonderful experience I knew it would be. A mere thank-you is not enough. Suffice to say, Jennifer has been one of my favorite editors for many years, but now she's one of my favorite people, too. This giddy, dreamlike gratitude is extended to everyone at William Morrow. I'm so proud to be a part of the family.

Finally, love and thanks to my spectacular wife, Emily, whose support is nothing short of staggering, and whose belief lights my way. And to our children, Lily and Charlie, who inspire and elevate me in every possible way.